Praise for *Sara's Sacrifice*

"Parfitt made early twentieth century Milwaukee come to life in this story of the hard work and sacrifice of Wisconsin's forward-looking suffragists. Readers will want to find out what happens…I thoroughly enjoyed it."

—Virginia McCullough,
Award-winning Author of romance and women's fiction

"The 19th Amendment to the U.S. Constitution didn't "just happen." In this fast-paced novel, set in Wisconsin, Flo Parfitt depicts the period of the suffragettes. The main character embodies the passion, courage and actions of women determined to secure their right to vote."

—Jacklyn Lohr Burkat,
Retired Librarian

Advance Praise for *Ella Endures*

"*Ella Endures* takes the reader on a journey back in time to experience the joys and trials of the Greatest Generation. The author draws from a deep well of historical knowledge and brings the past to life. I was immediately pulled into the story and connected with Ella. I didn't want to put the book down!"

—Laurie Winter,
Award-winning Author of the Warriors of the Heart series

"As someone who contracted polio in 1946, I can identify greatly with Parfitt's depiction of her young character, Henrietta Ellington, who endures living in an iron lung in *Ella Endures*. Readers will understand how horrifying it is to live in this breathing substitute and how important the eventual vaccines are to eliminate dreaded diseases. *Ella Endures* has so much humanity and love in it, you will be rooting for Ella and her family."

—Cookie Anderson, Polio Thriver

"This wonderfully written historical fiction, *Ella Endures*, with its engaging characters and iconic descriptions, takes the reader back in time in such realistic fashion that you will feel part of their lives and their fight. I have a much better idea of what my grandma and mother endured so I could have the freedoms I have today."

—Gail Buntin Blohowiak, Author and Playwright

"The Roaring Twenties have arrived and with it a face-paced, ever-changing world where Ella faces the changes with trepidation, determination, strength, and joy. As you read *Ella Endures*, you will find pieces of you so like Ella—able to endure what life brings your way. Flo Parfitt has written an inspiring novel!"

—**Deb Olsen,**
Elementary Teacher and Cancer Survivor

"With limited exposure to historical fiction, I opened *Ella Endues* with anticipation. Women's issues, family, and romance piqued my interest, but turn the page and I met intrigue. I'm hooked!"

—**Susan Teti-Finnegan,**
Natural Health Consultant

"Wow! In scenes from *Ella Endures* such as the bombing of Pearl Harbor, I felt like I was there. It was so real. I had a sense of pride in the nurses and what they went through. They endured an unimaginable situation. Being a former nurse, I can really appreciate their dedication and how Flo Parfitt wrote this story."

—**Elvi Ruotsala,**
a nonagenarian survivor from the Greatest Generation

"*Ella Endures* is a historical fiction gem that transports you to the Roaring 20s and incorporates historical events with a lovely tale of life, love, loss, and liberation. Ella Dewberry Ellington is an inspiring, strong female lead with gumption in spades and her family and friends will draw you in and make you want to be a part of their story."

—**Lindsey Marantos,**
Organizational Leadership & Effectiveness Consultant

ELLA ENDURES

Flo Parfitt

ELLA ENDURES

Book 2 of the Daughters of Evolution Series

Flo Parfitt

Green Bay, WI

Ella Endures: **Book 2 of the Daughters of Evolution Series** by Flo Parfitt, copyright © 2021 by Flo Parfitt. Author photo courtesy of Ambrosius Studios. Cover art design, interior layout design, chapter head artwork and logo © 2021 by Written Dreams Publishing.

Publisher/Executive Editor: Brittiany Koren
Cover Art Designer: Ed Vincent & Diedre Waite/ENC Graphics
Interior Layout Designer: Amit Dey
Ebook Layout Designer: Amit Dey

Category: Women's Historical Fiction
Description: Ella Ellington lives through the trials of the Greatest Generation during the Great Depression, the Dust Bowl, World War II, and a Recession, building a family together with John Ellington.
Hard Cover ISBN: 978-1-951375-62-1
Paperback ISBN: 978-1-951375-63-8
Ebook ISBN: 978-1-951375-64-5
LOC Catalogue Data: Applied for.

First Edition published by Written Dreams Publishing in December, 2021.
Ebook Edition published by Written Dreams Publishing in December, 2021.

Green Bay, WI

Books Written By Flo Parfitt

Sara's Sacrifice
Book 1 of the Daughters of Evolution Series

Ella Endures
Book 2 of the Daughters of Evolution Series

I dedicate this book to my grandmother, Emma Bloedorn Grunske, who endured the hardships of the Greatest Generation and showed me firsthand what it is to be a strong woman.

Author's Note

The "Greatest Generation" were the children of the 1920s, enduring the hardships of the Great Depression of the 1930s and through World War II in the 1940s. These were people of great fortitude who wouldn't give up. They were proud, they were strong, and they were survivors. Life was tough and so were they.

The Eighteenth Amendment, which ushered in Prohibition in January of 1920, and the Nineteenth Amendment giving women the right to vote in August of 1920, as well as the Fifteenth Amendment which gave Negro voting rights, which passed in 1870 were all still under debate. These Amendments were circumvented whenever possible and riddled with local qualifications or disqualifications by individuals or governments. In many cases, they were ignored, dealing with issues only when legally challenged. Most individuals possessed neither the means nor the resources to challenge the laws, making enforcement sporadic and difficult.

Some people maintained the dignity and propriety of the previous age. Others embraced the new-found freedom and carefree attitude of the Roaring 20s. Most people worked hard and were self-sufficient, having no government safety net for hard times. They relied on their own innovation and the community support of friends and family. There was great pride in self, community, and Country. And through it all, they endured.

Ella, the daughter of a suffragette, persevered. She was self-confident and independent. She endured much for her family, for her friends, for strangers, for her community, and her country.

This is Ella's story.

BOMBS

PROHIBITION

Chapter One

KABOOM!

A blast rippled through the city of Milwaukee, Wisconsin. The ground shook and people ran for cover. What was it? Were we being attacked? The Great War was still waging. Had it now reached our doorstep? Highly unlikely, but what was it?

It was 7:33 p.m. on a chilly November evening. Seventeen-year-old Ella Dewberry was on her way home in her family's one-horse surrey. Molly, the filly, bolted at the sudden noise and trembling of the earth. Ella pulled on the reins and calmed the steed. This was her first year at Downer College. She had stayed later than usual to do some research on a paper she was writing. She took the horse to the stable boy, who unharnessed her and brushed her down for the night.

Ella rushed to the house. Father would be worried.

Ten-year-old Elizabeth was clinging to her father, her eyes wide and her body trembling. Henry Dewberry, Ella's father, met her at the door. "Ella, I'm so glad you are home. Are you okay? What *was* that terrible noise?"

"I'm sorry, Papa. I...I lost track of time. The bang scared Molly, but I was able to calm her. It shook the earth."

"I know. It rattled the windows. I'm glad you're home safe."

"Me, too," Ella said as she went to the window and peered out, hoping to see some indication of what had happened.

People were gathering outside, stretching their necks to see if anything was amiss. In their neighborhood, everything was calm.

*   *   *

Across town at Broadway and Oneida Streets, the scene was quite different. The noise and effects were felt for miles around, but here, there was total devastation. The Milwaukee Police station had been bombed.

The scene outside the police station was total chaos. People were running and screaming. Fire fighters from far and wide arrived with sirens blaring. Wounded had stumbled from the building and were being treated. Bystanders stood in shock with eyes wide and hands covering their mouths. Others fled in fear there might be another blast.

The following morning, newspapers alerted the city to the tragedy that struck Milwaukee at 7:33 p.m. on November 24, 1917; a catastrophe that burned into the minds of its citizens forever. Nine police officers and one civilian had lost their lives. It was the largest loss of police officer lives in the history of the United States. Ella suspected the days to come would reveal more facts.

A package had been delivered to Father Giuliani's Methodist Church on Jackson Street. An eleven-year-old girl, Josie Spicciati, first noticed the package wrapped in brown paper and tied with twine. It was outside the church.

She alerted her mother, Erminia, the cleaning lady at the church. Her mother did nothing at the time, but as she was leaving later in the morning, she glanced at the package. It was not a normal package. It was the size of a half-gallon jar with another smaller bottle filled with liquid on top. There were metal plates on the top and bottom of the package. It weighed on Erminia's mind.

Later in the afternoon, Erminia told her daughter to return to the church and alert the organist and caretaker of the package. Before leaving, the organist, Maude Richter brought the package inside and placed it in the basement. Later, being suspicious, she called the police and spoke to the chief detective, who assured her someone would pick it up.

That evening, as the choir was convening for practice, Maude saw the package still there. At 7:10 p.m. a twenty-six-year-old choir member, Sam Mazzone, volunteered to take the package to the police station.

At the police station, the shift was changing, so Mazzone left the package on the floor by the desk of Sergeant Henry Deckert. Mazzone told him it was a bomb left at the church.

Detective Charles Andrews and Lieutenant Robert Flood instructed Mazzone to take it outside. However, Mazzone, who was Italian, was intercepted by two other officers, Detectives Arthur Burns and Bart Maloney to interpret an interrogation of a suspect they had brought in for questioning. Deckert took the package into a squad room to get it out of the way.

Meanwhile in the waiting area, a woman was seated on a bench ready to lodge a complaint against a man who had been harassing her.

The officers coming on duty joined Detective David O'Brien in the squad room where the package had been placed. At precisely 7:33 p.m., the earth shook as the explosion rocked the building. The bomb was at Sergeant Deckert's feet. He had begun to unwrap it when it detonated.

In a split second, seven detectives lost their lives along with Sergeant Deckert. The police alarm operator on the floor above and Catherine Walker, the civilian, were also killed. Others had minor injuries or were unscathed, including two who had been in the room with the alarm operator.

Detective Burns had left the squad room and stopped to talk to Lieutenant Flood on his way to get a container of water to place the bomb in. Lieutenant Flood, in his office across the hall, was thrown from his chair. The lights went out and the building was in total darkness. Flood ran to the squad room.

Firemen from Engine Company Number 1 were first on the scene. They, along with the jail, were housed directly across the street from the station. The firefighters spread out with lights to search the building.

Even the responders were shocked at what they saw when they entered what was left of the squad room.

"Glass, plastering, clothing, arms, legs, and papers covered the floor," the Milwaukee Journal reported.

Through the broken windows, a streetlight flickered eerily. Planks and chandeliers hung precariously from the ceiling. Detective O'Brien's body was found in the center of the room covered with debris. Officer Deckert's body was near the entrance, pierced by a piece of steel. The civilian, Catherine Walker's body was found lying near the doorway. Many of the bodies took days to be identified because of their horrific conditions.

The Journal kept the citizens abreast of the findings in the case, but the city of Milwaukee remained on high alert. Methodists in particular were wary. This seemed a targeted attack that went horribly wrong.

Ella and her family remained on edge. Any sudden noise caused her to jump. She cradled her younger sister, Elizabeth, when she woke up from nightmares. Ella wished her mother was there to hold her. *Where was she? Why wasn't she here?*

Sara, Ella's mother had been gone for three years. Or was it four? It felt like an eternity. *She said she would return. She might never return. It wasn't fair. She's out fighting a noble cause. Suffragettes! Fighting so women would have a vote, a voice.* "I hate her. Her place is here with us." Ella gulped.

She didn't mean it, or did she? Ella had always placed the blame on her father who forced her mother to leave, but now, now she sounded like him. She recalled him saying, "A woman's place is in the home."

Ella immediately felt shame. She was proud of what her mother was trying to accomplish, but...

"Oh Mother, I miss you so. Please come home."

Chapter Two

Ella and her sister slept together restlessly that night. The days and weeks ahead were precarious, but things gradually went back to normal. As normal as can be expected. On Thanksgiving day, just five days after the bombing, the family gathered and comforted each other.

Two weeks later, Ella decided to make Christmas a more joyful event. She needed to get out and do some holiday shopping. The snow was falling lightly, Christmas bells were ringing, and carolers were singing. There was a definite attempt to raise the spirits of the people in Milwaukee.

Ella dressed in a green empire dress with bell sleeves. Her hair was pulled back from her face and ringlets cascaded down her back. She pulled on her calf-length Victorian boots and tightened the laces. She thought about a hat, but instead donned her fox cape with a hood to ward of the winter temperatures, which hovered around 30 degrees.

The stable boy brought the carriage to the back porch. She greeted him with a smile and a cheerful "Good morning, Albert."

He helped her into the carriage where she pulled the horsehair blanket snugly around her legs and tightened the wool scarf around her neck.

"Mornin', Miss Ella. Goin' shoppin' today? Shoo is a good day fer it."

"Yes, Albert. Is Molly calm today?" Ella asked.

"The old girl's been mighty skittish lately, but she's been gentle all this week."

"I wish I were calm. I'm off to the milliner and I have to pass the police station."

"You jest hold on tight to the reins and talk to her kinda quiet like," Albert reassured her.

"Thank you, Albert." Ella clicked her tongue, and she was off down the drive and onto Astor Street.

*   *   *

Ella was coming up on the police station and she gasped when she saw the rubble and recalled the carnage that happened there. "Steady Molly, we're almost there." Ella was talking to herself more than the horse. Molly knew nothing of the horror that took place here, but Ella could barely breathe.

She sighed when she reached the milliner and hitched Molly to the hitching post. Ella, always on high alert, noted a man parking his vehicle just ahead of her carriage. She shuddered when she saw the crack, corner to corner in the Millinery Shop window cutting through the store decal.

She looked about as she stepped away from her carriage and saw the man exiting the vehicle in front of her. He was tall and impeccably dressed in a grey pinstripe double-breasted suit. He wore spats. He had on a burgundy ascot and a gray top hat, which he tipped as he nodded in her direction.

Ella smiled back. Very nice, she thought as she headed for the steps to the milliner's. She lifted her cape slightly to maneuver the step when suddenly, a passing automobile backfired.

Molly jolted. Ella screamed and fell backward off the steps and into the arms of the stranger.

"Gotcha," he said as his arms enveloped her waist and she fell backward into his chest.

She blushed and stammered, "So sorry." She looked up into a handsome face and into his penetrating hazel eyes. "Oh, oh. That was so clumsy of me."

"Are you okay?" His deep voice was filled with concern.

"I… I'm fine. Thank you so much." Ella straightened her cape; her hood had fallen back exposing her shiny brown locks.

"Always happy to aid a damsel in distress." He took her elbow and held the door for her.

"Thank you." She smiled coyly.

"Good morning." The milliner greeted them. "What can I help you two with today?" He greeted them as a couple.

"Oh no," Ella exclaimed. "We just met at the door."

"Very well, ladies first, what can I get for you today, ma'am?"

"Sir, why don't you help the gentleman while I look around. I am looking for several gifts today."

"Very well. Sir, what…"

The man interrupted, "That is quite all right, I am in no hurry. I'll just sit here." He pointed to a chair next to a mirror.

"Are you sure? I may be able to help you both," the milliner replied. The man did not immediately respond. "What are you interested in purchasing today?"

"I need a new top hat. In black, please."

"And what is your name, sir? I like to get to know my customers."

"Ellington, John Ellington. This is my first visit to your store, and I must say, I like what I see."

"Thank you, Mr. Ellington, let me bring a few top hats for you to try."

Ella had picked up a lovely fox hat that matched her fox cape perfectly. She placed it on her head, tilting it over her forehead.

"Lovely, simply lovely." John smiled.

She went to look in the mirror next to him. "I do like it." She tilted her head in several ways, admiring the hat. She wasn't sure from his tone whether he had referred to the hat or if he was referring to her. She placed the hat on the counter and went back to perusing other hats.

The milliner returned with two top hats. Mr. Ellington stood before the mirror and tried them on.

From across the small room, Ella side-glanced at him. "Definitely the second one," she advised and turned back immediately to admire the hats displayed on the wall.

"You have a very good eye." He smiled, enjoying the interchange.

She turned to face him. "Which one?"

John walked in front of her and gazed into her eyes. "They both look fabulous to me."

They both laughed.

"Shall I wrap this for you?" the milliner inquired of John while he held the hat in his hand.

John looked up. "Yes sir, put it in a hat box please."

Meanwhile, Ella picked up a knit hat with fur trim. She placed it on the counter next to the other hat. This would be perfect for Elizabeth.

"We have matching gloves," the milliner said and reached under the counter. He produced the item to complete the set.

"Yes, definitely." Ella smiled at the milliner. "I'll take those, too."

John paid for his purchase and picked up the hatbox.

Ella realized he was about to leave. "Wait," she gasped, not sure what to say next.

John broke the silence. "Yes?"

"Um, ah, I need to purchase a hat for my father. Maybe you can help me pick it out."

John placed his hatbox on the floor next to the chair. "At your service, madam."

"What type of hat do you have in mind?" the milliner inquired.

"Ah, I'm not sure. A top hat, I suppose. He's a stuffy banker." She giggled.

The milliner hustled into the back room and returned with three hats. What size hat does he wear?"

"Well, I'm not sure. About his size, I suppose." She nodded toward John.

Ella took one hat from the milliner and plopped it on her head. She admired herself in the mirror, making profoundly serious faces. "What do you think?"

John laughed. "Maybe a bit too stuffy. Try the one with the feather."

Ella reached for the hat with the small feather in the band and placed it on her head. She looked pleased.

"Looks great. You should get it for you."

"Hmm." She removed it and placed it on John's head. She stood back, studying it with her index finger at the corner of her mouth. "Nice, very nice."

Ella then reached for the third hat and placed it on her head. "The other looks much better on you."

"Come, let me see them side by side." John stood beside her, looking in the mirror.

Ella tapped an invisible cigar and imitated Groucho Marks, a vaudeville star she had recently seen. "I've made up my mind. If I didn't make up my mind, I wouldn't have one." She made another flick to the invisible cigar.

They both laughed.

She placed the hat on the counter and continued to talk with John. "Are you having a big family day for Christmas?"

"No, I'm afraid there is no family to celebrate. My parents died from typhoid a few years ago and I went to live with my Aunt Helen. She had a heart attack last year and died."

"I'm so sorry." She placed her hand on his arm. "You should have Christmas dinner with my family." Her purchases paid for, she reached in her purse and pulled out a calling card.

"Oh no, I can't do that." He glanced at the card that contained her name and address. "We just met. I don't want to impose."

"It's no imposition," Ella insisted. "We would love to have you."

John protested once again.

"Well, keep the card. I hope you change your mind. Come around noon. We would be delighted to have you."

John walked Ella to her carriage and placed the hatboxes inside. "I don't believe I'll join you for Christmas. I do have another invitation, but I would like to see you again sometime."

Ella's heart sunk and jumped at the same time. She likely would not see him for Christmas, but she held out hope that she would hear from him again soon.

"Have a safe journey home." Ella watched him go to his car and then trotted home with excitement in her heart. John would be all she thought about. *Ella Ellington.* She sighed. "Don't get ahead of yourself."

*   *   *

John did not come for Christmas. It was two days before New Year's when he called. Ella answered the telephone. "Dewberry Residence."

"Ella?"

"Yes, who is this?" Her heart skipped a beat. *Was it? Could it be?*

"This is John Ellington. Remember me?"

"John," Ella squealed. "Are you coming for leftovers?"

John laughed. "No, but I'd like to take you out for dinner. If you would," he added.

"I'd love to, John. But..."

"How about New Year's Day. We can welcome in 1918."

"I want to, but... I need to ask permission from Father."

"Is he there?"

"No, but I'll ask him tonight. Can you call back tomorrow?"

"Of course."

Ella had told her father about the stranger she had met, but she was only seventeen. She had not been on a date before. She paced nervously until Henry got home.

He barely got in the door when she said, "Papa, remember the stranger I met at the millinery shop? He called. He wants to take me to dinner. On New Year's Day."

Henry stiffened and was silent.

"He is calling back tomorrow. He really is a gentleman. I know you will like him."

"Let me think." Henry went to the library.

Ella went to her room and prayed. *Please, Papa, say yes.*

At dinner, they said grace and proceeded to eat the dinner that Ella had prepared earlier.

"About your gentleman friend...the answer is no," Henry said.

"But Papa, please reconsider. He is a good man. He is at the university. He is studying to be a doctor." Tears welled in her eyes.

"You can invite him to dinner here. When we get to know him, I will decide if it is wise."

Ella took a deep breath. She knew arguing would only make the situation worse. At least it wasn't a flat no. But John hadn't come for Christmas. Would he come now?

The next day, John called. Ella answered with trepidation. She explained, "Papa says he needs to know you before we can go to dinner. Can you come here instead?"

"Of course, Ella. Your father is being cautious. I understand that. I respect that."

Ella sighed in relief. "Please come New Year's Day. I'll cook ham. It won't be as good as Weiner schnitzel at Mader's but I'm not a bad cook. You will survive."

John laughed.

*　　　*　　　*

John showed up dressed in a gabardine three-piece suit, carrying a bouquet of fresh flowers.

Henry answered the door.

The gentlemen shook hands and Henry invited John into the parlor. He offered him a drink, which he declined.

Henry began inquiring into John's past, his plans for the future, and even his political and religious affiliations.

John answered confidently and willingly.

Ella was not sure if she should join them or wait to be invited. She decided to make an appearance.

When she entered the room, both men stood. She welcomed John, who presented her with the flowers. She commented on how lovely they were, thanked him profusely, then quickly excused herself and exited back to the kitchen to properly arrange the flowers, which she placed at the center of the dining room table.

They sat down to dinner, which was excellently prepared. She was pleased to see how famously the men were getting along. John was a perfect gentleman attending to Ella's chair, commenting with praises on her meal and how lovely she looked. He even gave Elizabeth her due attention. He was the perfect guest.

After dinner, Henry invited John to the library where he offered him a cigar. Once again, John declined, stating, "Thank you, sir, but I don't smoke."

The gentlemen continued their conversation while Ella waited nervously in the parlor. Soon they emerged, laughing.

Ella sighed, relieved to see things going so well. In fact, the conversation seemed to have turned to the subject of Ella, and Henry was touting her accomplishments academically and in the kitchen.

Once again, John complimented Ella on the meal and decided to broach the question of taking Ella to dinner to return the favor.

Henry was silent for a moment.

"You don't like my cooking?" Ella joked to fill the silence.

"Or we could…" John began, but Henry interrupted.

"I think that is a wonderful idea. However, John, Ella is still seventeen so we have some rules I trust you will abide by. She must be home by ten. There will be no alcohol and I expect you to be a gentleman and pick her up at the door. Or better yet, come in and tell me your agenda."

"Of course. Anything you say sir."

Ella was wondering if her father was going to monopolize the entire evening but shortly thereafter Henry excused himself. "I have some work to do, so you young folks can get to know each other." Henry exited to the library and shut the door.

Ella and John sat on separate chairs; not sure the sofa would be appropriate. They soon let down their guard. They talked about their families and about their hopes and dreams for the future. They talked about the bombing and laughed about their chance encounter at the milliner's.

Time flew by and John said he had better leave. He didn't want to press his luck and overstay his welcome.

They made plans for dinner on Saturday. John would be back to school in Madison and Ella's classes also resumed on Monday. They both knew they would probably not be seeing each other for a long time after that.

Chapter Three

John and Ella wrote often and counted the days until summer break. Then, when it came, their summer was filled with picnics, concerts in the park, days at the beach, trips to the planetarium and to the library.

Ella missed her mother dearly but was proud of her mother for her work as a suffragette. Still, she wished with all her heart that she would soon be home. Frequent letters arrived from her at the library, but she could never answer them. By the time Ella's letters reached the latest destination, her mother had moved on. She wanted so badly to hold her mother close and share her life with her. She treasured every letter, but they always brought tears to her eyes. She missed her mother so.

It was nearing summer's end and John would soon be returning to school in Madison. Ella, also, was corresponding regularly with her childhood friend, Rose, who had married and moved to Oklahoma. Rose was pregnant with her first child. She wanted Ella to be her child's godmother.

Ella had agreed to travel to Oklahoma to be there for the baby's birth. If everything were on schedule, she would arrive in mid-August and be home in time to be back at school. John took her to the train station and saw her off. A week later, he returned to Madison.

Much to Ella's surprise, Sara, Ella's mother happened to be in Boise City. A chance meeting between Rose and Sara occurred a couple of weeks prior to Ella's arrival. There was no chance Sara would miss a visit with her eldest daughter, so she postponed her travels and was soon reunited with her daughter.

Circumstances were complicated and after the birth of Rose's surprise arrival of twins, Ella and Sara returned to Milwaukee together. Reuniting Sara with Henry was a challenging time. However, at Christmas, Sara did meet John and was pleased with Ella's choice for her future husband.

Ella and John returned to their respective schools in January of 1919. Sara felt her work as a suffragette took precedence over everything else, but she now operated mostly from her home in Milwaukee.

In June, John returned home. The family gathered to celebrate the passing of the 19th Amendment and the State of Wisconsin immediately ratifying it. They were together for Sara's speech and the anticipated celebration. Though, joy was quickly snuffed out when Sara paid the final sacrifice with her life on the library steps.

Ella was inconsolable. She had waited so long to have her mother back in her life and she didn't even get a full year to reconnect with the mother she had longed to be with.

Henry was totally distraught. He suffered through the coming years with depression and bouts of anguish. Ella tried to seek some sort of normalcy. She would often sit with John, who curled her into his arms and comforted her.

Her father, however, ridden with guilt and loss sunk deeper into depression. Within three years, he suffered a heart attack and died at the age of forty-seven. Ella was sure her father's heart was not inherently weak but simply broken. It was impossible for him to go on without Sara.

*   *   *

Shortly after her father's death in the summer of 1923, Ella and John decided not to wait any longer and married at a quiet ceremony at the Presbyterian church. The Reverend Nelson officiated.

Fifteen-year-old Elizabeth was her bridesmaid. Ella was dressed in her mother's wedding gown that she resurrected from the attic. It fit her perfectly. The gown was of silk organza and fell softly against her body.

The veil fell from a crown of daisies and almost reached the floor. She carried a simple bouquet of wildflowers.

Liz admired her older sister. "Ella, you are so beautiful."

"And so are you." Ella took her sister's hands in hers. "Don't be afraid. I will always be here for you." They hugged and wiped away the tears.

"Stop, stop," Ella implored. "My face will be a total mess. Be happy."

Untraditionally, they'd walk the aisle together, along with Ella's brother Thaddeus, who was the groomsman. Ella was so happy her brother could attend. He didn't often get home from military school.

Before they entered the sanctuary, Thaddeus turned to his sister. "I don't think I have ever seen you so radiant." He kissed her on the cheek.

As they were about to make the trek up the aisle, Thaddeus in his mischievous way leaned over and nodded toward the groom at the front of the church. "Sis, you are about to knock that guy's socks off."

John stood with Reverend Nelson at the altar. At first glance, John gulped. Then, a smile crossed his face as he watched his new bride approach.

Only about a dozen guests were in attendance. John and Ella's reception was a dinner at a small inn at the edge of town. Their eyes sparkled as they enjoyed the evening.

*   *   *

Ella had graduated two years prior and took a teaching job at the local high school where Elizabeth attended. John returned to Madison for his final year of school, which provided him with his doctorate.

In 1924, Ella became pregnant and was not allowed to continue teaching. John was doing his residency in Milwaukee, but long hours didn't give them much time together.

In December, Ella gave birth to their first child. They named her Helen in honor of John's Aunt Helen who had raised him after his parents' death.

Finally, they were a family. It was a joyous holiday filled with love and joy. The dark shadow that had hung over them for so long had turned from black to gray. Ella and John were beginning to see the light again.

Chapter Four

In 1925, Ella Ellington sat on the old bentwood rocker beside the fireplace at her home on Astor Street in Milwaukee. The home she'd inherited from her parents, Sara and Henry Dewberry. Her baby daughter Helen was cradled in her arms, with her tiny fingers wrapped around Ella's little finger. The baby's big, quizzical eyes looked up at her mother as if to say, "Mother, I trust you. Will you always be here for me?" Or at least that was Ella's impression of what Helen was thinking. It was more likely Ella's own insecurities echoing in her baby's eyes.

The sting of her mother's death in 1920 still haunted her. Ella had looked after her little sister since Liz was seven. Elizabeth had now graduated from high school and was in Madison continuing her studies, fulfilling her dreams of becoming a nurse. She had been gone a mere semester, and Ella experienced a great loss. She was so proud of her sister. She missed Liz's bubbly personality and smiling face, and her almost unreasonable optimism.

Her brother had graduated from West Point two years earlier and was off to pursue his career in the U.S. Army Air Service. Thaddeus was enamored with airplanes. With the Great War over, she believed Thaddeus would be safe. She was always concerned for him because of his adventurous attitude. She knew if there was a dangerous mission, he would be first in line to volunteer. She worried about him.

John Ellington, Ella's adoring and adored husband had finished medical school and was serving his internship at Milwaukee General Hospital. When she fell in love with this charming and upcoming surgeon, she knew she would be spending a lot of time without him by her side. He almost didn't make it to Helen's birth. Luckily, he completed the surgical procedure he was assisting just in time to run to the maternity ward for the birth of his daughter.

He worked long, grueling hours, and when he was home, he was exhausted. If they could share one meal together in a week, she considered it a blessing. Ella longed for the day when he would be ready to open his own practice. She wasn't sure that would be any better, but she held onto the hope.

Ella rose from her rocker and placed Helen in her Jenny Lind cradle. Helen was sound asleep. The house was quiet, so Ella turned on the radio John had purchased for her this past Christmas.

The thud of the newspaper arriving on her doorstep startled her. She went out to retrieve it and took in a deep breath of cold spring air. She could smell the fragrant lilacs in bloom. She took the paper to the kitchen, poured a cup of hot steamy coffee, and proceeded to catch up on what the rest of the world was doing while she was at home doing almost nothing. Not that raising her daughter was nothing, but Ella wanted more.

Friday, May 29, 1925.

SCOPES INDICTED

Ella read with interest.

John Scopes, a Tennessee biology teacher, had been arrested earlier in May for teaching Darwin's Theory of Evolution. On the 25th, he was indicted.

"Hmm." Ella pursed her lips. "Tsk, tsk, tsk." She didn't know quite what to make of it. His arguments made sense, but the idea was foreign to her. She turned the page.

Trouble was brewing in China. Sun Yat-Sen, the founding father and first President of the Republic of China, had died on March 12, 1925. He was the forerunner of the democratic revolution in the Peoples Republic of China and instrumental in overthrowing the Qing Dynasty. He had been a uniting factor in Post-Imperial China and much revered. Now, other factions were at play. The KMT (Nationalists) and Communist parties (allied as the First Unified Front) were running a Soviet-backed administration in Guangdong. Anti-Western sentiment was gaining ground. Strikes were intensifying.

"Oh, dear. I hope this doesn't explode into a conflict here," Ella said.

She moved on to lighter news. *The Wizard of Oz* was a best seller. Ella smiled. She had thought about naming her baby Dorothy but had chosen Helen instead. Besides, it seemed like everyone was naming their baby girls Dorothy.

Ella turned to the classifieds.

There, in large print she read:

Milwaukee Journal is seeking freelance feature writers. If you have a background in journalism or if you possess excellent English Language skills, you may be qualified. Contact Editor, Milwaukee Journal.

Ella's interest was piqued. She had considered journalism when she was in school but had decided on teaching. *This could work.*

She put the newspaper aside, took out her professional stationery, and penned a beautiful résumé and cover letter. She addressed it to the Editor of the *Milwaukee Journal*. She wax-sealed the envelope and posted it.

Later in the day, Ella took Helen for a walk in her pram. They stopped at the post office and Ella dropped the letter in the letter slot. She smiled as she walked home, proud and excited. Could this be the beginning of a new career? When she sat down to dinner that evening alone, she wondered if she had acted in haste. Perhaps she should have discussed the matter with John first before applying.

"Pshaw, what difference could it make?" *It's a freelance position so it won't interfere in anything important. It is a feature story position. It will probably involve things like who attended social teas and the like.*

"Pretty boring stuff, but at least it will get me out of the house and give me a purpose, as mundane as it may be. Besides, I may not get the position," Ella rationalized. But all evening long her thoughts were on the byline, Ella Ellington. She fantasized one day she might be a great writer with numerous awards and accolades.

That evening as she pulled the covers up to her chin to fall asleep, her thoughts kept her awake with ideas of a great new career in the works.

*   *   *

Weeks passed, and Ella heard nothing. *What a silly goose I have been, thinking I had a chance as a writer.* She silently reprimanded herself.

She had just taken the clothes off the clothesline, and as she was folding the laundry in the kitchen, she heard the telephone ring. She hurried to answer, wondering who it might be. "Probably John saying he is working late," she surmised.

Helen was asleep in her cradle and the ringing of the phone startled her. She was beginning to squirm.

"Hello, is this Mrs. Ellington?" the voice on the phone cheerfully addressed her.

"Yes, this is she," Ella responded quizzically. She reached over and rocked the cradle gently as she spoke.

"This is Myron Wallace, Editor at the *Journal*. How are you today?"

"Oh, Mr. Wallace." Ella was pleasantly surprised. She pulled a sprig of hair back behind her ear. It had fallen across her face, and for some strange reason she felt she had to be professional in every way, including a sprig of hair out of place. "I am delighted to hear from you."

"Mrs. Ellington, I don't know if we have a position you would be interested in, but I wonder if you might be free tomorrow afternoon to come to my office to discuss the matter."

"Of course, of course," Ella responded enthusiastically. Then she realized perhaps she was a bit too anxious. "What time would work into your schedule?" she inquired more sedately.

"Shall we say two o'clock?"

"I believe I can manage that just fine," Ella responded. Inside, her heart was beating rapidly and she wanted to scream for joy.

"Two o'clock, then," Mr. Wallace responded. "I will see you tomorrow. Have a nice day, Mrs. Ellington."

"Thank you, Mr. Wallace. I will be there."

Ella hung up the phone, picked Helen up from her cradle, and danced about the room as she sang "Yes Sir, That's My Baby."

Should she tell John? No, she'd wait until after she spoke to Mr. Wallace.

Chapter Five

Ella arranged with Mrs. Johnson, her neighbor, to watch Helen while she went for her interview. Mrs. Johnson was a grandmother and had lived in the house next door for many years. She had been there when Ella was growing up, and she knew Mrs. Johnson was delighted with all children but especially fond of babies. She laughed at a memory that popped into her mind. When Ella was a little girl, she always made sure she was near Mrs. Johnson's house when she baked. The sweet, enticing smell of cinnamon rolls wafted through her kitchen window, and she was always willing to share the goodies with the neighborhood children.

Ella changed clothes a couple of times before putting on a conservative gray dress with sensible shoes. She decided to add a bit of flair with a red hat sporting a gray feather. Yes, this was no nonsense business attire but with a touch of adventure. It was perfect.

She took Helen next door and hurried to her Austin 7 automobile. They still had the Model T her parents had owned, but John drove it to work. He'd wanted to make sure Ella had a vehicle of her own. The Austin was an inexpensive vehicle but was very sporty with its yellow body and black fenders and top. Many considered it an extravagance to have two vehicles but understood John's profession required Ella to maintain some degree of independence.

Ella was soon at the Journal's building. She took a deep breath, checked her appearance in her compact mirror, and went to the receiving desk just inside the door.

The desk was unoccupied. A young man scurrying by stopped briefly. "Yeah, what can I do for you?" He seemed annoyed with the interruption.

"I am here to see Mr. Wallace," Ella said politely. "I have an appointment."

"Chief, someone here for you," the young man called out to what seemed like no one in particular.

An older gentleman with a balding head, well-trimmed beard, grey trousers and white shirt with sleeves rolled up to his elbows appeared in the doorway of an office across the room. He peered over his glasses. "Mrs. Ellington?" he inquired, looking in her direction.

"Yes, that would be me." Ella smiled as she headed toward him. "Mr. Wallace, I presume?"

Ella held out her hand, and then wondered if she was too forward. He shook her hand firmly.

"Come this way," he said, showing her to his office. "I like your assertiveness."

She gave a sigh of relief knowing so far, she was doing all right.

"Have a seat." He motioned to a chair across from his desk, which was piled high with reams of paper and a mess of pens strewn about helter-skelter. A typewriter sat on the back counter.

Her chair was somewhat stiff and uncomfortable. The kind of chair that said, "Come in and talk to me but don't take too much of my time."

"Do you have a portfolio for me to look at?" he asked hopefully, since it was obvious the only thing she carried with her was a small handbag.

"Ah, no," Ella said, hesitating. "I am afraid this would be my first position in journalism. I can write," she assured him. "I have a teaching degree and taught English at the high school level."

"Well, first, my dear, you are not applying for a 'position' here. We have an opening for freelance work. Do you understand what that means?"

"Of course," Ella responded somewhat indignantly. "If I can write, you will buy it. If I can't, I am gone. No contracts, no ties."

"Exactly." Mr. Wallace smiled slyly. "I won't waste your time, Mrs. Ellington. I am looking for five or six freelance writers for feature articles. Some features I will assign, others will be up to you to find something appealing enough for us to print. I just assigned a story on the Fourth of July celebration to one of my top writers. It is still a couple of weeks away, but I want him to be prepared.

"This week, I received a great article on the *Titanic* from one of my freelance writers. It won't be printed. The *Titanic* sunk in 1912. So, 1925 is not a significant anniversary. There is no new information discovered. The article is useless. Do you understand what I am getting at?"

"Absolutely, articles need to be interesting and timely," Ella agreed.

"Since you have not provided me with a portfolio, I want you to go find a feature article and have it back to me within two weeks. I suggest you write about something you know. It has been five years since the Nineteenth Amendment was ratified. Perhaps your mother's story needs to be revisited. I understand your husband, Dr. Ellington, did some interesting research on cancer. Find something you know about and bring me something worth publishing, and then, we will see if you have a job."

"Thank you, Mr. Wallace, I will." Ella left the room excited and somewhat terrified. This was a big assignment. Could she do it in two weeks? Then, she thought about her classroom. She gave writing assignments to her students, which were due in less time. She could do this. She knew she could.

*   *   *

Ella struggled with the assignment. It had to be interesting; it had to be significant. If she really wanted this job, she had to write something unique. "He said to write about something I know. Babies are interesting but not as a story," she surmised.

She explored idea after idea, but nothing seemed to have an impact. Nothing stood out. Her life was too mundane, bordering on boring to the outside world. Is this how her mother felt before she met the suffragettes?

What had Mr. Wallace suggested? Her husband's research work? Oh no! She knew nothing about that. Her mother's passion?

"Hmmm…maybe." Ella mulled it over for the rest of the day, reliving those years in her mind.

Sara had a vision, a mission. But now five years later, what had changed? Was it all for naught? Were all those years when the pain of not having her mother near tore at her heart all in vain? Was Sara's sacrifice worthwhile, was the world a better place because of it? Ella relived the agony of those years, relived the hopes and dreams of her mother, relived the heartbreak. After a few days, she finally had her inspiration and began to write.

The following week, two days before her deadline, Ella walked into the Journal's office. No one was at the front desk, so Ella called out, "Chief, Ella Ellington is here to see you."

Mr. Wallace peeked around his door, a broad smile across his face. "Let me see what you got." He motioned her into his office.

Ella took out several pages of handwritten copy from her satchel and handed it to him. He put on his glasses and began to read as Ella sat quietly on the chair that said to her, "Come in and talk to me but don't take too much of my time." She fidgeted as he read.

Sara's Sacrifice
By Ella Ellington

Sara Dewberry, a prominent suffragette in Milwaukee, paid the ultimate sacrifice on June 10, 1919 when she was gunned down after a stunning speech announcing the Wisconsin ratification of the19th Amendment to the Constitution, which gave women the right to vote.

Today we ask, was her suffrage in vain? After five years, has anything changed? We still live in a male-dominated world. In March of 1921, police in Sunbury, Pennsylvania issued an edict requiring women to wear skirts at least four inches below the knee.

In 1923, Black women in this country were still denied their right to vote despite the compassion and hard work of Tillie Morgenson and Sara Dewberry, who raised awareness of their plight. Women still find it difficult to find productive work and are denied jobs in certain fields because they are women. Women are paid far less than men and are expected to be subservient to male employees and employers. They are often faced with sexual harassment and made fun of by their male counterparts.

Other women, in fact, look down on working women as unfit mothers and poor housewives, not taking into consideration the many women who are the breadwinners in their family due to varying circumstances. Many women are relegated to sweatshop-like conditions.

Women, there is hope. In 1910, Carrie Chapman Catt was instrumental in forming an organization called The League of Women Voters. This organization was formed to enlighten and prepare women for their role in government. They provide information to help women be informed in a non-partisan way. They rally to certain causes and support issues which improve conditions for women and for the public in general.

Change is coming. Sara did not die in vain.

Mr. Wallace put down the papers and looked at Ella. "Do you recall what I told you about the *Titanic* story?"

"Yes, Mr. Wallace, I do. You said it was old news and untimely." She waited in anticipation.

"Second lesson, Mrs. Ellington… You have written a good editorial, and that is where it will go—in the People's Forum. It is not newsworthy."

"I don't understand," Ella said, puzzled.

"It is an opinion. You have not backed it up with fact. Well written, but irrelevant for a newspaper. Ask yourself: who, what, where, when, and why? We want to know facts backed up with proof. We don't want conjecture or opinion in our stories. You have given facts. You started out well by citing a police edict and by giving a date when Negro women were recognized, but then your story fell apart. Who is being harassed and in what way? We want the full story behind the facts and...or... statistics and proof your statements are accurate. I like your information about the League of Women Voters. It alone could be a feature. On second thought, I won't publish this in the People's Forum. Go home and write a story on the League and dig into it. Find out everything you can."

Ella was disappointed, but she could see her work was lacking. "Thank you, Mr. Wallace. I will show you I can write for the *Journal*." She picked up her satchel and headed for the door.

"Mrs. Ellington," Mr. Wallace called after her, "one more thing. Buy a typewriter."

Chapter Six

"Buy a typewriter? Buy a typewriter. Is the man insane? I don't know *how* to use a typewriter," Ella mused as she drove home. "I don't even have a job and I have to *buy* a typewriter. This is ridiculous. I don't need this job! Why would I want to buy a typewriter? I have perfectly good handwriting. I taught penmanship. They reset the words to print anyway. Typewriters are expensive. What nerve. And he didn't even ask, he demanded," Ella muttered as she parked her car. Then she walked around the block to Gimbles Department store, where she headed to the typewriter department.

"May I help you, ma'am?" the friendly clerk inquired.

"Yes, please," Ella stated curtly. "I need a typewriter, an Underwood."

"Very well, ma'am." The clerk led her to the counter with several typewriters. "The Underwood is very nice. We have several other less expensive brands. This Corona typewriter is very popular, and it is ten dollars cheaper." He pointed out the shiny black Corona. "Most of our Underwoods are sold to professionals."

Ella stood up straight. "I am a professional and I would like to purchase the Underwood," she announced confidently.

"Very well," the clerk beamed. He moved to the left and swept his hand in the direction of the Underwood. "This is our best model, and it sells for seventy-five dollars." He lowered his head and peered at Ella above his glasses. "And what is your profession, madam?" he inquired.

"I am an up-and-coming reporter for the *Milwaukee Journal*," Ella stated proudly. "I will take it."

Ella ran her fingers over the keys. "Would you mind getting me a new one, please? This model appears to have all of the keys in the wrong places."

The clerk smiled knowingly and placed the typewriter on a nearby table. "Ma'am, this is the qwerty keyboard used by all professionals. It is designed so you can type rapidly." He sat down at the typewriter and his fingers flew across the keyboard. "Would you like to try?"

"No, thank you," said Ella. "I will practice at home." *Good Lord, how will I ever learn this? Ella Ellington, what are you getting yourself into?*

"Please bill my husband, Dr. John Ellington," Ella stated much less confidently. "We have an account."

"Will you want it delivered?" the clerk asked.

"No, I will take it with me. I have my automobile."

"Well, then, let me carry it to your automobile. It is quite heavy," the clerk offered. "And Mrs. Ellington, I will include an instruction manual, which gives you the operational details of the machine but also includes a small learner's handbook."

Ella showed him to her vehicle and thanked him graciously.

When she arrived home, Ella opened the passenger door of her Austin to remove the typewriter and almost dropped it, not realizing how heavy it was. She got a good grip on the machine and struggled up the front steps. She placed it on the porch swing while she opened the door. She retrieved the typewriter, then took it to her husband's office and placed it on the corner of the table under the window. She cleared the space around it and made a pleasant work area for herself. Next, she went to Mrs. Johnson's house to fetch Helen.

"I think our little Helen is cutting teeth. I know she is only five months old, but she has been a bit fussy today. When she bit my finger, I felt a sharp edge," Mrs. Johnson reported. "I think she is hungry, too."

"I am sorry, Mrs. Johnson. My errands took a bit longer than I anticipated. Thank you so much for watching Helen for me. Do come for dinner on Sunday. Liz should be home from school tomorrow, and I know she'll want to see you."

"I would be delighted to come." Mrs. Johnson smiled. "Liz was such a joy as a child and has grown into quite the young lady. I do so want to see her."

"I need to rush. I am running late, and John promised he would be home for dinner tonight. I am sure it won't be until late, but I will be so happy to spend a little time with him. Thank you again." Ella hurried home to feed Helen and to prepare dinner.

When they arrived home, Helen was in a full torrent of tears. Ella changed her and sat on the bentwood rocker to feed her. She knew Helen would soon be fast asleep, and then Ella would be able to look at the typewriter in the office while dinner was in the oven. Helen settled in and suckled while Ella rocked.

"Ouch!" cried Ella. "I guess you won't be nursing much longer," Ella reprimanded her adorable baby girl.

Helen opened her big eyes and gave her mother a cheeky grin.

*   *   *

Soon, Helen was fast asleep. Ella cut up potatoes and carrots and proceeded to make a pot roast. She mixed the dough for fresh biscuits and put it aside, so they could go in the oven just before dinner. John loved hot rolls slathered with fresh butter.

Ella checked on Helen, who was still fast asleep in her crib. She headed for the office and sat down at her new Underwood typewriter. She took paper from John's desk and wound it into the roller of the typewriter, then lightly tapped a key.

Nothing happened.

She tapped again a little harder and the letter touched the paper, but still nothing printed. She took out the owner's manual and scanned the instructions.

"Ah, here it is. Place the ribbon in the machine." She rummaged around in the packing materials and there it was—a brand-new box with typewriter ribbon. Ella breathed a sigh of relief. For a moment, she thought she would have to return to purchase the ribbon and her brand-new Underwood would sit idle for a couple of days.

She struggled with the instructions and ribbon for a bit but managed to get it in place. Once again, Ella tapped a key. And again, nothing happened.

She looked at the instructions and figured out she had placed the ribbon in upside down. Again, Ella went through the process and tapped a key.

There was a slight sign of print on the paper but so light. Ella, in her frustration, hit the key several times, each time a little harder. There it was on her sheet of paper. FFFFFFFF.

Ella smiled. She was ready to type. The instruction book on learning to operate the typewriter was very helpful. It told her where to place her fingers on the crazy mixed up keys. Exercise one was learning the alphabet, letting her fingers rest on the home keys.

"How silly," she said. "If they had put them in order, I would know where they are."

She was getting impatient, so she decided to move on to lesson two.

Ella read aloud, "With your fingers resting on the home keys, type the phrase 'The quick brown fox jumps over the lazy dog.'"

What a strange sentence. The book explained this sentence was a good practice sentence because it used every letter of the alphabet. Ella became engrossed in this silly sentence. As she plunked away, typing the words over and over again, Helen slept peacefully. Nothing split the silence except for the sporadic clacking of the typewriter for the next two hours. Then, Helen stirred and began to fuss. Ella jumped up and went to her side.

She went to change Helen's diaper, and when she was about halfway through, the pungent aroma of something burning invaded Ella's nostrils. "Oh dear, my pot roast!"

Ella squealed, "No, no, no." She ran from the room, leaving Helen half-diapered.

Smoke filled the kitchen. Ella grabbed a towel and pulled the roast from the oven, burning her thumb in the process. She let out a scream and dropped the pan on the sideboard. She opened the window and began clearing the air with her towel.

Helen, being terrified by the sudden abandonment and the shrieking and strange odors, screamed from her crib.

Ella called out, "It's okay, Helen. Mother is here." Then, Ella dropped to her knees in tears, recalling the times as a child she wanted to call out to her mother, but her mother wasn't there.

She ran to her child and cradled her, comforting her, cooing to her until the baby felt safe in her arms.

Then as Ella had learned early in life, she pulled herself up and went about diligently cleaning up the mess she had created. "Damn typewriter!" she said under her breathe.

*　　　*　　　*

Ella placed the roast in cold water and began to cut away the burned parts of the meat. She cut the remaining pieces into cubes, cut up new vegetables, which she cooked while Helen was propped up in her pram close enough, so they could keep an eye on each other.

Luckily, it was a warm June day, so the doors and windows could be opened to clear and refresh the air. She lit a cinnamon scented candle to replace the charred air with an odor which permeated the atmosphere like freshly baked pie. She got some beef stock out of the ice box and prepared gravy. In no time, she had a wonderful beef stew ready for dinner. To make the pie smell more authentic, she put together a quick apple crisp and whipped some cream for topping.

Ella set the dining room table, and then went to her room to freshen up herself and Helen.

John arrived about an hour later to the smell of apple pie and a wife who looked and smelled equally sweet in her burgundy pinafore style dress with a matching ribbon tying back her brown locks. Helen was in a long cream eyelet trimmed night dress with a ruffled collar.

John was exhausted yet energized by his beautiful loving family. He took Ella in his arms and said, "Hi beautiful, what's cooking? It smells scrumptious in here."

"Pot roast, um stew," Ella corrected. "You sit for a minute while I bake the biscuits."

"Can't sit or I will fall asleep," John stretched. "Guess I will check the mail." He yawned as he went to his office.

Ella was in the kitchen when she heard John's voice. "What is this contraption in my office?"

Ella called back, "What contraption, dear?" Knowing full well what he was referring to.

"This thing on my table, which now appears to be your table."

"Oh, that's just my plant and some pictures. I thought it was pretty," Ella responded coyly.

John came into the kitchen. "I was referring to the typewriter on the table."

"Oh yes, that *is* a typewriter." Ella smiled.

"I know it is a typewriter." John smiled back. "What is it doing in my office?"

"Well, I suppose it is not doing anything—unless you are typing." Ella smiled even broader.

John walked behind his wife, put his arms around her waist, and nuzzled her neck. He whispered softly in her ear, "And I suppose there is a story here you are not telling me?"

Ella put her hand on his cheek, turned and kissed him gently on his other cheek, and chuckled. "I have some wonderful news and I will tell you all about it at dinner. Go open the wine on the table and we can talk. Dinner is almost ready."

"Just don't tell me you are going to jail. This is prohibition, you know."

"Oh please, please don't turn me in," Ella teased.

John poured the wine and said, "Okay, tell me the news."

They sat down to dinner.

"Oh, where to begin," Ella sighed. Then she told him the whole story starting with the ad in the newspaper, the interview and Mr. Wallace… "And so, I bought a typewriter!" Ella exclaimed.

"And when were you intending to tell me?" John inquired.

"Why tonight, of course," Ella stated as though it was the most natural progression.

"That was a month ago, Ella. I know I have been gone a lot, but I *have* seen you in the past month," John said incredulously.

"I know," Ella explained, "but you have so much on your mind. I didn't want to bother you with such trivial matters."

"I don't think you getting a job is a trivial matter, Ella. What about Helen?" John stood and began to pace.

"Don't be silly. Helen is too young to work," Ella tried to joke. She wanted this whole thing to be light and insignificant in his eyes.

"No, Ella, this is serious. Have you thought about Helen? What will she do while you are working?"

Ella knew joke time was over. "Yes, of course I have," Ella said, serious now. "Mrs. Johnson will watch Ella when I have to be at an appointment. I can take her with me when I am doing research, and with the typewriter here, I can work at home. We won't be apart much at all." Ella reassured her husband by patting his hand.

"Do you even know *how* to type?" John reasoned.

"I do now," Ella said proudly. "I can type the quick brown fox jumps over the lazy dog in less than three minutes."

"I saw your paper. Keep practicing. Maybe soon we will be able to read what you type." John raised his glass. "Here's to my little newshawk. May you never get your wings clipped." John shook his head.

With that, Ella knew she had her husband's approval. She rose, raised her glass to his, and sealed it with a kiss.

Chapter Seven

It was noon on Friday. Ella was in the office practicing on her Underwood typewriter. Using the morning newspaper as practice, she'd placed it beside the typewriter while she typed the articles from it. She was beginning to find it fun, although she was not as fast as the clerk at the store. But she knew if she kept practicing, she would soon become an expert typist.

Helen was on a blanket on the floor also practicing her latest skill, learning how to crawl. She could get up on her hands and knees and rock, but she couldn't quite get the hang of forward movement.

It was a warm June day. The windows were open to a soft breeze gently playing with the lace curtains on the windows. Suddenly, a horn blasted *ooga, ooga*. There was the sound of clunking and jubilant laughter and then the chuga, chuga of the motor car leaving.

"Ella, Ella," cried Liz from outside.

Ella went to the window. Liz was standing in the front yard among containers filled with all her belongings from school. Seeing Ella peek through the window, Liz called out, "Ella, I'm home. Come help me get these things inside."

Ella glanced toward Helen on the blanket and felt sure she was safe. She flew out the screen door and down the steps, calling, "Liz, Liz!"

They hugged and danced about the bags, almost falling over them in their exuberance.

"Come quick, you have to see Helen. She is trying to crawl." Ella grabbed a satchel in each arm and Liz dragged the heavy trunk toward the steps. They clamored up the steps. "She hasn't quite gotten the knack of it yet."

"Can't wait to see my niece."

Ella dropped the large satchel on the porch, opened the screen, and helped Liz drag the trunk backward into the parlor. Liz followed behind her and dropped the smaller bag Ella had been carrying and let out another squeal as she dashed to her niece, who was on all fours in the doorway of the library. She reached down and swung the pudgy baby into her arms, much to the delight of Helen.

Ella looked bewildered. "That is *not* where I left her."

Helen smiled and clapped her hands, applauding her own performance.

"She couldn't wait to see her Aunt Liz!" Liz exclaimed proudly.

Helen had found her mobility and there was no slowing her down.

After a lunch of chicken dumpling soup and fresh salad, Ella put Helen down for her afternoon nap, leaving Ella and Liz to catch up on news. They had corresponded almost every week, but it had been almost three weeks since their last letters. Ella had so much to tell her sister about the past month and Liz had her own stories to share. First, however, was the matter of getting all of Liz's things up to her room.

"By the way," Ella began, "I heard a motor car outside dropping you off. Who was that?"

"Oh, that was Charlie." Liz smiled coyly.

"And Charlie didn't help you with your bags?" Ella questioned disapprovingly. "Is Charlie another student?"

"Oh no," Liz responded. "I met Charlie at a speakeasy on State Street. He was kind of in a hurry."

Ella had noticed her little sister had changed from the giddy little girl who left for school the past fall. She had grown at least two inches. Her dark hair was clipped to a short bob, popular with the flappers of this decade. Her long dark lashes and brilliant blue eyes made her quite attractive, and Ella began to be concerned about her little sister. When she left home, she was interested in bugs and bandages, but now there was Charlie. "Oh dear."

Liz was smart and had graduated high school a year ahead of her peers. She'd already completed one year of college, but she was barely eighteen.

After Liz's things were deposited in her room and properly put away, Liz and Ella sat in the parlor to talk over a cup of tea. Ella sat in the bentwood rocker and Liz sat on the floor in front of the fireplace, hugging her knees, which were tucked up under her chin.

*   *   *

Ella had picked up her knitting and was knitting furiously. Liz instinctively knew this to be a clear sign something was troubling her sister.

Never one to mince words, Liz blurted, "What's eating you?" She was concerned perhaps her sister was having marital problems. She hadn't heard John mentioned since she arrived.

"Tell me about Charlie," Ella responded equally blunt.

This brought a smile to Liz's face. "Charlie? Charlie's the cat's pajamas." Liz giggled.

"Tell me more," Ella prodded. "How did you meet? He's not a student, so what kind of work is he in? Where was he going in such a hurry? And…what were you doing in a speakeasy?"

"Oh Ella, don't be such a prude. Everyone is doing it."

"Doing what, my dear sister?"

"Going to speakeasies, of course. It is a great place to meet friends and dance the Charleston. Some joints even have great jazz musicians. It's a hoot." Liz was thrilled with her new lifestyle.

"But it *is* dangerous. I hear illegal liquor flows and women, well, women are loose and available. I don't want you to get in trouble and ruin your life," Ella said maternally.

"Ella, it's *not* dangerous. Yeah, there is liquor, but the police just turn their heads. As long as there are no fights or trouble of any kind, they don't care. In fact, after their shifts they sometimes join us."

"Ehh," Ella breathed out. "What is this world coming to?"

"It is coming to reality. Mother died to give us emancipation. She fought for women's rights," Liz countered.

"Mother fought for women's right to vote, for women's voices to be heard. Not for promiscuity and loose living."

"Well, it is the twentieth century and women are free to do what they choose. Thank you, Mother!" Liz shot back.

Ella was standing over Liz now and a tear fell from her cheek. "Liz, I love you and I don't want you to be hurt. I don't want you to spoil your dreams with the likes of Charlie."

Liz jumped to her feet. "You don't even *know* Charlie."

Ella sat down, placed her hands in her lap. "Fair enough, tell me about Charlie."

Both women sat back, sipping their tea. Ella was a bit stiff but willing to hear out her sister. Liz was enamored and anxious to have her approval.

"Ella, you'd like Charlie. He is handsome and funny. He works hard and is very successful. He travels a lot for his job, so he has a very nice automobile. He had to meet with 'the boss' today and he was running late. That's why he was in such a hurry."

Ella relaxed a bit. "And where does he work for 'the boss'?"

"Well, I don't exactly know. Charlie doesn't like to talk about work, but I know they deal in beverages because he said they had a supply ready to go to Chicago. I think Charlie is more in the banking division because he said he had to go collect on a loan. I told him my father used to be a banker. He seemed very interested in the bank and asked me a lot of questions about the bank security."

"Hmmm…" Ella's curiosity was piqued. "And what is the company name? Who oversees the beverage um, banking company?" This seemed an odd combination.

"I really don't think you would know them. Father has been out of banking for several years and lost contact with all the new bankers long before he died. I don't think it is a regular bank anyway, more like a loan company. I don't think he ever said a company name. He doesn't have an office. He is more…um, independent. The boss tells him where to collect bad debts and he goes out and collects. He says he gets paid very well. He is good at what he does. He says he is very persuasive."

"And what is his boss's name?" Ella inquired.

"Well, I guess he is a pretty strict boss because they call him Touhy the Terrible. Charlie said I will probably never meet him, but if I do, I should call him Mr. Touhy. He must be a successful man because Charlie says someday everyone will know his name." Liz seemed impressed.

"So, what is Charlie's surname?" Ella pressed on. "And where is he from?"

"His name is Charlie Rosario. His father emigrated from Italy around the turn of the century. They live on Bowen Street in Milwaukee. Charlie says when he gets done with this job, he will take me down to the neighborhood. I want you to meet him, too. You'll see what a great guy he is. I know you'll like him."

Ella was still very skeptical, but she was willing to give her sister the benefit of the doubt…for now. Their conversation drifted back to Helen since she was awake now, fussing and squirming in the bedroom.

Liz jumped up and dashed to the baby's side. "Good afternoon, my little niece," she cooed. She welcomed the disruption to their conversation.

Chapter Eight

John arrived home late from work; Helen was tucked in for the night and Ella and Liz had settled into the parlor after a brisk walk in the summer air. A slight breeze had picked up, which was a welcome relief from the heat and humidity they had endured throughout the day.

John kissed Ella and then twirled his sister-in-law around. "Welcome home, Sprite," John greeted Liz with his favorite nickname for her. "My, haven't you grown into a lovely young lady. College is treating you well. I may have to find a new name for you. How do you like Lady Sprite?" John teased.

Liz giggled.

John went back to Ella, and with his hands on her tiny waist, he swung her around, gazing deep into her eyes. "And you, my love, are a sight for sore eyes." He gave her another kiss.

"Aren't you the charmer this evening? Had a good day?" Ella inquired, happy to see her husband in good spirits. Lately, when he came home, he was so exhausted, they barely had time to enjoy each other's company.

"Do I need to leave you two alone?" Liz inquired with a sly grin.

"Actually, I have some exciting news to share with both of you." John could hardly contain his enthusiasm. "You know old Doc Mallory on Water Street? Well, he is making plans to retire in five years and is looking for someone to join his practice, and later take it over. I met with him today and he would like that person to be me!"

Ella left out a squeal and joined in his excitement. "When will you start? What about your residency? Do you know anything about Dr.

Mallory? Tell me about him. Is there a Mrs. Mallory?" Ella was happy for John but happy for herself, too. Maybe now she would get to see more of her husband and Helen may get to know her father.

John explained, "Dr. Mallory is seventy-five-years old, and his patients love him. He treats them all like family. He is a brilliant doctor, and I can learn a lot from him. He wants to give up the surgical part of his practice as soon as possible. His eyes are growing dim and his hands aren't as steady as they once were."

"I know Dr. Mallory," Liz interjected. "I met him when I volunteered at the hospital. He is a wonderful man. I think his wife was a nurse, too. She gave up practice when her first son was born but she still volunteered at the hospital. She is so sweet."

"I guess I am the outsider here," Ella commented. "Tell me more about his family."

"They have three sons and a daughter," John said. His oldest son joined the Mayo Clinic staff in August of 1914 after their newest facility was completed. They are on the cutting edge of research and care of critical cases. It is quite an honor to be part of the growing staff of the Mayo Clinic. The young Doctor Mallory was just thirty-nine when he went to Mayo. Our Doc Mallory prefers the hometown feel of private practice and his long-term patients, but he is very proud of his son's accomplishments."

"Are all of his children doctors?" Liz asked.

"No, their second child died of scarlet fever when he was just a child. Their daughter is married to a judge in Tulsa, Oklahoma I believe. Their other son, the youngest, is an architect in Chicago. They have twelve grandchildren, but they don't get to see them very often. Their daughter Mary visits on occasion and brings her four children, but the gentlemen of the family don't have that luxury in their chosen professions. The one thing Doc Mallory is looking forward to...visiting all his children and grandchildren. Soon his grandchildren will bless him with great grand-children. In fact, I believe there is one on the way in Minnesota."

"What do you know about his wife?" Ella wanted to know.

"Margaret is a kind, sweet woman. She spent most of her life caring for her children and housekeeping, but she made time to volunteer at the hospital and orphanages. I understand she is an excellent cook. Doc says it is her fault for his rather rotund frame. You will get to meet her on Saturday. We're invited to their home for dinner at seven. Do you think Mrs. Johnson could watch Helen for a few hours?"

"Oh, don't worry about it. I can watch Helen," Liz offered.

"I invited Mrs. Johnson to have dinner with us on Sunday," Ella recalled. "Looks like this will be a busy weekend."

"Mrs. Johnson? That's terrific." Liz was elated. "I haven't seen her for about a year. I can't wait to see her again."

"She is equally happy to see you, although I can't imagine why. You used to bring all sorts of bugs to her door to show off your latest find."

"But she loved my bugs."

"No, no." Ella shook her head. "She hated your bugs, but she was too kind to disappoint you. She knew how proud you were to show them off."

"Really? Guess I owe her an apology. No bugs at dinner, I promise."

"Absolutely no bugs at dinner." John ruffled Sprite's hair and headed for the library.

*   *   *

Saturday was a wet one. Thunder rumbled throughout the day. An occasional bolt of lightning lit up the house, followed by an enormous boom. When it first started, Helen began to cry out in fear of the strange sounds crashing all around her. Ella held her close and comforted her with soft humming of familiar songs. Liz came down to the kitchen where Ella and Helen sat near a warm oven filled with the delightful treat of hot cross buns.

"Let me take her," Liz prompted.

"She is so frightened of the thunder," Ella said.

"Don't you remember what mother did when the thunder came?" Liz asked. "She embraced it."

It seemed so long ago, but Ella remembered. The next time the lightning struck, together Ella and Liz counted. When the boom hit, they both shouted, "Kaboom" and laughed heartily.

The next time they did the same thing until Helen found it to be a wonderful noisy game, and they all played together.

Soon Helen was clapping in anticipation. "Boo, boo," she prompted, hoping she could create another kaboom to make the game go on. Each clap of thunder startled her, but it was no longer out of fear.

"Good thing I went shopping yesterday," Ella said as she gazed out the window to see if there was any break in the clouds.

"What did you buy?" Liz wanted to know.

Ella needed something festive for their dinner engagement. Her clothes seemed so outdated.

"I bought a royal blue satin sleeveless chemise and a cloche hat with a blue feather. I will wear the blue Tiffany necklace father bought mother and the blue sapphire earrings." She was pleased with her selection.

"That sounds lovely. I need to go shopping soon, too," Liz said. "Can't wait to see it on you."

*   *   *

John went to work on Saturday but promised to be home by five. It was now 5:10 and John was nowhere to be seen. Not wanting to be the reason why they were late, Ella went upstairs to dress. At 6:30, Ella came down to see Liz for her final inspection.

"Not bad." Liz put her index finger at the corner of her mouth. "I would have gone for fringe and a lower neckline."

"And I would have gone for a higher one," Ella responded.

"Could be about four inches shorter," Liz nodded to the hemline.

"Eehh!" Ella rolled her eyes.

"Where is that husband of mine?" Ella was getting concerned. "We are going to be late."

Just then, she heard the old Model T pull into the drive. John ran into the house.

"Better hurry," Ella said as she held the door for him. "Your clothes are all laid out for you."

John changed quickly and rushed down the stairs, tying his ascot. "You look fabulous," he said to Ella as he grabbed their rain gear.

They were on their way and arrived at the Mallory's home at 7:05.

After introductions and small talk, Mrs. Mallory announced dinner was ready. John was right. Mrs. Mallory was an excellent chef. The meal began with Vichyssoise, a French potato soup, and a mixed green garden salad with a vinaigrette dressing. The main course was Chicken Marsala served with wild rice and a vegetable medley. The meal was superbly prepared and delicious.

After dinner, the gentlemen retired to the library where Dr. Mallory professed to have the finest Cuban cigars. John rarely smoked but had taken to occasionally smoke a pipe or a good stogie.

While the gentlemen discussed the terms of their new joint venture, Ella and Margaret became fast friends, despite the differences in their ages. Margaret told Ella how fascinated she was with Sara Dewberry and her work with the suffragettes. "You must be so proud of your mother. Her death was such a tragedy. It must be very difficult for you, dear. I am so sorry for your loss."

"Yes, it is difficult. It has been five years, yet it seems like yesterday. We had been apart for so many years when Mother was traveling the country and we were just beginning to look forward to making up for lost time. Unfortunately, it was not to be." Ella wiped a tear from her eye.

"There, there." Margaret patted Ella's hand. "I am so sorry to have opened old wounds. I know no one can replace your mother, but if you ever need a shoulder to lean on, mine are strong and willing."

Ella smiled. "Tell me about yourself," she prompted, anxious to move on to less painful topics.

They talked about Margaret's work with orphans. Ella was very curious about the children in their care and thought what an interesting topic to write about for the *Journal*.

Margaret was intrigued with Ella's new venture with the Milwaukee Journal and was equally intrigued with a possible piece on the orphanage. Any publicity would bring added funding they so desperately needed.

The evening flew by, and Ella was excited about the new partnership John would have at the Mallory/Ellington clinic. She was even more excited about the new friendship she and Margaret had made.

Chapter Nine

Helen was tucked into her crib and sound asleep. Liz had donned her nightgown and was curled into the arm of the davenport with a copy of the *New York Times* best seller, *The Great Gatsby* by F. Scott Fitzgerald. The rain splashed on the front porch with an occasional rumble of thunder breaking the night silence. Liz had left the front door open since the evening was still quite steamy. She loved the sound of the rain and the fresh clean smell from the huge raindrops washing the earth.

It was dark, and Liz expected John and Ella would soon be home. It wasn't their custom to stay out late. The grandfather clock in the hall struck ten o'clock. She heard a car pull into the driveway. She'd left the back entry unlatched since it was the shortest access from the garage and expected they would dash in to avoid being drenched.

She heard the door open but not the familiar chatter or Ella's voice calling out. Liz put down her book and headed for the kitchen where there was just a flicker from the kerosene lamp on the dining room sideboard. She started to cross the dining room on her way to the kitchen when someone grabbed her from behind and swung her around. She let out a blood curdling scream, and then immediately saw the intruder.

"Charlie! You scared me to death!" Liz was torn between indignation and pleasure at seeing the familiar face. "Charlie, don't you ever do that to me again. I thought you were going to be gone until next weekend."

"Aren't you happy to see me?" Charlie beamed. "I'm happy to see you." He winked, and pulled her close.

Liz returned his kiss. Then, she realized her attire was inappropriate and causing quite a stir in Charlie. She blushed and pulled away.

"Charlie Rosario. You are incorrigible." Liz moved back to her spot on the davenport, motioning him to a chair by the fireplace.

Charlie didn't take the suggestion but instead sat next to her on the davenport. He leaned into her, taking her face in his hands, and kissed her gently.

"Charlie!" Liz reprimanded. "I need to change my clothes." She moved to get up.

He pushed her back gently and nuzzled her neck. She knew she should get up, but she was enjoying his attention.

Charlie pulled his body onto hers and kissed her passionately, finding his way past the scoop neck of her nightgown to her breast. They were so engrossed in each other, they didn't hear the door open.

Suddenly, they realized they were not alone. Liz and Charlie jumped up and adjusted their clothing.

"Ahh," Liz stammered. "This, th…this is Charlie Rosario, Charlie, this is my sister Ella."

Ella was frowning. "So, this is the mysterious upstanding Charlie," she mocked.

John was half turned with a smirk on his face.

Liz went on, "And this is Dr. John Ellington, my brother-in-law." She coughed.

Charlie offered his hand. "Pleased to meet you."

John shook his hand but said nothing.

After a brief awkward silence, Charlie said, "I got back in town early and dropped by to say hello to Liz. I really must be going."

"Quite a hello." John stared at Charlie, his eyebrows slightly arched.

"You better go," Liz encouraged.

"Good-bye then," Charlie stammered. He bent to give Liz a peck on the cheek but seemed to think better of it. He backed out the front door, nearly falling down the steps.

He barely made it to his car when Ella began her scolding. "Young lady, we left you in charge of our baby. Have you even checked on her? Or have you only checked out Charlie? You have some explaining to do."

Liz stared at her sister, her eyes big.

An awkward silence ensued. Finally, Ella shook her head and said, "Better turn in for the night. We will discuss this in the morning."

Liz was relieved to make an exit.

Ella turned to John and said, "Dr. Ellington, in your expert opinion, how do you think we should handle this situation?" She took a deep breath and exhaled loudly.

"Let's go to bed and talk about it." John grinned. "I can explain to you all about hormones."

Chapter Ten

Sunday was a beautiful sunny day. The family dressed in their Sunday finest and headed for church. The morning had been tense.

They arrived at church and exchanged pleasantries with the other parishioners and took their places in their familiar pew. People nodded and smiled, acknowledging Liz's presence.

Reverend Nelson began the services, welcoming everyone. When it came to the sermon, Ella secretly hoped for a sermon on the damnation of carnal sin. Instead, Reverend Nelson delivered a message of tolerance and forgiveness.

John had given Ella some advice last evening, which she found difficult to accept. "Sprite is not a child anymore. She is a young woman, a beautiful young woman. You are not her mother. You may *think* you are, but in truth you are not. She has been raised well. *You* have raised her well. She needs to make her own decisions."

"Yes, but I don't want her to get hurt," Ella protested.

"She may get hurt, but hopefully she will learn from her mistakes. I must admit, she can be a little naïve. Counsel her, warn her, guide her, but Ella, don't judge her. And certainly, don't try to control her. Controlling her will only drive her away and push her further towards danger," John advised.

"But the world is changing so quickly. There is so much more freedom for women and so much more temptation." Ella was so worried for her sister.

"True," John agreed. "That's why you need to *guide* her. There is a fine line between guiding and controlling. If she thinks you are teaching and concerned, she may listen. Note I said *may*. I can tell you with all certainty if you try to control her, she will run to Charlie, and you could lose her. You know firsthand how it works. Your father tried to control your mother. Everyone was hurt. She went on her mission and grieved the loss of her children, he grieved the loss of his wife, and you grew up without a mother. Maybe if he'd had more tolerance in the beginning and approached his fears differently, there would not have been so much sorrow in your childhood."

Ella sat in church listening to the word 'tolerance' once again as Reverend Nelson spoke about self-serving demands on others and judgment of things that are different. He read from scripture, Matthew 7:1-5.

Liz looked at her sister. Ella looked away.

Pastor Nelson's message was clear. We do not have the right to judge others, particularly those we know nothing about. Do we know why the thief steals? Do we know what is in the heart of an adulteress? Do we know a person is bad simply because he was born a different color or raised by another prophet? Who are we to judge? Only God can see into another's heart. Only God has a right to judge.

The family greeted the pastor on their way out. Ella and Liz walked side by side as they continued to the automobile. She reached out and squeezed Liz's hand.

Liz smiled knowingly, and they both ran to the vehicle much as they had when they were small children. Liz's hat flew back but was secured at her neck with a pink ribbon. Ella clutched her own hat as they ran laughing all the way.

"Hey, wait for me," John called as he carried a squirming Helen in his arms.

Ella felt much better and told herself things were going to be just fine. John talked a good talk but let's not be fools. She could sense John harboring his own reservations about Charlie.

Chapter Eleven

Ella was back in Editor Wallace's office within a week. In her hand was a simple one page, poorly typewritten article with a headline.

WOMEN VOTERS RISE TO THE CHALLENGE

By E.J. Ellington

Mr. Wallace, with some flourish began to read aloud.

"February 14, 1920, before the Nineteenth Amendment, giving women the right to vote passed, the League of Women Voters was established under the direction of Carrie Chapman Catt in Chicago, Illinois. The purpose of the organization was to provide experience and education for women to assure the success of democracy and educate the populace in a non-partisan fashion to the issues facing our great nation. The Wisconsin Chapter of this organization was founded in the same year, dedicated to improving our systems of government and impacting public policies through citizen advocacy and education.

"Looks like you did your research." Mr. Wallace smiled and continued reading to himself.

Ella tried to analyze his expression to see if he liked what he read. It was impossible, so she sat at the edge of the chair in anticipation. The article went on to explain the function of the organization.

"The League of Women Voters provides information on the issues of the day so women will be educated and informed voters, free to select the parties of their choice. Maude Wood Park was the first president of the National Association. She made it clear from the beginning the League was not focusing on women's issues but issues affecting all the electorate. It neither supports nor endorses any political candidate. Currently, the League is organized in 346 of the 443 congressional districts."

Mr. Wallace peered over his glasses at Ella, still not revealing his opinion. In the article, she had written about the issues facing them today.

"Issues being tackled by the organization include such things as: child welfare, education, the home and high prices, women in gainful occupations, public health and morals, and independent citizenship for married women. These are a few of the almost seventy topics addressed by the organization. The League provides classes to train volunteers for citizenship, schools and groups to study defects in our government. They provide surveys, lobby for causes, and hold forums to provide information about candidates. This is an enormous undertaking, which has received great support and enthusiasm among all women. Although the organization is for women only, men are being educated on the issues as well."

Ella sat back and watched Mr. Wallace. She fidgeted as he finished reading the article.

He put the paper on his desk and gave her a stern look. "Mrs. Ellington!" There was a long pause. "This article," he hesitated again, "will run in the Saturday edition of the *Journal*. I'm afraid, I may be keeping you very busy. I trust that will be fine with you?" he inquired.

"Yes, yes." Ella could not contain her pleasure. She put her hands to her mouth stifling the squeal of delight begging to be let loose. "I can't wait for my next assignment!"

"I noted you used initials in your byline, can you tell me why?" Mr. Wallace was curious, considering her obvious advocacy for women's recognition.

"Umm, well, mm, Mr. Wallace," Ella stammered. "I would like to pursue some articles on more controversial issues, and it might be better if my gender were not known. Is that a problem?"

"Can you tell me what exactly you have in mind?" Mr. Wallace asked.

"I can't say for certain, but you did say I could pursue articles on my own, did you not?"

"Well, yes, I did, but be careful. Controversial could mean danger-ous. You must have some ideas in mind," he asked, pushing for a little more insight into her thoughts.

Ella glanced away a moment. She cleared her throat. "Umm, well, umm… I thought I might look into the workings of the Italian commu-nity in our city and umm…"

"Oh, no, Mrs. Ellington, I think that is a very *unwise* idea." He frowned. "Why would you want to do that? You know the Italians were behind the bombing at the Milwaukee Police station a few years ago. 1917 to be exact. You could get in trouble sticking your nose into their business. No, no, I don't think so. It is far too dangerous."

"I promise you I will be careful, and I will only rely on sources I know."

"M-M-M-M-M." Mr. Wallace shook his head. "Let me find a more appropriate topic. You'll be hearing from me soon." He took her hand, shaking it.

Lightening the mood, he added, "And by the way, Mrs. Ellington, you could bide your time better by brushing up on your typing skills."

Ella waited until she was out of his office before she permitted herself to roll her eyes at his suggestion. She knew her typing skills needed work. She couldn't let go of her investigation idea. She needed to know if for no other reason, to protect Liz. She sighed. *What to do, what to do.*

Chapter Twelve

That evening, Ella had a talk with her sister. "I know you are headstrong, Liz, and I know you care about Charlie, but please be careful. You are young and beautiful. Sometimes, that can lead you to trouble. You should keep focused on your career and your future. If Charlie is going to be a permanent part of your future, he will respect you. He'll wait for intimacy. Abstinence is a virtue, you know."

Liz rolled her eyes. "Ella, you are so old-fashioned. It's so cute, but I can take care of myself."

"I don't think you *do* understand." Ella took a breath, remembering John's caution about being controlling. "Mistakes could ruin the plans you have for your future. Bad choices could ruin your reputation. Please, be careful."

"Don't worry, I won't get pregnant. I've taken care of that."

"What?" Ella was shocked. "What do you mean?"

"I saw a doctor. I have what I need."

"What do you mean? Who did you see?" Ella was even more concerned now. "Maybe you should talk to John. He can explain what you are getting into." Ella was sure John could set her on the right path.

Liz laughed. "What doctor did you *think* I saw? John fitted me for a diaphragm and gave me a supply of condoms…in case Charlie forgets."

"*What?*" This was not the path for Liz. "Oh my!"

Liz smiled at her sister's frustration. "Welcome to the Roaring Twenties."

Not knowing what to do or say, Ella welcomed the stirring of Helen from the bedroom and exited to get her child.

"Oh, dear Helen, don't ever grow up," she said to her daughter. "I don't think I am ready for this."

*　　　*　　　*

John arrived home late, exhausted from a long day at the hospital. He was hoping to have a drink and go directly to bed. He was not at all prepared for the cold reception he got from his wife. Sensing a problem, he asked, "Is something bothering you?"

"Yes, John," Ella barked at him. "You didn't *tell* me you met with Liz. You didn't *tell* me you supplied her with contraptions for birth control. What were you thinking?" Ella slammed down the book she held in her hand.

"Of course, I didn't tell you," John said. "It's called doctor-client privilege. If Helen were older and came to me as a doctor, I wouldn't tell you, either."

This incensed Ella even more.

"Helen is my child, and I forbid you to withhold that kind of information from me."

"Ella, you know I never discuss patient information with you no matter who it is. I treat all of my patients with the confidentiality they deserve, and I treat them to the best of my ability."

"You enlightened me to the nature of hormones, and it is clear you also discussed hormones with my sister."

"No, my dear, I discussed hormones with you and with a patient whose name will remain anonymous, although you continue to refer to her as your sister."

"But why, John? Why did you encourage this behavior by giving her birth control?"

"Because first of all, it is her choice. Second, we want the same things for Sprite. Once she has crossed that line, there is no putting the genie back in the bottle. It's that hormone thing. Would you rather have her out there playing Russian Roulette or give her the means to be protected from pregnancy and disease."

"Disease, oh my God," Ella said. "Oh John, this is way too much for me. I can't fathom what that girl is getting into or what this world is coming to."

"You don't have to, my dear, it is not your problem. Love Sprite and be good to her. She is smart. She will figure it out." He patted her on the shoulder. "We don't want to see our babies grow up, but they do. We have to trust they will make good choices, and if they don't, we at least can try to cushion the fall."

"John, how come you can make things seem so simple?"

"Education, my dear. You can never get enough of it. Would you like to learn about condoms? I think I have some in my bag." He grinned.

*   *   *

Ella laughed. She was getting nowhere with John on the issue of morality. As Liz had reminded her, it was the Roaring Twenties and life as she knew it was changing rapidly. It seemed to Ella that it was spinning out of control.

Maybe her husband was right. The answer to all questions was in education. And she was about to be educated. It was a scary thing for her, but she needed to find out for herself what all the hoopla was about.

"Yes, my dear, why don't you show me how condoms can be used." Although this was an uncomfortable situation for Ella, she gave a show of bravado and winked at him. *Good Lord, what is this world coming to and how will I ever survive it?*

*   *   *

Charlie had been in Chicago for some time but was expected back on Saturday. Liz was going to see Charlie on Saturday night and they were going dancing.

"Liz, this might be a bit awkward, and I don't want to chaperone you, but do you think I could go with you and Charlie on Saturday? Just for a little while?" Ella asked.

Liz was taken aback for a moment. "Well, uh, sure," she replied hesitantly. "To the speakeasy?"

"Oh, I don't want to interfere, so check with Charlie first to make sure it's okay. You seem to like the speakeasies and dancing. Maybe I would, too, but how will I know unless I try?"

"I'm sure Charlie won't mind. He wants to get to know you better," Liz lied. After the awkward moment on the davenport a few weeks ago, the last thing Charlie wanted was to get to know her sister better.

"What should I wear?" Ella asked.

"Let's check your wardrobe," Liz volunteered, almost a little giddy at the prospect of showing her big sister a new lifestyle. Ella was a vivacious and outgoing person. Liz knew she would not be an embarrassment, but still wondered what Ella's response would be to this new world.

They tore through Ella's wardrobe, but Liz determined nothing would do.

"Come with me," she said and charged down the hallway to her room, Ella in tow. "I have some things that should fit you."

In moments, they had laid out three dresses that made Ella roll her eyes. They were shorter than the length she was used to with fringe everywhere.

Liz made Ella try on the red one first, but it was clearly a bit more than Ella could take. The black one was very chic but way too provocative.

The forest green one was perfect. It accented Ella's chestnut locks, wasn't too short or too fringy, and it fit her perfectly. She could pair it with their mother's emerald earrings and a long set of pearls, which Liz insisted was an essential part of her wardrobe. She would wear her black heels with the ankle straps.

Liz was beginning to feel good about this new adventure. She might be disappointed if Charlie said no.

*   *   *

Charlie called Liz on Friday morning. "Hey, chick, looks like my work will be done early. Want to go for a drive Saturday morning?"

"Sure thing, Charlie boy," Liz said, giddy with the news. "We can drive by the Lakeshore and have a picnic in the park. I'll bring a basket. I have wonderful news to share."

"Whazat? Got some hooch in your basket?" Charlie teased.

"You'll never guess. Wanta guess, Charlie boy? Here's a hint. It is about my sister." Liz giggled.

"She's got a bun in the oven?" he asked.

"No, sweetie. Get this. She wants to go to the speakeasy with us on Saturday. You don't mind, do you?"

The line went silent.

"C'mon, it's okay. She is trying to be open-minded," Liz urged.

"Why? She was about to crush my nuts a couple weeks ago. This can't be good."

"Give her a chance. You'll like her once you get to know her. Ella wants to get to know you. *Please*… C'mon, please? She only wants to go out for a little while. John is in Madison at a conference this weekend. She can get a sitter till eleven and then the rest of the evening is ours."

"All right, babe. I can't resist your baby blues."

"Oh Charlie, you are so silly. You can't see my eyes through the telephone." Liz giggled again. "I'll tell Ella you think we will have a delightful time."

"Yeah, do that." Charlie sighed. "Wear the little red number you had on when I met you. We'll go to the Manhattan Club, it's a classy joint. No blind pig for your sister cuz if she's disappointed…"

"What?"

"Nothin'. Just check her bag to make sure she's not carrying a nutcracker."

Liz laughed. "Whatever you say."

Chapter Thirteen

Saturday was a hot and steamy kind of day, and the speakeasy was crowded. They entered the front door of the Manhattan Club where people were coming in from every direction. It was early but the smoke from cigarettes and cigars hung in the air, creating a fog in the dim lit, sultry room. The bar was crowded with patrons ordering cool mugs of root beer or seltzer.

A jazz band was getting warmed up, but no one was on the dance floor. The saxophone cried out a bluesy tune Ella didn't recognize, though so far, she was enjoying the jovial atmosphere. People were engaged in conversations and laughter.

Belle Richards sauntered over, loosened Charlie's tie and told him to ditch the jacket. She was dressed in a tight red dress and bustier. The black lace covering her bosom hid little and was designed to attract attention. Ella and Liz looked on with raised eyebrows.

Belle turned to the ladies. "Which one of you fine ladies is the lucky captor of this handsome gent?" She nodded toward Charlie.

Liz smiled broadly and staked her claim. "He's mine." She sidled up to Charlie, wrapping her arm in his.

"Keep an eye on him, honey," Belle said and smiled. "He's fair game here."

"Not on my watch." Liz stood all of her five-feet-two inches tall and faced Belle's five-feet-ten looming frame.

Belle laughed raucously. "Honey, he's all yours. I got my own man. This is my establishment and I aim to keep my customers happy." She looked Ella up and down. "Mmm, honey, you are a sight for sore eyes. We'll have you fixed up in no time."

"Ah, ah, no!" Ella protested. "I'm already spoken for."

Belle looked down at the ring on her finger. "Where's your man, honey?"

"He's not here tonight. He's away at a conference," Ella explained.

"Uh, huh! That's what they all say. Don't you worry, girl. There's plenty of fish in the sea." Belle sauntered off, chuckling to herself. "You all enjoy yourselves," she called over her shoulder.

They found a place at a small table and Charlie excused himself after ordering a root beer for each of the ladies. He headed off to the back of the bar and was soon out of sight.

*   *   *

In the back, Charlie knocked three times on the door, stopped, and then rapped four more times. A Negro gentleman opened a small, frosted window in the door and peeked out.

Charlie did not hesitate or wait for a greeting. "It's raining in Vegas," he said, and the door creaked open.

In the middle of the room was a poker table with four gentlemen sitting at it, their jackets off and their sleeves rolled up.

"New blood?" the big fellow on the right questioned. He was clearly the big winner.

"I'll be back later with my broad. Just came back here to get a real drink." Charlie lit up a cigarette.

"What you havin'?" the colored man nodded toward the small bar in the corner.

"You got hooch?"

"Moon shinin' bright tonight! Got some good stuff."

"Yah?" Charlie nodded. "What's yer name, my man?"

"The name's Albert," the colored man replied. "Jigger or snifter?"

"Well, Albert, make it two snifters but put it in a tumbler. I'm takin' it out to the floor."

"You got it," said Albert and filled a tumbler.

*   *   *

At the table, Ella and Liz had attracted some attention. Two fellas spotted the ladies alone and wasted no time being charming.

"Hey, you sweet things sitting here all by yourselves. That just ain't right. I'm Norman and this here is my brother, Harold. Do you mind if we sit?" Not waiting for a response, they each pulled up a chair.

Ella, having no idea they were being picked up, gave a welcoming response. "I'm Ella and this is my sister, Liz."

Liz kicked her big sister under the table.

"Well, wad d'ya' know," Norman went on. "Imagine that, sisters and brothers. We already have something in common." Norman reached over and patted Ella's arm.

Harold was next to Liz. He pulled his chair closer and put his hand under the table.

Liz spoke up. "It is nice meeting you gentlemen, but we have fellas." She gave Ella a glare.

Finally realizing what was happening, Ella chimed in, "Yes, I'm married." She shook her ring finger for them to see. "And Liz's man, Charlie, is in the rest room."

Norman chuckled. "I think Charlie must have diarrhea; he's been gone a long time. We saw him go out the back way. Don't think he's coming back."

Ella was alarmed. "Liz, did Charlie leave?" She scanned the room but saw no sign of him. She wanted to tell Liz to go find him but didn't want to be left alone with Norman and Harold.

The trombones broke into a rendition of the Charleston and Norman leaned into Ella. "Wanna dance?" he asked. He grabbed her hand

and before she knew it, she was on the dance floor with several other couples.

She was not very good with this new dance, but neither was Norman.

*   *   *

Liz not wanting to be alone with Harold's wandering hands and regretting she was wearing such a short dress said, "Harold, let's dance," and headed to her sister's side on the dance floor. At least this dance did not require touching your partner.

Charlie, where are you? She gritted her teeth when she realized he was still nowhere in sight.

Liz no more than reached the dance floor and the music changed tempo as "Stardust" was being played by the band.

Harold and Norman grabbed their partners and pulled them close.

"My feet are killing me in these shoes," Ella lied and broke away, about to head toward their table. She turned to Norman, upset yet trying to be discreet. "Look, Norman, I am married and I don't appreciate your advances. I think you better move on." Norman gave her puppy dog eyes, but she was not about to give in.

Meanwhile after a sort of wrestling match on the dance floor, Liz had had it. She didn't know whether she was madder at Harold or Charlie, but Harold was the closest target. She pulled away and slapped him across the face. In no uncertain terms, she told him to get out of her life, drawing the attention of others on the dance floor.

"Okay, okay," Harold said as he held his hands in the air defensively. "I'll get my things from the table and go." He followed Liz back to the table. Apparently, he couldn't resist one last gesture as he grabbed her behind.

Charlie was finding his way back to the table and saw Harold in action. He raced across the room, grabbed Harold by the collar and yelled, "Keep your hands off my woman."

Liz wasn't sure where Charlie had come from, but she was glad he was there.

Charlie drew back his arm and slammed his fist into Harold's chin. Harold never knew what hit him. The second blow sent him careening across the next table. Drinks went flying into the air. Harold was out cold.

Norman went to the aid of his brother and Belle came running over to see what the commotion was about.

She poured a cold drink on Harold. Norman managed to get his brother on his feet and assisted him out of the club.

"Well, well Charlie," Belle said and smiled. "I think you owe these nice people drinks at this table you destroyed. Do you think we can tone it down for the rest of the evening?"

"Never mind about the rest of the evening," Ella commanded. "Charlie, please take us home."

Liz agreed. This was not the night she had expected.

When they arrived home, Ella made her way into the house to thank Mrs. Johnson for babysitting Helen.

Liz lingered with Charlie in the automobile but decided not to return to the speakeasy with him. They had thought the venue they chose would be more subdued than some of the other speakeasies. As it turned out, Liz wasn't sure if Ella would ever approve of Charlie or speakeasies in the future. She held her head in her hands and let out a low whistle as she walked to the door. What a disaster this night had been. She took a deep breath and went to see how upset her sister was and who she was blaming for this fiasco.

But Ella had already retired to her room. Cooling off might be good.

Chapter Fourteen

The next day at breakfast, Liz tried to make light of the situation. "What a night! We have never been to the Manhattan Club before, but Charlie says word around town is it's a classy place."

"Well, if that was classy, I don't want to see the seedy side!" Ella exclaimed.

"Charlie feels awful, and he wants to make it up to you. He has invited us to the speakeasy in his neighborhood. He wanted me to meet some of his family and friends anyway. Perhaps John could join us next Saturday?" Liz asked, hoping her sister would not refuse without some consideration.

Ella hesitated as she seemed to think about the invitation. "Well, Charlie apologized all the way home last night and he did seem sincere. I do believe in second chances," Ella pondered.

"Please, Ella, please?" Liz begged. "It would mean so much to Charlie and me."

After a bit more silent consideration Ella said, "Okay, I will check John's schedule and let you know for certain." Ella seemed to mull it over. "If Charlie had not disappeared or those horrid brothers showed up, it might have been a pleasant evening. The band was good, and everyone seemed to be enjoying themselves," she reflected. "Yes, it's worth another try. But there won't be another after that."

When she told John about it, he was less than enthusiastic. He finally agreed but said they would drive in separate cars in case an emergency arose.

*   *   *

They were to meet at the neighborhood clubhouse at six p.m. There would be a welcome home party for Charlie's Uncle Frank and the tables would be spread with a grand buffet to celebrate such an event.

John was not disappointed. In the ballroom, tables were filled with ham and fried chicken, casseroles, salads, and desserts. It looked like enough to feed an army. This was quite appropriate since Frank was being welcomed home from the army.

Frank entered the ballroom in a rickety wood wheelchair. He was missing a leg.

John was touched and had many questions about Frank's care. He immediately went to the man's side and introduced himself.

"Looks like you've been through some rough times. How did this happen?" John asked and pointed to Frank's stump.

Frank looked up at John. "Doctor you say?"

"Yes, Dr. John Ellington," John repeated and reached to shake Frank's hand.

Frank smiled and said, "Pleased to meet you. Guess I'll be needing a doctor here. Are you that kind a doctor? Medical, I mean?"

"Yes, I am," John said. "Can you tell me what happened?"

Frank sighed and shut his eyes, clearly reliving the horror. "Twas the Muese–Argonne offensive in France. We were up against the Germans. It was a bloody battle." Frank hesitated. Pain was written on his face as he recalled the battle. "General John J. Pershing led the battle. Don't think he knew how bad it would be."

"Were a lot of lives lost?" John asked.

"So many!" Frank shook his head. "I was one of the lucky ones. More than 26,000 men lost their lives. So many." He hesitated again as a tear ran down his cheek. "My pal, Fred. Fred Thompson. Fred died in my arms. The Germans got him good. I think he was shot two, maybe three times. He fell on me, and I was covered with his blood and guts. No other way to describe it. Fred was a good man. He didn't deserve to die. Neither did the thousands of others."

John listened patiently, placing his hand over Frank's. "It was a terrible war."

"That it was." Frank took a deep sigh.

"So, tell me, what happened with your leg?" John pressed on.

"I was shot in the leg and Louie came to get me, but then he was shot in the back and head. He fell on me, and I guess he saved me. Louie had a wife and two kids at home. It should have been me what died."

"I think God had other plans for you," John reasoned.

"Lot of good it'll do with one leg and a wheelchair...a rickety one at that. They needed a lot of wheelchairs. Over 95,000 soldiers were wounded. Sure, the offensive was over in 100 days, but the last days were the worst. Bodies everywhere. Some bad, some not so bad. I hear it was the bloodiest battle in the whole war."

"When did this happen?" John asked.

Frank chuckled. "We may be banged up, but we knocked the hell out of them Germans. That battle ended the war. Forty-seven days we fought. Forty-seven. General Pershing arranged the Armistice on November 11, 1918," Frank said. He seemed proud despite his anguish. He chuckled again. "I lost my leg on November eighth. Too bad the damn war wasn't over a week sooner."

"So, what happened then?" John asked, still wanting to know about his treatment.

"Well, sir, the guys put a tourniquet on my leg and gave me water. It was so silent. All we could do was wait. There were so many needing medical attention. It was impossible to get everyone out at once. They took the most critical first. The pain was real bad at first but after a while it didn't hurt at all. I couldn't feel my leg so I couldn't get up or walk. I just laid there for days."

"How many days?" John was horrified.

"Don't rightly know," Frank said as he thought back. "Three, maybe four. I lost so much blood I wasn't always conscious. Maybe five."

John knew that was far too long for a good outcome. *What a decision it must have been to decide who gets help first and who had to wait.*

Ninety-five thousand men! It was beyond his comprehension. And that's just our allied forces. Think of all of the opposition lives lost, too.

John's heart was heavy. He had pledged his life to saving lives and here were so many lives destroyed too quickly. Many thought it a needless waste. Some thought for economic gain. How foolish it all seemed to him.

John pulled a chair over so he could sit at Frank's level.

"Tell me, Frank, what happened then? Where did you go, what treatment did you receive?" he asked, curious.

"They flew me out on one of those airplanes. Some went by airplane and some by ship. Guess I was one of the lucky ones. Went to a hospital in Washington, D.C. They operated on my leg and dressed the wounds. Then, it was a matter of waiting and hoping it wouldn't be infected. They had some pretty nurses there who helped but they didn't give me much hope."

"How did they treat you? Do you know? What medications did they use?" John was interested in learning.

"Well, first they gave me some shots to stop the infection. I think they said bromide. But it didn't work too well. Gangrene set in anyway."

"Yes, that method was used in Civil War hospitals, and it had some good results. Dr. Goldsmith applied it in over 330 cases and mortality was under three percent. It is still quite effective, but the prognosis is much better if the treatment had been done much sooner. Your tissue was already starting to die before you got there." John had feared this was going to happen when Frank indicated it was days before he got medical attention.

"Well, sir, they said they had no choice but amputation."

John nodded in understanding. "I'm afraid that's probably true."

"So then, they kept me until they were sure there would be no more gangrene. It took two more operations. One to clean out more tissue and the next was another amputation. The whole leg pretty much had to go."

"How long were you there?"

"Don't recall exactly but it was a long time. But those pretty nurses stayed close by. Wouldn't let me smoke, though."

"Did they do rehab with you?"

"Some," Frank said, "but when they were pretty sure the gangrene was taken care of, then I was moved to the National Home for Disabled Volunteer Soldiers in Hot Springs, South Dakota. Was there I think six years? Got to be like home. Lots of soldiers sharing war stories. I'd just as soon forget. But I'm a lucky one. Louie's family can't forget."

By the end of the evening, John and Frank were fast friends.

*   *   *

Meanwhile, Liz was captivated by the attentions of Charlie's friends. He stuck close by her throughout the entire evening.

Liz saw Ella had made friends of her own in Charlie's sister and mother.

This didn't seem at all like a speakeasy…and for this night, it was not. The clubhouse was periodically used for private parties. Lots of neighborhood friends stopped by to pay their respects to Uncle Frank, to indulge in good food, and imbibe the liquor that flowed rather freely. Prohibition was in force, but you would never know it. The party was private, and no one was rowdy. It was a party to pay respects for the men in uniform.

Time flew, and the party was nearly over. People were beginning to leave.

Charlie's mother gave her son a big kiss on the cheek and said, "Charlie, will we see you at mass tomorrow? Bring Liz and her family."

Ella spoke up and said, "Oh, but Mrs. Rosario, we are Presbyterian."

"Protestant?" Mrs. Rosario was shocked. "Methodist?" The air now had a definite chill to it. "Get out!"

Ella and Liz looked at each other in surprise.

"No, we are Presbyterian," Liz echoed.

"Same thing!" Mrs. Rosario shouted. "Go back to your Father Giuliani. I thought we were done with Methodists."

Father Giuliani. Father Giuliani. Where did I hear that name before? Liz grimaced.

But Ella remembered. Giuliani's mission work incited the Italians of this neighborhood to plant a bomb in the Methodist church in 1917. Although the Italians were not formally charged, many were jailed and deported.

John took Ella by the arm and ushered her from the clubhouse.

"Liz, come with us, please!" Ella called to Liz.

Liz looked to Ella and then back to Charlie, obviously torn.

Charlie took Liz's arm and led her to John's automobile outside. "You better go with your sister. I'll telephone you tomorrow."

It was clear Charlie didn't want to leave Liz, but he seemed afraid of what might happen if she stayed or if he left with her. There was bad blood between Catholics and Protestants, and especially Methodists, in the Italian community. Although the Dewberry/Ellington family had heard of the conflict, they were immune to the intensity of it all.

Up until now…

Liz waved good-bye through the window at Charlie, hoping he'd still call her.

Chapter Fifteen

Charlie didn't call Liz for two days. It took that long to calm the storm in his house. He was a dutiful son who attended mass on Sunday morning with his mother, who insisted he spend the rest of the day with Uncle Frank. She knew then he was not off with that *despicable protestant*, "that WASP." Mother Rosario was not simply prejudiced; she had a personal grievance to bear.

Finally, on Monday, Charlie telephoned Liz.

*　　*　　*

Liz had been searching her mind to figure out what went so horribly wrong. She knew the Italians had a religious rebellion happening, but she never dreamed it was this intense and so broadly focused. She thought for sure she could endear herself to Mrs. Rosario, and in truth until that fatal moment, they had gotten along beautifully…at least Liz had thought so.

"Hello," Liz said into the telephone, her voice weary.

"Hi, Sweetheart." There was a pause. "I'm so sorry," Charlie said. "It seems like all I am doing lately is apologizing. To your sister for the speakeasy, to you for my mother's reaction…"

"I thought we were doing so well. What happened?" Liz asked. She truly believed there was something more than her religion to provoke such a reaction.

"It's kind of a long story. Can I see you?" Charlie sounded weary, too, not his usual playful self.

"Of course."

"I'll be right over."

Within a half hour, Charlie was at her doorstep with a gigantic bouquet of flowers.

She put the flowers in a vase, making small talk while she arranged them.

"Let's go sit on the veranda," she suggested. John was at work, and Helen and Ella were down for an afternoon nap. It was a warm sunny afternoon with a slight breeze. The wicker rockers were arranged near a fountain surrounded by summer blooms.

Liz sighed. "So, what did I say that was so horrible?"

"Liz, I need to tell you something." Charlie shifted in his chair and cleared his throat. Slowly, he began, "My family came here from Sicily when I was a young boy. We are related to the Genna family, who came to America around the turn of the century. They joined the Unione Siciliana, an organization dedicated to helping poor Sicilian immigrants. Prohibition brought an opportunity for these immigrants to make money in the bootlegging business. As time went on, there were other opportunities in gambling and extortion. The leader of the organization was shot, and my uncles, the five Genna Brothers, took over and operated out of Little Italy."

Charlie took a deep breath, then went on. Liz shifted slightly in her chair wondering where this story was going.

"Turf wars broke out and many were killed, including some of the brothers. My father, Giuseppe Rosario, was an expert in firearms and explosives. The gangs were mostly family, and although some were recruited from without, family loyalty prevailed. The Genna Brothers knew things were tough in our neighborhood, so they asked my father to make bombs for them. They paid well. We were finally able to live a good life, out of poverty. Uncle Frank joined the military during the Great War, but my father was waging his own war at home, providing bombs for the anarchists. Since we live in Milwaukee, my father didn't have any direct involvement in the Chicago gang wars, but he made many contacts. Bugs Moran visited often to get 'supplies,' as they called them."

Liz was speechless. Her mouth dropped slightly.

Charlie seemed to be gauging her reaction before he went on. "My father taught me how to make bombs." He hesitated once again.

Liz looked on wide-eyed.

"In 1917, my father made the bomb that destroyed the Milwaukee Police Department." Charlie looked away, embarrassed.

Liz gasped and put her hand over her mouth. "Your father bombed the police department?"

"No, no. Not directly. He made the bomb. Someone else delivered it to the church but then someone else took it to the police department where it exploded."

"Who took it to the church, Charlie? Who?"

"We don't know."

Liz worried Charlie may have delivered it but when he said he didn't know, she believed him. "Why is your mother so angry with me?"

"Father Giuliani was warned several times to leave and stop harassing the Italian Catholics, but he and the other Methodist Missionaries wouldn't listen. They kept coming to the neighborhood, preaching and causing trouble."

He blew out a breath. "After the bombing, several of our neighbors and relatives were arrested. My brother Anthony was deported. My father was distraught because a friend of his, Mario Stephano, had been shot by the police and died. His son was jailed. My father was teaching a neighbor to make bombs. They were making a bomb for the Chicago gang, and he was distracted by Father Giuliani and his missionaries. The bomb went off and my father was killed. My mother blames the Methodists."

"Oh, Charlie, that's horrible. But they didn't detonate or even make the bomb? Why does she blame the Methodists?"

"If Father Giuliani had left us alone, none of it would've happened. I know it doesn't seem reasonable, Liz, but she needed someone to blame in her grief. There was bad blood between the Catholics and Protestants before all this. My mother needed someone to blame, and Father Giuliani and the Methodists were an easy target. Grief does that." He pushed his hand through his hair.

"Charlie, you need to get away from that hostility. You need to... Oh, my gosh Charlie, you are working with the mafia. You are doing business in Chicago. Oh, my gosh." Liz couldn't catch her breath.

Charlie took Liz into his arms, but she was rigid and scared.

"Charlie, you need to stop. You need to stay away from them. You're smart, you can find other work," she pleaded.

"You don't understand. There is only one way to quit the gang...in a box," Charlie explained. "I would leave but I can't. I don't kill people, but I do make and deliver the bombs, and sometimes, I collect debts owed to the mob. I take bombs to them and bring back alcohol to Milwaukee. You can't tell anyone, Liz. Do you hear me? You can't tell anyone, not even your sister or I'm a dead man."

Liz broke into tears. "Charlie, Charlie, how could you?"

"I didn't have a choice. My father was in the bomb-making business and he taught me. The mob knew this, and they knew I knew everything. I had no choice. I had to be with them or against them, and if I were against them, I would die."

She pulled away from him and ran toward the house. "Leave, Charlie, now!" Liz shouted through her tears.

"Liz, please," Charlie begged.

"I need time to think," Liz said as she turned to look at him before she ran into the house. She couldn't be in love with a criminal.

Chapter Sixteen

Liz stayed in her room for the rest of the day. When Ella came to check on her, she said she wasn't feeling well and would skip dinner.

A few days later, Charlie left for Chicago. He called Liz when he was back in town, but she refused to see him. She couldn't...

Summer ended, and Liz returned to school in Madison. She became engrossed in her studies. She had no interest in speakeasies or any of the men on campus who found her attractive. Charlie was in love but so was she. Her heart broke every time she thought of him, but she dealt with it by pouring herself into her studies.

In November, about a year after she had met Charlie, Liz got a call from him.

"Can we meet for coffee? Please, Liz?" he asked.

They talked for a while, and eventually, she gave in and agreed. She needed to see that he was okay.

On Friday morning, the week before Thanksgiving, they met at Butch's Café on State Street for breakfast. Liz sat in a booth, waiting. She looked up when the bell over the door jangled. There was Charlie, so tall and handsome. Her heart skipped a beat.

They ordered the breakfast special and sipped coffee, first exchanging small talk about the weather and their families.

"I have something to tell you and something to ask you," Charlie began. "First, I am quitting the gang. I will be going to Chicago today and I plan to talk to the boss. I'm going to tell them I am ill and can't work anymore. I will tell them I have tuberculosis. Liz, please help me. Tell me everything you know about tuberculosis."

Her breath caught in her throat. "Charlie, I..."

He held up a hand. "Then, I will come back here and figure out what to do for an honest living. I have a pretty good stash saved up, so I don't have to work for a while. I will tell them I am in Madison to be near the hospital. I need to know everything about the disease. What medications, what therapy. It must be believable. If it is believable, I think I can pull this off."

"Charlie, you must know tuberculosis is contagious! You will have to wear a mask, cough a lot. Tell them it is in its early stages, and you will have to go to a sanatorium. There are medications, but I don't know what they are. I am just a student, but I can find out."

"No, I don't have time. I am leaving for Chicago today. I will tell them a treatment plan is being set up," Charlie replied nervously.

"You need fresh air and bedrest. Lots of bedrest." Liz winked as she gave him a sly grin.

"I can't be without you any longer. Liz, I have something to ask you." He took her hand and held it in his own.

"About tuberculosis?" she asked.

"No, I want to know if I get clean, will you marry me? Will you wait?"

She nodded. "Of course, Charlie, but you must be free from the gang. You must get out of this mess. We need to start life fresh. I will wait for that day," Liz promised.

She glanced around the restaurant, then at him. "I will be going home for Thanksgiving. Can you come for Thanksgiving?"

"I will see you with bells on. Eh...you didn't tell Ella or anyone, did you? About the business, I mean."

"No, it will be our secret," Liz said, then smiled and winked at him again.

Charlie tossed some bills on the table, then got up to leave.

Liz walked with him out to his automobile.

He took Liz in his arms and kissed her passionately. "Till Thanksgiving, my future Mrs. Rosario. I love you."

Liz said, "I love you, too."

He got into the automobile and was about to leave when Liz called after him. "Be careful!"

Liz pulled her coat tight around her and walked to campus for her next class.

"Mrs. Rosario, hmm…" She was a bundle of emotions; happy Charlie was back and would soon be free but scared to death with worry something might go wrong. She shivered. She prayed Charlie would pull this off.

Chapter Seventeen

Charlie stopped at the drugstore to pick up a couple of surgical masks. He threw them in the glove box of his 105 Talbot automobile. He had just purchased this sporty four-seater touted to be the fastest vehicle to race at Brookland's track in Surry, England. It was a first edition and Charlie had to have it. Convertibles were head turners. It was too cold today for a convertible, but there would be plenty of time to delight in the amenity come summer.

Charlie enjoyed the ride to Chicago, feeling a weight lifted from his shoulders. He had thought this story out and rehearsed what he would say to the boss. He even practiced coughing and brought with him a phlegm-filled handkerchief.

When he got to the outside of Chicago, he stopped for gasoline. He pricked his finger and placed a few drops of blood on the same handkerchief to make it look more authentic. He wasn't sure it would work so he ate some jalapeño peppers and dressed in extra warm clothing in hopes he would perspire and appear feverish when he arrived. He popped several peppermint drops to cover the odor of the peppers. Before he went to see the boss, he stopped by the nearest facility and dampened his collar and disheveled his normally impeccable attire. It was showtime.

He hadn't seen the boss in over a month. They were to meet at the Hideaway Speakeasy on Jackson Boulevard. It was dusk. Too early for the party crowd but dark enough to be less visible in the dim backroom where the boss conducted business.

Charlie entered the room with his bloody handkerchief over his mouth, hacking and bending over in a deep wheeze. He stood after a minute or so, pulling the surgical mask over his face.

"So sorry, boss..." He once again wheezed out a deep cough, pretending to deposit chucks into his handkerchief.

"Nasty cold you have there," Big Al said and looked up from the papers he had been shuffling over his desk. He stood.

Big Al was never alone. His two henchmen were there, one by the window peering out. The other with his back turned to Charlie, seeming to be polishing his piece. Neither muscle wanted to be anywhere near whatever bug Charlie was carrying.

"S'what I came to see you 'bout," Charlie said breathlessly.

"I ain't no doctor." Big Al laughed.

Charlie wheezed again, holding up his hand as though to say, "give me a minute."

"Been to the doctor. Says I got tuberculosis. Got to go to a sanatorium," Charlie coughed again and put the handkerchief to his mouth, feigning chucking up more phlegm.

"Holy Christ, stay away. That stuff's contagious, you know." Big Al motioned one of his muscles over to the corner where they whispered in private while Charlie was doing the performance of his life.

"Charlie, I got one last job for you till you recover. Sam here will drive you to the docks. They know you down there. Got a package for you to pick up. Introduce them to Sam. He can take over while you're gone."

"Sure, boss." Charlie swallowed deep and made himself appear out of breath.

*   *   *

They went to Sam's vehicle. "Sit in the back. I don't want what you got!" Sam said disgustedly.

They drove in silence to the docks. Then exited the vehicle. It was dark now and Sam instructed Charlie to lead the way.

Sam removed a Colt 1911 from its shoulder holster. "Don't like this part of town. Too dark. Too many thugs," Sam explained.

Charlie walked ahead toward Pier 12 where pickups normally took place.

"The boss feels really bad about your illness. And Charlie?"

Charlie turned back to face Sam. "Yeah?"

"The boss says he doesn't like to see you suffer." He lifted the gun.

"No!" Charlie saw a flash of light and heard the crack of the Colt. Then, he fell to the ground.

He watched as Sam walked back to the car. "Terrible thing, tuberculosis. It's a shame. You were a good man, Charlie."

Charlie lay there in a pool of his own blood, unable to move or call for help. He died moments later.

Sam watched from the car. You never leave until you are sure the deed is done. Sam was sure.

Chapter Eighteen

Thanksgiving came, but Charlie didn't show up for dinner. Liz didn't know if he was held up, if he changed his mind, or if something had gone horribly wrong. Since Charlie didn't telephone, Liz suspected the worst. She paced, then stared out the window, hoping his automobile would magically appear.

There was no news for a few days. Then, on the weekend a story hit the Milwaukee papers.

MILWAUKEE MAN SHOT DOWN
MOB CONNECTION BEING INVESTIGATED

Charles Rosario was found dead Thursday morning in a dark passage near the freight pier.

Liz could read no further. Tears welled in her eyes, and she fell into deep shaking sobs.

Ella ran to her sister's side. "What is it?"

Liz couldn't speak. She pointed to the article, and then the words poured out between sobs. "Charlie…is dead…and it's my fault."

Ella's comforting attempts could not console her.

*   *   *

After a few days, Liz regained some control and spilled the whole story to Ella. She left nothing out.

Ella was aghast. She didn't know what to think or how to react. Her first thought was, *How could Charlie get Liz mixed up in this lifestyle?*

After she thought about it further, she realized Liz was a willing participant. Liz and Charlie were in love. They had been trying to fix the situation but only made things worse. What to do now?

Ella read the article. The funeral would be held at Sacred Heart Catholic Church on Tuesday. Liz insisted on going and Ella agreed to go with her.

Tuesday morning, they entered Sacred Heart Catholic Church dressed in appropriate black mourning attire. They saw Mrs. Rosario standing next to the casket. They went up to her to offer their sincere condolences. Liz tried desperately to hold back tears as she wiped her eyes.

Mrs. Rosario glared. "Haven't you Protestants done enough? Must you come here and torment me more?"

"Mrs. Rosario," Liz pleaded. "I love Charlie and I am hurting as much as you are. Pleeease understand."

Mrs. Rosario turned away. "Ushers, please have these women removed."

Not wishing to make a scene, the sisters quietly left the church.

"We will visit the cemetery later," Ella consoled Liz. "Perhaps tomorrow."

*   *   *

Liz spent the next few days hating Mrs. Rosario, then hating the mob, then hating herself. All the hate welled up inside her and she couldn't move, couldn't think.

Ella didn't know how to console her sister. The one thing she did know was it was not Liz's fault, but still, Liz was riddled with guilt. She told Liz over and over again she was not guilty, but Liz couldn't be convinced. She felt she'd pushed Charlie into the dangerous situation that got him killed.

Finally, Ella realized she couldn't fix this situation. She asked Liz to speak to Reverend Nelson.

At first Liz saw no point, but Ella was quite convincing. She went to the church at ten in the morning with the saddest face on the planet.

"Good morning, Liz," Reverend Nelson said and took Liz's hand. "Have a seat."

The reverend motioned for her to take the chair next to him. "Can I get you a glass of water?"

Liz nodded.

He poured a glass of water and set it on the table beside her.

Liz glanced around. The room was sparse. Reverend Nelson's desk sat at one end of the room with two comfortable chairs and a small table at the other end. The table held a kerosene lamp and a box of tissue. On the wall was a picture of Jesus, the Shepherd, tending sheep and carrying a lamb in his arms.

Liz, so far, had remained silent.

"Your sister told me a bit about your situation when she scheduled this appointment for you," Reverend Nelson said. "Can you tell me more? How are you coping? What are you feeling?"

Immediately Liz's eyes filled with tears that escaped down her cheek. "Pastor Nelson, Charlie is dead and it *is* my fault. He met with the people who killed him so he could be with me. I encouraged him to go."

"But Liz, you didn't *know* he would be killed, and you didn't pull the trigger. It is *not* your fault." Reverend Nelson placed his hands over her trembling ones. "Your intentions were good. You did try to save him; you tried to save him from the evil surrounding him. In you, he only saw good—the good he wanted for himself. It was Charlie's decision to escape the evil."

"But why did he *have* to die?" Liz sobbed.

"I can't answer that. I can only tell you Charlie made the right decision and because of that decision, he will be in God's hands in Heaven. We can't have all of the answers because we are all sinners." Reverend Nelson passed the tissue box to Liz.

She took a tissue and wiped her eyes. "But this hurts so much," Liz sobbed.

"I know it does. It takes courage and commitment, and Charlie had both. He didn't die because of you, he died *for* you. Because in you he saw beauty and love and all that is good."

"But now that he is gone, how…can I go on?" Her voice caught, and after a moment she sipped the water Reverend Nelson had placed on the table.

"Look at that picture, Liz." Reverend Nelson pointed to the Good Shepherd on the wall. "See the lamb he is carrying? That's you, Liz. He will carry you when you need to be carried and he will lead you when you want to be led. Trust in Him."

Liz blinked and tried to smile. A tiny whimper escaped her. She nodded her head in affirmation.

"You think about it, child, and come back to see me in a few days. We can talk again." Reverend Nelson stood and walked her to the door.

Liz still had a heavy heart but somehow it all seemed a little clearer.

In time, she felt the burden of Charlie's death slowly lifting from her shoulders.

*   *   *

Meanwhile, Ella had spoken to John about the situation. He was her rock and always knew what to do.

"Sprite is so young. She'll bounce back," John assured her. It may take some time, but I am confident time will work its healing magic. It would be nice if we had a magic pill to cure heartache, but this is one thing I don't have a cure for. I can give her phenobarbital to help her sleep, but that's the best I can do."

"I can't help thinking about Charlie's family," Ella said, concerned. "Do you think they are in danger? If the mob thinks they know too much, what might they do? And what about Liz? Should we be worried about her?"

John sat thoughtfully for a while as he put down the morning paper and pondered the idea.

Ella could see she had opened a new concern that was on John's mind as well.

"I will be seeing Frank at the clinic next week. Let me check if the family feels in danger. For now, we should keep a close eye on Sprite."

*   *   *

On Tuesday, two weeks after the funeral, Frank Rosario bounced his rickety wheelchair off the buckboard, which had transported him to the clinic. The makeshift ramp at the back worked well. A rope was fastened to the wheels of his chair and tied to the front rails of the buckboard. The friend who drove him offered to try to lift him into his buggy instead, but Frank assured him "The buckboard will work just fine."

It was a warm day for December, if you can call 42 degrees warm. Frank had bundled up in wool blankets. Fortunately, it wasn't very far to the Mallory & Ellington Clinic.

"Frank, it's good to see you," Dr. Ellington greeted his patient.

"Hey Doc, how's it goin'?" Frank responded.

"Let's take a look at those legs. Any problems? Any pain?"

"No Doc, 'cept sometimes I feel like they are still there. I feel a little pain, and I reach down and then I remember. I'd just as soon forget," Frank confessed.

"It's not unusual. It's called phantom pain. If it hurts, you might try repositioning yourself or put ice on it," Dr. Ellington advised.

"Doesn't happen often but it sure is peculiar," Frank observed.

After the exam was complete, John addressed the other issue. "Say Frank, since Charlie died, do you and your family feel in danger? I'm a bit concerned for your safety."

"Naw, Doc. I was in the military when all of this was goin' down, so I don't know nuthin'. Bess, Mrs. Rosario, is a little worried 'cause the stuff is in her house. They worked out of the basement there, you know.

The mob's code is strict. When yer in the mob you don't talk to no one but them about their business, and I doubt they'd suspect any family member of having any information. Charlie knew the rules. B'sides, ya' don't exactly keep records in this kind of business. It's pretty much cash and carry."

"But I read in the newspaper that they killed Charlie. He wasn't a threat to them," John reasoned.

"Ya', but Charlie knew too much. They keep tight reins on their people. He could have a deathbed confession and finger them. That's why mobsters don't tell stuff to their families or their molls. They could get loose lips, and then all *hell* would break loose."

John was quite sure Charlie's family would be safe, but Charlie spilled the beans to Liz who told Ella, who told him. Was *his* family safe? Did the mob know about Liz? John was more concerned than ever.

That night, John warned Ella they could be in danger. "Take precautions, don't say anything to anyone about Charlie or the mob. Liz is sleeping now but we must warn her. Maybe she should change her appearance, dye her hair, or wear a wig. Carry a parasol or something to hide her face if she goes out. This is serious, Ella, and I am worried." John paced the room. This was one-time he had no answers.

*　　　*　　　*

Ella didn't sleep a wink all night. She wasn't too concerned for herself, but she was worried for Liz. They would talk with Liz in the morning. Something more needed to be done, but what?

During her sleepless night, Ella had an idea.

The next day, she asked Liz to stay in and watch Helen while she went to the newspaper. If anyone would know what to do it would be Mr. Wallace.

Chapter Nineteen

"Hey Chief, Ella Ellington here!" Ella called to Mr. Wallace in her usual cheerful tone as she entered the Journal's reception area. Her voice didn't reveal the butterflies in her stomach.

"Mrs. Ellington, come right in. What gems have you brought me today?" Mr. Wallace asked.

Ella sat down, placed her elbows on his desk and her forehead in her hands, then drew in a deep breath. She exhaled and sat thoughtfully for a moment, contemplating where to begin. She raised her head and sat upright. "Mr. Wallace, I need your advice," she sighed.

"What have you gotten yourself into now?"

Ella suspected Myron Wallace had learned in a short time this woman was not a wallflower and had a knack for sticking her nose where it didn't belong. But that's what he liked about her. She had the nose of a reporter. She wasn't afraid to go places her male counterparts shied away from. She was a woman after all and a charming one at that.

"You know the idea I had about the Italian community?" she began cautiously.

"Oh dear," Mr. Wallace gasped. "You didn't pursue that, did you?"

"No, but I'm afraid it pursued me, or rather…my sister, and I am worried for her safety. I have an idea, but I need your help."

Mr. Wallace got up and shut the door. "Okay Ella, call me Myron. Tell me the story."

Mr. Wallace paced the floor, shook his head, and gasped as Ella revealed all she knew to him. Mr. Wallace seemed as perplexed as John was on how to keep Liz safe, but he had in his lap a story that could be a blockbuster.

"I have an idea," Ella continued.

"Shoot," Mr. Wallace said, hopeful. "Right now, I will listen to anything but I sure as hell hope it's a good one."

"Do you have a contact at the police station that will work with us but not reveal the source?" Ella questioned.

"I think we need to go directly to the chief. But remember, the mob will know someone squealed. Will this make things worse? For Liz or for Charlie's family, I mean?"

"Here's what I was thinking," Ella continued. "If the police do a raid on the house where the bombs were made, they might be able to solve the police station bombing. Then, we can do a story emphasizing the family had no part in any of this and Charlie's girlfriend was equally in the dark. We can say the tip came from a totally unrelated source."

"Mrs. Ellington—Ella—I think you may have something. Let me get Chief Jansen over here as soon as possible." Mr. Wallace reached for the phone on his desk.

In less than a half hour, the Chief of Police was in the Journal's office. Mr. Wallace told him on the phone he had an anonymous tip regarding the police station bombing and the informant was in his office. It was enough to cause the chief to put everything else aside.

*   *   *

The chief said he would go back to the station and do an investigation based on the facts Ella had provided. They had sufficient reason to believe it was a credible report.

A raid was conducted the next day. They wanted to act before evidence was destroyed.

Mr. Wallace had the scoop of the year. "It's your story, Mrs. Ellington. Have it ready for press."

That evening, the headline read:

POLICE RAID MAY REVEAL SOURCE
OF MILWAUKEE POLICE STATION BOMBING

The article was published without a byline. It stated the anonymous tip that led the police to the bomb site was not a family member or anyone directly associated with Charles Rosario.

All family members were shocked and couldn't believe Charlie had any connection to the underworld.

The mob never retaliated, and the families never spoke of it again.

Except John, who looked at Ella and shook his head. He repeated the words he spoke when he first learned she was working for the newspaper. "My little newshawk, may you never get your wings clipped."

Then he added, "But don't ever do that to me again or I will clip them." He was upset with his wife's involvement. At the same time, he knew if she hadn't used her powers as a reporter Liz could be in absolute danger. "Do you think for a while you might stick to ladies' teas and bar mitzvahs?"

Ella gave him a peck on the cheek. "I'm exhausted. Let's go to bed."

They all slept well that night. It was their first night of peaceful sleep since the news of Charlie's death.

But there was never any doubt for Ella that life would never be dull in the Ellington household.

ORPHANAGES

POORHOUSES

Chapter Twenty

The next morning, John poured a cup of coffee and sat down to breakfast. "Well, my dear, will you be writing more articles, or have you had your fill of journalism?"

"I think I will take a break until after the holidays," Ella said with a smile. "Liz needs someone to lean on, and I think preparing for Helen's first Christmas might be just the ticket to get my sister out of her slump."

"It will take a long time for Sprite to heal, but you may be right," John responded.

That Christmas was the most somber Ella experienced since the first Christmas when her own mother was not home for the holidays.

Helen clapped for the tree lights and was enamored with everything Christmas. She got excited and bounced when she heard "Jingle Bells" on the radio. She took a few steps on Christmas Eve. The tree ornaments were too irresistible for Helen to ignore. The ornaments had to be plucked, felt, looked at and even tasted. She needed to explore every beautiful addition to their home. It was a wondrous time of the year.

Helen received many gifts, including books and rattles and stuffed toys, but nothing compared to the intrigue of the tree.

Ella gave John a beautiful fountain pen to replace the dipping pen he had used in the past. She said it was time he moved into the current century and use the more resourceful and less messy pen now available.

They didn't know what might please Liz, so John decided it would be encouraging for her to have her very own stethoscope. She couldn't have been more pleased.

Liz had not been in the mood for shopping, but she turned to the Sears Roebuck catalogue that carried everything. She could mail order purchase anything from underwear and kitchen appliances to cars and even houses. After much thought, she decided shiny, new brass tools for the fireplace would be a nice addition. She chose a set with bellows, poker, broom and pan, along with a pewter log rack for John and Ella.

John surprised Ella with a new kitchen stove, which arrived the day before Christmas. Forget all that wood burning mess. Ella's new stove was a special gas range with temperature control. Not only that, but it was also a beautiful enamel piece of furniture with ivory doors trimmed in black, two ovens to the right of the cooktop, as well as a broiler below. The stove stood on fashionable skinny legs.

Ella was excited about preparing Christmas dinner in her new General Electric oven. She could set the temperature and forget the turkey, except for periodic basting. That gave her time to visit the poorhouse and orphanage with John. Liz stayed behind to keep an eye on things until she returned.

They were pleased this year because Ella's brother Thaddeus was able to join them for several days. He wouldn't arrive until Christmas day, but he assured them he would be there before dinner and would bring a hearty appetite with him. He survived on military mess but a home-cooked meal with family…well, Thaddeus couldn't think of anything he would enjoy more.

Mid-morning Christmas Day the unmistakable thump up the steps came with Thaddeus's call of "Anybody home?" as he burst through the front door.

The familiar sound immediately brought Liz out of her slump. She squealed, "Thaddeus, Thaddeus, Thaddeus," and ran to greet him. She grabbed him around the neck and didn't let go.

Finally, he peeled her away.

"Hey kid," Thaddeus greeted his little sister. "Let's take a look at you?" He walked around Liz as though he were a drill sergeant making a routine inspection of the troops.

"Don't be creepy!" Liz smacked her brother on the shoulder.

"Feisty as ever, I see," Thaddeus said and smiled. "C'mere." He grabbed his sister and gave her a kiss on her cheek.

"Lookin' good, Liz." He smiled as he drew back to take another look. "All grown up. Mmm… I should be here to keep an eye on my little sister. Nobody better break her heart," he teased.

"Too late for that," Liz said and sighed.

Thaddeus noticed tears well up in her eyes and put his arm around her shoulders. "What's the story?" he encouraged. "I'll teach him a lesson if you tell me where he is."

"Oh, Thaddeus, Charlie's dead," Liz confessed. "He was shot by the mob in Chicago. They didn't need to kill him." She turned her back to him. "I don't want to talk about it."

He respected his sister's wishes and changed the subject. "Where's the family? I only have a seven-day leave. I need to be back on Wednesday, but at least I get to be home for Christmas." Thaddeus fist bumped Liz's cheek as he glanced about.

"They went to take some gifts to the poorhouse. Food and presents for the children."

"Did they save some food for me? I'm starved," Thaddeus said, half-kidding. He hadn't eaten since yesterday except for a candy bar on the train. It was ten in the morning and some delightful smells were wafting from the kitchen.

"Dinner will be a bit late today, but I think we can find you a hot cross bun left from breakfast." Liz grinned.

There were three left and Thaddeus devoured all of them. He and Liz spent the next two hours catching up on recent activities at school and their careers, then reminisced about the past.

Time flew by and soon the rest of the family was home. Ella swore her brother grew a foot since they last saw each other. She threw her arms around his waist, and he bent to kiss the top of her head.

John put Helen on the floor, and she made a beeline to the Christmas tree. They all laughed at her enthusiasm.

"Welcome home, soldier," John said and shook Thaddeus's hand.

Liz scooped up Helen before she took the tree down and introduced her to her uncle.

Thaddeus raised the baby high into the air and tossed her to the ceiling, catching her firmly as Ella gasped. Helen squealed with delight.

Liz hurried to the kitchen and soon returned, announcing dinner would be ready shortly. She and Ella tended to the last-minute chores of making gravy and setting the table. The smells were mouthwatering.

Christmas dinner consisted of roast turkey, dressing, mashed potatoes, canned green beans (from last summer's garden), homemade cranberry orange sauce, and hot rolls. Ella had made a fresh apple pie with cheese warmed on top for dessert, a delightful treat in the dairy state.

During dinner, Ella and John told stories, both happy and sad about their encounters at the poorhouse.

"Everyone there is in desperate need of clothing. They have a working farm, some meat, vegetables and dairy are in sufficient supply for the most part, but special treats beyond the basics are non-existent," Ella explained. "I gave one small girl a lollipop and her eyes got as big as the sucker. It felt like she was afraid to eat it."

"Or maybe she wanted to make it last," Thaddeus interjected.

John, concerned with sanitation, observed, "They don't have running water, so their drinking and cooking water is pumped from the cistern in the basement. The toilet facility is a two-seater outhouse down by the barn. They have beds for their 50 residents, but children often share three or four to a bed. Laundry is done with water heated on the cook stove in a boiler. Baths require the same process. Families bathe in the same water, starting with the oldest and going down to the youngest. Occasionally, a fresh tea kettle of hot water is added between bathers. Of course, by the time the last child is in the tub, it is difficult to tell if the water is cleaning or just smearing the dirt around."

Ella added, "That prompted the phrase, 'Don't throw the baby out with the bath water.'"

They all laughed.

"The phrase is funny, but their situation is sad," Ella said.

"The children, of course, were very excited to see us bearing gifts. We brought tops, yo-yos, toy trucks, dolls, colors, pencils, tablets, books, and other goodies. We even brought some taffy and Christmas hard candy. Without these gifts, the children would have gone with nothing for Christmas," John said.

"We should all be grateful for our blessings," Liz acknowledged.

"Oh, they find ways to amuse themselves without the trappings," Ella went on. "Summers they played stick ball, catch frogs and fireflies, climb trees, jump rope with old clothesline. In the winter, there are snowball fights, sledding on old pieces of cardboard, building snow forts, playing king of the mountain, and of course, there is tag anytime of the year." Ella laughed, giving her brother a look. "The gifts we brought were simply a delightful diversion. These children understand Christmas is not about the gifts but the birth of Jesus."

She glanced at her daughter. "I wonder," stated Ella, "whose children are richer?" *I must do a story on this.*

Of course, everyone was anxious to hear about Thaddeus's adventures and how he was faring in the army.

"Thaddeus, tell us about your experiences in the military," John encouraged.

"When I return," Thaddeus said, "I will be training on a new military aircraft, the P1 Hawk. It's a biplane single engine, single seat fighter. It was designed to be a frontline fighter in all the armed services. I'm excited to have this opportunity."

He explained he had previously flown the Martin MB1 twin engine bomber, which began mass production in 1920. It was the first U.S. designed bomber. "I feel so comfortable in the air. I'd always dreamed of flying and now that dream is coming true."

"There is no question of your courage," Ella commented. "No way would you get me up in one of those contraptions."

Ella was proud of Thaddeus's accomplishments and happy for him but felt uneasy that he could be pressed into a military conflict. The

Great War was over, but there were still many conflicts around the world. So far, the United States was not directly involved in these conflicts, but she recalled the politics of the last decade had led them into a war that was unpopular in the United States and not anticipated by the public based on President Wilson's adamant opposition to involvement. That is, until he was re-elected. She smiled at Thaddeus's enthusiasm but secretly prayed her fears were unfounded.

"What do you think of your commander-in-chief?" Ella inquired.

"Coolidge?" Thaddeus contemplated the question. "Don't quite know where that is going. He sure isn't Harding. Since Harding had the heart attack and died, it's been completely different. Harding was somewhat of a bumbling…well, in my opinion, he swayed with the wind. Not a very effective president. Coolidge on the other hand is a minimalist and wants to cut back on aid everywhere. He cut the farm relief bill, which hurt Wisconsin and rural areas across the nation hard. He liked business, but so does most of the country. As far as the military, I'm not sure."

"No one wants war," John said.

Thaddeus stared at him. "The message loud and clear to Europe and other nations is 'Fight your own battles'. I'm not sure where it leaves the aircraft program. Under Harding, several nations have agreed to disarmament but that hasn't hurt much because we were going to cut some of the old battleship fleets anyway. Personally, I think General Billy Mitchell had it right."

"But wasn't he court-martialed earlier this year?" Ella recalled the news story. "Incompetence and insubordination, I believe."

"Yes, he was, but for him it was pure frustration. Battles have been fought archaically for centuries. Troops line up where they can see each other and perform a bloody massacre. At night, they go to sleep and at dawn they repeat the process.

"Billy had a vision with an air force fighting battles. It would profoundly change the battlefield. While men died on the battlefields, people at home were going on with business as usual. Politicians were making decisions, but they had no personal investment. It was a move on the chessboard. During the Great War, Billy had the idea of using an airplane to fly over and drop troops behind the lines, essentially blocking the enemy in. But the people in charge felt it was an unfair loss of lives and used the plane primarily for reconnaissance. Using planes for actual fighting meant civilians could be hurt, cities could be demolished, and for God's sake, even the people who sent the men off to die could be targeted.

"Billy knew if they felt the pressure, maybe they would think twice before putting battles on the table. Also, if Berlin were bombed, it would have been a quick end to the war. I think he's right."

"The war ended. Wasn't that enough?" John asked.

"Not for Billy and his followers." Thaddeus laughed and slapped his knee. "They towed several captured German battleships out to sea and sunk them by dropping bombs from airplanes. The public was impressed but the military hierarchy was not. Billy was frustrated, so he took the issue public, going over his superiors' heads and alleging military incompetence." He shook his head. "Guess he asked for it. He was charged with insubordination. I still think he was right and someday the world will know it.

"As for Coolidge, I doubt he will do anything worthwhile. He won't listen to Billy's ideas, and he won't go to war. He is a very congenial fella. He has a lot of friends in Washington."

"How about some dessert?" Liz wanted to bring the mood up.

Everyone groaned, rubbing their full bellies, but in the end, no one could resist the delightful smells of fresh apple pie wafting from the kitchen. It was still warm from the oven.

Thaddeus continued on a lighter note. "Coolidge has a childlike sense of humor at times. Did you know he was so enraptured by the trappings of his office he sometimes presses all the buttons on his intercom just to see all the staff scurrying in to do his bidding? I doubt he even wants to be president."

Everyone laughed. They enjoyed Ella's delicious dessert and the rest of their time together.

Thaddeus only had a seven-day pass, but it was enough to cheer up Liz. They had always shared a mischievous bond and this year was no exception. During his stay, they went ice skating, played Monopoly, and saw a movie.

Seven Chances was playing at the Bistro. It starred Buster Keaton, which meant it would be a laughter-filled comedy. The funny tale had Liz giggling and forgetting her woes. It was about a man who found out he would inherit seven million dollars if he was married by seven p.m. on his twenty-seventh birthday. This was his twenty-seventh birthday and his longtime girlfriend turned him down. He was on a quest for a wife and pursued by hundreds of marriage-minded women.

Thaddeus was glad that was showing and not *The Merry Widow*. Time with family was precious.

Chapter Twenty-one

When the new year began, Liz returned to school, Thaddeus returned to his post, and Ella spent time at the poorhouse. She recruited the ladies of the church to make quilts. She helped at the soup kitchens. She organized clothing drives to provide clothing for those in need. In the spring, Ella returned to the Journal.

"Hey, Chief, Ella Ellington here," Ella called to Mr. Wallace.

"I was beginning to wonder if you'd had enough of the journalism field." Mr. Wallace smiled. "Are you ready to get back to work?"

"Have you got an assignment for me?" Ella inquired anxiously.

"I think you've had enough adventure for a while, but I don't think we can ever get you back to the mundane society pages. I was thinking about an article you mentioned about the orphanages. Would you like to pursue it?"

"I'd like to do it," Ella said and smiled. It was something she would find rewarding, and maybe, it would make a difference.

Later, when she sat down to dinner with John, she told him of her assignment. It put John at ease. He had been somewhat concerned Ella would continue to stick her nose where it didn't belong. It all felt so safe, so warm and fuzzy, but Ella didn't know what she was about to get herself into this time.

*   *   *

Ella began by meeting with Mrs. Mallory. It was a conversation at the dinner party with Dr. and Mrs. Mallory where Ella first became interested in the goings on of orphanages.

"Why don't you come visit the orphanage with me? I go there every Tuesday," Mrs. Mallory suggested.

"That would be wonderful," Ella said enthusiastically. "Do you think I could bring Helen along? I can get a babysitter, but I hate to impose on Mrs. Johnson. Since Liz is back at school, I prefer to leave Helen with her only when necessary. I don't want to impose on her kindness."

"Of course, I think the other children would be delighted."

On Tuesday, Ella dressed Helen in a simple frock and a lovely bonnet. Ella wore a plain straight black skirt and a white blouse with a ruffled collar. Over this, she wore a tweed jacket and donned a wide-brimmed hat with a feather. She had strapped sandals on her feet.

Helen rode in the back seat of her automobile. She found it great fun to climb on the seat and stand to see the world go by from the back window. Ellen picked up Mrs. Mallory on the way.

"You look lovely this morning," Ella complimented Mrs. Mallory on her colorful dress.

"Thank you." Mrs. Mallory glanced at Ellen's attire. "You look very professional. For future visits, you might find a more casual dress to your liking."

"Oh dear," stammered Ella, "is my attire inappropriate?"

"Heavens, no," Mrs. Mallory assured her. "It's just that, well, you may find the children very boisterous and a bit messy."

They arrived at the orphanage by mid-morning. The children were dressed and had been fed breakfast. The older children were attending classes and those under six were preparing for playtime in the yard. At the age of three, Helen fit right in.

Helen was delighted to be around people closer to her own size and the children were equally captivated by their new visitor. Interested in Helen's clothing, they all took turns trying on her bonnet.

The play yard was fenced in. There were two swings suspended from the big oak trees and a seesaw a local farmer had made for them. Mostly, the children played games of tag or leapfrog. Of course, with visiting volunteers, they wanted to enlist the help of their visitors.

A charming three-year-old grabbed Ella's hand and dragged her across the muddy yard to a vacant swing. "Push," she demanded.

Ella soon discovered what Mrs. Mallory was referring to regarding her choice of clothing. The heeled sandals had to go, as did the confining jacket and jaunty hat.

They stayed through lunch and helped to feed the children. Bowls of porridge and somewhat stale buns were set before the hungry children. The children ate heartily. Some wiped their mouths on their sleeves, others had to be washed clean since their porridge was spread from cheek to cheek. Fresh milk was provided. Today, they were lucky to have an apple for dessert. The wee ones needed to be hand fed and then cleaned up.

After dinner, they were all put down for a nap. Babies with their bottles and some of the other tykes satisfied themselves by sucking their thumbs. When they were all sleeping, it was like seeing a room of angels Ella observed. Ragamuffin angels.

Helen, too, had been exhausted by all the activity and was sound asleep in the back seat of the automobile on the way home.

"This has been an inspiring day," Ella said. "Will all of the children be placed in good homes?"

"Well, we try but I am afraid we fall short. The babies and those under three are usually placed within the first year unless they have special needs. As you noticed, there are also several Negro babies. They are more difficult to place. I am afraid the chances for older children is bleak."

"But the twins I met, Johnny and Jimmy are adorable. They are just seven. Do you mean to say they will spend the rest of their lives in the orphanage? There must be people who would take them. They are so polite and bright."

"Yes, but did you notice Johnny has a club foot. It is a birth defect that can be somewhat corrected with special shoes as an infant, but most families don't have the means or the desire to spend the money. Besides, at the age of seven correction becomes more difficult and expensive."

"But they are children, not defective merchandise," Ella said. "Even with a club foot, Johnny could have a good life and a successful career. He is very smart, you know. He read a book to me and showed me his writing assignment. He is smarter than most at his age. I suppose, because while the other boys were out playing kickball he is reading."

"Be that as it may, Ella, chances are Jimmy will find a home, but Johnny will be left behind." Mrs. Mallory sighed.

"What? They could be separated?" Ella was appalled.

"It's not unusual. Families are quite often separated. Even twins."

"That's so sad." Ella wanted to gather up all the children and take them home with her.

"Do you know about the orphan trains?" Mrs. Mallory inquired.

"I've heard about them in Michigan and Illinois. I understand there are too many street children in New York, abandoned by their parents. They are placed on trains and taken out west where they find foster homes. Some are adopted. I believe Aid for Dependent Children is running the program."

Ella recalled reading a news article about it in the *New York Times* newspaper. She would often pick up newspapers from New York and Chicago at the library. News seemed to hit the metropolitan areas before the locals got wind of it. Since she was working for the *Journal*, she would check the Associated Press articles where news came much quicker. The big news was published locally but feature items for the *Journal* were usually regarding local events. Yet the larger newspapers had become a research source for her.

"You are correct, but there have been train stops in our area as well. In fact, next month we expect to have a stop here. Maybe you should check it out."

"I will," Ella said. "Thank you for letting me go with you today."

"My pleasure. Come as often as you can. I go every Tuesday."

Ella made several more visits to the orphanage. She got to know many of the children, and they looked forward to her visits. Jimmy and

Johnny entertained her with their antics, even presenting her with the gift of a frog they had named Herman.

She and Helen laughed at this hopping, croaking creature. It soon escaped through the fence.

*   *   *

The orphan train was scheduled to arrive on the first Tuesday in March. Flyers were sent out to persons who had made inquiries about it. Some just showed up at the station. Everyone interested in taking a child had to register. Those who inquired in advance were given a basic background check, namely to determine if they had a home and no criminal record. Methods of checking were limited to records in the county. Those who just showed up were given a questionnaire and asked to disclose any irregularities and swear they had no criminal records. Their records would be checked later. Both husband and wife were requested to come but if one or the other didn't show up, they would ask for the reason for the absence. Excuses ran the gamut from illness to farm chores.

When the train stopped, the nervous children stared out the windows. Some smaller children clung to older siblings or a chaperone. They were ushered off the train and told to line up on the platform. Prospective foster parents looked them over, walking among them, checking their muscles if they were older boys, or checking their teeth and seeing how plump they were. Most were undernourished but recently cleaned up for display.

Some adults attempted to make conversation with the children, but most checked them out like they would livestock at a market.

Ella overheard some of the conversations. Mrs. Mallory stood quietly beside her.

A farmer spoke to a strapping sixteen-year-old teenager. "What's your name, boy?"

"Marvin," the boy said sheepishly.

"Speak up, boy," the farmer commanded. "Ever work on a farm?"

"No, Sir," the boy said. He held the hand of a younger boy who stared down at the platform.

"Want to learn?" the farmer asked.

"S'pose," the boy said.

"K, ya' can come home with me." The farmer turned to get the paperwork.

"What about Toby?" Marvin motioned toward the younger boy. "He's my brother; he works hard. He's stronger than he looks."

The farmer took another look, pinched Toby's arm.

Toby pulled away.

"Naw," said the farmer, "he's too scrawny."

"Then, I don't wanna go." Marvin placed his hand on Toby's shoulder.

"Boy, one mouth's enough to feed," the farmer said. "Yer a strappin' fella. I suspect you can pack away a good portion of food, maybe two."

"I'll share my portion with Toby," Marvin argued.

The farmer shook his head. "Can't, boy. The missus would be furious."

Just then, another man stepped up and smiled a toothless grin. He grabbed Toby by the ear. "I'll take the young un." The man staggered a bit and left out a loud alcoholic burp.

"Watcha want with him?" the farmer asked.

"Ain't got no missus. He can wash dishes and hang laundry. Maybe tend the chickens. Know how to cook, boy?" the man asked.

"You ain't takin' him," the first farmer said, taking Toby by his free hand. "Yer goin home with your brother."

"What about yer missus?" Marvin asked.

"Toby can help her," the farmer said pensively. "Come along."

The farmer took care of the necessary paperwork and got in his buckboard. "Hop in the back," he told the boys, and they were off to their new home.

"What kind of life will they have?" Ella asked Mrs. Mallory.

"Those boys are indentured servants," Mrs. Mallory stated. "They'll share a bed, have food to eat, and some education. Most of the time, they will be farmhands."

"They are children!" Ella shook her head sorrowfully.

"It's a better life than they had in the streets, scraping garbage cans for food, sleeping in alleys, begging, and never getting a bath."

"But why? Where are their parents?"

"Some families are so poor they can't afford to feed all the mouths. People feel sorry for the kids that are alone and provide them with morsels. Some parents feel they are better off on the streets. Many times, the mothers die in childbirth. The fathers can't cope; they send them to live with friends or relatives who soon grow tired of the children. Other children have abusive family lives and decide to take their chances on the streets. They find the streets more tolerable."

"They can't possibly expect babies to survive on their own," Ella said, incredulous.

"They are survivors. It is quite amazing, but it is also a problem. That is why the Children's Aid Society came into being. It has been in existence since about 1855 to address the issues of street children. Charles Brace, a Yale graduate and philanthropist, is the father of the foster care system. The orphanages had no room, and he felt the children were better served living in real homes. He established a group of foster families willing to take in children. Unfortunately, there were not enough homes for the number of children in need. He then had the idea of orphan trains."

"But who monitors them? How do we know the children are safe?" Ella asked.

"We don't always know. There are not enough agents to follow up, but the children are not slaves. They can leave whenever they choose. Many do."

"What happens to them then?"

"Some end up back in the hands of the Society, most hire out to other farmers or find their way in the world on their own."

Just then, Ella noticed an argument ensuing between a man and a woman over a blue-eyed blonde girl about five years old. The woman was claiming she had priority on a child of this description. She had placed an order and was waiting for such a child. The man was claiming he had spotted her first and the girl belonged to him.

Ella was quite sure the child would be better off with the German lady. She was well-dressed and quite smitten by the child. The man may have spotted the child first but didn't seem the gentlemanly type. Ella looked about but didn't see a wife.

The chaperone took the little girl aside and talked to her alone. She told the adults to stand aside and wait until she returned. They smugly stood their ground, temporarily ceasing their dispute.

Finally, she returned and stated unequivocally the child wanted to go with the lady, and that is the way it would be. She had the child speak to the lady while she led the man away, explaining to him that had his wife come with him, he would have had a much better opportunity. Under the circumstances, they could not release a little girl to a man who had no wife present.

"Perhaps another time when your wife is available," the chaperone smiled at him.

Ella was relieved. It was quite possible the man was decent and his wife had a valid reason for not being here. She was comforted, feeling the little girl would be safe in a loving home…or so she chose to believe.

The crowd was disbursing except for a few still dealing with paperwork. The train would soon be leaving the station with the children who were not chosen. Their next stop was in Iowa.

Ella looked at Mrs. Mallory. "Let's go home. I don't know whether to be happy or sad. It is good to hope the placed children will have a family to take care of them. But it is so sad they have no family to love them."

"We can hope," said Mrs. Mallory. "We can hope. Go home and pray for their well-being."

Ella smiled, again thinking of the little girl. "I will."

Chapter Twenty-two

Ella continued visiting the orphanage during the next year. She wrote several articles about the orphanage and the orphan train hoping to find more people interested in finding homes for the children. In that time, she saw children come and go. For every child who left with happy parents, two or three new scared faces arrived.

Jimmy and Johnny were about to celebrate their eighth birthdays. Ella baked two huge cakes for dessert that day, one for each of the boys to share with their friends. They played pin the tail on the donkey and had a great time. Ella placed eight candles on each cake and told the boys to make a wish.

Jimmy was quick to make his wish. "I wish this year I will find a family I can go to live with."

Johnny shouted, "NO!" and hobbled from the room.

Ella dashed after him and knelt in front of the boy, who had tears streaming down his face. "What is wrong, Johnny? It was a wonderful wish."

"I...I...I don't want Jimmy to go!" Johnny stammered.

"Maybe a wonderful family will come along and adopt both of you."

"Nobody wants me," Johnny sobbed.

Ella gathered Johnny into her arms. "Johnny, you are very special, and everyone would love to have a boy like you." She comforted Johnny, reassuring him. After a while, she took his hand. "Come now, let's get some cake."

Johnny's cake with its candles was undisturbed at the table.

"Let's light these candles and hear your wish." Ella lit the candles and Johnny took the deepest breath he could and blew them all out.

"What did you wish? What did you wish?" the children shouted.

"I wished Mrs. Ellington will take me home to live with her." Johnny looked up at Ella with the broadest grin she had ever seen.

Helen clapped and laughed. "Johnny come home, okay, Momma?" Now Jimmy was the one standing back, shuffling his feet, and feeling alone.

She took Johnny and Jimmy by their hands. Johnny grasped Helen's hand when Ella said, "Let's go sit and talk a minute." She led them over to a table and had them sit quietly.

Ella paced back and forth in front of them in her teacher stance with her hands on her hips, deep in thought. She reached up and rubbed the back of her neck with her hand. Her mind raced.

She had grown to love these boys. She cared what happened to them and didn't want them to be separated. Helen loved them, too. This was a big step. What would John think? Could she manage three children and a career? She remembered what her rough and tumble brother Thaddeus had been like as a boy and imagined how having boys around would change their household.

What about the boys? They had been in the orphanage for over four years? Would they adapt to private life in a family situation? Would they like John?

She stopped pacing, pursed her lips, and in a single thought she answered all the questions. John was the easiest person to get along with and he would love having sons. The boys would have a family. Helen would have big brothers to watch over her. It would be a house filled with love. Her career…damned her career. It was only to give her something worthwhile to do and what was more worthwhile than bringing up a family. Besides, she had only written ten articles in the past year and four were on the orphanages.

She turned to the children who were waiting for Ella to say something.

Helen spoke first. "Momma, can Johnny come home with us?"

"Not today, sweetie," Ella began.

All three faces looked somber and looked at the floor, dejected. "Maybe both boys can come Sunday…for a visit," she added.

She was used to making decisions on her own but increasing their family was way too big a decision to make without consulting John first.

*   *   *

John came home to a lovely dinner of baked cod with a béarnaise sauce, Brussel sprouts, and rice pilaf. A glass of white wine was beside his plate, candles were lit, and fine china was on the linen tablecloth. Helen was already asleep.

John greeted his lovely wife. She was dressed in a shimmery chemise which outlined the soft curves of her body.

"Oh my," John whispered and gave a soft whistle. "I know I was tired but am I dreaming?"

He took his wife in his arms and kissed her gently. "If I am, don't wake me up."

Ella smiled up at him and said, "Come sit, dinner is ready, and we don't want it to get cold."

They sat across from each other and made small talk for a while. Eventually, John's patience ran thin. "So, tell me what this is all about?" He circled the table with his hands. "Did I forget our anniversary? I thought it was in June. Or your birthday? Isn't it in August? Helen and mine are in December." John had perfect recall. "What am I forgetting?"

"Nothing, dear," Ella said and grinned. "I have wonderful news and I thought I would preface it with a delicious dinner. If you are finished, let's take our coffee to the parlor."

This has got to be good or, oh no, what has Ella gotten into now?

They sat on the davenport. John at one end and Ella cuddled up next to him with her stocking feet curled up on the sofa beside her. John put his arms around her shoulder, lifted her chin, and kissed her gently. He pulled away and said, "So, Mrs. Ellington, what's your news?"

Ella began slowly, "Well, as you know, we discussed having more children and you know Helen is almost three now…"

"Oh, oh!" John beamed. "Oh my gosh, you're pregnant."

"No, no. Oh, no, no," Ella responded.

"You want to get pregnant?" John winked. "What are we doing in the parlor, although I have no objections."

Ella laughed. "No, no. I'm not, I don't, I mean…"

"You don't want to have my baby?" John asked, bewildered.

"No, I mean yes, I mean no."

"Well, which is it?" John was thoroughly confused.

"Um, let's start over. I am not pregnant, yes John I want your babies, but I have ah, another idea."

"Ella, I am a doctor. I kind of know how this works. You want someone else's baby?" John chuckled, still confused.

"Yes!" Ella exclaimed.

John was shocked. "This I want to hear…I think."

"You know I have been visiting the orphanage and I…"

"Ah, I see where this is going, but Ella, there are lots of loving people who are waiting for babies at the orphanage. We can have our own. Unfortunately, there are couples who can't."

"I know, John, but there are kids who will never be chosen. Healthy babies are adopted, and older boys can be farmhands, but kids between those ages are lost kids no one wants."

John reached for her hand. "Ella, honey, you can't save the world. We can't adopt them all."

"No, but there are two boys I want you to meet. Their names are Jimmy and Johnny."

"Two? You want to adopt two? Or do you want me to pick?"

"It has to be both. They are twins. I don't want you to say you will adopt them. I want you to say you will *meet* them."

"I can see this means a lot to you. How old are they?"

"They turned eight today. Can we bring them home for the weekend? Just for a visit? Please? I'll go in the morning to make arrangements… just for a weekend."

"First, tell me about Jimmy and Johnny."

Ella, in a state of euphoria, told John everything she knew about the boys.

When it was time to turn in, John inquired, "This doesn't mean we won't have babies of our own, does it?"

Ella laughed. "Of course not. I would like at least one more."

"Times flying, Helen is going on three, so we better get started." John swatted his wife on the behind as they went upstairs to the bedroom.

"We've got some catching up to do." John winked at her.

Ella giggled.

Chapter Twenty-three

John consented, and over the weekend Jimmy and Johnny were with the Ellingtons. Both boys were a little shy and quiet all the way to the big house on Astor Street, and when they saw it, both boys were astounded.

"This is your house?" Jimmy asked. "How many people live here?"

"Just us," Ella replied, "but I grew up here. We had six people at one time."

"I think there is room for 20 people." Johnny was stunned.

The boys grabbed their overnight sacks from the automobile and looked about as they went up the stairs to the front porch. Johnny spotted the porch swing and couldn't resist a quick rock.

John led the way with a sleeping Helen in his arms. "I'll put her down for a quick nap. You boys can explore."

"Come in," Ella encouraged, "and I will show you to your room." She had five bedrooms in the house but decided the boys would feel safer sharing one room.

"We have a room just for us?" Jimmy asked, not quite believing it was true.

Ella had not thought about it before, but the boys were used to sharing a room with up to ten other boys. Most of the time they shared a bed.

They were in the room that once belonged to Thaddeus. It had pictures of airplanes on the walls, a passion the boys shared. The room also had a few remnants of toys left over from Thaddeus's childhood. Ella had long since stashed them away in the attic but retrieved them for this occasion. There were a couple of toy trucks, a gyroscope, an erector set, and a jar of marbles.

The boy's eyes widened. Not even Christmas was this fantastic. Their eyes perused the room. They were not sure if the things were just to look at or play with, but it was clear they were thrilled.

"There is a bureau over there." Ella pointed to the wall next to the bed. "You can put your things in the drawers." Thaddeus had a full-size bed with a puffy featherbed mattress. "I think you boys can share a bed tonight."

Jimmy put their things in the drawer of the bureau while Johnny jumped up on the fluffy down-filled bed. He couldn't stop laughing. Then Jimmy joined him, and the gales of laughter continued.

Ella suspected this was quite different from the hard rope tied cots of the orphanage.

"You can play for a little while with the toys. I'll fix lunch," Ella directed.

"Yes, ma'am," the boys said in unison.

John and Ella went downstairs while the boys played.

"They do seem happy and are quite polite," John observed. "I must say, I had anticipated boisterous ill-mannered ruffians and I admit it concerned me about their influence on Helen."

"They are a delight," Ella agreed, "but mark my words, they are boys. They are on their best behavior. By the end of their visit, we'll see their true nature." She laughed.

John called the boys downstairs when lunch was ready. Ella made stew from yesterday's pot roast, along with hot biscuits and poured cold milk.

The boys clamored down the stairs, then stood silent awaiting instructions.

"You can sit across from each other." John motioned to the two empty chairs. "Helen will sit next to her mother."

John held a chair for Ella. "I will sit here at the head of the table." He took his place while the boys looked on in silence.

Ella dished up bowls of hot stew. Jimmy placed his spoon in the dish and was about to take a bite.

"One minute, Jimmy," instructed John calmly. "We must say grace."

Jimmy shouted "Grace" and once again picked up his spoon. He looked across at his brother and said, "Say it, Johnny, so we can eat."

"No, no, no," John said, and Ella and he both laughed.

"We need to thank the Lord for this food," Ella explained.

"Is He here, too?" asked Jimmy. "Where will he sit?"

They laughed again.

"Jimmy, do you know who Jesus is? Do you know how to pray?" Ella inquired.

"Yeah," said Johnny. "We know about Jesus. He was born at Christmas. We pray at the orphanage and ask Him to come, but he never does."

Ella was puzzled. "What do you mean, Johnny? Jesus is always here."

"Well," said Jimmy, "I guess if he has dinner here, he can't make it to the orphanage."

"What makes you think that?" John, too, was puzzled.

"Every day, Sister Theresa tells us to bow our head and close our eyes. Then, we all say, 'Come Lord Jesus, be our guest,' but he never comes. When we open our eyes, he's not there so we go ahead and eat anyway."

Ella smiled. "I think we better talk later; our stew is getting cold. John, would you please say grace. I mean, can you pray for us?"

"Boys, fold your hands and close your eyes," John said. "Heavenly Father, thank you for the food we are about to receive. Thank you for allowing Jimmy and Johnny to spend a couple of days with us. We are blessed to have them stay in our home. Amen."

Ella said "Amen" and the boys followed suit.

"Now, let's have some of that delicious stew," John directed, and the boys dug in.

Johnny looked around and shrugged his shoulders. "Guess Jesus can't make it here today, either."

Ella tried her best not to laugh.

After they enjoyed their meal, the boys went outside to play. Helen took a nap and Ella needed to have a heart-to-heart talk with John.

"What do you think about the boys?" she asked.

"I think they are smart and curious. I think they are polite and wonderful. I need to examine Johnny's foot. It looks bad, but I think it can be fixed. I don't know if he can ever walk without a limp, but I can check it out."

"Helen loves them. Particularly Johnny. I'm not sure why. Perhaps, because he is not as boisterous as the other boys. She can keep up with him. John, I think we can make a big difference in the boys' lives. Will you think about it?"

John chuckled. "I can see they have found their way into your heart, but this is a huge decision, Ella. Will *you* think about it? Let's not rush into anything."

"I will," said Ella, "but can we talk to the Director of the orphanage at least?"

John gave Ella a kiss on the cheek. "Yes, but let's take it slow."

Ella's heart skipped a beat.

*   *   *

Late in the afternoon, Ella sat down in the parlor with the boys. She pulled her bible from the bookshelf and explained this special book has the answers to almost everything. She opened it to the book of John.

"John was an apostle," Ella said. "An apostle was a very wise man who wrote things in the bible. Here in Chapter 14, Apostle John said…"

"He has my name," Johnny interrupted her.

"Yes, so you have a very important name."

"What about my name?" Jimmy asked, not about to be left out.

"Why, yes, James is also in the bible. In fact, a few people were named James and one of them was a fisherman who became a disciple of Jesus."

"A dis-ci-ple?" Jimmy asked, taking his time saying the word.

"Yes, a disciple was a follower of Jesus. He went wherever Jesus went on earth."

"Was there a disciple named Johnny?" Johnny asked.

"Well, no, but there was another important man named John the Baptist. Someday we will read about him, but today I want to tell you about Jesus."

She tucked the boys under her arms as she read from John 14. Ella's King James Bible was way beyond the boy's comprehension.

"Here, Jesus is saying wherever you go you will never be alone. Jesus will always be in us if we love him and welcome him. So, you see when we pray, we are welcoming Jesus in us. Even when we are alone, and sometimes, we can feel very alone and unwanted. All we must do is ask Jesus to be with us and he is with us. He will help us get through anything."

"So, when we ask Him to come to dinner, he is with us even if we can't see him?" Johnny asked.

"Yes, that's right," Ella said.

"And if we ask Him for a mother and father, He will help us get some?" Johnny asked.

Ella nodded. "If He can find the right ones for you, He will. But remember, even if he can't find some good enough, he will be there to keep you safe or to help you through any problems you have."

"Can he help with arithmetic?" Jimmy asked.

Ella laughed. "He can't give you answers because you have to learn how to get the answers. If you want him to help you learn and you really mean it, he will help you."

"I get it now. So, if I ask Him for a BB gun, he will get me one," Jimmy said. "I mean it. I really want one."

"Well, Jimmy, if Jesus thinks you should have a BB gun, then you will get one, but maybe He doesn't think you are ready for one yet. He would rather keep you safe and make you wait."

"Shucks," said Jimmy. "I may have to wait forever."

"The important thing to know is Jesus is always with you wherever you go, whatever you do. You are never alone." Ella hoped both Johnny and Jimmy would soon be theirs, but she was aware of the possibility it might not happen.

On Sunday, the family went to church together. Afterwards, Dr. John looked at Johnny's foot. It would take a long time to correct, but he had seen remarkable results with braces and therapy.

Later in the day, they returned the boys to the orphanage. Sister Theresa welcomed the boys back. They were happy to tell the other children about their exciting weekend.

"How were the boys?" Sister Theresa inquired. "Well behaved, I hope."

"They were wonderful. Can we meet with you later this week? We have some questions." Ella smiled broadly.

"Oh?" Sister Theresa raised an eyebrow.

"About adoption," Ella said.

"Let me look at my schedule." Sister Theresa shuffled a few papers on her desk and came up with her calendar. "Do you have a time in mind?" She peered above her round glasses. "I know Dr. Ellington has patients to see and we can work around his appointments, I'm sure."

"Since he is in a clinic, Dr. Ellington tries to take off Wednesday afternoons. Would that be convenient?" Ella asked.

Sister Theresa checked her book. "Yes. Would two o'clock work for you? Most of the tots will be asleep and the older children will be in school."

Dr. Ellington had been dragged away by Jimmy and Johnny, who were showing him their beds and the playground.

"I think that will work just fine," Ella stated. "Thank you."

Sister Theresa and Ella spotted the boys by the swings and walked out to join them.

"We have to leave now." Ella made a sad, pouty face. "I will be back on Tuesday for playtime, and we will both be back on Wednesday for a meeting." She directed the last half of her sentence to Dr. Ellington. She didn't want to get the boys' hopes up by telling them the news just yet.

"Come give me a hug," Ella said, opening her arms to welcome both boys.

She held them tight and kissed the tops of their heads. Even if they couldn't talk about it just yet, in her mind and in her heart, the boys were theirs.

John picked up Helen and swung her high on his shoulders. "Goodbye, boys," he called out as he turned to leave. Helen waved bye-bye above his head.

Ella added her good-bye, but she wished she could scoop them up and take them back home with her.

Chapter Twenty-four

Ella tried to keep her Tuesday visit with Mrs. Mallory as normal as possible, but she couldn't wait until her meeting on Wednesday.

On Wednesday, Sister Theresa was prepared with applications and information on hand. "Please fill out the application. It is pretty straight forward, and I see no reason why you should not be approved as adoptive parents. Have you decided if you would like a boy or girl baby?"

"Oh no," Ella stammered. "We want Jimmy *and* Johnny."

"My, my," sighed Sister Theresa. "I assumed you would want a baby. You do realize there are special challenges in adopting an older child."

"We are quite aware of their needs, physically and psychologically," John interjected.

"As a doctor, of course, you are. This will require a bit more paperwork and some discussions, of course. First, as a matter of procedure, we will do a background check. I would waive that in your case, but we are bound by certain regulations. They are simple, you understand, but rules are rules."

"Of course," Ella said, quite confident. "What will you need from us?"

"Your completed application will be sufficient. I will also give you a questionnaire which will let us know your intentions with regards to the children, where they will attend school, what work you will require of them and your religious affiliation, among other things."

"We would not require them to work," Ella said, alarmed. "They are only seven, I mean eight. Naturally, we would expect them to do certain chores around the house, such as making their beds and perhaps carrying wood for the fire, but they are children after all."

"Many of our parents are looking for farm labor or maid services. This is common when children are taken from the orphan trains. Adoptive parents generally are making a more permanent commitment, but many are looking for helping hands," Sister Theresa said honestly. "It is a joy when we can place older youngsters in a loving Catholic home. Especially one willing to accept Johnny with his disability."

"But Sister, we are not Catholic; we are Presbyterian," Ella coughed. She had visions of the chaos the last time those words were mentioned to Charlie's mother.

"Oh dear," said Sister Theresa. "That could be a problem. We only place children in good Catholic homes. I might find dispensation for Johnny since he is considered unadoptable, but Jimmy is a healthy young child. We couldn't..."

"But Sister, they are twins. They are brothers. They shouldn't be separated," Ella pleaded.

"I'm sorry. I will do what I can, but I can't be too hopeful. Rules are rules you understand."

"Of course, we understand," said John.

"I don't understand." Ella was upset. "Rules are made to be broken." Tears welled in her eyes.

"Let me take it to the bishop," Sister Theresa said and sighed. "I'll see what I can do. Please fill out the application and questionnaire so I can present them with my plea."

"Please, Sister, please," Ella begged. "Do everything you can. It is important for the children's welfare."

John and Ella left the meeting with a heavy heart. They didn't ask to see the boys before they left. Ella was sure she would cry and didn't want to upset them.

*   *   *

Weeks went by and still no word came from the bishop. Ella continued her volunteer work and tried to keep her anxiety level in check. A month later, when Ella was there on her volunteer Tuesday, Sister Theresa called Ella to her office.

"I'm afraid I have some bad news for you. We have potential adoptive parents for Jimmy. They are a lovely German family in the Chicago area who are interested in him. They have a five-year-old boy and two girls, seven and two. They would like another boy and Jimmy fits their required blue eye, blonde hair profile. The man works for a large corporation and his wife is a stay-at-home mom. He would look like the rest of their children."

"What?" exclaimed Ella. "They have placed an order for a matching set. I assume they will all be dressed alike, too. Did they have his IQ tested to make sure he fits the intellectual profile as well?"

"As a matter of fact, they did. He is quite intelligent and athletic. He should be a role model for their little boy."

"And what if he doesn't perform to their expectations? Will they relegate him to the position of stable boy? I suppose they rejected Johnny as defective merchandise." Ella was indignant.

"They realize Jimmy will need to be properly groomed regarding mannerisms and habits, but they are prepared to have him professionally coached in social graces and speech. They are quite wealthy, you know."

"And what about Johnny? What will happen to him?"

"Johnny will stay in our care for at least another year. If a proper Catholic home is not found for him, the bishop will again consider your request."

"A year? You would keep him from a loving family for a year? And if we have changed our minds about him, what would happen to him then?" Ella asked, indignant.

"Perhaps he will be transferred to a station in the monastery or to another orphanage. Are you thinking you could change your mind?" Sister Theresa inquired. "You are not certain?"

"We are certain. We will wait as long as it's necessary. When will Jimmy be leaving?"

"This coming Monday if it is convenient for the parents. If not, it will be the following Sunday."

"Convenient? If it is convenient?" Ella was aghast. "Sister, please understand. I love both boys and I want them to be happy. I don't want to lose either of them. Do you think they might be able to stay at our home this weekend?"

"Both boys? Well, I don't know. It is highly irregular since Jimmy has been spoken for," Sister Theresa stammered.

"We would love to make it a special day for them."

"I suppose it is not against the rules and it would be nice for the boys to spend one last weekend together. Yes, I think we can arrange it." She smiled.

*   *   *

Saturday was a cold day in February. The previous day brought a thick layer of fresh snow. The bright sun made it seem warmer than its 25 degrees. A perfect day to get out and enjoy the crisp winter air.

Through the weekend no mention was made of the boys's separation. They played outside in the snow. They made snow angels and snowmen, built a fort, and rolled in the snow and laughed until they could hardly breathe. They drank hot chocolate by the crackling fire and read books until they fell sound asleep.

Sunday was equally fun. They went to a local ranch to take a long sleigh ride through the dell since the Ellingtons had long since gotten rid of their own horse and buggy. The boys took their turns at the reins and were sad when Sunday night came. It was time to return to the orphanage.

Ella grabbed both boys and gave them a huge hug. She hugged Jimmy tight and told him, "No matter what life brings to you, Jesus will watch over you. Always remember how much I love you."

She turned to Johnny and said, "Be strong, your time will come."

"Yes, ma'am," Johnny said, not quite sure what Ella meant. He reached up and wiped a tiny tear that had fallen from her eye. "Don't be sad, I'll see you Tuesday."

"Me, too," said Jimmy.

That made Ella's heart hurt, because she knew that he didn't know what fate had in store for him.

Chapter Twenty-five

Tuesday arrived, and Ella went to the orphanage with a heavy heart fully expecting Jimmy not to be there and Johnny to be heartbroken. She was partially correct. After she entered the orphanage and stomped the snow from her boots, ready to hang up her coat, both boys came running toward her with a big hug.

Ella was both surprised and delighted. She looked up at Sister Theresa with a puzzled expression.

"Can I speak to you a moment?" Sister spoke softly.

"Certainly," Ella said, and took a deep breath, wondering if the family or the bishop had a change of heart.

"Run along boys, I will be there soon," she addressed the boys and hurried to Sister Theresa's office.

"It seems the adoptive parents were not able to make it yesterday due to some pressing business. They will, however, be coming on Sunday."

Ella's hopes were shattered but she realized this would give her a little more time with both boys.

"Jimmy knows he will be leaving. I thought you should know because they may discuss it with you." Sister Theresa sat up straighter. She cleared her throat. "I know this is difficult but please do not be too affectionate. It will make it more difficult for them."

"How do the boys feel about this?" Ella needed to know.

"Quite frankly, they are both upset. Jimmy is unhappy because Johnny will not be going with him, and Johnny is disappointed because Jimmy is leaving. He has no desire to go with his brother but wanted him to come live with you as well. Mrs. Ellington, did you tell Johnny he would be coming to live with you?"

"Oh no, of course not. I would never do that unless it was a certainty. It must be the birthday candle wish," Ella surmised.

"Good," Sister Theresa sighed in relief. "If you had offered such encouragement, I am afraid we would have to terminate your visits or limit them to times when the boys are in classes. It would be cruel to give them false hopes."

"I agree," Ella stated. "I want only what is best for both boys."

"Fine, the boys are waiting to see you. Please try to make it a pleasant visit, and if possible, encourage them to accept their destiny."

Encourage them to accept their destiny? What did that mean? It seemed rather ominous to Ella but the last thing she wanted to do was plant seeds of doubt and despair in the young boys.

"Of course," Ella said. She turned to leave the office only to find both boys waiting outside the door with hopes of their own.

Jimmy swallowed hard. "Did they change their minds? Can we go home with you?"

"Oh Jimmy, I'm afraid not. But we have the whole day. What would you like to do today?" she asked, smiling down at their sad faces.

"What would you like to do today?" Jimmy asked. "You pick."

"How about if we draw? I need some pictures to take home," Ella encouraged. This could be her last picture she'd ever get from Jimmy.

*   *   *

They sat at a table with tablets and colors. "What should we draw?" asked Johnny.

"Whatever you would like me to keep?" Ella answered. "Valentine's Day is in a couple of weeks, so maybe we could all make valentines."

"What is Valentine's Day?" Jimmy asked.

Ella remembered Sister's caution. "Well, let me think." Ella sighed. "St. Valentine lived hundreds of years ago. He loved everybody. When he died, people missed him. So, on the day of his death, February four-teenth, we all tell each other how much we love them. You remember everyone important to you, like Sister Theresa and each other, and to show how much you appreciate them, you give them a card you make to tell them how important they are to you."

"Oh," said Johnny. "So, we draw a pretty picture to give them?"

"Right," said Ella, "and sometimes we add words. But the picture is enough."

For the next hour, they worked diligently making cards. While they drew, they talked. Ella started her paper with a big heart and the boys did the same. Everyone was engrossed in the project when Jimmy said quietly, "I don't wanna go."

"Look at it as a great, wonderful adventure," Ella encouraged. "You will have lots of new toys and clothes, and you'll learn lots of new things. You will have a brother and sisters..."

Before she could go on, Jimmy pouted, "Already have a brother, don't want new ones."

"They ain't come for him yet," Johnny said hopefully. "Can't we both come live with you? If you don't want me, it's okay. You can take Jimmy."

"Oh Johnny, nothing would make me happier than to have both of you but..." Ella remembered Sister Theresa's caution. "But there are rules that say Dr. John and I can't take you."

"Why?" both boys chimed in unison.

Ella cocked her head to the side, thinking. She took a deep breath. "Well, it is complicated and too much for you to understand, maybe too much for me to understand, but we have to follow the rules."

"Dumb rules," Johnny said and wiped away a tear that rolled down his cheek.

"Yeah, dumb," Jimmy agreed and tried to swallow past the lump in his throat.

Ella wanted to hug them and cry, but she knew it was up to her to put a smile back on their faces.

"We have today, and we are together, so let's make today a happy day," Ella repeated. "Tell you what... Let's each make two valentines. One for each of us. Jimmy, you make one for me and one for Johnny. Johnny, make one for me and one for Jimmy, and I will make one for each of you and we will keep them forever. If we ever get lonesome, we can read them and know somewhere out there is someone who loves us."

The boys thought it was a fantastic idea. They worked diligently. When they were finished, each of them treasured the valentine they were given and promised to keep it forever.

That day, it was difficult for Ella to leave. She gave Jimmy a big hug and said, "Well little man, you are off on a new adventure. Be strong and be happy. If you are happy, it will make me happy."

Then, she gave Johnny a hug and promised to see him soon. Afterwards, she went to Sister Theresa's office before she headed home.

"Sister, what if we became Catholic—John and I, could we adopt the boys then?"

"Oh Mrs. Ellington, it's not that easy. Jimmy has already been chosen."

"But it doesn't matter that we would take both boys and they would not be separated?" Ella prodded.

Sister Theresa pursed her lips together. "I am afraid not, Mrs. Ellington. You see, you and your husband would have to be selected to join the church. That takes time. There would be instructions in the faith and then Father would have to feel certain you are dedicated to Catholicism and not using this means to adopt."

"I don't understand. If we became Catholic, we still couldn't adopt?"

"Not immediately. You see, we have to make sure you will remain Catholic."

"You have no guarantee with any adoptive parent, why would we be different?"

"True, but the likelihood of your returning to your faith is an imminent concern. Once you have practiced the faith for a sufficient amount of time to show your commitment is valid, it is another story, but naturally it would take a substantial amount of time."

"So, you are telling me I will not be able to adopt either child." Ella shook her head in despair. "Can I at least see the boys another time this week?"

"Mrs. Ellington, I am sorry, but it would be more difficult for the boys if you continue to see them. After Jimmy is gone, you may resume your volunteer duties on Tuesdays if you desire."

Ella went home with a heavy heart. That night, after she put Helen to sleep, she cried silent tears. She didn't sleep a wink. Her tears soaked her pillow. How could they separate the boys? How could they be so cruel? Why didn't they see what was best for the boys? Was there an answer?

She returned to the orphanage the following Tuesday. Johnny was happy to see her, but he was depressed by the loss of his brother. They sat on the porch swing and Johnny buried his head in Ella's side, crying. She rocked him gently, silently, deep in their own thoughts.

Chapter Twenty-six

Meanwhile, in Chicago, there was much excitement and gayety at the Schmidt home. Jimmy learned he would have a new name. He would no longer be Jimmy Kraus; he would hereafter be named Samuel Schmidt. His new siblings were Anna, Rachel, and Robert. Anna and Rachel looked at him as a strange curiosity. They giggled at his tattered knickers. Robert, being only five, had no interest in such trappings and found it fascinating another boy was part of the household.

Mr. and Mrs. Schmidt shuffled Samuel off with their housekeeper, Harriet, who took him away to be bathed and re-clothed. She had a fresh set of clothes laid out on his new bed. She explained he would have all new clothes. They would be found in his wardrobe and his drawers. She took his old clothes away in her fingertips, avoiding touching them for fear of contamination. She provided a warm bath with plenty of soap and instructed him to scrub properly. She would inspect his hair upon completion of his bath to be sure there were no fleas, lice, or other vermin.

When she was satisfied he was properly cleaned, she told him to get dressed and meet the family at the bottom of the stairs in the parlor.

Jimmy said not a word but dutifully did as he was instructed. After a long period of time, he heard Mr. Schmidt call from the bottom of the stairs, "Samuel, we are waiting. Please come downstairs."

Jimmy felt scratchy in his starched shirt. His shoes were stiff and uncomfortable. He did as he was told and slowly proceeded to the parlor.

"Come here, Samuel," Mrs. Schmidt commanded.

"Yes, Ma'am," Jimmy responded quietly.

"Let me straighten you up a bit," Mrs. Schmidt said.

Jimmy had loosened his collar, hoping the scratchiness could be relieved.

Mrs. Schmidt tugged the collar straight and placed a bow tie around his neck, assuring the collar would remain snug in place. "Now you look presentable," she said and smiled.

She seemed like a nice enough person but why did she insist he wear these ridiculous clothes, and why had they decided to call him Samuel?

The only Samuel Jimmy knew was Samuel Clemens and he was called Mark Twain. Jimmy decided if Samuel Clemens could be called Mark Twain, Jimmy Kraus could be called Samuel Schmidt. He didn't know why people had to change their names, but he supposed if there was a name Samuel might not be too bad. He liked Tom Sawyer and Huckleberry Finn, and if Samuel knew them, he was okay with it.

The next day Jimmy was hustled off to his coach, who was going to teach him about proper etiquette. He wasn't sure what *etiquette* was, but it seemed mighty important to the Schmidts. He thought it must be a foreign language since Mrs. Schmidt insisted he learn etiquette before he was introduced to their friends.

After a few weeks, Jimmy was getting tired of being Samuel. It seemed nothing he did was right and nothing he said was right. Most of all, Jimmy hated those starched collars the Schmidts liked so much.

Jimmy missed his brother and the kids at the orphanage. He missed the Ellingtons, too. He asked Mr. Schmidt if they could go back to visit his brother sometime.

Mr. Schmidt replied, "Samuel, you don't have a brother at the orphanage anymore. That was a previous life. Your only brother is Robert."

"Do, too," said Jimmy defiantly.

"Samuel, don't talk to me that way. Show respect. What did you learn from your coach?"

"I learned you are stuffed shirts!"

"What? Come here." Mr. Schmidt reached for Jimmy, but he pulled away.

The man grabbed Jimmy and placed him across his knee and gave him three swift whacks on the behind. "Now, go to your room."

Jimmy refused to cry and ran up the stairs. Once he was hidden away in his room he realized he may never see his brother again. Tears flowed down his cheeks. Jimmy also knew if there was ever any way to get to the orphanage, he would find it.

He had several books in his room, and one was written by Mark Twain. It was *The Adventures of Huckleberry Finn.*

Jimmy read the book over and over and decided if Huckleberry Finn could do the things he did, so could he. He didn't think he could build a raft and he didn't think the Chicago River would take him to Milwaukee, so he devised his own plan to get there.

As soon as the first signs of spring showed, Jimmy set out to find his brother. He had taken some clothes out of the laundry and rinsed them to get the starch out. He hung them out the back window to dry after it was dark. He didn't want the scratchy starched clothes he normally was required to wear.

In the morning, the clothes were still a little damp but softer, so it was fine with him. He loved the feel of the soft fabric.

He snuck down to the kitchen before Harriet, the housekeeper, was out of bed. He made himself a sandwich and found a twig and a piece of cloth. He tied the sandwich in the cloth and hung it on the twig just like Huckleberry Finn had. Before dawn, he was on his way.

Unfortunately, Jimmy didn't know where Milwaukee was, but he knew it was a long drive from Chicago so he suspected it would take him a long time.

I wish I made an extra sandwich, Jimmy thought. Oh well. He would find some food along the way.

He went by way of the back alleys because he didn't want to be recognized and taken back to the Schmidt's house. Once he reached the edge of town, he managed to catch a ride on the back of a buckboard. He told the farmer he needed to get to his sick grandmother's house. When the farmer reached his destination, Jimmy asked, "How far is it to Milwaukee?"

"You don't mean to tell me your grandmother is in Milwaukee?" the farmer asked.

"Oh no," lied Jimmy. "She is just a short way up the road. I was just curious about Milwaukee. That's where I was born."

"Well," said the farmer as he pulled off his hat and scratched his head, "can't zactly tell ya' where Milwaukee is. Never been there. All I can say is due north more 'n a hunert miles."

"Hundred miles?" Jimmy was shocked. A hundred miles was incomprehensible. At least he knew it was due north. "Thank you, sir."

"You take care o' yer gramma now. Hope she's done ailin' soon."

"Sure thing. Bye, mister," Jimmy called over his shoulder as he trotted due north. At least he assumed it was north since the farmer looked in that direction when he'd said 'due north.'

That night, Jimmy slept in a barn, thankful he had taken his jacket. It was spring, but the nights got pretty cold. The barn hay, along with his jacket, made it tolerable. His tummy gurgled. He had eaten his sandwich several hours earlier. He sure wished he had saved part of it.

*   *   *

The Schmidts awoke to a frantic cry from their maid, Harriet. "He's gone, he's gone," she shouted.

Mr. Schmidt rushed into Samuel's room. His bed was made but nothing appeared to be missing…except Samuel. "Tarnation, what is that boy up to now."

Mr. Schmidt ran from room to room calling out, "Samuel, Samuel. You better come out or you are in deep trouble."

Mrs. Schmidt wrung her hands and peered out the window to see if he might have gone outside.

After a search of the house and the neighborhood, Mr. Schmidt summoned the police. When the police arrived, they inquired of the family about friends he might be visiting.

They all assured the officer that Samuel had no friends. The children also had no clue where Samuel might be. After exhausting all possibilities where he may have gone, the police determined that Samuel was a runaway. There was no sign of foul play.

Mr. Schmidt became even more angry with Samuel. He paced the room. "When that boy is returned he will be sorry he pulled a stunt like this."

Mrs. Schmidt simply wiped away tears and kept praying that God would keep him safe. "He is just a little boy. He must have gone out and got lost. He must be frightened."

"Troublemaker," Mr. Schmidt mumbled.

The police told him they'd have a lookout for him and let them know as soon as he was located.

*   *   *

The next morning, Jimmy woke up really hungry. He heard a farmer starting his morning chores. Jimmy went down to check out what the farmer was doing and to see if he could earn breakfast.

"Hey, mister," Jimmy called out. "I'm lookin' for work. D'ya have some chores I can help ya' with?"

The young farmer looked at the scrawny eight-year-old. "Where you live, boy?"

"Up the road a piece. I'm staying with my uncle for the summer." Jimmy shuffled his foot on the barn floor.

"That right? Don't yer uncle have work for you?" The farmer pulled a bit of straw from Jimmy's jacket.

Jimmy shook his head. "No sir, he has hired hands."

"Well, hmm…" The farmer stood there thoughtful for a moment. "Are ya' hungry?"

"Yes sir, left before breakfast this mornin'."

"Well, how about we have us some breakfast, then you can help me clean out the barn. After that, I need to take a ride into town. I'll give ya' a lift back home when I go."

The farmer's wife had prepared scrambled eggs and bacon and hot biscuits. The farmer brought in a bottle of fresh milk, but Jimmy drank the cold milk from the ice box.

"Don't always have chilled milk," the farmer said. "Ice man only comes this way once a week."

"What do you do if he doesn't come? Your milk will spoil."

"No, we take the bottle down by the stream. Spring water is always cold. We make sure it is wedged between the rocks so it doesn't drift away, but it stays pretty cold there."

While the farmer and his wife were busy, Jimmy stuffed two biscuits in his jacket pockets.

After breakfast, Jimmy helped the farmer clean the barn.

"Ready to go?" the farmer inquired. He removed his hat, scratched his head and sighed.

"Naw," said Jimmy. "Think I'll keep lookin' for some more work."

The farmer pursed his lips, shook his head. He reached into his pocket and pulled out a quarter. He handed it to Jimmy. "This should be a good amount for one day's work. Maybe we could stop by and see if it's okay with your uncle if you ride into town with me. You can help carry supplies."

"No, my uncle is gone today. I need to stay and keep an eye on things 'til he gets back."

"Well, you ain't exactly doin' that, are ya'. Maybe I should get you back home so you can be watchin' things."

"No, I don't have to be there now. I have to feed the chickens later and gather eggs."

"Maybe we could talk to yer aunt about that?" the farmer asked.

"Can't, ain't got no aunt. She passed last year."

Still prodding, the man asked, "What's yer uncle's name? Maybe I know him. You know, we kind of take care of each other in these parts."

"Umm," Jimmy hesitated. "Don't think you know him. He just moved here. His name is MacDonald." Jimmy wondered why that popped into his head. He supposed it was because he learned the song "Old MacDonald's Farm" in school.

"Well, alright then," the farmer said and went to his truck. "You come back in the morning, and you can help with the morning chores. Then, maybe we can get some plowing and planting done." He waved good-bye. "Get here early, we're up with the chickens. Our chickens get fed early."

Jimmy liked the farmer and his wife, but he needed to move on. He got back on the road and headed due north.

Several hours later, the sheriff drove up as Jimmy was sitting on the side of the road nibbling on a biscuit.

The sheriff stopped his car and walked over to Jimmy. "Hey boy, what's your name?"

"Jimmy," Jimmy said solemnly.

"Sure it isn't Samuel?" the sheriff looked directly in Jimmy's eyes.

"Nope, it's Jimmy."

"It's a funny thing," the sheriff continued. "There is a family named Schmidt outside of Chicago looking for their boy, Samuel. What is funny is Samuel is wearing the same clothes you have on. Then Mr. Thomas, a farmer in these parts, told me a young lad with the same clothes did some work for him this morning. What do you make of that?"

Jimmy shuffled his feet, looking at the ground. He said nothing.

"Well, Jimmy, suppose you tell me where you live, and we can go talk to your parents."

"I live in Milwaukee in an orphanage, and I want to go back there," Jimmy sobbed.

"Get in the car, Jimmy," the sheriff said softly.

Once in the car, the sheriff told Jimmy, "I can't take you to Milwaukee, but let's go back to the station and talk about it."

Jimmy was silent all the way back to the station.

The Schmidts were excited and happy to have Samuel found safe. "Don't ever scare us like that again," Mrs. Schmidt said.

But that was not to happen. Jimmy continued to run away, always to be brought home to the Schmidts.

Needless to say, the Schmidts were soon weary of going to the police station to retrieve their son. This continued for more than a year.

Then, Jimmy decided running away was getting him nowhere. He realized the only way he would ever be released would be if he became unmanageable, and unmanageable he was.

He picked fights with his sisters, he harassed his little brother, he spoke back to his parents even though he knew a punishment would ensue. He got in trouble at school, and he stole from the local market. His grades deteriorated. He was miserable and everyone around him was miserable as well.

The final straw was the day the Schmidts brought home a new leather sofa. It was quite expensive and something they took great delight in. Before he left for school that morning, he took out a knife and slashed the sofa several times.

For this act, he was punished severely by his adoptive father. Mr. Schmidt took Samuel over his knee, stripped down Samuel's britches, and gave him a sound trouncing.

That evening, Jimmy was sent to his room without supper. "Young man, you have reached my limit of tolerance. I cannot abide this behavior a moment longer." He stormed out of the room, leaving Jimmy to consider his fate. He refused to cry and, in fact, took a degree of pleasure in knowing this time he really had gone too far.

The following morning was Saturday and there was no school. Mr. Schmidt had discussed the matter with Mrs. Schmidt. They called him into the parlor for a discussion. Mrs. Schmidt was wiping her eye with a handkerchief.

Jimmy felt bad for her. She had done nothing terrible to him, so a feeling of remorse crept into his heart.

Mr. Schmidt cleared his throat. "Son," he cleared his throat again. "We have tried to give you a good home and opportunities for your future. It is clear you do not appreciate our efforts. You are disruptive, destructive, and belligerent. Mrs. Schmidt and I had a long conversation about your future. I'm afraid we can no longer tolerate your behavior in our home. We've considered strongly about sending you off to boarding school."

Jimmy looked on in silence.

"However," Mr. Schmidt said and wiped his brow, "that would get you out of our hair and perhaps teach you some discipline, but we still don't feel you will ever fit into our family."

Jimmy looked down silently at his shoes. The shiny new shoes the Schmidts had purchased for him.

"Do you understand what I am saying?" Mr. Schmidt inquired.

Mrs. Schmidt choked back a sob.

"Yes, sir," Jimmy replied with a mixture of joy and sadness. "You're giving me back to the orphanage?"

"Not exactly," Mr. Schmidt said with a stern look. "You won't be going back to St. Joseph's."

Jimmy looked up at him. "But that's where Johnny is, that's where Mrs. Ellington is," he said and panicked. "I need to go to Milwaukee."

"Well, Samuel, you need to learn there are consequences to your actions. I'm afraid St. Joseph's coddled you. You will be going to a public orphanage in Cook County. They have a strong disciplinary program, and hopefully, you will learn how to become a productive member of society. It is unlikely you will be adopted since you are already nine, but if you would like, Mrs. Schmidt will visit you on occasion and assess your development."

"I hate you. I don't want to ever see you!" Jimmy lashed out. He ran back to his room and sobbed into his pillow. This was not what he expected.

The next day Jimmy was taken to Cook County Orphanage and left in the hands of a matronly woman who reminded him of a crow. She had a large beak-like nose, and her dark hair was pulled back in a bun. Jimmy was already planning his escape.

*   *   *

Ella and John continued to see Johnny as often as they could. Sister Theresa saw a sparkle in his otherwise sad eyes anytime he saw the Ellingtons. She looked at their visits as healing for this grieving boy. He'd especially developed a strong bond with John, who began calling him Little Buddy. Soon everyone called him Buddy, which he responded to with pride.

As time passed on, it became more and more evident that Johnny would never be adopted. On his ninth birthday, they celebrated at the Ellingtons. When Buddy blew out the candles on his cake, he wished that he could see his brother.

"I wish I could make that wish come true." Ella hugged Buddy. "Someday, you will see your brother. It may not be for a long time but one day you will be together."

"Promise?" Buddy asked.

"Promise."

John shot Ella a stern glare.

That evening after the children were fast asleep, John confronted Ella. "Why did you promise Buddy something that you know is not likely to happen. It's been a year and Jimmy's family has not reached out. We can't access the adoption records and I am sure his new family would respond badly if somehow you could."

"I told Buddy it could be a long time."

"A lifetime." John sighed. "When they are of age probably, though I am sure they will meet again. I know they will both be changed but twins can never be separated. There is research that substantiates that, but it isn't easy with the confidentiality surrounding adoptions."

"John, I am really worried for Buddy." Ella looked down, her fist cuffed over her mouth to stifle her emotions.

"What is the problem?" John sat next to Ella and put his arm around her shoulder.

"Buddy is not likely to be adopted and when he turns ten, he will likely be removed from the orphanage," Ella said. "He could be put on an orphan train or more likely sent to a monastery or other facility. He could be put in an institution for the disabled. Perhaps even a mental institute."

"Well, that's not likely. Buddy is very smart. He misses his brother, but he has us. I don't think he will suffer that fate."

"You're right, John. He has us now but what will happen if he loses us, too? How much loss can a child take before it tears at his mental health? We can't let that happen to Buddy. I don't know what it will do to my mental health. We've lost Jimmy. I can't take losing Buddy, too."

*   *   *

A few days passed before John came home with a smile on his face. He put his hands on Ella's slim waist and swung her around. "I have the answer."

"You have the answer to what?" Ella asked, surprised.

"Money talks. Money always talks. The bishop will listen if the price is right."

"What? You are going to *buy* Buddy?" Ella was aghast.

"I'm not going to buy Buddy. I am going to buy his freedom...if I can."

John immediately set up an appointment with the bishop. He did not reveal his plan but indicated that he was prepared to make a substantial donation to the orphanage or the church. The appointment was quickly set up.

*   *   *

The bishop greeted John warmly and shook his hand profusely. "Welcome, welcome Dr. Ellington."

The conversation began with small talk about the weather, the foliage and other trivial matters. "Dr. Ellington, I know you are a busy man and I'm sure you are not here to discuss our giant spruce tree."

"You're right, Bishop Lofton. I have a matter of grave concern. You have a young boy in your orphanage, Johnny Kraus. You may have heard that my wife and I have a great fondness for the boy. No, not fondness, much more than that. We would like to adopt him."

"Wonderful, wonderful." The man smiled. "Sister Theresa can take care of that for you. I am pleased for the boy. You will be wonderful parents."

"You see, there are issues. My wife and I are not Catholic."

"Oh, I see. That is a problem. I'm afraid…"

"Before you go any further, I want you to know I am prepared to donate a sub…"

"Oh no, Dr. Ellington, we can't bend the rules. This is highly unusual."

"Yes, Bishop Lofton, this *is* highly unusual. You see, Johnny is in need of surgery and time is drawing short to successfully perform that surgery. I know the church is struggling to support the orphanage. These are desperate times financially. If we could adopt Johnny, his surgery would be taken care of, and you would have one less mouth to feed. Johnny would have a home where he is loved and cared for."

"But…"

"It is a win-win for everyone. Johnny would have a family and the medical attention he needs. My wife and I will have the child we want. The church will benefit financially."

"But what of Johnny's religious beliefs? Money is good, but faith is more important than a few hundred dollars."

John shook his head. "I am talking thousand, not hundreds."

The bishop choked. He placed his hand over his mouth, then looked at John to make sure he'd heard correctly.

"Thousands?"

"Yes, three thousand."

"Three thousand?" He cleared his throat. "I…I need to discuss this with others…the board. You make good points regarding Johnny's medical needs. Yes, yes. It would not be fair to deny Johnny the help he needs. Can I get back to you tomorrow?"

"Absolutely, Bishop." John stood with his hat in his hand. "I look forward to hearing from you. Good day."

"Good day, Doctor." The bishop extended his hand. "I believe I will have good news for you."

John and the bishop shook hands. John placed his hat on his head and left.

That went better than expected, he thought. *I was prepared to offer five thousand if necessary.*

The next day, the bishop called to inform the Ellingtons that they would soon be parents. The paperwork was expedited, and Johnny became John "Buddy" Ellington.

The surgery on Buddy's foot was completed soon afterwards, leaving Buddy with just a slight limp.

On Buddy's tenth birthday, the celebration was filled with joy. Buddy blew out the candles and once again wished to see his brother.

"You will, Buddy, you will. Be patient." Ella hugged him tight. "I want to see him, too."

Chapter Twenty-seven

Jimmy bided his time, carefully planning his escape. He tried running away a few times but just like in the past, he would be caught and returned to the orphanage. This orphanage was more troublesome than St. Joseph's in Milwaukee. It was overcrowded and understaffed. There were no nuns to take care of things and give them attention. Jimmy didn't need attention, though he often thought of the hugs Mrs. Ellington would give him and longed for her personal touch.

The work was harder here. The older children had to do most of the labor. He would soon reach his tenth birthday, so the tasks became harder. There was some talk that after he was twelve, he might be put on an orphan train to go out west to work on a farm. Since Jimmy had some experience on a farm, even though it was just a couple of days, he might be sent at eleven or maybe even ten.

At first, he thought perhaps he could get on a train going to Milwaukee and make his escape there, but if the train went west, he might not ever get back to Milwaukee.

Among Jimmy's belongings was the valentine he had made with Mrs. Ellington before he was taken to the Schmidt's house. He also had the quarter he had earned from the farmer for his day of work over a year ago.

He had an idea. The orphanage sometimes had paper and colors. They were there for the smaller children and doled out sparingly. They were kept under lock and key and only brought out when there were school activities. He had to devise another plan.

When the opportunity came, he was able to get a pencil from the penmanship class. He took out the valentine late at night and with the pencil, he wrote a letter on the valentine to Johnny.

Johnny, I miss you. I am not with the people anymore. I am in Cook County orphanage. I want to come see you. I run away but they always find me. Say hello to Mrs. Elenton. I love you and miss you so much.

Jimmy

Jimmy addressed the letter to Johnny Kraus, St Joseph's Orphanage, Milwaukee. Now, how could he get a stamp? He had the money. Stamps were only two cents and Jimmy had a quarter. He wondered if it would get there without an envelope, but he decided if he had a stamp he could somehow find an envelope.

*   *   *

Jimmy talked to Mrs. Crowley. She was the orphanage matron. The kids sometimes called her 'the warden.' The kids were referred to as inmates, so they felt calling her the warden was fair. It was kind of a prison with the inmates sentenced to hard labor.

Mrs. Crowley was the lady he had met on the first day who reminded him of a crow. He thought Crowley was the right name for her since she also cackled like a crow. But despite this, Mrs. Crowley wasn't so bad. She liked well-behaved children who minded their manners and volunteered for jobs.

Jimmy became endeared to Mrs. Crowley, addressing her as Ma'am, flattering her whenever he could. Or at least trying to.

"Good morning, Ma'am, your nose doesn't look so big like everyone says. I bet it is good to smell with."

"Good afternoon, Ma'am, you shouldn't worry about fat, it will keep you warm in the winter."

"Good evening, Ma'am, can I carry that package for you? Old people shouldn't have to carry their own packages."

Mrs. Crowley had told him she was only thirty-five. She would laugh silently after each encounter, no matter how much his words took her aback. She was strict. It was the only way to maintain order under the trying circumstances at the orphanage, but she couldn't help but laugh at Jimmy's attempts at flattery.

One day, Jimmy had an idea. "Mrs. Crowley, someday I would like to be a postman. Do you think I could help with the mail? Sort it? I read real good. I could lick the envelopes and stamps. I have lots of spit. Deliver it where it needs to go? I run real quick."

"Well, Samuel, I could use some help. You can start tomorrow."

Jimmy was still Samuel Schmidt, even though he didn't want to acknowledge it.

The next day, Mrs. Crowley handed Jimmy a stack of envelopes and a page of stamps. "Put the stamps on the envelopes and seal the envelopes," Mrs. Crowley directed.

Jimmy took the envelopes and stamps to a table and proceeded to do the task as directed. The temptation was very great to take one of those stamps. He just needed one. If he asked Mrs. Crowley for one, she would want to know why. He didn't think she would approve.

The next day, Jimmy stood outside waiting for the postman. When the postman arrived, Jimmy handed him the stack of envelopes to be mailed.

He took out his shiny quarter and asked the postman if he could buy a stamp.

"Why, sure," he said. He reached into his bag and took out the stamps. "It is two cents for just one, did you want more?"

"No, one will be fine," said Jimmy.

The postman reached into his pocket and gave Jimmy twenty-three cents change.

"Thank you, Mr. Postman," Jimmy said excitedly and placed the stamp in his pocket, along with the change. Then, he proceeded to run back to the orphanage.

"Hey, boy," called the postman. "Didn't you want your mail?"

"Oh yeah," said Jimmy as he ran back to get the mail.

"Good-bye now, see you tomorrow," the postman called after Jimmy, who was running back to the orphanage.

"Good-bye," Jimmy called over his shoulder.

Jimmy sorted and distributed the mail. Then, he hurried to his bedroom, reached under his cot, and pulled out a cigar box that held all his treasures. In it were the valentine, the pencil, and a marble Johnny had given him the day he left St. Joseph's.

He deposited the twenty-three cents from his pocket. He removed the valentine from the box and wondered how he would find an envelope. Then, he put the valentine back into the box. He had an idea.

*   *   *

The next day when he reported for duty, Jimmy asked Mrs. Crowley if she had an old envelope left over from her opened mail.

"Why do you want an old envelope?" Mrs. Crowley inquired.

"Thought I'd make a paper airplane," explained Jimmy.

"Samuel, that's a wonderful idea. I'll save all my old envelopes for you and maybe you can have a contest with the other children. You can see who makes the nicest airplane or whose plane flies farthest." Mrs. Crowley was delighted with Samuel's innovativeness. She was also pleased with the work he was doing for her.

"Would you, ma'am, would you?" he asked.

After the mail was finished, Jimmy couldn't wait to see how many envelopes Mrs. Crowley had saved for him. He dutifully ran out to meet the postman and sorted and delivered the mail. He gave the neatly stacked envelopes to Mrs. Crowley.

"Thank you, Samuel. I have something for you." Mrs. Crowley reached into her drawer and pulled out four envelopes, then handed them to Jimmy. "You may have to save these until you get enough for all of the boys," she encouraged.

"Here is a box to store them in." Mrs. Crowley took out an empty shoebox and handed it to Jimmy.

"Thank you, thank you," Jimmy said. He was so excited he scampered back to his room without even inquiring if there was more work for him to do.

"You're welcome," Mrs. Crowley shouted after him.

*   *   *

Jimmy pulled out the valentine and compared it with the envelopes he had. There was one he decided would fit it perfectly. He only had to fold the valentine once.

He reread the message to make sure he didn't forget anything and placed it inside the envelope. It fit with a little room to spare, but there was a problem. The envelope had Mrs. Crowley's address on it.

He thought about it for a while, and finally, he had the answer. He spent the next hour trying to take the envelope apart. Some of it opened but most of the seams were securely glued. He would have to cut it apart.

He got a scissors and a jar of paste from the classroom. He cut along the seams, being extra careful not to be wasteful. He turned the envelope inside out and refolded it, so he had a nice new envelope, which he carefully pasted together.

Now, the valentine wouldn't fit.

He took the scissors and trimmed the valentine and was thrilled to see it fit. He placed the envelope on top of the box under his bed to dry overnight.

The next morning, he took the envelope out, wrote the address on it. Johnny Kraus, St. Joseph's Orphanage, Milwaukee, Wisconsin.

He didn't know the street, but he was sure everyone in Milwaukee knew where the orphanage was. He carefully pasted the envelope shut and placed the two-cent stamp on it.

He hid the envelope under his shirt all morning. Later, Jimmy stamped and licked several envelopes Mrs. Crowley had prepared the day before. He added his envelope to the pile and ran out to meet the postman.

"Hello, Mr. Postman," Jimmy said. He pointed out the top envelope. "This one is very important. Will you make sure it gets delivered as soon as possible?"

"I'll do that, young man," the postman replied. "What is your name, boy?"

"Jimmy Kraus," Jimmy replied proudly. "I'm from Milwaukee."

"Well, I will see you Jimmy Kraus from Milwaukee." The postman patted Jimmy on the back. "You have a good day."

"I will, Mister Postman."

Jimmy ran back to the orphanage with the mail in his hand and a smile on his face, ready to sort and deliver the day's work for Mrs. Crowley.

"Samuel, I enjoy having you assist me but I'm afraid next week school starts, and you won't be able to help me in the morning. You will have to be in classes and mail can't wait. I will have to do it myself. I want to let you know how much I've enjoyed having you help me, though. I will keep the used envelopes for you, so stop by after class to pick them up."

"Okay, Mrs. Crowley," Jimmy said, nodding.

He liked his job, but it was okay. He knew as soon as Johnny knew where he was, someone would come get him.

Chapter Twenty-eight

⁂

For the remainder of the summer since the valentine was mailed, Jimmy ran to meet the postman, sure one day a letter would arrive addressed to him. It never happened. He thought about writing to Johnny again, maybe this time getting the correct address.

*   *   *

In Milwaukee, the mail arrived on Sister Theresa's desk. As she shuffled through it, she saw a crudely made envelope addressed to Johnny Kraus. There was no return address. She knew Johnny Kraus well. He had been with the Ellingtons for more than a year now.

She wasn't sure what to do about the letter. Johnny had recently had surgery to correct his foot and Mrs. Ellington was not volunteering at the orphanage until Johnny had fully recuperated.

Adoptions were kept confidential. She didn't want to destroy the Schmidts' privacy, if by chance the letter had come from Jimmy. She didn't know what was in it, but she didn't feel it was her place to open it.

On the other hand, if the letter had come from Jimmy and Johnny's mother or other birth relative, she was bound to keep the children's whereabouts a secret. She couldn't return it since it had no return address. She set it aside. More pressing matters were awaiting her.

Later that day, she picked up the envelope again and pondered it for a moment.

Who could it be from other than the options she'd already considered? No one, and in either case would she be allowed to disclose to the sender any information about Johnny. At first, she was going to throw it in the waste basket but then decided to place it in Johnny's file where it was soon forgotten.

*   *   *

After some time, Jimmy became disheartened. He asked Mrs. Crowley if she would let him do mail duty on the days he was off from school. That didn't allow for much time since the postman never delivered on weekends or holidays.

Time passed, another summer arrived, and Jimmy tried again. He got his old job back handling the mail.

Once again, he approached the postman to purchase stamps. This time, he asked for three. The mailman gave him four cents change from his dime.

Jimmy chose a larger envelope and used it for stationary. He folded it and placed it in another envelope he made.

"Please, Mr. Postman," Jimmy pleaded. "Make sure this letter gets delivered. I don't think the last one arrived."

The postman looked at the envelope. "Well, let me see." He turned it over in his hand. "It doesn't have an address on it."

"I don't know the address, but the Milwaukee postman must know where St. Joseph's Orphanage is."

"I think you're right, Jimmy. Let's try it one more time."

Jimmy said a prayer that night. "God, please help the postman find the orphanage."

*   *   *

Once again, Sister Theresa didn't know what to do when a letter arrived. Mrs. Ellington was volunteering at the orphanage on Tuesdays. She would have a talk with her on the following Tuesday.

When Ella arrived at the orphanage, Sister Theresa called Ella into her office. "Mrs. Ellington, I have a dilemma." Sister placed her hand over her mouth and thought for a moment.

"What is it, Sister? Have I done something wrong?" Ella asked.

"Oh no," Sister Theresa assured her. "It's just... I have an ethical dilemma." She hesitated a moment. "You know the rules of adoption are very strict. I cannot release the name of adoptive parents to anyone. Nor can I release the name of biological parents to anyone, including the adopted child. We must protect the child's identity at all costs."

"I understand. Is someone looking for Johnny?" Ella guessed.

"I'm not sure. I received this in the mail." She held up the makeshift envelope.

"Looking at the construction, I will assume it is either from Jimmy or the children's biological parents. If the content divulges the names of Jimmy's adoptive parents or the biological parents, I am bound to secrecy. However, I do not know the contents of the envelope and there is no return address to respond to. The letter is written to Johnny, and I have no right to open it without your permission. I would like to have your permission, so I know what, if any, of the contents can be relayed. Do I have your permission?"

"Absolutely," replied Ella, sitting on the edge of her chair.

Sister Theresa tore open the letter. It was indeed from Jimmy. She read it to herself. A tear rolled down her cheek as she handed it to Ella. Jimmy had made no reference to the Schmidts.

Ella read silently.

Dear Johnny,

I miss you so much. I hope the Ellingtons were able to adopt you. I'm not adopted anymore. I am at the Cook County Orphanage in Chicago. We are eleven now, so they might send me on the orphan train. I ran away to see you, but the sheriff always brought me back to the family. If I know where you are, I will try to run away again. Please let me know where you are so I can find you.

Jimmy

"Oh, Sister, do you have an address for the Cook County Orphanage?" Ella asked, her heart going out to Jimmy.

"I will try to find it before you leave today."

"Thank you, thank you," Ella said as she grabbed Sister Theresa's hand, excited about the prospect of finding Jimmy. "God bless you."

Ella generally stayed two hours at the orphanage. She watched the clock, but it didn't seem to move fast enough. At precisely three in the afternoon, Ella was at Sister Theresa's door. "Did you find it?"

"Yes, I did," said Sister Theresa. "I have written it down for you."

*   *   *

Ella raced home. She couldn't wait to tell John the news. As soon as he returned home from the clinic, she pulled John into his study so the children couldn't hear. She didn't want to get Buddy's hopes up only to be dashed. After a discussion, they decided to tell Buddy and Helen, and planned a road trip to Chicago the following weekend. Johnny couldn't sit still; he was so excited to see his brother.

The trip was on good roads, but it took them almost four hours going thirty miles per hour. The orphanage was north of Chicago and proved quite easy to find.

They arrived close to noon, so they decided to have a picnic lunch before going to the orphanage. It was a good idea, but no one had much of an appetite. They were all just anxious to see Jimmy once again.

*   *   *

The Ellingtons approached the entrance to the orphanage. It was a typical two-story asylum with austere dark brick. There was a wide stairway leading to a large door, also dark and uninviting. A circular drive led to the front entry. The children peered out the side window of their touring car in silent awe.

Eleven-year-old Buddy asked, "Where are the kids?"

Six-year-old Helen echoed, "Nobody's here."

John looked at Ella and said, "Maybe they are still at lunch."

Ella shrugged.

They exited the automobile and walked up the steps. John knocked on the front door. They waited anxiously as a young woman in a print house dress answered it.

She looked in awe at the children dressed in their finery and inquired, "May I help you?"

"I am Dr. John Ellington, this is Mrs. Ellington," John motioned toward Ella, "and these are our children Helen and Buddy, ah Johnny. We would like to speak to the person in charge of this facility."

"You mean the orphanage? Or the poor house? We have both here," the woman said.

"Oh? The orphanage," Ella stammered, clutching Jimmy's letter in her hand.

"That would be Mrs. Crowley. I don't think she is available, but I'll check."

"Miss, if you don't mind," John interjected, "we have come all the way from Milwaukee, and it is quite important. Please be sure to tell Mrs. Crowley it is very important we speak to her today."

"Come in and have a seat in the parlor." The young woman pointed the way.

The Ellingtons sat and fidgeted while they waited for what seemed like an eternity.

Helen questioned once again, "Where are the children, Mama?"

"I'm not sure, Helen." This was a much bigger facility than St Joseph's in Milwaukee, so Ella supposed the children were housed in another wing.

After almost an hour, Mrs. Crowley arrived to the parlor. She appeared austere in her pulled back bun and black attire. "I am Mrs. Crowley, the director of this facility. How can I help you?" She pulled back a sprig of hair that had managed to escape.

"Where are the children?" Helen once again inquired.

"Hopefully resting peacefully," Mrs. Crowley sighed. "I'm afraid we are having an epidemic of Cholera. We aren't allowing the children out until the issue is resolved. We are also not allowing visitors in, so I hope your visit is not of that nature."

Ella and John looked at each other.

"Well, we were hoping to see one of your children, Jimmy Kraus," Ella said. "More than that, we would like to adopt him. He sent a letter to his brother Johnny." Ella pulled Johnny to her side.

"Hmm," Mrs. Crowley pondered. "We don't have a Jimmy Kraus here."

"Are you sure? Johnny received this letter last week." Ella pushed the letter toward Mrs. Crowley.

She perused the letter and returned it to Ella. "No, I am sure we have no one here named Kraus. We have two Jimmy's; one is three, the other is sixteen." Mrs. Crowley shook her head.

"He is eleven," Ella offered. "Do you think we could possibly see your eleven-year-old boys?"

"I'm afraid it will be impossible; we have twelve eleven-year-old boys and at least six of them have cholera."

"Mrs. Crowley, Jimmy and Johnny are twins," John said. He pulled Johnny forward. "Please. Take a look. Do any of your eleven-year-olds resemble him?"

Mrs. Crowley took another look. She tilted Johnny's head and examined his face. "Maybe. No, I don't think so. Samuel is much thinner and perhaps a bit taller. Although, they do share similarities. Samuel is much darker, but he does spend a lot of time outdoors."

"Might we see Samuel?" Ella was so excited she couldn't sit still.

"I'm afraid not," Mrs. Crowley replied sadly. "Samuel is a great helper, but I'm afraid he has been stricken with cholera. He is in quarantine. Perhaps you can come back in a couple of weeks. He could be better then."

"Mrs. Crowley, perhaps you didn't understand me when I introduced my family. I am Dr. John Ellington with the Mallory & Ellington Clinic in Milwaukee. I would like you to remand Samuel to my care. Certainly, you can do that. My family can remain here. Please allow me to examine the patient."

Mrs. Crowley was a bit flustered now. "Well, I don't know you, Doctor Ellington. We have our own doctor, and Samuel is his patient. I don't think it would be ethical to declare you as Samuel's physician. We don't even know if Samuel is the Jimmy you are seeking."

"Mrs. Crowley, I'm sure we can simplify this. Unless Samuel is in a coma and cannot speak, will you please ask him if he is Jimmy Kraus?"

"Well, I guess I can do that, but it will take a while because I need to scrub and put on a sterile apron."

"We will wait here," John instructed. "Take your time."

Mrs. Crowley scurried away.

After several minutes, Mrs. Crowley hurried back.

"Dr. Ellington, Dr. Ellington. It's Jimmy, it's Jimmy. I told him there is a Dr. Ellington here to check him out. He jumped up and asked, 'Dr. Ellington, Dr. John Ellington?' I said, 'Yes, but he calls you Jimmy Kraus. Is that you?'"

She stood in front of them now and went on. "He said, 'Yes, yes, can he come now?' and I said, 'In a little while. You stay in bed. I will bring him.'"

"Oh, John, it's him," Ella said, relieved.

Mrs. Crowley finally took a breath. "Hurry, Doctor, Jimmy is waiting."

She turned to Ella and the children and said, "I am so sorry, only the doctor is allowed."

*   *   *

John followed Mrs. Crowley to the infirmary. He scrubbed, donned a surgical jacket, and went to Jimmy's bed. Jimmy was about to hop from his bed into Dr. John's arms, but John warned him to stay there. Instead, he sat on the edge of Jimmy's bed and the boy wrapped his arms around John.

"You came, you came," Jimmy sobbed.

John held him close and comforted him.

"Lay back, Jimmy," Dr. John instructed. "Let me check you out."

Jimmy was running a 103 degree fever. He could tell Jimmy was severely dehydrated and his records showed symptoms of diarrhea.

"You are a very sick young man," Dr. John said seriously. "I think we can make you well again so you can come home with us. Not today," Dr. John cautioned, "but soon. I need to talk with your doctor."

"But you are my doctor," Jimmy said, smiling despite his ailments.

Dr. John laughed and continued to examine Jimmy's eyes and ears. "You don't appear to have any other problems, so I am going to prescribe a medicine to get you well quick. Jimmy, make sure you take all of your medicine and drink lots of water."

"Okay, I will. Can I see Mrs. Ellington and my brother now? Mrs. Crowley told me they came with you."

"Yes, they are here, too. I am afraid that will have to wait for now. You are very sick and in quarantine. You can't have visitors."

"But...you are visiting me," Jimmy pleaded his case.

"That is because I am a doctor. Doctors have to take a chance and we take many precautions."

Jimmy hung his head low. Johnny was so close, yet he was still denied his wish of the past three years. "Okay," he said somberly.

Dr. John lifted Jimmy's chin. "Follow doctor's orders and you will be out of here in no time and we will be back to get you."

"Promise?" Jimmy asked and smiled.

"Promise!" Dr. John grinned back and gave Jimmy another hug. Then, he turned to go. "We're gonna git ya' back up on yer horse, cowboy." Dr. John poked his finger like a pistol as he turned to leave.

Jimmy tried hard not to laugh.

Dr. John asked the nurse in charge to let him talk to the house doctor.

"I'm sorry, the doctor isn't here now," she said. "He isn't a house doctor. He stops in when he gets time and when we summon him if there is an emergency."

Dr. John understood but was a little troubled that with so many sick children there was no doctor on staff. "How might I reach him?"

"Just one minute." The nurse scurried away, soon returning with a slip of paper with the doctor's clinic name and address.

John met up with his family and gave them all the details about Jimmy as they piled into the car. Then, John explained the situation as he drove to the clinic of Dr. Robert Johansson.

Ella recalled stories her mother had relayed about Chicago. She, too, was aghast at the beautiful tall buildings and the hustle of people, cars, and a few horses, and the fresh smell of air wafting over Lake Michigan as they drove along the Lakeshore to meet the doctor.

They went into Dr. Johansson's small clinic. Dr. John introduced himself to the receptionist at the desk and was told to have a seat.

The receptionist disappeared and returned in a minute stating, "The doctor is with a patient, but he will work you in as soon as possible." She explained he was setting a broken arm, so it would be a while.

A short while later, Dr. Johansson came out and introduced himself to the Ellingtons.

He spoke quietly to his nurse and then asked the Ellingtons to follow him to the back of the building to the doctor's home. It was just two small rooms, a kitchen, and a bedroom. There was a curtain pulled across the bedroom and they were invited to sit at the table, which only had three chairs. The two doctors and Ella sat while the two children were allowed to exit to the steps outside.

"I'm sorry. I only have a few minutes to spare, but what can I help you with?" Dr. Johansson got right to the point.

John explained who they were and expressed their intent to adopt Jimmy Kraus also known as Samuel Schmidt as soon as possible. He provided Dr. Johansson with a quick update on Jimmy's condition and asked him to provide the prescription he recommended.

"Hmm," Dr. Johansson pondered. "That is an arsenic-based product. I hesitate to prescribe it to children."

"I realize that," John said. "I am recommending it in very small doses. However, he is also dehydrated, so most importantly he needs water… lots of water…good water."

"I concur; however, the orphanage is concerned about the water quality. There is much water contamination. We are wondering if it could be causing the cholera and diarrhea, so we are restricting its consumption until this epidemic ceases."

"The children *need* water," John insisted. "Dehydration can lead to death very quickly in youngsters."

"I agree. That is why we are limiting but not ceasing its consumption."

"Isn't that prolonging the problem?" Dr. John was getting a bit frustrated. Was there a solution? "Respectfully, Doctor, I understand your dilemma. I would like your permission to remand Jimmy's care to me. I would like to have him return to Milwaukee as soon as possible."

"I'm afraid I cannot do that. First, there will be a procedure for you to have the child and second, releasing a child in quarantine would be foolhardy."

They were at an impasse. Obviously, they had differing opinions, but neither were totally wrong. It was clear this conversation was going nowhere.

"Thank you for your time," John said as he stood up.

Ella retrieved the children, and they left Dr. Johansson's office having accomplished nothing.

They stopped by a small stream just outside of town to have a picnic dinner before heading home. There was a narrow waterfall of fresh water nearby. Dr. John took a cup from the picnic basket and filled it with the fresh cold water. He took a sip. Here was an endless supply of lifegiving water.

"Taste this," John said as he pushed the mug of cold water into Ella's hand. "Don't drink it all."

Ella dutifully took a sip. "Ah, it's so refreshing."

She was not sure what was on John's mind. He was babbling away about 'nectar of the gods' and 'saving the children' and all sorts of nonsense. Surely one mug of water was not a lifesaving gesture.

"Hurry, children, hurry Ella," John said, clearly on a mission as he gathered up the picnic supplies and placed them in the automobile.

"Watch for a pharmacy," John demanded.

In minutes, they found one.

John grasped the cup of water in his hands and dashed into the pharmacy. He went to the counter and asked to speak to the chemist.

"Please," John pleaded, "can you test this water immediately? I need to be sure it is not contaminated."

"Do you suspect anything in particular?" the chemist asked.

"I just want to know if it is safe." John was expecting a good report, but he didn't want to influence the chemist in any way.

The chemist took the cup into the back room.

Meanwhile, John was checking out the supply of jugs and other containers for sale in the store. He gathered them all together at the counter as he awaited the test results.

The chemist returned with a smile on his face. "This is the purest water on the face of the earth," he stated confidently.

"That is good news. I want to purchase all of these containers," John said, excitement in his voice. He had gathered more than 20 jugs.

"All of them?" the chemist inquired, raising an eyebrow.

"All of them," John said and grinned. "Do you know where I can get more?"

"You can try Steffens Hardware Store down the block," the chemist said, and pointed to the right. "That will be five dollars for these containers."

John took out his money pouch. "And the test?"

"Test is free."

"Thank you, thank you. You are truly a lifesaver."

John hurried from the store, handing each of them as many jugs as they could carry. He stuffed them wherever they could find space in the automobile. Then, he drove a block east to the hardware store. He purchased eighteen more jugs there.

Jugs were everywhere, piled high to the auto's ceiling, on laps, tucked around their feet. Anywhere there was a space, there was a jug.

They had to pass the orphanage on their way back to the stream. John stopped at the orphanage and told Ella to take the children inside to the lobby. "Tell Mrs. Crowley to begin the paperwork. Tell her to put a rush on it because next weekend we want to bring our new son home."

Ella and the children exited the car, climbed the steps to the door, turned to wave to John, but he was already headed down the driveway.

John went to the stream and filled all the jugs with fresh spring water. He stacked them everywhere. There was more room without passengers but still he struggled to find room for all of them.

He hurried back to the orphanage and began to remove all the jugs from the car. When the caretaker spotted him, he came with his wheelbarrow, and together they loaded and wheeled all the jugs to a porch behind the kitchen.

John hurried inside to find Ella in Mrs. Crowley's office.

"Mrs. Crowley," John said, "please listen to me carefully. On your back porch, there are thirty-eight jugs of lifegiving fresh water. Try to keep it cool. It is cold in the evenings, so it will be fine where it is. Cover it if the sun shines on it. Give it to the children generously. At least eight glasses a day for the older ones, five for the youngsters. It will bring down their fever. It would be good to provide them with medication as well, but Dr. Johansson and I disagree on the type of medication to use. I agree the medication I recommended can be harmful to some and would have to be monitored carefully. Dr. Johansson has some methods he feels are safer, so I will defer to him on that level. The water I insist is necessary and I do know Dr. Johansson will agree."

"I will speak to the doctor," Mrs. Crowley said seriously. "We've had some concerns about our water supply, and Mrs. Ellington has explained the water has been tested."

"Yes, that's correct," John said.

"I have started the papers for the background check. Since you already have Johnny, I anticipate no problem whatsoever. Please sign here." Mrs. Crowley pointed to a line on the paper.

John read the paper quickly and signed it without hesitation.

"If Jimmy's fever has gone away, will we be able to retrieve him and bring him home next weekend?" Dr. John inquired. "Assuming the background check is satisfactory of course," he added.

"I believe that is possible; I will telephone you."

Later in the week, Jimmy's fever broke.

On the following Saturday morning, Jimmy and Johnny were reunited, and the Ellingtons were well on their way to being a family of five. The boys couldn't stop giggling all the way home. All their birthday wishes had come true.

DUST BOWL

GREAT DEPRESSION

Chapter Twenty-nine

Jimmy adapted well to life with the Ellingtons. Helen was overjoyed at having two brothers. She was becoming quite a tomboy. She loved climbing trees, playing stickball, and exploring the neighborhood. And Buddy, who had only a minor limp since the surgery correcting his club foot, played right along with them.

* * *

It was June of 1929 and there were definite signs of the economy sliding. Dr. John's practice was growing but it was suffering, too. More and more patients were unable to pay their bills. Sometimes, patients would pay with chickens or eggs, and he'd take them home for Ella. He was more concerned with the well-being of his patients than their ability to pay.

He'd enjoyed some lucrative years of practice and had invested their money well. He was interested in the growth of technology, believing it was the future of the world. He invested in Edison General Electric and in a growing company called International Business Machines. With the growing interest in electricity, many people were wiring homes and businesses with lights and telephones.

International Business Machines, commonly known as IBM, concentrated on business needs and provided time-recording devices for workers called punch clocks. They also manufactured scales and tabulating machines, such as calculators and cash registers. John saw nothing but continuing growth from this innovative company.

What machine had been more useful in this time than the automobile? Horses and carts were now in the minority after General Motors was introduced in 1929. The company grew out of a brainchild of William Durant, who had owned the Durant-Dort Carriage Company. Durant purchased many companies: Oldsmobile, Buick, and Cadillac, and had built an automobile empire. In 1929, a deal to buy out Ford failed. Along with that, Durant's position was eliminated. General Motors, now the largest conglomerate in the automotive business, had good management and innovative people at the helm, so it seemed sensible to have a piece of the pie. John made it part of his portfolio.

Not all his investments proved to be as fruitful. He invested in a helicopter company and a lamp company, but neither panned out. Soon after the depression hit, those companies folded.

On October 27, 1929, Black Thursday happened.

A run on the banks left bank customers with pennies on the dollar. Although John was in a better position than most, his bank holdings crashed along with most of the population. The Great Depression hit hard. He still had enough paying customers so he could keep his head above water, at least for now.

*   *   *

John tried to assure Ella they were okay, but she could see the world was not okay. It was times like this that they both treasured time with the children. She prayed often for all the children and families devastated by the Great Depression.

Ella continued to volunteer at the orphanage and was beginning to see an influx of children. At one time she was concerned, because for every child who left, two more appeared. Now even fewer left and each one was replaced with five or six more. People could not afford to take in another mouth to feed and many parents could not afford to take care of the ones they had. People were being laid off from their jobs, losing their homes, and finding the only sustenance they could at the local soup kitchen.

Ella decided to help at the soup kitchen and learned quickly it was not unusual to feed a hundred people in one day. Sometimes, they had to water down the soup so everyone got some. Even so, there were times they ran out. Days like that, Ella wondered if those they turned away ate a meal at all.

*   *   *

They made it through 1930, and in 1931, Ella received a letter from her old friend Rose who was living in Boise City, Oklahoma. She could tell Rose was attempting to be upbeat, but it was clear things were deteriorating even faster in the plains.

My dear friend Ella,

I hope this letter finds you in good health. It has been some time since I wrote but we are trying our best to make the most of these hard times. It has been so dry our crops were barely able to survive. Most of them didn't. We sold half of our cattle since there was not enough food for them to survive the winter. Cody had to go to Texas to find a buyer since all the farmers here are in the same boat. Ha, ha. Boat is a funny word to use. We can hardly keep afloat.

The kids are okay. The girls are now eleven and a big help. David and Michael are growing like weeds, but they don't like staying indoors much. They are so full of energy that I would love it if they could play outdoors but the dust storms here are so bad it is hard to even see walking from the house to the barn. It is no fun to get sand in your eyes.

We have tried to be careful but some of our neighbors are in bad shape. Since their crops have failed, they have no money to pay their mortgages. Many have lost their farms. They are moving to other states where it isn't so bad. Some have tried to sell their land, but everyone is feeling the pinch. They can't afford to buy property, especially unfertile property.

I may not be able to send you letters so often. I must pinch the pennies to keep food on the table. I know postage is only pennies, but I save every penny to survive.

Don't worry. We are stoic plains people, and we can handle almost anything.

I hope you and your family are fine. Congratulations on the adoption of the boys! I can't wait until we can see each other again and have our children meet.

God bless you.

Forever friends,
Rose

Ella put the letter down and wondered if she *should* be worried. Rose sounded okay, but her words left doubt. Things are so tight she can't afford a stamp. Ella resolved to answer Rose's letter soon and send her a stamp. She should do more, but she didn't want to offend her friend. Was sending a stamp offensive?

She prayed aloud. "Dear God, please heal this country and help Rose's family to survive. Amen."

A few days later Ella wrote a letter to Rose.

Dear Rose,

I was surprised and happy to find a letter from you in the mailbox. It has been months since I heard from you.

She wanted to go on, but she couldn't find the words. She put the letter down and went about her other tasks, but Rose and her family stayed on Ella's mind.

A few days later she began again.

My dear friend,

I have been struggling with the words to continue this letter. I don't wish to offend you, but I cannot bear to think of you in the plight you and your family are facing. Times are tough all over, but I am counting my blessings. John doesn't like to share financial difficulties with me. He always assures me we are fine, but I know we have lost a great deal in this depression. Nevertheless, in terms of economic stability we fare better than most.

You are like a sister to me and if you are in financial straits, please let me know what I can do to help. Your letter indicated you still have half your herd, so I assume you have enough to eat but from an agriculture standpoint I am not sure if your soil is providing vegetables to see you through. If I can help in any way to supplement your losses, I will try to do what I can.

I know you are proud and will not accept charity. We could call it a loan you can pay back after you are back on your feet. I am hopeful we will see an end to this crisis soon.

I miss the wonderful times we had when we were growing up in Milwaukee. We were always there for each other and wanted only the best for one other. I recall when you talked to my mother about making me go to the Academy when I didn't want to because it meant we would be in different schools. You wanted what was best for me. As it turned out, you got the best of the deal since you found your beloved Cody as a result. I want to be there for you if you are in need. Please let me know what I can do.

The boys are adapting well, and Helen enjoys having two big brothers.

All my love to you my forever friend,

Ella

Ella posted the letter and placed a stamped envelope with a blank sheet of paper inside. The only thing Rose needed to write back was a pencil.

Ella waited but a response didn't come.

Many months passed, and Ella sent another letter and then another. Still, a reply didn't come from Rose. Oh dear, had she offended her friend?

Chapter Thirty

Elections were nearing. Ella was fed up with the Hoover administration and campaigned for FDR and his new deal. She had hopes for a brighter future. In 1932, Ella proudly cast her vote for President Roosevelt. She thought of her mother briefly as she did so, and all that she had sacrificed. The chaos of the world in the past decade had to end. The poorhouses were overflowing, crime was rampant, jobs were nowhere to be found. Hoover tried to improve the economy by building the National Park system. It wasn't enough. Roosevelt came around with "A New Deal" and it gave hope to a struggling society that had lost hope.

John was continuing his medical practice, sometimes still being paid in chickens and vegetables. They tightened their belts during the hard times but were lucky they had funds to sustain them. Many folks weren't so lucky. Times were getting tougher.

Ella had slipped into the role of mother of three with ease. Her teacher training was put to good use, even though she had not been allowed to teach in the school system. Married women were still banned from that role.

Thaddeus had risen through the ranks and had a career as a pilot in the U.S. Army. He was now ranking Lieutenant Commander Thaddeus Ellington. He couldn't partake in the Ellington Holiday Season since he was on a reconnaissance mission in parts unknown. It was always great to see family, but Thaddeus's life had become very distant and secretive of late. When they did get together, he was his normal boisterous self and cheered up everyone with his antics. The children couldn't wait for Uncle Thaddeus to come home again.

After Liz graduated from nursing school and took a job at the Red Cross in Madison, she was able to still get home on holidays. It was bittersweet to spend time with Ella's family, wishing for her own.

In 1934, after Thaddeus had lured her with talk of travel and adventure, she had decided to join the Army Nurse Corp. After a military tour on the mainland, Liz was stationed in Pearl Harbor. Pearl Harbor was a bustling military base in the beautiful Island of Oahu in the U.S. Territory of Hawaii. It was a paradise in the tropical islands.

Ella felt a tiny bit of jealousy. Liz was following her dream of nursing and was stationed in a tropical paradise. But her jealousy was far overshadowed by the pride she had for her sister.

Dr. John's practice was growing. The Mallorys had moved on to enjoying their family and Dr. Mallory's only role at the clinic was as a consultant. John was capable of handling all cases in the clinic, though sometimes he called on Dr. Mallory to reaffirm a diagnosis, to reassure his elderly patients who were given peace of mind talking with their long-time physician, or simply to chat with his friend and mentor. As his clinic grew, so did Dr. John's hours. It was getting to the point John was contemplating adding another doctor on staff.

The children were healthy and growing. Buddy had a few surgeries and had walked with braces for some time but now he was able to walk with only a slight limp. He was a bookworm and showed interest in following his dad's steps into the world of medicine.

Jimmy was athletic and strong. He was enthusiastic about the star hitter for the New York Yankees, Babe Ruth. He also had an interest in a new football team, the ACME Packers from Green Bay. They had formed a team in 1919 and were developing a strong following. Surprisingly, even though the men were from a small city, they won the National League Championships in 1929, 1930 and 1931. There was talk of them coming to play in West Allis, a suburb of Milwaukee. Ella thought what a thrill that would be to see with the family!

Academically, Jimmy was leaning toward becoming a lawyer or a politician. However, both boys were going on fourteen, so careers were a distant dream.

Helen changed her mind on a weekly basis regarding her future. At nine years of age, she was more interested in playing careers than planning for one. She would play teacher, nurse, secretary, store clerk but saw draw backs to all of them. Teachers still couldn't work if they got married; she didn't like blood and the thought of giving real injections was disturbing; a secretary had to sit at a desk all day; and a store clerk? Well, she thought she would rather buy than sell merchandise. She was content looking forward to age ten. Ella couldn't blame her. Being an adult was nowhere near as fun.

*   *   *

Ella continued to volunteer at St. Joseph's Orphanage while school was in session.

One day when Ella arrived at the orphanage, she noticed a tiny wisp of a girl with curly blonde hair and big blue eyes sitting alone in the corner. She clutched a teddy bear and sucked her thumb.

Curious, Ella went over to her and tried to develop a conversation. The girl sat in silence but in spite of coaxing, she said nothing.

Sister Theresa saw Ella and said, "I would like you to meet our new resident. This is Shirley. She is four."

Ella smiled. "Hello Shirley, my name is Mrs. Ellington. How are you today?"

Shirley continued to sit quietly.

"Would you like to color with me?"

Still no response from Shirley.

"Can you come to my office, Mrs. Ellington?" Sister Theresa motioned to Ella.

"I'll be back soon," Ella said and winked at Shirley.

Still no response from the girl.

"I want to talk to you about Shirley," Sister Theresa said when they were alone in her office. "Shirley, as much as we can tell, has never been held or cuddled. She was fed sporadically, and we found her in a pile of filth eating dirt off the floor. She was severely malnourished and has some bruises. We have not determined if they were inflicted on her or if they were self-inflicted."

"Self-inflicted? Why would you think that?"

"She has bruises on her head. Often children in these circumstances will bang their head on a wall or the floor. We think she may have had one or more concussions and we are not sure if she has brain damage."

"Were there other bruises on her body?" Ella asked, concerned.

"She had one rather large bruise on her buttocks but again, we don't know how it occurred. It is suspicious. She has also lost two front baby teeth; we don't believe it is a natural loss. She is too young and new teeth are not yet protruding. She grabs food and hides it. It's a survival instinct since she doesn't know when she will be fed again. We are not sure if she is deaf mute or if she chooses not to speak."

"What about her parents?"

"From what we've learned, her mother passed away in childbirth and her father had no interest in taking care of an infant. He passed her around to relatives for a while and then he started to put her in a cage when he was gone. Sometimes he would feed her and sometimes he would drink himself into a stupor and forget to feed or change her. She is still in diapers. No one put forth an effort to train her. Her whole life has been filled with neglect and abuse."

"That's horrible. She is adorable. She looks like Shirley Temple. How could anyone hurt such a beautiful baby?"

Sister Theresa pursed her lips together. "Unfortunately, we see this all too often. The father blames her for her mother's death. He wants nothing to do with her because babies are dependent. The only thing he has taught her is fear. I'm not sure she knows what love is."

Ella glanced through the office window at the girl. "What can be done?"

"You may be our only hope. Would you work with her? You have a way of connecting with children. If we can make progress, perhaps someone will adopt her. If not, she will be placed in an asylum for the rest of her life."

"No," Ella shook her head. "No! That can't happen."

"I was hoping you would say that. Perhaps if you can work it into your schedule…if possible, you could spend more time with us, with Shirley."

"Of course. I'll do what I can."

Ella spent the next two hours sitting next to Shirley reading to her, not knowing if she heard or if she understood anything she said. She mixed it up with simple children's songs. Ella made sure she could see the pictures. Sometimes Ella laughed. Shirley showed no emotions.

Ella visited daily for two weeks.

When it was time for Ella to leave one day, she knelt before her, placed Shirley's arms around her own neck and gave her a gentle hug. At first, Shirley's arms were limp but then she tightened her arms.

Ella picked up Shirley with the little girl's arms still around her neck. She placed Shirley on her lap and rocked her gently, singing a soft lullaby. Ella didn't leave that day until Shirley was sound asleep.

*   *   *

That evening, Ella told John about the little girl. "We don't know if she can hear. We don't know if she can talk. We don't know if her brain is damaged. Today for the first time in her short life, she felt what love is like when I held her. She is so tiny and so hungry."

"Hunger we can take care of. We can test for some of the other senses but some problems we can't fix, Ella," John explained. "I wish I had better advice to offer."

"It's okay. I understand."

He patted her hand. "You have such a big heart, my love. I could examine her if the orphanage would agree. But Ella, don't have too much hope for her. If her brain is damaged, there may be little we can do."

"Would you, John? It would mean so much to me. I can't stand the thought of throw away children. If there is any hope, we need to find it."

It was then Ella decided today was the first day of Shirley's life and she would live, and she would thrive. Was it possible? Ella had no idea, but she sure as heck was going to help the little girl try.

The next day, Ella got her children off to school and went directly to the orphanage. She found Shirley huddled deep in the corner of her chair, hugging her teddy bear and sucking her thumb.

She hugs her teddy. Ella thought about it a minute.

Instinctively, Shirley did *know* what love is.

Ella hurried to Shirley and tapped her on the shoulder. Shirley was startled when she looked up.

Ella reached out her arms and Shirley immediately reached out to her. Once again, they continued the routine of singing and reading as they snuggled together in the rocker. But still, Shirley said nothing.

Now Ella thought of another thing. She washed Shirley's dirty face and hands. No one had been allowed to do that since she had arrived. Forcing her only led to more trauma. But Shirley tolerated Ella's soft touch.

Then, Ella brushed her hair, being careful not to pull too hard on the curly snarls. She showed her a mirror and had Shirley look at her reflection.

Shirley was fascinated.

Ella guessed she may have never seen her reflection before. She pointed to Shirley and said, "Shirley," then she pointed to the mirror and said her name again, "Shirley."

Ella got into the mirror's view herself and pointed to her own reflection. "Mrs. Ellington." Ella got a thin smile as Shirley pointed to Ella and then to her reflection in the mirror.

Relief flooded her. Progress at last.

Once again, Ella stayed until Shirley was fast asleep.

Gradually, Ella added baby activities. They played peekaboo and did hand clapping. Shirley was very good at aping the things Ella did, but still, she did not speak.

Ella moved on to toddler activities of stacking blocks and coloring, which the little girl seemed to enjoy. She was told Shirley had stopped hoarding food, but she ate crudely with her fingers. Ella taught her how to use utensils to eat. She also taught her how to brush her teeth.

Ella visited every day for at least an hour, often longer. Mrs. Johnson looked in on Helen and the boys after school.

After a few months, Ella asked John if he could visit the orphanage to test Shirley. She needed to know if Shirley could hear and if Shirley had the capabilities to talk.

On Monday, John went to the orphanage with Ella.

Ella went into Shirley's room and said, "Shirley, this is Dr. John."

Shirley immediately crawled back to the comfort of the chair in the corner and put her thumb in her mouth.

Ella wanted to pull her out, but John stopped her. "Let's try something else first. She is afraid of me."

John spoke softly to Ella, saying things that might provoke a response in Shirley. "Let's go away and not come back." "Let's get some ice cream."

There was no response.

Then, Dr. John picked up a heavy metal poker from the fireplace and dropped it to the floor. It landed with a loud crash. Everyone in the room jumped, including Shirley.

"She hears," he said and smiled. "Now, we have to find out how much she can hear."

Chapter Thirty-one

Now that they knew Shirley could hear, Ella tried to get her to speak. She read books with illustrations of animals. She would point at the animal and say its name "cat," then she would make the sound a cat made. She would repeat the word *cat* over and over again. Then, Ella would repeat what other animals were and point at the picture.

After repeating *dog* several times, she would make a noise as close to the real sound the animal made. Then she would point at Shirley and repeat her name several times.

Still, she received no response.

Finally, she decided to use herself as an example. Mrs. Ellington seemed too long a name for someone who didn't know how to speak. So, Ella pointed to herself and said "Mama." After doing the exercise many times, she pointed to herself and put Shirley's hand to her mouth and said mama again. It was a tool used with blind people who could speak and hear.

She knew Shirley wasn't blind, but she was running out of options. Then she said "Shirley" and put Shirley's hands on her own mouth.

Shirley did not respond at first but eventually put her hands over Ella's mouth and said, "Mama."

It surprised Ella so much she smiled broadly and gathered Shirley into her arms in a giant hug. They were both beaming, and Shirley was soon repeating mama repeatedly.

It appeared Shirley had never communicated and was left alone so much she didn't have anyone to teach her. She had learned not to cry or laugh because there was nothing to cry or laugh about in her cage. It also appeared if she did show emotion, she was punished. She had finally learned to trust, and under Ella's guidance, a whole new world opened to her.

Shirley thrived.

After a few months, Ella asked Sister Theresa if she could take Shirley home for a visit.

The visit wasn't tragic for Shirley, but she was wary of the boys. She was terrified of Dr. John. Whenever he was around, she quivered and ran to Ella's arms, which was her safe place.

"She'll come around," John encouraged. "Give her time."

Ella didn't give up.

After a year of adjusting, Shirley was a shy but happy five-year-old. She was beginning to open up to the boys with a degree of cautiousness and would eat with Dr. John at the table but stayed close to either Helen or Ella.

She observed the joy the other children felt in Dr. John's presence and seemed to like his pleasant manner, but she was so uncertain. In spite of this, she enjoyed her visits with the Ellingtons. It was a happy place.

They tried to have her visit often until the point they became her foster parents. There was some objection from the powers-that-be at the orphanage, but considering her progress and the unusual circumstances of Shirley's case, they finally agreed it was in the little girl's best interest. John's continued generous contributions to the orphanage didn't hurt.

*   *   *

One day while Ella was in the kitchen preparing dinner, Dr. John came home early and found Shirley in the parlor alone. She was about to make a hasty exit to the kitchen, but Dr. John got down on one knee in front of the doorway, blocking her exit.

"Come here, Shirley," he said, quietly holding out his arms.

Shirley inched cautiously toward him.

Dr. John said, "Let's talk." He scooped Shirley up and sat on a parlor chair, putting her on his lap.

Shirley tensed.

"You don't need to be afraid anymore. I am big and strong, and I will never let anyone hurt you ever again. I will always protect you and keep you safe. I promise, Shirley."

Somehow, Shirley believed him. She reached up and put her arms around his neck and hugged him.

They both smiled.

"C'mon, let's go see what Mama is doing." He stood up with Shirley in his arms and walked into the kitchen.

Ella was taking a roast out of the oven and had her back turned to them.

"Look what I have, Ella." John smiled.

Ella turned and almost dropped the roast. She placed it on the sideboard and ran to them, adding her own hug to theirs. Tears were in her eyes.

It wasn't long after they started planning the official adoption of Shirley to their family. By Christmas, they were a family of six. This time, there was no question by the diocese. The adoption was granted immediately. Ella and John were overjoyed.

Chapter Thirty-two

Chaos was erupting across the globe. In other parts of the world, poorly regulated markets led to high consumer debt, over optimistic loans by banks and a lack of high growth industries. All these factors had contributed to the 1929 start of the Great Depression. The downfall was blamed partly by Congress and partly by Executive Order. It was a hard time and difficult to stop the fall of the economy. Here it is 1932 and it seems it will never let up. Even Ella the eternal optimist was beside herself in despair. "What will become of our children's hope for the future? Will this never end?" she asked John.

John reassured her, but she knew he didn't have the answers this time. Roosevelt had a plan, and like any plan it took time. Unemployment reached an all-time high. The new year brought no relief. By 1933, twenty-five percent of the work force was unemployed. Ella placed her hope in this new president and his New Deal.

The Twenty-first Amendment was passed, ending prohibition. Roosevelt was instrumental in pushing for the repeal. This was a major component in getting him elected. Prohibition was not entirely a failure according to statistics. Prohibition resulted in a loss of liquor tax income. This resulted in the need to impose an income tax. The tax was limited to the wealthy and was even looked at as a status symbol by some. Of course, Ella disagreed. How could anyone look for status symbols when the majority of the populous was so devastated.

Alcohol tax revenues increased substantially from four million to thirteen million, giving a great boost to the economy. Additionally, jobs became available for brew masters and barrel makers. The cities of Milwaukee and St. Louis were two of the leading beneficiaries of the repeal. Taverns, supper clubs, and other liquor store revenues increased as well—all contributing to the economy. Was there finally a glimmer of hope?

Yes, a glimmer of hope sparked in Wisconsin, but other parts of the country were still struggling, and the effects were felt all over the nation. Some states chose to continue the ban on alcohol. It was a state decision. Those who chose to imbibe went across state borders to make their purchases.

In 1935, the country was deeply immersed in the problems of the Great Depression. They had hoped it would soon pass but it only seemed to be getting worse. Everyone tightened their belts. The soup kitchens were busier than ever. Poorhouses were overflowing and Potter's Field, the local cemetery for the indigent, was filling up with those who didn't survive, many of whom committed suicide. The orphanages were at capacity, many beyond.

The market was in dire straits and the investments John had made were losing their value. He was forced to cash in some stocks, even though it was not advisable by the brokers' standards of buy low, sell high. He didn't have a choice. Many of Dr. John's patients still couldn't afford to pay. He had to do something to support his growing family.

The only profession that seemed to be riding it out with little pain were lawyers. Many times, foreclosures were collected in property, which they knew would one day be worth more than the current value. Also suits won took precedence over any other debts owed. Even when payment was not forthcoming, it was money in the bank to them. It seemed the world was becoming sue happy. Although the norm once was to help your family and neighbors, desperation had brought out greed, or maybe it was survival. Ella shook her head when reading the headlines.

One day in August, a letter came in the mail. It was a desperate cry for help from Rose.

July 8, 1935

Dear Ella,

It is with a heavy heart and desperation for my children that I write this letter.

Last April 14, the worst dust storm in American history came upon us. I don't know how much news you get about this part of the country, but that day is now called Black Sunday. Thousands of lives have been lost in the past year and I fear many more will come. We lost all our herd. Through most of last year, we had something to eat but this land of dust will not sustain crops. There is no food for the animals. We couldn't sell them for much because they were no longer producing milk and they were so skinny they had no value for meat.

But Ella, that is not the worst. The dust has been so bad we can't leave our homes. We have to cover our faces, so we do not breath in the sand. Michael didn't make it. A small child couldn't possibly understand the danger. He died a tragic death coughing up black phlegm.

Cody was devastated. He felt a failure for not being able to protect and provide for his family. Last week, he went out to the shed and shot himself. I ran to the shed when I heard the shot, hoping he had shot a rabbit but found his still body there. Ella, it was terrible. We had his funeral yesterday.

When I was preparing for the funeral, the undertaker took note of my cough and feared I too might be afflicted by this terrible condition brought on by malnutrition and the consumption of my lungs by the dust. I pray he is wrong, but I fear the worst.

The girls have been diligent in protecting themselves from the elements, but they are very thin since food is scarce. We have been surviving with rabbits and squirrels and soup I am able to make from the carcasses. We have a few potatoes and carrots in our root cellar, but we will soon be out of that as well.

I know it is a lot to ask, but for the sake of my children I must. Is it possible for you to provide us with money to buy a train ticket back to Wisconsin? I will try to pay you back in the future. Maybe I can get a job as a housekeeper or a seamstress. I hope we might be able to stay with you for a few days until I can pay for lodging or find a poorhouse to take us in.

I wish my mother were still alive to take us in, but as you know, she passed several years ago. There was little inheritance and it is long gone.

I hate to ask this favor of you, but I need to think of my children. Ella, I am so afraid.

All my love,
Rose

Ella dropped the letter to the floor and choked back sobs of anguish for her friend. To lose her husband and child was unthinkable. Of course, she must rescue Rose immediately.

John was home early that night and Ella was at the door to meet him. "Oh John, I have very bad news."

"What is it?" John reached out and took Ella by her arms to keep her from falling, she was shaking so much.

"It's Rose." Ella broke into sobs. "Read this." She thrust the letter into John's hands.

*   *   *

John led Ella to a nearby chair while he read the letter. "This is bad," John said somberly. "Of course, we must get her and her children to safety."

He thought for a moment. "I will wire money to Boise City first thing in the morning. We can send a telegram to her immediately."

John reached for the telephone. Then he hesitated. "How much money will she need?"

Ella had stopped shaking but tears still rolled down her cheeks. "I don't know. I think it is about two cents a mile. That would be about $20.00 each. The fare for four would be, oh I don't know, maybe $100.00. They will need food and maybe some fares are more. I haven't traveled there in ten years. Can we double it?"

John nodded. "I think that is best. I will cash in ten shares of General Electric stock. The stock split last year so it will pay for this, and we will be fine."

John glanced at the envelope Rose's letter had come in showing the return address, then picked up the telephone and spoke to the operator. "Operator, give me Western Union."

"Hello, this is Dr. John Ellington. I need to send a telegram please to Mrs. Rose Corrigan, Route 5, Boise City, Oklahoma."

"Go ahead," replied the Morse Code operator.

"ROSE STOP HELP IS ON THE WAY STOP GO TO YOUR WESTERN UNION STATION TOMORROW NOON STOP MONEY IN THE AMOUNT OF $200 WILL BE THERE FOR YOU STOP BUY TRAIN TICKETS AND BE ON THE NEXT TRAIN TO MILWAUKEE STOP BUY FOOD WITH REMAINING MONEY STOP ANXIOUSLY AWAITING YOUR ARRIVAL STOP ELLA."

"Sent," said the operator. "Hear things are terrible out that way. Family?"

"Practically," replied John. "How much for the telegram?"

"That'll be, um $2.59."

"I'll stop by tomorrow morning and pay for the telegram when I wire the money."

"That will be just fine. With times so tough, I would ask for money up front but for you doctor, I'll make an exception."

"I appreciate that. I'll see you tomorrow."

"Good-bye, Dr. Ellington."

"Good-bye, my good man." John hung up the telephone.

He turned to Ella and held her chin. "Don't you worry, everything will be fine."

"No, it won't," Ella sobbed. "Michael and Cody are gone. Rose is devastated and ill."

"We can't change what is done, but we will do all we can for the future." He hugged her until her crying subsided.

*   *   *

It took ten days for Rose to arrive with her children. It felt like an eternity to Ella. Rose was first to descend the platform. Emma Sara and Ella Sue were almost sixteen years old, David just twelve. Ella's joy at seeing them was tempered by their appearance. Rose was the same height and age as Ella and had always outweighed her by at least ten pounds. Now the friend she saw was a fragile woman with grey hair tied back in a bun, her face drawn. She must've weighed 90 pounds, hardly anything for her five-foot-six frame. The girls were equally emaciated with dull brown hair, braided, and wrapped about their heads in an attempt to make them presentable. They wore plain sack dresses presumably made from flour sacks but showing the wear of hand-me-downs. David was a ball of energy despite his tiny frame. He was a ragamuffin straight out of Dickens' novels.

Ella ran to her friend and wrapped Rose in love and compassion, feeling her bony structure in the process. It made Ella want to cry. But this was not the time to cry. She had to be strong for Rose and her children.

"My, aren't you girls lovely," Ella hugged Ella Sue. "My darling goddaughter. And Emma Sara, my sweet surprise." Ella recalled her visit to Boise City to help Rose with her firstborn child, only to find they had arrived before she did and not just one but two.

"Whoa, whoa," she called to David, who was running circles around them. All those days of sitting had made him rambunctious. "Hey little man, how old are you?"

"I'm all growed up," he announced. "I'm twelve, almost thirteen. I can rope a steer."

"Well, I'm afraid we don't have many steers in Milwaukee," Ella replied, "but we do have boys and I think you will get along just fine."

"Come," she turned to Rose. "Let's get home to have a cup of tea and chat."

Rose nodded.

"Where is your luggage?" Ella inquired.

"This is it." Rose shrugged as she lifted the carpetbag she'd brought with her.

Ella swallowed hard. "Well good, then we are ready to go."

She led the way to her automobile. There wasn't much room for all of them but with so little luggage, they managed fine.

*   *   *

"Come children," Ella called out. Children scrambled out from everywhere. Ella called them out by age. "These two fellas are Jimmy and Buddy. They are sixteen." Then she turned to the two girls on the other side of the room. "This is Emma Sara and Ella Sue. They will be sixteen in August." The girls shuffled shyly.

"I'm Jimmy, I like to play sports...and I like girls." Jimmy grinned.

Ella Sue and Emma Sara blushed, and Rose pulled her girls closer.

Ella had coached her children to talk about themselves but hadn't rehearsed what they would say. It took Ella aback for a moment, but she laughed and went on. "Buddy likes to read."

"I have a lot of books, you can read them if you want," Buddy said cordially.

"This is Helen, she is ten." Ella pulled Helen to her side.

"Pleased to meet you," Helen said courteously. "I have lots of clothes, you can try them on if you like. I think they will fit." Helen meant to be gracious and polite, but Ella feared under the circumstances it might have come off as snobbish.

"And this is a little jumping bean. His name is David and he is twelve." She hoped to lighten the air and make it a fun meeting.

But Rose broke in, "I'm sorry, I will try to control him."

"Oh no you won't, we love him just the way he is." She smiled at Rose. "He reminds me so much of Thaddeus."

This shook a spark in Rose. "Oh Ella, how is Thaddeus? I think he was twelve when I last saw him."

"We don't see much of him, and I do miss him. He is in the army. He's an aviator. We are very proud of him. But we can't talk about Thaddeus now, we have one more in our family. Come here, Shirley."

Shirley was hiding behind the curtain. She came out and hugged Ella's legs. "Shirley is almost six and she is a bit shy. Give her some time and you will get to know her. She is very sweet."

Ella clapped her hands together.

"So, children, you can explore. Jimmy and Buddy, show the guests around while Rose and I catch up. There are cookies and milk in the kitchen. I'll get them out while I make the tea."

Ella disappeared into the kitchen, the children following her. Then they all went outside where they found swings and teeter totters, balls and jump ropes. Shirley stayed close to Ella and went back into the parlor with her.

In the parlor, she found Rose coughing and gasping for air. "Oh dear," said Ella, "are you okay? Is there something I can get for you?"

Rose wheezed, waving her hand in denial. "No, no. I'll be okay."

Ella poured the tea and offered Rose a cup. "Maybe this will help." She had poured a little honey into the tea and handed it to Rose.

"Thank you, Ella. I hate to impose on you in this way. We will try to be out of your hair as soon as possible."

"No, Rose, you will stay as long as you need to," Ella insisted. "You will not go to a poorhouse. You need to get well, and your children need to feel safe. I will hear no more of your leaving. It has been more than fifteen years since we saw each other, and I am not about to have you struggling on your own. You are like a sister to me. I consider you family and family takes care of family in need."

"But Ella, we are imposing. There are four of us and you already have four children. You have been so kind, and I do appreciate it, but we can't take advantage of your kindness."

"Pshaw, there is plenty of time to talk about your future. For now, let's just take care of your children. They are much better here than in some institution."

Rose bowed her head. "Ella, I don't know what I would have done without you."

Ella reached over and squeezed Rose's bony hand. "You are safe, my friend. You are safe."

Rose and Ella spent the rest of the day talking about the plight of all the people in Boise City. Ella had no idea how tough things were in that part of the country. She had heard some news, but now she was hearing about real life strife.

"Why don't the people leave?" Ella asked.

"For some, it is their homeland. Others are too sick to leave or have no means to leave or no place to go. For many, it is Armageddon. They look at it as their last plight before the Judgement Day and feel there is no escape. Some have tried and died in the dessert that lied before them or didn't survive the dust storms. It is horrible. Dying in a storm is a terrible death. Most have no money to purchase transportation out and have no one to turn to."

"Since you wrote, I have done some research. I understand the death toll is at three thousand and rising. Every family is affected."

"I believe it," Rose said. "So many have suffered. I'm so glad to be back in Wisconsin again. I am so grateful."

*   *   *

Hours later, Ella called the children for dinner. She had prepared a dinner of fried chicken, roasted potatoes, creamy gravy, fresh beans from the garden and apple pie she had baked the day before.

The children sat at the table wide-eyed to see such a display of food on one table. David drooled in anticipation but waited patiently.

Ella announced, "We will not wait for Dr. John. He is late with patients, but we will invite our Lord and Savior to join us."

Jimmy felt the need to explain the process he had learned several years earlier. "We always ask Jesus to join us. I used to think he never came but Mama explained even if we can't see him, he is here."

Ella asked everyone to join hands and she prayed, "Dear Jesus, please be with us tonight. We are sharing this meal with our new and old friends, who are in need of your help and guidance. Please show them the way to health and happiness. Please sustain their bodies with this food we are about to enjoy. Thank you for bringing them into our lives and thank you for being here for us."

Everyone joined in and said amen.

It was clear to Ella that David couldn't wait for the plate of chicken to be passed his way. He reached for the biggest piece on the plate and then glanced at his mother to see if it was okay.

She nodded, and he took it joyfully. He heaped the rest of his plate with potatoes and vegetables and ravenously consumed every bit on his plate.

They were all very hungry and before long, the serving dishes were empty. Such a feast was beyond their imaginations.

Why this was enough food to feed everyone in Boise City, David thought.

Even Shirley seemed to enjoy herself.

Chapter Thirty-three

It was quite a boisterous evening with the children getting to know each other and Ella and Rose catching up, reminiscing about old times while trying to keep upbeat and confident in the future. Through it all, pain and concern were on everyone's mind but there would be time enough to address that tomorrow. The evening was drawing to a close and the long trip from Oklahoma had taken a toll.

"You must be very tired." Ella directed the bedtime arrangements. "The boys will share a room at the end of the hall." It had been Thaddeus's room. "Buddy and Jimmy, please take David with you and show him the washstand and get him a fresh toothbrush from the cabinet."

Turning to Rose, Ella explained they had brought in a cot for David. "There is plenty of room for everyone."

The boys were clamoring up the stairs as Ella called after them. "Boys, I expect you to go right to sleep. There will be no horsing around, do you hear?"

"Yes, Mama," the chorus rang out as the boys giggled all the way up the stairs. "C'mon, David. Last one in bed is a rotten egg."

"Emma Sara and Ella Sue, you will share a room with Helen. I'm afraid there is only one bed in the room, but it should be quite sufficient for the three of you to share. If it is a problem, we will see about adding a cot in there as well. Helen, check to see if we have enough toothbrushes to go around. I believe there are two nightgowns in the hall closet that belong to Liz. They may be a tiny bit large, but they should do nicely.

She is stationed in Hawaii, and I am sure she won't mind sharing them with the girls."

The girls headed up the stairs and Ella cautioned again that she didn't want to hear a peep.

"Yes, ma'am," Emma Sara and Ella Sue replied.

"Yes, Mama," said Helen.

The girls had decided earlier that two Ella's in the same house was too confusing, so they would call the twins by their middle names.

"I'm sure they will be sleeping in no time. It has been a long day," Rose yawned. The yawn ended in another cough.

"Rose, I'm afraid the small bedroom upstairs is a bit disheveled since I have made it into a sewing room. There is a daybed in the room. I have found sheets and blankets, so you should be quite comfortable there, though a bit crowded."

"Oh my, Ella, any space is just fine. I believe I could sleep standing up, I am so exhausted." Rose began yet another lengthy siege of coughing.

"Tomorrow, we will have John check you over. That's a nasty cough. Is there anything we can do for it? I have some Vicks Vapo-rub."

"No, no," Rose reassured her. "I am sure I will be fine once I get some sleep." She gasped for air.

"I left a nightgown and robe on the chair in your room. They are mine, but I think they should be quite comfortable. You may drown in them, but I am sure they will work. You will find toiletries in the upstairs bath along with washcloths and towels."

"Ella, you thought of everything. I am so grateful." Rose stood and gave Ella a big hug. "Thank you so much."

Rose started up the stairs and then remembered there was still one other child to be bedded. "What about Shirley? Are we imposing upon her space?"

"Oh, no," Ella assured. "Shirley will be in the maid's room off the kitchen. She often crawls in bed with John and I because she has nightmares. We are trying to keep her in her own room. We made up the maid's room so we are not very far away. She is getting much better."

"Ella?"

"Yes, Rose?"

"If something should ever happen to me, my children have no one. Will you...?" Rose began to cry, and then coughed.

"Rose, nothing will happen to you, but yes, of course, now that we are closer again, I will do anything to help you and the children. Now, go up to bed and get some rest." Ella smiled kindly at her friend. The rest could wait until tomorrow.

*   *   *

Relieved, Rose crawled into bed exhausted. Hmm, a maid, she thought. She recalled Ella's mother having her maid, Claudia. *Wonder if Ella has a maid? This sure ain't Boise City.*

Her head hit the pillow and Rose fell fast asleep. She awoke several times during the night with a coughing spell. She tried to stifle it in a handkerchief so as not to awaken anyone.

Her handkerchief felt wet. She lit the kerosene lamp by the bed.

Black phlegm. She felt her damp forehead and realized she was running a fever. She poured a glass of water from the pitcher Ella had left by her bedside.

Rose prayed aloud, "Dear God, please help me. My children need me."

Chapter Thirty-four

The morning sun glistened through the red and yellow leaves on the oak and maple trees. There was a tiny nip in the air signaling autumn had arrived. It was Saturday, and everyone slept in a little later, including Dr. John. Ella had asked him the previous evening to check out Rose's cough.

Today, Ella was the first to rise. She put on a pot of fresh coffee. The sweet smell of maple smoked sausages frying in the pan was beginning to permeate the air and it was a wake-up call to the others in the house. She turned the burner off and covered the pan to keep the sausages warm. The nutty blend of fresh ground coffee called to John, and he was soon padding barefoot into the kitchen wearing his pajamas and robe.

"Ah, couldn't resist the smell of coffee, give me a cup of Joe," he said, standing behind Ella by the stove. He held out his cup.

She took the percolator off the stove and filled his cup to the brim. "It's hot. Don't burn your mouth," she warned.

John set the cup down on the table. "Something smells very sweet, and I am not talking about the sausages." He smiled as he wrapped his arm around Ella's waist. "Come sit and have a cup of coffee with me." He pulled her down on his lap as he sat on the kitchen chair.

"I have lots of work to do," she protested. "We have ten mouths to feed."

"They can wait a minute." He nuzzled the back of Ella's neck.

"Oh John," she once again reprimanded him as she turned her head to accept his affections.

Just then, the boys came clamoring into the room. Ella jumped up from John's lap.

Buddy and Jimmy were pleading for pancakes. David sat quietly, not saying a word.

"Pancakes it is," Ella responded and began whipping up the batter. She poured fresh milk for the children.

The boys, still in their pajamas, began to gorge themselves with pancakes. As soon as one pan was emptied onto the plate, they were ready for another.

"I can eat more than Little Black Sambo," Buddy announced.

"I can eat more than you," countered Jimmy.

David continued to sit quietly. It was clear he was just delighted to see the pancakes stacked on his plate with warm maple syrup oozing off the top. The cool and refreshing milk was something he hadn't had in many months. David ate until he could eat no more.

"Okay boys, rinse your plates and you can go out to play. It's a bit nippy this morning, so put on a sweater. I'm sure you can find one that fits David."

"Oh boy, stick ball," Jimmy announced. "Maybe some other boys will be out."

"Let's go." Buddy was at his heels. "C'mon, David."

The door slammed and the boys were off for a morning of fun in the neighborhood.

Soon the girls were coming down the stairs, giggling and peeking around the corner with their new surprise. They strutted around the kitchen showing off their clothes. Ella Sue was dressed in a blue pinafore over a blue and white striped dress. Her brunette hair was brushed and went down to her shoulders. The kinks from her braids gave it a wavy appearance. She had a blue ribbon holding her hair back behind her ears. She sashayed from the door and around the table while Emma Sara stayed in the entry.

"My, aren't you lovely," Ella observed.

Then, Emma Sara came into the room wearing a yellow dress with tiny white flowers and a white sash. Her hair was shoulder length also and tied back in a white ribbon. The dress was a bit tight, but she managed to get into the fashion walk and stood tall and proud.

"You are both very lovely," Ella gushed. "Let me look at you." She took their hands as they stood in a circle. Ella looked down and noticed both girls were barefoot. "Where are your shoes?"

"We can't wear our ugly shoes with these beautiful dresses," Emma Sara replied, "and Helen's shoes don't fit us." They all giggled.

Helen came in wearing a navy-blue striped jumper made from sack cloth. She had made a poor attempt at braiding her hair. The girls helped but Helen's curls were way too short.

Ella giggled and hugged her daughter.

She addressed all of the girls when she said, "You are all beautiful. Your beauty inside far outshines anything you wear." She wanted the girls to know she loved them all, no matter what they wore.

Then, Rose came into the kitchen wearing the nightgown and robe Ella had left for her. Her hair was soaking wet, her face was flushed with drops of moisture on her forehead. She was coughing worse than the night before, if that was possible, and she was shivering.

"Come here, Rose, sit." Ella pulled out a chair for Rose to sit down. She put her hand on Rose's forehead. "You are burning up."

She poured a glass of apple juice and handed it to her friend. "Drink this, we need to cool you down."

Rose took the juice and then saw the girls. "Girls, take those clothes off immediately. They are not yours." Then she began coughing.

"It's fine, Rose. They are just playing dress up," Ella explained.

"No, it is *not* fine. We will not impose further." She gave her girls a stern look.

Ella glanced back at the girls. "Okay lovely ladies, please change into your own clothing and we will resume dress up another time. Besides, we have pancakes for breakfast, and you wouldn't want to spoil your lovely frocks. Come back before the pancakes get cold."

The girls scampered off and Ella turned her full attention to her friend's health. "Rose, I am very worried about you. John went up to get dressed but will be back shortly. He will have you checked out before he heads to the clinic."

Rose couldn't catch her breath before another coughing spell started. Each seemed worse than the one before if that was possible. Ella felt helpless. Rose held her handkerchief over her mouth. She pulled it away and Ella caught a glimpse of the black phlegm with a red streak through it. Rose was coughing up blood.

John came down the stairs minutes later and Ella met him and spoke to him in a hushed voice. "John, I am really afraid. Rose is burning up and she is coughing up blood."

John rushed to the kitchen and helped Rose to a couch in the parlor. She was shaking. "Rose, let's take a look." Dr. John took out his medical bag and removed a stethoscope and thermometer. "Try not to bite this off." He smiled as he placed the thermometer under her tongue. Then, he put the stethoscope on her chest and listened carefully.

Within minutes, Rose was coughing again.

John took the thermometer and let out a slow breath. "Whooo." The thermometer read 105.6. "Rose, I am afraid you have pneumonia. I suspect it is dust pneumonia. You will need oxygen. I need to get you to the hospital now."

"But I can't…the children," she insisted.

Giving her a firm doctor look, he said, "You can, and you will. Ella can mind the children. We need to get you well and it can't wait."

"John, I know all too well the prognosis is not good. I watched my son Michael die earlier in the year."

"Then you know this is your only choice." He patted her hand. "Let me help you."

She nodded. "Okay, but…"

"I'll be right back, Rose." John explained the situation to Ella and then he helped Rose into his car.

"But I can't pay," Rose worried.

"Don't you fret about that," Dr. John stated. "It's a problem for another day. We will figure it out later. Right now, we need to take care of you."

John suspected her condition was probably far too advanced to treat, but he knew they had to do what they could.

That night Rose died. John held her hand as she breathed her last breaths. He left the hospital with a heavy heart.

When he arrived home late that night, he gathered up Ella in his arms in their bed to tell her the news, but he didn't have the words. He knew she would be devastated to lose her friend when they had just gotten reacquainted. "I'm so sorry, my love. I'm so sorry. Rose is..."

"Oh, John, no! She can't be." Ella's eyes welled up with tears.

"Her condition was far too advanced. There wasn't much we could do."

"Oh, John. How will we tell the children? Can they take yet another loss?" Pulling away from him, she sat up and said, "John, the children have no place to go. Rose had nothing left. The dust bowl took everything from her. And...I made a promise."

"And we will fulfill that promise. We will open our hearts and love her children as we do our own." He held her tight.

She sobbed through the night. How *will* Ella tell the children? It seemed an impossible task. John held her the whole time and tried to reassure her. "It'll be okay, Ella. We'll be okay."

Chapter Thirty-five

Wiping tears from her eyes, Ella gathered the children together the next day and told them the tragic news. The girls huddled together, consoling each other.

David cried softly. "I hate Jesus," he shouted angrily.

How could Ella argue with that, and how could she ever explain to a small child why his mother, his father, and his little brother were all called to heaven by Jesus. It wasn't fair.

Helen stayed near and comforted Ella Sue, Emma Sara, and David as best she could, which Ella appreciated.

Over the next two days, Ella and John arranged for a funeral service for Rose. The children kept their emotions in check, but now and again they sobbed alone in their grief.

Ella assured them they were all safe and they would not be placed in an orphanage. She and John had discussed the situation and decided the children would stay with them. It seemed almost impossible, but within two years they had gone from a family of three to a family of nine. She opened her heart and hoped Rose knew she would love her children as her own.

*   *   *

At the funeral, the family took up more than one pew. Ella and the girls sat in the front pew and John sat in the row behind them with the boys. One of the songs they sang was, "What a Friend We Have in Jesus."

David crossed his arms and said quietly, "He's not my friend."

Over the next few weeks, David refused to say prayers at dinner and became adamant it was Jesus' fault his mother was gone. He expressed hatred toward a god who was so cruel.

Ella tried to console him. She told him Jesus needed his mother and his father and his brother in heaven and someday we would all be together in heaven. It was no consolation for David and his anger continued to grow.

Soon, Ella realized she did not have the answers needed to help this little boy through his grief. She contacted Reverend Nelson.

"Hmmm," Reverend Nelson said. He scratched his head and grimaced. "Why don't you bring David to my office on Thursday. Perhaps, we can work our way through this." He heaved a heavy sigh. "To be sure, Ella, it will be difficult for an eleven-year-old suffering from such stupendous grief. Why wouldn't he blame God? A god he had always been told would answer his prayers and keep him safe."

Ella left confident Reverend Nelson, who was always her rock in hard times would once again come to her rescue. She left the church with a bit of the weight off her shoulders.

*   *   *

Getting David to agree to see Reverend Nelson was quite a challenge for Ella.

"Don't wanna go," David protested. "Reverend Nelson believes in God and maybe he lies or maybe he is just stupid. I don't even want to go on Sunday, but Mother always said we had to. They lied to her, too. She believed in a good God, but God isn't good. If he was good, he wouldn't take my mama and papa...and my brother. They never did God no wrong."

"David, God *is* good. We don't know why God needs the people he takes but he takes care of them, and he takes care of you, too. We love you, David. God made sure you are with a family who will love you and take care of you. He didn't leave you out in that awful dust storm. He brought you to a place where you will be safe."

"But my mama and papa *did* love me. I know they did. I don't think there is a God. I think he is just make-believe." David folded his arms across his chest in defiance.

"Well, David, if that is what you believe, you should tell Reverend Nelson. Listen to him carefully and then make up your mind. Can you do that for me?" Ella pleaded.

"For you, Mrs. Ellington, I'll see him but 'twon't do no good."

"Well, let's see about that." Ella smiled. She gave David a hug and sent him off to wash up for dinner.

At the table, David sat politely with his hands in his lap while the family prayed. But he did not participate, not even to say amen.

The next day was Thursday. Ella had shopped for clothes for the children. When it was time to see Reverend Nelson, Ella asked David to dress in a new pair of overalls and a denim shirt.

"Don't I gotta dress up?" David asked.

His only experience in Ella's church was for his mother's funeral and Ella had purchased dress clothes for the occasion.

"No, not this time," Ella explained. "This is not a church service. Reverend Nelson wants to have a chat with you. He has some things he wants to explain."

David and Ella were both a little nervous as they entered the church and found their way to Reverend Nelson's office.

*　　*　　*

"Good morning, Mrs. Ellington. Good morning, David," Reverend Nelson cheerfully greeted, then asked them to sit. After some brief comments about the weather and the beautiful fall leaves, he turned his attention to David.

"How are you this morning, David?"

David sat stone-faced with his arms folded across his chest.

"Oh, I see, don't feel like talking. Hmm? That's okay. How about we take a little stroll in the garden?" He didn't wait for a response. "Mrs. Ellington, you can wait here. Help yourself to some coffee." He took David's hand.

David stood but withdrew his hand.

"You don't have to talk. I'm pretty good at talking without people responding. Sometimes, they even fall asleep in the pews," Reverend Nelson snickered as they walked outside.

"Come and sit here," Reverend Nelson directed David to a bench in the garden. "Mrs. Ellington told me you might not believe in God. Well David, I think I can prove there is a God."

David seemed curious but remained silent.

"In the Bible, the very first story is about God creating the Earth."

"I don't believe it. That story was all made up like *The Wonderful Wizard of Oz*. Maybe God is that kind of wizard."

Reverend Nelson laughed. Partly because of the analogy and partly because David was talking.

"Okay, let's talk about that for a minute. We know the wizard wasn't real because he had no real power. In the Bible, it tells how God created the heaven and earth, the sky and the water, the stars and the moon, plants, animals, and people. Now think hard. Who created all of those things if there is no God?"

David thought for a minute. "They just were, nobody created them."

"Hmm, I find that hard to believe. Let's talk about one of those creations. Which one do you want to talk about?"

David tilted his head to the side. "Animals."

"Which animal?" Reverend Nelson asked.

"A cow." David's interest was piqued having been raised on a ranch.

"Okay, what do you know about cows? A dairy cow."

"They're big, they make milk, sometimes they are spotted and sometimes they are just brown. They eat grass...or oats or corn. They have four legs with hoofs on them, and they have small ears and a big nose." David hesitated.

"Anything else?"

"Yeah, they say mooo."

Reverend Nelson looked down at him. "How do you suppose that happened? That a cow is like that?"

"Just happened," David responded, a little less sure.

"Hmm…" Reverend Nelson rubbed his chin. "So…a cow eats grass and makes milk. Sounds like a miracle to me."

David shrugged his shoulders.

"Do you think maybe God had a hand in that?"

"I don't know."

Reverend Nelson went on to explain other miraculous unexplainable things, like the seasons, how our body works, that a caterpillar turns into a butterfly. "I don't know anyone who can make things so miraculous. All those things are God at work."

David was amazed. "Really?"

"Really! You can ask Dr. John if you don't believe me."

"Dr. John is really smart."

"Dr. John is smart, but you know it takes someone even smarter to make a cow. Cows and people have hearts and lungs and other organs that work together to make us grow strong and help us breathe and live healthy lives. Oh yes, and don't forget our ears and eyes and tongue and nose. They let us hear and see and taste and smell. Now, aren't they wonderful things?"

Curious, David asked, "Did God do that, too?"

"Yes, David. It's why I know there is a very, very, *very* smart god."

"Even smarter than Dr. John?"

"Yes, even smarter than Dr. John. But you know what David, here is the sad part. Sometimes, things go wrong. That's where Dr. John comes in. Sometimes, we get sick or have accidents. Dr. John gets to fix the things that go wrong. But sometimes, Dr. John can't fix everything. Sometimes, the problem just can't be fixed. That makes Dr. John sad, and it makes God sad, too. Sometimes, God has to take people to Heaven to fix them."

"After he fixes them, can they come back home?"

"No, I'm afraid not. Heaven is such a beautiful, wonderful place where we can never be sad, and you never get sick there. And the most special thing is when we are there, God will be there with us."

"So, my mama is not sad, and she won't cough there?" David asked.

"That's right. And your mama knows you are going to be sad and miss her, but she wants you to know she wants you to be happy, too. She knows Mrs. Ellington and Dr. John will make sure you have everything you need here on Earth until you can all be together in Heaven."

"You're not just telling me a fairy tale, are you?" David was still a little skeptical.

"No, David, it is true. I promise."

"Cross your heart?" David squinted up at him.

Reverend Nelson put the sign of the cross over his heart and then over David's. "Cross my heart."

Reverend Nelson thought for a moment. *So that's where the saying comes from. Cross my heart and hope to die. Christ's cross. Guess God taught me something today, too.*

"I enjoyed our talk today. Now, let's go back to see Mrs. Ellington. Anytime you want to have a talk, you come see me. Okay?"

"Okay," David said.

*   *   *

David came back to the room with a smile on his face. Ella sat in her chair, satisfied that it was the right decision to bring David here today. Sometimes, a different perspective helps to get us through the hard times.

Chapter Thirty-six

David told Ella all about his conversations. He shared with the other children the facts he had learned about cows, and he told Dr. John he wasn't the smartest, but he came close.

Ella continued to bring David to meet with Reverend Nelson. He still missed his mother desperately and would pray to Jesus every night asking Him to watch over her.

About two weeks after Rose's death, Ella became ill. She felt faint on occasion and was vomiting. One morning, she was feeling horrible and couldn't get out of bed. "John, can you get the children off to school? I am feeling very faint."

Ella was not one to complain, so John knew this was significant. Soon, everyone was on their way except Shirley, who was now almost six but not ready to face a classroom yet.

John turned his attention to Ella.

"You don't think what Rose had was contagious?" Ella asked, concerned.

"Absolutely not," John assured her. He listened to her heart, checked out her breathing, checked her blood pressure, and poked around as doctors tend to do.

"Hmmm," he pondered, looking very concerned.

"Is it serious?" Ella asked.

"I am afraid so…"

"What is it?" she asked, trying not to panic.

"Oh no, it...it's not serious for you but I am afraid a rabbit has to die."

"Whatever are you talking about?"

He smiled. "A few years ago, the University of Pennsylvania developed a test. It hasn't been used extensively yet. You inject a woman's urine into a young female rabbit. They have done it with mice in the past, but they are now trying it with rabbits. It takes a few days to get the results. They then operate on the rabbit to determine the results. I'm afraid the rabbit is going to die."

"John, please tell me." Ella was now envisioning some rare and toxic disease.

John reached over and took Ella's hands in his, looked deep into her eyes and said, "Honey, my preliminary diagnosis is you are pregnant."

"John!" Ella slapped him on the arm. "You had me scared. What? I'm pregnant? Are you sure?"

"I will be as soon as I do the rabbit test."

Ella put her hand to her mouth. "Oh my, John, we already have seven children."

He cocked his head to the side. "Are you saying you don't want this one?"

"Oh my gosh, no, I mean yes. I mean, of course I want this one. I didn't think it would ever happen again. Helen is ten. Oh my gosh." She let out a squeal and wrapped her arms around John's neck. She kissed him and squealed again. "Oh John, I am so excited. A baby!"

Her squeals woke up Shirley, who padded into the room yawning.

"I am excited, too." He picked up Ella and whirled her about the room. Unfortunately, whirling was not a good thing for Ella today and she rushed off to the bathroom.

"Me, too," Shirley said and lifted her arms for John to whirl her around, too. "What are we excited about?"

John picked her up and tossed her high into the air. "Oh, Shirley, we are so happy today." John laughed.

"Me, too." Shirley laughed, not having a clue.

Ella returned to the happy scene.

John placed his arm around her waist and took on the Dr. John role. "You will need to stop by the office today for a proper exam and to provide a urine sample. I would advise you to drink some ginger tea to calm your stomach. For the next three months, don't do anything too strenuous and take a nap in the afternoon if you can."

Instinctively, Ella and John both knew the first few months were critical and making an announcement at this point was ill-advised.

He turned to his daughter. "Shirley, you can be my nurse today. Mama is a little bit sick, but she will be fine. You make sure she takes a nap in the afternoon. You can take a nap together, okay?"

"Yes, Dr. John. I'll take good care of her."

"Thank you, Nurse Shirley." John gave Shirley a tweak on her nose. "And you, Mrs. Ellington, you need to follow Nurse Shirley's advice. Also, you should see about hiring a housekeeper. I think you need a little help around the house. We don't want you to be over-taxed. I need to go but I want to see you in the office. Come around eleven this morning. See if Mrs. Johnson can watch Shirley."

John gave Ella a special good-bye kiss before he headed off to the clinic. He whispered in her ear. "I love you...so much."

Shirley seriously took on the role of Nurse Shirley. She advised Ella to sit on her favorite rocker. She gave her an afghan to cover her legs and went to the kitchen to prepare breakfast.

Ella had made biscuits the day before. Shirley brought her a biscuit slathered with butter. "Do you want tea?" Shirley asked.

"No, sweetie, I'll make some later." Ella was a bit thirsty but didn't want Shirley trying to heat the teapot. "Perhaps just a glass of water please."

"I'm not sweetie, I'm Nurse Shirley." Shirley skipped off to get the water and then disappeared.

She returned to Ella dressed in a plain blue dress which she had covered with a white dish towel apron. "I don't have a nurse's hat," she announced sadly.

"Well, that will never do. Go get me a large piece of paper from Dr. John's office and a scissors." Ella cautioned, "Be careful with the scissors and walk, don't run."

Ella took the paper and scissors and within minutes she made a nurse's hat. She secured it on Shirley's head with bobby pins from Ella's own locks. It was difficult to secure in Shirley's fine hair, but she managed. "Now you are officially Nurse Shirley," Ella announced.

Shirley catered to Ella's every need that morning, bringing her books to read and handiwork to keep her busy. She tucked her blanket and fluffed her pillow so she would be comfortable. When Ella went to the bathroom and then to the kitchen to prepare tea, Nurse Shirley was right there to help her back to her place in the parlor. Ella had to convince her it was all right and she needed a little exercise.

At ten-thirty, Mrs. Johnson came to collect Shirley. "Ella, you said you are going to the clinic. Are you okay? You are not ill, are you, dear?"

"No, no Mrs. Johnson, I am fine. I think my iron is a little low. Dr. John wants me to have a test. I have been a little sluggish lately."

"It's no wonder with all the work you have with all of these children. I don't know how you do it."

"They are quite a handful, but I will be looking into hiring a housekeeper. I could get a nanny, but you know I was a teacher, so the children should be no problem. I just need some help with the household chores and such. Maybe a little childcare when I have appointments to tend to."

"Are you firing me?" Mrs. Johnson chuckled.

"Oh, Mrs. Johnson, you have been a delight and a lifesaver. I don't know what I would have done without you. But bless your heart, you are nearing seventy and I think it is high time we start watching over you."

"I am doing quite well on my own, thank you. Although, I do appreciate the boys coming over to mow my lawn and shovel snow. I can still tend to my flowers and take care of my house, but I have to admit it sometimes is a bit taxing."

"You wouldn't happen to know of a good housekeeper, would you?" Ella asked.

Mrs. Johnson thought about it for a minute. "I just might. This depression has taken quite a toll. Companies have laid off people and individuals have tightened their belts. The Martins who live on Lakeshore Drive kept their nanny but have let the maid go. She is a sweet lady, around forty-five. Her husband passed away last year from lead poisoning. She has children of her own, so she would have to be home in the evening. Her son Tom is our paperboy. He is the youngest."

"I know Tommy. I'll try to catch him tomorrow. Shirley, go with Mrs. Johnson and I'll see you in a little bit. Okay?"

Ella went off to her appointment and stopped to browse in a store at baby clothes before she headed home.

The next morning, Ella was up before dawn. She had no more than put on a pot of coffee when she had to run to the bathroom with her morning heaves.

John came scurrying down the stairs to assist her with the morning task of feeding seven hungry children and getting them off to school.

"Just watch for Tommy," Ella called to him. "I don't want to miss him. He should be here any minute." He delivered papers before he went to school so typically, he was there between 5:30 and 5:45.

Just then John saw Tommy's bicycle swing by the driveway. *Whack*, the paper hit the porch with perfect aim and just like that, Tommy was gone.

*   *   *

The following day, John was on the doorstep waiting to flag Tommy down.

"Hi Dr. Ellington." Tommy smiled at John.

"Hi there, Tommy. I understand your mother might be interested in a job."

"Yeah, but she don't know nuthin' about docterin'. 'Cept tendin' to cuts 'n stuff like that."

"Does she know something about housekeeping?" John asked with a wink.

"Oh, she knows lots 'bout that stuff. She gets mighty put out when us kids make a big mess whilst she's gone. She sure does make a good apple pie, too. I like it hot with cheese melted on it."

"Well, Tommy can you have her call me or Mrs. Ellington please?"

"Cain't do that, sir. We don't have a telephone."

"I see." Dr. John paused a minute. "Well, can you ask her to stop by today or tomorrow to talk to Mrs. Ellington? We need a housekeeper and Mrs. Johnson next door," John pointed to Mrs. Johnson's house, "said your mama might be available."

"Sure thing, Dr. Ellington. I'm almost done with my route. I'll tell her right away."

"Thanks, Tommy."

"Thank you, Dr. Ellington. Bye."

John waved, but Tommy was already halfway down the street.

That afternoon, John called Ella to tell her the pregnancy was confirmed, and they were officially a family of nine and a half.

Ecstatic, Alice Davis was hired by Ella that same afternoon.

Ella liked her immediately. She knew it was the right thing to do. During the interview, Ella had informed Alice that they had seven children and one on the way. She explained the new arrival would not be here until June.

She also explained it was a secret and for now, she didn't want others to know. She gave Alice a list of chores she was expected to do, and the woman said she would be there the next day to begin her job.

That evening as they sat down to eat, John offered up the mealtime prayer.

Shirley added, "And Jesus, please hurry and send us our new baby."

Ella's jaw dropped and she realized Shirley must've been playing in the next room when she was in conversation with Mrs. Davis.

The children looked at each other with grins on their faces.

John shrugged, and they all burst into happy laughter.

Chapter Thirty-seven

The next two months were a whirlwind of activity. Since there was no bedroom space left, Ella and John decided to do a little shifting. They would move Shirley into a room with Helen. Then, Ella moved her sewing things down into the maid's room off the kitchen, and Ella Sue and Emma Sara would share the old sewing room upstairs.

Ella would make a space for the baby in their room, and eventually, decide how the space could best be used when it was time for the baby to move to a crib. A bassinet fit in the cut-out space in front of the bow windows, but a crib would be too large.

John went into the attic to find all the baby furniture they had for Helen. He found the bassinet, a crib, a small dresser, and a highchair. The crib was the one Ella's mother Sara had used for all her children. It had seen better days but was still sturdy. He decided all it needed was a new coat of paint.

He took it out to the stable house, where the stable boy had lived before they turned in the horses for horseless carriages. A few weeks later, John was refinishing the crib on a Saturday morning. It was a rather brisk day. Winter would soon be here. The leaves were all raked, and the children were playing in the yard jumping into the gigantic leaf pile, filling the air with laughter.

He could smell Alice's famous apple pie cooling in the window as Shirley peeked into the door of the stable house.

Tears welled in her eyes as she asked John, "What is that?" She pointed to the crib.

"That's a crib for our baby. It's a place for the baby to sleep."

Shirley ran from the stable house, crying hysterically.

John realized immediately something was terribly wrong and followed Shirley into the house.

She bounded into the kitchen and ran to Ella, who was talking with Alice. She wrapped her arms around Ella's legs and sobbed. Her tiny body shook but she didn't speak.

John went to Shirley's side, but she wanted nothing to do with him. "What's wrong?" John pleaded, but his pleas were met with even stronger sobs.

"Come, shush, shush." Ella ushered her into the parlor and sat on the bentwood rocker with Shirley on her lap, rocking and cooing to her gently. When she quieted, Ella turned Shirley so she could see her face. "Now tell me. Did someone hurt you?"

Shirley shook her head but continued to sob big sobs. Finally, she got out the word *baby*.

"Baby?" Ella had to be sure. Could she not *want* the baby? It didn't make sense. Shirley was the first to want the baby.

John had stayed out of the room to give Ella space, but now peeked in to ask, "Is everything all right?"

On seeing John, Shirley burst into another rush of tears. Ella motioned him out of the room.

Once again, Ella calmed Shirley down and placed her on the davenport. "Stay here, I'll be right back."

Ella went to the kitchen where John was talking with Alice, puzzling over what went wrong.

"John, tell me what happened." She sat at the kitchen table with great concern. "Shirley is treating you like the time she first met you. She is afraid of you. What did you do?"

John placed both hands on each side of his head. "I don't know. I was finishing the old crib when she came into the stable house. She already had tears in her eyes when she asked what it was... Oh my god, Ella. That poor child."

"What? What?" Ella asked anxiously.

"I told her I was making it for the baby. It's a cage."

Ella went pale. "Oh dear. Stay here, John."

She ran back into the parlor where Shirley was rocking with her thumb in her mouth, tears rolling down her cheeks.

Ella gathered her into her arms. She was shaking. "Shirley, listen to me. Daddy will never ever hurt you and he will never ever hurt our baby."

"B...b...but he is is...making..." Once again, the sobs came uncontrollably.

"Yes, he is making a crib, sweetheart. A crib is very different from a cage. The crib is to keep a baby safe. It's the baby's bed. It will be soft and warm. It has sides on it so the baby can't fall and get hurt. It is to keep him safe," Ella repeated. "It has no top. In fact, we will put a toy on the top so he can play with it if he wakes up. And when he is awake, we will take him out of the crib. It is just his bed. Sweetheart, his *safe* bed."

"Why does he need bars?"

"Babies try very hard to learn to sit and walk so they roll around a lot. If they don't have sides on their beds, they would fall out of it. If they did fall, they would get hurt. We don't want him to get hurt, do we?"

"We could watch him and keep him safe," Shirley said.

"But honey, we can't watch him all of the time. At night when we are all asleep, he needs a crib to keep him safe. Tell you what. Let's make it your job. You can be in charge of keeping the baby safe and happy. If anyone upsets the baby, you need to report it to me, and I will make sure it stops."

"Okay." Shirley nodded, still sniffling. "Mama, are we getting a boy baby?"

"We don't know, but whether it's a girl or a boy we will love it and keep it safe. Now, let's get Daddy and go to the stable house and really check out what he is doing."

They met John in the kitchen. She winked at him and squeezed his hand. "Come, let's check out your project together."

Shirley was one of the true snifflers. Ella smiled as she saw Shirley still had a bit of a sob left. It would continue for at least another ten minutes, ending in hiccups. Shirley took her hand, and they all went to the stable house together to assure John he was once again on solid ground.

Chapter Thirty-eight

The heat wave of 1936 brought record high temperatures across the nation. The heat and dry spells which had plagued the great plains and created the Dust Bowl were affecting the rest of the country. The Midwest was no exception. In June and July, Wisconsin experienced weeks of record high temperatures over 90 degrees Fahrenheit, even reaching 108 one day.

Ella was miserable. She had anticipated the birth of her child at the end of June but now it was July, and still no baby. John was a little concerned for Ella's sake, but the pregnancy was progressing well.

July fourth was as hot as the rest, but Ella had a sudden burst of energy. She decided the family had been confined long enough. Fireworks would be on display in the city park only a few blocks from their house. A late afternoon picnic, fresh cold ice cream from the vendors while listening to the band playing under the gazebo, and an evening of fireworks seemed just the ticket.

"Are you sure?" John inquired. He reached down to check her ankles. They were a tiny bit swollen but not enough to cause undo pain.

"I'm sure," Ella said. "The children need to get out of the house, and it would be a shame for them to miss the festivities. This is a special year. It is the 160th anniversary of our country. We should experience it."

She had Alice make a special birthday cake for the occasion the day before. Ella prepared some chicken sandwiches and Alice had two large picnic boxes ready to go before she headed home to her family.

"We'll take the red wagon to carry the baskets. If the little one gets too tired, she can ride on the way home."

"Sounds like you've made up your mind." John smiled. "You've thought of everything."

They told the children, who were ecstatic.

Before they left, Ella had a word of caution. "Okay boys, stay out of trouble, stay away from the water and keep an eye out for each other. Jimmy and Buddy, you watch David. Emma Sara, Ella Sue, Helen. That means the same for you. I will keep an eye on Shirley. Don't go too far. I may need to have you take her to the playground and watch her there."

"Aww," pouted Helen. Ella raised her eyebrows and stared at her daughter.

"Oh, all right," Helen conceded.

"Of course, we will," Emma Sara spoke first.

"Don't you worry, we will take care of her," Ella Sue mimicked.

Although the twins were adapting very well to their new environment, they were still on their best behavior. Ella encouraged their feelings at home but understood their reluctance. Everything was still so new to them. It was going to take time…lots of time to adapt.

David, on the other hand, seemed to be adapting well with the help of his coaches, Jimmy and Buddy. They had become the proverbial three musketeers.

They had a wonderful time at the park. The ice cream was refreshing. They laid out the blankets they had placed in the wagon and prepared to watch the fireworks display. Everyone was engrossed in the magnificent display when Ella began to feel a pain. It was a small pain, so she decided to ignore it.

A few minutes later, she had another much larger pain. She snuggled closer to John. Then, she felt wetness where she was seated. She reached down to see if it was her imagination.

The fireworks were exciting. Shirley jumped at each boom but sitting in the comfort of Emma Sara's lap made her feel safe. Their laughter and squeals of joy made her feel it was all good fun. Still, each boom startled her. The grand finale boomed and boomed. The children jumped up in excitement, and Ella let out a scream she tried to swallow as she dug her fingernails into John's arm.

"We have to go," she gasped. "My water broke."

John gathered the children together and gave them strict instructions on going directly home and to alert Mrs. Johnson that he and Ella would be at the hospital. "Ella Sue, Emma Sara, Jimmy and Buddy, you need to make sure everyone gets home safely. Watch the traffic, it will be heavy since people are starting to leave."

Shirley appeared puzzled and a little scared.

John looked down at her and gave her nose a little squeeze. "It's time to go to the hospital to get our baby," he announced.

"Me, too?" Shirley jumped up and down in excitement.

"No, I'm afraid only Mama and I can go. As soon as the baby arrives, I will be home to tell you. You be good and mind Emma Sara and Ella Sue. Will you do that?"

Shirley nodded, wide-eyed. "Hurry, hurry," she said as the children scurried home.

John looked across the parkway and spotted a constable. He left Ella on the blanket for a moment and hailed the constable, who rushed to Ella's side.

"I have radioed an ambulance to come for you," he announced.

"John, this is coming too quick," Ella said and winced as one pain seemed to follow another.

John asked the constable to hold up the blanket for privacy as he examined his wife. "We need to get to the hospital immediately. I am not sure we will make it in this traffic."

John was right.

Ella let out a loud cry and very soon a new Ellington joined the world just as one final stray firework lit up the sky.

John had tried to carry it out discreetly, but a small crowd had gathered around. He held up his sweet baby girl wrapped in his shirt.

The crowd gave a loud shout and applauded vigorously. This was one celebration the people would not soon forget.

The medics who'd been summoned by the police arrived. One took the baby while John helped Ella to her feet and led her to the emergency vehicle. The crowd applauded as they drove off into the night.

At the hospital, the doctor and nurses tended to the usual birthing procedures, checking out the baby fully. She was a healthy seven-pound, three-ounce girl. They took her away to wash her and tended to Ella, who also checked out fine. Father was fine but a bit dazed.

He smiled at Ella and whispered, "Ella Ellington, the love of my life, you are absolutely amazing." John placed a kiss on each of her eyes and stated in his doctorly wisdom, "You are exhausted. Get some sleep and I will get home to the children." He didn't leave however, he sat by her bedside until she fell asleep.

"It's a girl," John announced as he bounded up the steps and into the house at three a.m.

The older children were still awake, waiting for word. Helen, David, and Shirley woke when they heard the commotion.

"Where is my baby? Where is Mama?" Shirley wanted to know.

"She will be home in a few days, if everything goes well," John assured her. "Now, let's all get to bed and get some sleep. We have work to do. We have to think of a good name for her."

*   *   *

There were no shortages of names for the baby.

John said, "There are already three boy names starting with J and three girl names starting with E or S. I think this girl should start with H to go with Helen."

Buddy piped up, "Or we could rhyme with Helen, so we would have three. Helen, Ellen and…"

"Melon!" Shirley squealed. Shirley was just learning about rhymes.

"Oh, no," everyone chimed in. They concentrated on H. Harriett, Hannah, Hope, Henrietta, Hazel, Helga, and Hilda.

"Heidi! It's my favorite story," Emma Sara added.

"Happy." Shirley made another contribution.

Everyone laughed. "We'll make her happy but Happy can't be her name." Everyone preferred their own selection, so a decision was impossible.

"How about if we make a list and let Mama decide?" John suggested. They all agreed that was the best solution.

Once she was home from the hospital, Ella perused the list, considering each name. "Hannah is a name in the bible. It is a beautiful name. Heidi is a lovely book and a lovely name. Hope is eternal. We all have hope. Hilda and Helga are strong names. We certainly want our little girl to be strong. Hazel is a beautiful tree and a beautiful color, and she is a beautiful baby. Harriet and Henrietta are from boys' names, Harry and Henry. Hmmm…" Everyone awaited her choice.

Ella didn't want to disappoint anyone, but she had made her selection. She kissed her baby on the forehead and said, "Good morning, Henrietta."

A chorus of "Aww…" came from all who didn't select the winning name, but no one claimed the winning entry.

Then, Ella explained she'd chosen Henrietta in honor of her father. "I'd already decided if it was a boy his name would be Henry."

Everyone smiled.

A few weeks later, the baby was christened Henrietta Louise Ellington. Louise in honor of John's mother who had passed away from typhoid when John was a teen. He'd been devastated. Someone must find cures for all the diseases plaguing the world and taking away our loved ones. It was one of the reasons he'd decided to become a doctor. He believed his mother would have loved her granddaughter being named for her.

Chapter Thirty-nine

⸻ ❦ ⸻

Franklin D. Roosevelt's advent of Social Security in 1935 gave the country hope. FDR's theme song "Happy Days Are Here Again" resonated amongst the people. He won by a landslide in 1936.

This was a year of joy for the Ellington family as well. Dr. John's business was thriving, his investments were increasing. The children were growing, and Rose's children seemed to be happy in their new lives. This is not to say there were no aftereffects of their troubled pasts, but they appeared to be adjusting well.

Roosevelt put programs into effect to rectify the country's situation. The New Deal program had to include getting the people back to work. Unemployment was at an all-time high of twenty-five percent in 1933 and had dropped to fourteen percent in 1937. A far cry from a little over three percent in 1929 but comfortably on its road to recovery. Roosevelt's WPA program initiated in 1935 was working to create jobs, which in turn boosted the economy. The Works Progress Administration employed millions of workers on public works projects, rebuilding roads and public buildings. Almost every community had a new school, bridge, or park. It began with primary needs of roads and electricity in rural areas, water conservation and sanitation, and flood control. It was now expanding into public transportation, airports, museums, and other projects, which improved the lifestyle of the communities and instilled a sense of pride for those who had previously felt hopeless.

Ella had never felt hopeless, but she wasn't unaware of what was happening, either. She was happy someone had taken a real interest in making their country a better place to live.

*   *   *

Things were going very well for the Ellington family. It was the summer of 1937, and the circus was coming to town. Ringling Brothers Circus had combined with the Barnum and Bailey Circus in 1908 to become the greatest show on Earth. Every year, the circus would travel by rail from its home in Baraboo, Wisconsin to the circus grounds on the Lakefront in Milwaukee. The circus employed hundreds of people who traveled with the show. In addition, they hired from the local population on each of its stops. The entire family was excited and anxious for its arrival, but none so thrilled as David. This would be his first circus.

David was fourteen now and some of his friends from school were planning on being at the circus grounds early to help set up. There was lots of work to be done and many hands were needed. Tents needed to be set up, plus concession stands, rides, and side shows. Yes, indeed it was a thrilling time.

The circus train arrived early on Friday morning. The crew had already begun setting up the day before. David and his pals had been first in line and spent all of Thursday raising tents, erecting fences, setting up bleachers, and lending a hand wherever they were needed. Often it was necessary to do the entire set up in the morning and be prepared for a late afternoon show. Having the extra time meant they would be able to watch the circus train arrive. For their efforts, they were each paid a dollar and told to return the next day for the show. If they wanted to help after the last performance, they could help the roustabouts break down.

The Big Top was at the middle of the lot. The front lot consisted of side shows, concessions, and rides. The back lot housed the animals, the performers, and crew. It was hard work, but David thought it was something he would love to do every day. He admired the people who got to travel with the circus, and he didn't mind hard work.

Friday morning, the boys were waiting as the train roared down the track. The troupes of performers rode in passenger cars. Some animals were in elaborately colored wagons, which had been placed on flat cars. There were about 50 cars on the train. Thirty flat cars carried approximately 60 wagons. The wagons contained elephants, tigers, lions, and horses. Most of the animals were transported in stock cars for the long trek.

A calliope hailed their arrival as a crowd of adults and children cheered. Toddlers were on the backs of adults to get a better view.

Horses pulled the wagons from the flat cars the short distance to the circus grounds. Now, the grounds were ready for the animals. The cages were secured, feeding troughs and water supplies waiting. The fuel had arrived the day before and the generators were ready to provide the lighting and other power necessary to run the show.

The Ellington family was enthusiastic. They would be attending the second performance of the day at 6:30 p.m.

"Hurry everybody, hurry," David prompted. "We don't want to be late."

At five o'clock, the family was in line to pay their entrance fee. As they entered, the sounds and smells were mesmerizing. Popcorn, hot dogs, cotton candy, roasted peanuts. The smells combined, drawing the people in while vendors hawked their wares. Ella and John decided to start with hot dogs all around.

As they continued down the midway, vendors called out to them.

A fellow in a striped shirt juggling three balls in his hands yelled, "Right this way, folks, three chances to win this big teddy bear." He poked his baton at the biggest teddy bear Shirley had ever seen. It was bigger than her! Her eyes grew wide, and she wanted that bear more than anything.

It was ten cents to try. Jimmy, Buddy, and David all gave it their best shot, but no one was able to win the bear. They had to knock over three wooden bears to win the prize. Jimmy got one down and got to pick a consolation prize. They all thought the game was rigged. "Bet some of those bears are nailed down so they won't fall," David surmised. "I hit one dead on."

They tried their skill at a few more games as they made their way down the midway. They even did the strong man challenge, hitting the gong with a mallet.

David won a kewpie doll he gave to Emma Sara. "You'll have to share, I only got one." He shrugged.

They got to the dunk tank and Jimmy and David were both able to dunk the clown. Buddy didn't win anything, but he was the first to admit the other boys were much more skilled at athleticism.

They were entering another area and heard a hawker, "Come one, come all. We have sights you have never seen." He was showing off the fattest lady they ever saw.

Shirley's eyes got big. The lady was sitting in a chair on a scale reading 650 pounds. She was eating a doughnut.

"There is a lesson for you kids," Dr. John cautioned. "Eat healthy or you will end up in a side show." They all laughed.

The hawker went on to encourage them to come inside and see a four-legged girl, a dog-faced boy, Siamese twins, a two-headed goat, and more…

It was nearing 6:30 and the show in the Big Top would soon be starting. The family found good seats at the center so they could see all three rings. The clowns were working the crowd. One clown was dressed a lot like Raggedy Andy with a big red nose and stopped in front of Henrietta. He made balloon dogs for Shirley and Henrietta. He flirted with Ella and the other girls and pretended to be intimidated by the boys. Then, he ruffled David's hair and disappeared into the crowd.

The ringmaster entered the ring to roaring applause. "Ladies and Gentlemen and Children of all ages, welcome to the Ringling Brothers, Barnum and Bailey Circus." Loud music sang out and the crowds shouted. Small dogs following a lovely lady pushed carriages around the ring.

"Ladies and Gentlemen, bring your attention to Ring One with José Vitero and his wild lions."

The lights went up on the ring to the right and all eyes focused on a cage filled with roaring lions and a man with a whip. He didn't hit the lions, but the crack of the whip brought the attention of the lions to their various tricks. They climbed up on stands and stood on their rear legs. Then they laid down, rolled over, and one at a time, jumped over three lions lying side by side on the floor of the ring. In the finale, they all jumped through a ring of fire.

Occasionally, they appeared to defy the trainer, showing their teeth and lashing out with their paw, roaring ferociously. Everyone was at the edge of their seats.

Next came the elephants circling the Big Top, holding the tail of the elephant ahead with their trunk as they circled the arena. They came together in Ring Three. The Ringmaster announced their performance and the elephants bowed to the audience and began their routine of standing on small boxes, standing on their front feet, and raising their rear feet high into the air. They were the gentle giants of the circus.

A beautiful young woman stood on one elephant trunk. The elephant lifted her to his head. She comfortably rode around the ring, waving to the crowd. She did some acrobatic stands on the elephant's back and he gently lifted her back to the ground where they both bowed to the audience.

The center ring had high wire walkers and trapeze artists keeping everyone's heart in their throat, fearing they would fall to their death on the ring floor.

Dog acts and clown acts made it the greatest show on earth. Everyone was enthralled.

When they left the big top, it was dusk. The neon lights lit up the rides and the midway. The family stayed to enjoy the end of this splendid day. They walked home, filled with the ecstasy and thrills the shows offered. It was a fantastic day. It was ten p.m. and they were all tired. By eleven most were fast asleep.

David had written a note he'd left in the kitchen. He packed a small bag with pajamas and a clean set of clothes. He spoke to Mr. Morgan the Circus Advance man earlier about a job.

"Can I come back to help pack up the show? Do you think maybe I can get a job with the roustabouts? I work hard."

"I don't know, kid. Yer a hard worker and I can use some hands, but what'll your mom and dad say?"

"Don't got none. They both died. I'm staying with friends. I don't belong ta nobody and I really want ta belong here."

"Hm," said Mr. Morgan. "Well kid, if they let ya' come at midnight to break down, I guess there is no harm in your coming along. We can give you a bedroll and you can bunk with the other rousties. Some camp out when we stay over and some bunk in the train. Everyone sleeps on the train when we are travelin'."

David was there at midnight. The work was hard, but it was quicker than set up. In four hours, they were on the train and pulling out of town. Their exit was much quieter than their welcome to the new town. Since it was the dead of night, the animals were sleeping and so were the townspeople. Only a few were awake to watch the train pass by without all the hoopla.

David was out on a new adventure. Down deep, he knew Ella and John would not let him go, but being the adventurer he was he was ready to step into this new role, this new life. He would write. They might be sad for a while, but when he assured them he was happy and well he was sure they would understand. Or would they?

*   *   *

The next morning was Saturday and Dr. John was up early to make his morning calls. Ella yawned. She pulled on her robe, put on her slippers, and padded to the kitchen to make coffee and prepare breakfast for her husband. She called to him in the bathroom. Ella could hear him shaving. "Would you like eggs and bacon this morning?"

"That would be wonderful, dear. Thank you," he said.

Ella saw a folded sheet of paper on the counter but paid it little mind. She put on the coffee and took a basket of eggs from the ice box. She cracked several eggs and began to mix them for scrambling. She added some chives from her garden to the mixture, then took out the bacon and began to fry it up.

While the bacon was frying, she mixed up biscuits and heated the oven. When the bacon was crispy, the biscuits were ready to go into the oven. The coffee pot was gurgling. She took it from the burner and poured a cup for John and herself. Just then, John came into the kitchen, and she handed a mug to him.

"Smells fantastic in here." He took the cup and reached around her to pick up the cream. He spotted the folded sheet of paper. "What's this?" He put the pitcher down and picked up the paper.

"I suppose one of the kids left it there," Ella commented, thinking it was a picture. Shirley often left pictures for her.

John unfolded it and said, "It's from David."

"What is it?" Ella was curious. Did he get up early to go fishing? Was he back at the circus grounds with his friends?

John read the note aloud.

"Dear Mama Ella and Papa John,

When you read this, I will be gone. I have joined the circus. Don't worry about me. I don't know where I will be, but I will write you when I can. I'm fourteen now, so I should be earning my own living. The circus pays me and feeds me, so I will be fine.

Love, David."

Ella was alarmed. "John, we need to find him now before the circus leaves."

"I'm afraid we might be too late. They'd leave before dawn unless something holds them up. I'll go there right now. I'll be back soon."

John grabbed his satchel and was out the door and in his vehicle. He wondered why he'd grabbed his satchel, but he guessed it was second nature. He drove the lakeshore route for any signs of anyone from the circus but there wasn't a soul around.

John headed home to deliver the news to Ella. She would be devastated.

He went into the house, and Ella ran to the door when she heard him. He looked at her and shrugged his shoulders. "There's no sign of them."

Tears streamed down her face strained with worry. "We have to find him, John. We *have* to find him."

"We will need to learn where the circus went from here. I'll call the mayor."

"Hurry John, we have to bring him home."

"Ella, he is fine," he said firmly. "We will find him, but it isn't a crisis. We know where he is, we just have to find the circus."

"Go now," Ella urged. "Please, John."

"Ella, the mayor won't be in his office before nine if he goes in at all. It is Saturday."

Beginning to calm down, she said, "I suppose you are right. But promise me you will check immediately at nine."

"I will." John hid his smirk. *Dang, that kid is full of mischief. What kid doesn't want to join the circus, but he did.*

Ella finished making breakfast. The other kids were beginning to get up and they all wanted to know what was happening. Emma Sara and Ella Sue were a bit concerned but the others all thought it was a hoot and laughed vicariously, enjoying David's adventure.

At nine, John was at the mayor's office, but no one arrived that day. John tried to call the mayor, but he evidently did not want to be disturbed. When he finally reached someone from the mayor's office, he was informed the mayor was out of town but would be back on Monday. That meant a long weekend of Ella being worried about David and not a thing John could do about it.

On Monday, the mayor wasn't very helpful. He did not have the circus schedule, but he did provide John with the telephone number for Ringling offices in Baraboo.

John called the office in Baraboo and a man picked up the line.

"This is Dr. John Ellington. I am looking for our son, David. It seems David joined the circus when it was in Milwaukee last Friday. We are trying to reach him and bring him back home. He is just fourteen."

"Just a minute, you say the circus was in Milwaukee last Friday. Ah yes, that train moved on to Ohio. It should be back in Chicago next weekend. You could catch up with it then."

"Is there any way I can speak to the circus manager before that?" John asked, annoyed.

"Well, that would be Mr. Morgan. I can get word to him to call you. There are no phones on a circus train."

"Please do. My number is Pleasant 6693."

"Dr. Ellington, you say? And the boy is David Ellington? Let me write this down."

"Yes, that's right but the boy's name is David Corrigan," John corrected the man.

"But you said he is your son?"

"Well, yes I did. He is, but I am his legal guardian."

"I'm afraid we would need to speak to his parents. Is he a troublemaker or does he have a medical issue we need to be aware of?"

"No, no. He is a healthy, mischievous boy who lost both his parents due to the dust storms out west. We are the only parents he has."

"Maybe the boy doesn't like his new family, hmm. That may be why he decided to run away."

"I assure you, sir, that is not the case. You can ask him. He has an adventurous spirit, and the circus is a great adventure."

"Fine, fine. I'll have Mr. Morgan call you."

Two days later, Mr. Morgan called, and John answered the line with his usual, "Dr. John Ellington speaking."

"Damn, you're a real doctor. I expected that to be a fake story. You lookin' for David Corrigan? He told me his parents were dead."

"Yes, that is correct. I am his legal guardian. How is he?"

"He's great. He is a real hard worker. That boy knows how to handle a lasso. And man, he can ride a horse, too. It's like he was born in the saddle."

"He practically was. He grew up in Oklahoma."

"Well, Mr. Ellington, ah Dr. Ellington, can I give you a bit of advice?"

"Sure, what do you have in mind?"

"We have three more weeks on the road and then we will be headed back to Baraboo for the winter. We do shows at the Circus Museum there, but by summer's end everyone is exhausted and ready to stay in one place. Madison will be our last show in August. Leave the boy with us for the summer. We'll have him back before school starts."

"I don't know," John said, hesitating. "Mrs. Ellington is frantic to get him back home safe."

"He is safe here. Norma the tattooed lady has been watchin' over him. I tell ya'. A lot of kids *want* to join the circus, but they soon find out it is a lot of hard work. If you get him now, he ain't broke in enough and will want to come back. Another week of blisters and sore muscles might make him homesick. In a couple weeks, he should be missin' his comfy bed and his family. He'll be ready to go home. And I can use the help. He likes feedin' and waterin' the animals, but we'll make sure he gets plenty of bull work, too."

"Mr. Morgan, I appreciate your thoughts. You could be right. Let me talk with my wife about your suggestion. How can I reach you?"

"Well, you can't. No phone on these empty lots. I check in every day with the office from a public phone. I'll call you in a couple of days when we reach Chicago."

"Great. I think you are on to something. I will try to convince Mrs. Ellington but it will be quite a task. I look forward to speaking with you." John hung up the telephone and took a deep breath. Ella wouldn't be thrilled about leaving David at the circus.

Chapter Forty

The telephone rang, and Ella jumped to answer it.

"Hi honey," John said.

"You sound chipper, do you have good news?" Ella asked.

"Yes and no."

Ella was frantic. "John, tell me. David is Rose's son and I vowed to my best friend I would take care of her children. Now David is missing. Lord only knows what he has gotten himself into and we don't even know where he is." Ella paced while she twisted the phone cord, blinking away tears. "Is he okay?"

"He's fine. The circus is in Ohio. When they finish there, they'll go to Illinois and be in Chicago next weekend."

"Did you talk to David? Can we get him from Chicago?"

"I didn't talk to him, but I had a good talk with Mr. Morgan, the circus manager. He says David is doing well and is a hard worker. He praised his skills with animals and wants him to stay on for three more weeks until they return to Baraboo for the winter."

"Absolutely *not*, John," Ella said in a stern tone. "David needs to be here with us."

"Ella, listen to me. Mr. Morgan made a lot of sense. It's hard work and soon the adventure will wear thin. He'll *want* to come home. If we get him in Chicago, it will be an uncompleted adventure. The next time the circus is in town he may do this again. Maybe it is best to let him finish. He will have enough of it and want to be back home. He will be missing us and his siblings, and he will be home before school starts."

"I don't know. What if he doesn't grow weary of the circus? What if he decides *not* to come home?"

"Mr. Morgan has more experience with this than we do, honey. He is not going to go easy on him. He says most runaways have second thoughts after about two weeks, unless of course they have no family waiting for them. Let's discuss this more when I get home tonight. I just wanted to let you know that David is okay."

After he got home, with much persuasion, John convinced Ella that David would be fine. He'd instruct Mr. Morgan to let them know if David changed his mind.

The next day, a letter arrived from David.

Dear Mama Ella and Papa John,

The circus is neat but hard work. It's okay, I'm strong and I can handle it. I am being paid a whole dollar a day. I showed them some tricks I can do with a lariat, and they liked it a lot. I get to see the circus every day! I feed the horses and the elephants, and sometimes I even get to ride them. Elephants are fun to ride but I mostly like the horses.

I am meeting lots of people. The tall man picked me up on his shoulders and I could see forever. I kind of feel sorry for the fat lady but she is funny and makes me laugh. The clowns are funny in the show but some of them are not so funny as real people. The Siamese guys stay by themselves and the four-legged lady kind of scares me. It is just too weird. I like the tattoo lady. She is nice. She makes sure I get food and sleep. Mostly, I sleep with the roustabouts, but on a nice night I take my bedroll down by the animals and lay on the ground gazing at the stars. It's kinda like Oklahoma before the dust. I like it here. Tell everyone I say hi.

Love, David

Ella read the letter to the children at dinner time. They said grace asking God to take care of David and bring him home safely.

Ella went about her daily activities, but her mind was always on David. It was going to be a very long three weeks.

*   *   *

A few days later another letter arrived from David.

Hi everybody,

This is David and I am fine. I have made some new friends. They are roustabouts like me. Most of them are older. There are a few sixteen-year-olds. Tony is sixteen. He is really strong. He doesn't have a family. He came from Tennessee and grew up on a farm. He has been alone for two years. His maw died and his dad is in prison. He was gonna join the hobos, but the circus came to town, and he decided to do that instead. He thinks this winter he'll be a hobo.

Being a hobo sounds kinda fun but kinda scary, too. You ride the rails until you decide to get off or they kick you off. Then, you find some nice folk who will give you a sandwich or an apple. He says, sometimes you run into an orchard, and you can take all the apples you want. Most farmers have a pump where you can get a cup of water or else you find a cool spring to take a drink. You tell folks you'll work for food, but most are kind enough to feed you anyway. But sometimes you need to knock on a few doors before that happens. Otherwise, you find a church and they will feed you for sure. At least, that's what Tony told me.

Big Earl is from Alabama. He is a darkie, but he is just like the rest of us. He sometimes joins the hobo thing, too, but it is harder for him to find food. He likes it better up north. He says people are kinder there. He likes the circus and hoboing 'cause he says his color makes no mind to those folks. He says he thinks white people are stupid 'cause they think a darkie's brain is smaller 'cause they are black. But it just ain't true. What do you think, Papa John?

Well, I best get the elephants fed. They sure eat a lot. I kinda miss playin' games and swimming. We ain't got much time for kid stuff here. We'll be in Iowa tomorrow. By the time you get this letter we will be gone.

Love, David

Ella pressed the letter to her heart. One week down, two more to go. The days seemed to drag, but three days later another letter arrived.

Hi everybody,

The weather has been terrible. It has been raining cats and dogs. The work is harder in the rain and wind. The wind is the worst. We get soaked, but they say the show must go on. We don't get as many people when the weather is bad, so the bosses get a little cranky. They say it cost a lot of money to run a circus, so when the people don't come it gets hard to pay the bills. The tattoo lady explained it all to me. She says maybe they will make it up at the next stop if the rain lets up.

Sometimes, the animals get spooked when there is a thunderclap. There was a loud thunderclap when the elephants came into the show tent last night. They started to run. It was scary, 'cause if they stampeded no one can stop them and people would be hurt. Good thing there wasn't another clap 'cause the workers were able to get them back out to their cages. They had to skip the elephant act for that show. They almost had to shut down the show, but it was just a shorter show than usual. They had to shut down some of the rides because of lightning. It wasn't much fun. Pretty soon we will have to pack up in the rain so we can move to the next city.

Hope my pajamas didn't get wet. It's kind of cold, too. I miss my warm bed. I love you all.

David

"Well, well, the appeal of the circus is starting to dim," John said and smiled at Ella. "I think in another week David will be happy to come home."

The other kids had mixed emotions for David's adventure. At first, they wished it was them but now were not so sure. Buddy and Jimmy thought it was crazy. They had looked for a home and David was running away from one. Ella Sue and Emma Sara were just worried about their brother and prayed he would be safe. Helen admired David's spirit. Shirley wasn't sure what to make of it but worried right along with Mama Ella. Henrietta was too young to care. Ella had flashbacks of her brother Thaddeus. *This is exactly the kind of thing he would do.* John took it all in stride.

Then, another letter arrived from David. Ella read it aloud at dinner and again afterwards.

Hi Everybody,

It's me, David. After all the rain we had I got a cold, but in the circus you can't take a day off. It's like farming, Ella Sue and Emma Sara. There are chores to be done and the animals need to be cared for. I can handle it, but I sure miss Mama Ella's chicken soup. I didn't like the awful stuff she put on my chest but some of that would be real nice about now.

One of the clowns got sick and they asked me to go perform. I did some of my rope tricks and roped another clown. The people

laughed but boy, was I scared. The tattoo lady said it's called stage
fright. Well, they can keep it. I almost puked.

I like the animals, but the people are getting short-tempered. I
guess it is the long hours and bad weather getting to them. I don't
think I'm cut out for circus life. Hoboing doesn't sound much fun,
either. When we get to Baraboo next week, do you think I could
come back home? I miss you all and I think I will even like getting
back to school.

I thanked Mr. Morgan for giving me the opportunity but roust-
aboutin' is not for me. And performing sure ain't. He said he
would call you to let you know when the circus will arrive. I have
lots of money, so I can catch a train home. They paid me but I
didn't have no place to spend it except at the circus and I got tired
of wasting it on the midway.

Mama Ella, don't be too shocked if I don't smell very good. I'll be
sure to take a good bath soon's I get home. That is, if you will have
me. I'm so sorry if I caused you any worry. I am fine, but I miss
you all.

Love, David

Mr. Morgan called John the next day and advised him of David's
homecoming. He offered to get David to the train station, but John told
him they would make it a family outing to visit the Circus Museum in
Baraboo.

Ella Sue, Emma Sara, Jimmy and Buddy were all preparing for their
freshmen year at college so they had decided to pass on the trip but
instead would prepare a wonderful welcome home party for David.

John, Ella, Helen, Shirley, and Henrietta all piled into John's new
1935 Packard Super Eight Club Sedan. John estimated it would take five
hours round trip at 35 mph with pit stops, so they planned a two-day

trip. They arrived in Madison on Monday, where they toured the state capitol in the afternoon.

The Ellingtons arrived in Baraboo early on Tuesday, anxious to be reunited with David. David saw his family and ran to greet them, welcoming them with hugs all around. David acted as their own personal tour guide.

He explained that on Monday, the circus arrived at the museum in Baraboo at dawn. The crew stowed the equipment, got the animals housed and began the task of cleaning up cages, wagons, etc. There were costumes to wash properly and maintenance to do. The crew had a farewell dinner to say good-bye on Monday night to those who would be going on their way to new adventures.

A few would remain at the museum, which held daily performances for visitors. It was good to be home, but it was also sad to say good-bye to those they worked and lived with for the entire summer.

David introduced his family to people along the way, telling behind-the-scenes stories as they went. They ran into Mr. Morgan in the Big Top. It wasn't time for a show, but Mr. Morgan stood there silently assessing the scene.

David called, "Mr. Morgan, I want you to meet my family."

Mr. Morgan crossed the tent to meet them. "Dr. Ellington, Mrs. Ellington, it is so good to meet you."

"And you as well," John said. He made introductions of the children.

"When we visit Milwaukee with the circus, come see me, Dr. Ellington. I will give you free passes for your whole family."

"Under one condition," John added. "Only if you promise never to hire this young man again." He ruffled David's hair.

"Well, don't know if I can do that," said Mr. Morgan. "He was a good worker and never complained."

"I don't think you need to worry about that, Papa," David replied, and reached out to shake Mr. Morgan's hand. "Mr. Morgan, thank you for the opportunity but…I think one circus adventure is enough."

WAR

RECOVERY

Chapter Forty-one

Things were heading back to normal. The economy was slowly recovering, but change didn't happen overnight. There were still soup kitchens to be manned and uneducated citizens who required assistance to get the help they so desperately needed. Ella was interested in reconstruction projects and helped illiterate workers fill out paperwork to find jobs.

Roosevelt was doing his best to bring order back in the country and looked toward a prosperous future. However, a full recovery would be many decades into the future. In1939, with the return of rain to the plains states and the soil conservation measures initiated by the Soil Conservation Act, which President Roosevelt signed in 1935, as well as creating the Soil Conservation Service (SCS) in the U.S. Department of Agriculture, the crises of the Dust Bowl was declared over. Over 7,000 people had lost their lives, mostly children and elderly. And sadly, many had been suicides.

Roosevelt still resisted the notion the United States would be drawn into the escalating battles in Europe. In May of 1940, most of France was occupied by German forces, who devastated Great Britain with air strikes. It was beginning to look less likely the United States could remain out of the war. Roosevelt tried to support the U.S. allies with supplies but had no interest in the United States' participation in the war.

People were still reeling from their own hardships of the Depression and recalled the aftermath of the Great War, now sometimes referred to as World War I because there were signs the war with Japan and Germany would turn into World War II. Ella worried. Thaddeus was in the forefront of her mind. *Will he be safe?*

Thaddeus was a seasoned pilot in the military now and had been sent overseas due to the war escalation there. Times were tough. Ella knew he was tough, too, and would be first to volunteer on dangerous missions where the fighting was happening in England and France. The thought kept her awake at night.

Ella prayed often Thaddeus would be safe, but she knew his love of adventure and airplanes. She tried not to think about it. Roosevelt had provided arms and equipment to Britain, and in spite of this, it appeared they were losing the battle. Thaddeus never left her mind.

*   *   *

In 1940, Liz reached the age of thirty-two. It had been fourteen years since Charlie had died. Charlie's memory was beginning to fade from her life, except whenever Liz was alone. Then, her heart ached for him. She didn't think she could ever love again. She began to date but no one could ever replace Charlie.

It was a rather sticky day in July. A tropical breeze cooled the evening air and after a hectic day at the hospital, Liz and three of her friends had decided an evening at the officer's club would be fun.

She and her friends changed from their nurse uniforms into fashions of the day. Liz always knew exactly what to wear. Her knee length red polka dot dress with puffy sleeves and a low scooped neck drew attention from the time she stepped from her barracks. It was only a few blocks to the club and the walk was met with a choir of wolf whistles.

At the club, a handsome gentleman held the door. Another offered to buy each of the ladies a drink. Eyes were on all four of them from everywhere in the room.

"Feel like fresh meat?" Evelyn whispered into Liz's ear.

"Kinda," Liz replied.

They took a seat at a table near the door.

Agnes had already exited to the dance floor with a lieutenant. Soon, Evelyn disappeared onto the dance floor.

A gentleman tapped Liz's shoulder. "Care to dance?"

"Thank you, but I think I will stay here with Millie for a while," Liz stammered.

"Fine with me, the name is Ben. My pal Ed and I just arrived on base. We don't know anybody yet. Do you mind if we join you?" Ben motioned Ed over.

"Suit yourself," Millie said and smiled while she snapped her gum. She gave Liz a nudge under the table. They seemed like nice enough fellas.

After a few drinks and many dances to the songs of Glen Miller on the juke box, Millie disappeared. Ben was gone, too. Liz found a note under her glass. It was from Millie.

Corporal Ben and I are taking a stroll in the moonlight.

You should try it. See you later, Alligator.

Much later.

Millie

Liz smiled and turned to Ed. "Guess it is just you and me."

Liz switched to root beer. Ed switched, too, but he switched from beer to boiler makers…a shot of whiskey with each beer. He also seemed to be downing them quicker. He staggered to the bar, leaned across to the bartender and said something Liz could not hear. His motion in her direction followed by uproarious laughter signaled to Liz this evening was over.

When he returned, she made it clear. "Ed, it is late. I've enjoyed your company, but I must get up early tomorrow." She looked around to see if Agnes or Evelyn were still there, but her friends were nowhere to be seen. Liz pushed away from the table, but Ed reached for her hand.

"Whoa…" He smirked. "Sweet stuff, you can't leave now. The party is just beginning."

"Another time," Liz replied.

"'Kay," he burped. "I'll walk you back."

"No need, it isn't far," she protested.

"I insist." He put his arm around her shoulder as they headed to the door. She didn't know if it was a friendly gesture or a means of stabilizing his inebriated body, but she let it be.

As they reached the exit, his arm slipped and he grabbed her ass.

Catcalls erupted, and she bolted forward.

She slapped him across the face as the swinging door slammed behind them.

In response, he put his hands on her shoulders and pinned her against the outside of the hut. She squirmed and attempted to scream, but he pressed his mouth against hers. It reeked of alcohol and tobacco as he tried to initiate a sloppy kiss. She pushed him away, but he was too strong.

Liz attempted to knee him in the groin as he tugged at her dress, trying to lift it. Tears burned her eyes as she pushed against his chest heaving out a yell, which he again tried to stifle with his mouth.

Just then, Liz felt his body jolt away and heard a loud crash as Ed hit the ground. "The lady said get lost."

Liz looked up into the gray blue eyes of the most gorgeous man she had ever seen.

"Lieutenant Richard Cornell, at you service. I don't think this fella's going to be a problem for you. I believe he will be sleeping for a while. You should be able to be on your way without any trouble but if you would allow me to escort you, it would be my honor."

Catching her breath, she said, "Lieutenant Cornell, my knight in shining armor, I would be delighted. Thank you."

They talked as they strolled to the barracks. Just outside, there was a park bench situated under a palm tree.

"It is such a lovely evening," Liz said. "Would you care to sit a while, Lieutenant Cornell?"

"Only if you will call me Richard." His beautiful smile melted her and made her legs shaky. Could this be her second chance at love?

It was the beginning of a beautiful romance. Liz continued to work at the hospital, patching up various injuries and occasionally tending to casualties who were flown back from war zones.

Richard was stationed on the *U.S.S. Arizona.* Whenever they had a weekend pass, they would steal away to Maui or Kuai or any place they could be alone together. Richard was thirty-five and planned on making the military his lifelong career. He was a navy man through and through.

Marriage was not in the cards. Liz had over a year left on her commitment to active duty and she was confident that she wanted to make it her career. Women in armed service could not be married. Richard understood and respected her choice, but his heart broke. He soon discovered this was the woman he wanted to marry.

Chapter Forty-two

⁓

News of the war via radio waves and newsreels at theatres were disheartening, but the Ellingtons made the most of Christmas in 1940, making it the best Christmas ever. Relief from the Depression was evident in the songs and spirit of the season. Store fronts were dressed in holiday cheer. Santas were in the stores, handing out candy canes and delivering their Merry Christmas greetings as bells tolled and snowflakes covered the city in a blanket of white snow. Spirits were high and holiday cheer was evident in the carols of the year— "Santa Claus Is Coming to Town" and "Jingle Bells." Also, Bing Crosby's "Winter Wonderland" and "Looks Like a Cold, Cold Winter." And, *Twas the Night Before Christmas* enthralled every young child dreaming of sugar plums, or more likely dolls, wagons, and sleds. Older boys longed for a train set or a BB gun.

The Ellington household was no exception—the house was inhabited by a rowdy bunch of siblings. Ella Sue and Emma Sara were now twenty-one as were Jimmy and Buddy. All four were enrolled in local colleges but still living at home. The girls were pursuing teaching careers. Buddy was interested in a medical career, while Jimmy thought he'd like to be a lawyer.

David was seventeen, soon to be eighteen, but had already graduated from high school. He wasn't sure college was for him, so he found a job in construction.

The Ellingtons couldn't afford to send all the kids to prestigious colleges, but it worked well for them to attend local schools while living at home. Helen was fifteen, Shirley ten, and little Henrietta was just four.

Liz had called, and she and Richard were making their way home for the holidays. Liz was excited to show off the man in her life and to see the children. My, how they had grown in the two years she had been away. Ella had sent a photograph a year ago, and even then, Liz said she barely recognized them.

Ella and the girls had retrieved ornaments from the attic and the fellas were about to leave on their annual quest for the perfect tree when Thaddeus burst through the door.

"Ho, Ho, Ho and a Merry Christmas to all!" He dropped his duffle bag on the floor and held out his arms. He was about knocked over by the ladies rushing into his arms, Ella leading the pack.

"Thaddeus!" she shrieked. "Come warm yourself by the fire." She took him by the hand and led him to the parlor. She sat on the bentwood rocker, and he shrugged off his coat and muffler, tossing them onto a nearby chair. He took a seat on the hearth.

"Ella, Ella, Ella. It is so *good* to see you. You look fantastic. Motherhood has done you well." He looked so handsome in his dress uniform.

Ella Sue picked up his coat and placed it on the rack by the door.

"Helen, go fetch some tea. No…hot chocolate for Uncle Thaddeus. It's always been his favorite." She reached for his hand again and shook her head. "Oh Thaddeus, we've missed you so. I worry about you all the time."

Helen brought the hot chocolate and a plate of biscuits baked earlier that day.

"Are you hungry? I can fix you something," Ella said.

"I am, but this will do just fine. These biscuits smell delicious." Thaddeus grabbed one and savored it.

The children were clamoring around, full of questions about the war and the planes and the places he had been and the things he had seen.

John came down the stairs dressed in his warm coat, carrying a cap and a new pair of galoshes.

Thaddeus stood.

"Hey, Thaddeus." John dropped the hat and boots at the bottom of the stairs and put out his hand, drawing Thaddeus in for a hug. "You're just in time. We were about to get the tree. Want to come along?"

"Wouldn't miss it." Thaddeus grinned. "Maybe I should change." His wardrobe was very sparse of civilian clothes, so he returned in minutes in his fatigues and army boots.

Thaddeus looked around. "Is Liz here?"

"Not yet, but they are on their way. It's a long trip from Hawaii. She should be here this afternoon."

Thaddeus tapped David beside his head. "Okay men, stop standin' around. We got work to do." The five men thumped out the door, laughing and challenging each other to the task at hand.

"Well ladies, we have about an hour to get this place in order," Ella instructed. "Emma Sara and Ella Sue, can you girls tend to the banister? Helen and Shirley, we need to string popcorn and cranberries for the tree."

"Me, too!" Henrietta exclaimed.

"You, too," Ella assured.

"C'mon, Ella Sue." Emma Sara grabbed the box of pine boughs they had gathered the day before. "I'm sure glad I don't have to string popcorn this year."

"We will make it beautiful," Ella Sue sang as she twirled with the strings of ribbon and bows.

When the men returned with the tree, the banister and front entry were a gorgeous array of Christmas cheer. The popcorn was ready to be hung on the tree and a pot of soup was simmering on the stove.

"I'm hungry as a horse," Jimmy announced.

"Me, too," said Buddy.

John lifted the cover on the pot and took a deep whiff. "Looks like that's what's for lunch. Horse stew." He chuckled. The men all guffawed.

"You boys get cleaned up. The biscuits are going in the oven and will be out in just a few minutes," Ella said.

The girls set the table.

Soon, they were devouring every drop of soup and every biscuit, but no one left the table hungry.

After lunch, the men tackled the tree and wrestled it into the parlor. It was a beautiful Norway pine but had to be trimmed down to make room for the star. All took credit for finding the magnificent specimen. The banter continued through the early afternoon.

At two-thirty, the doorbell rang.

Helen was first to the door. There stood Liz with Richard, their arms full of bags and boxes of things wrapped in holiday paper.

"Aunt Liz," Helen squealed.

Ella was right there with her and let out her own happy greeting.

"Come in, come in, let me help you with those packages." Ella took them one by one and passed them to Helen, who passed them to David, who passed them to Ella Sue and Emma Sara, who placed them in a corner of the parlor. When the last package was retrieved, Ella grabbed Liz and squeezed her, not wanting to let go.

Liz introduced Richard to Ella, who immediately gave him a welcoming hug.

Just then, Thaddeus bounded down the staircase with John close behind.

"Liz," Thaddeus shouted as he grabbed her and twirled her around before setting her back down again.

"Sprite," John said, putting his arms around her waist as she introduced Richard to them. John reached out his hand as did Thaddeus, warmly welcoming Liz's beau.

John squeezed Liz and smiled down at her. "Welcome home."

As tradition dictated, the afternoon was filled with chatter and the decorating of the tree. There was the traditional walking to church and as luck would have it, a light wafting of snowflakes on the way home.

Henrietta made Christmas special. Christmas glows in the eyes of a child. She was still enamored with the gifts and the holiday glitter. For the others, the joy was in sharing time with each other.

*   *   *

On Christmas Day, after exchanging gifts early in the morning, they all gathered around the table for a light breakfast. Henrietta was too excited to eat. She was delighted with the Betsy Wetsy doll and doll cradle. She couldn't wait to play house. Santa knew just what she wanted.

The rest of the family were engrossed in stories of their lives, and reminiscing. They had exchanged lovely gifts for each other, which they'd oh'd and ah'd over, but for them no gift could compare to sharing time together. Precious time that seemed to fly by.

Ella had a goose cooking in the oven, filling the house with delightful odors. The fresh baked pies from yesterday still permeated the air. Thaddeus and Liz volunteered to set the table for dinner.

"Liz, what's on the docket for this afternoon?" Thaddeus asked.

"I don't know," she said. "We will have to see if Ella has plans."

"Is the skating rink still there? Can we go ice skating?"

Liz laughed. "I believe it is, but Thaddeus, we don't have skates."

"Ella never throws things out. I bet our old skates are tucked away in the garage attic. Let's go look." He finished the last place setting.

They exchanged the same mischievous glances they had when they were kids, grabbed jackets from the hook by the back door and ran outside to the old stable house, which was now a garage.

Liz stopped short. "Thaddeus, my skates aren't going to fit. I wasn't much more than a kid. That was 20 years ago. You and I both went off to school a few years after Mom died. I never got new skates."

"Don't worry if yours don't fit, maybe Mom's or Ella's skates will."

They climbed the ladder to the loft and began to look around. There was no electricity out here, just an old lantern. Thaddeus lit it and they began their search.

At the top of the stairs was Helen's crib John had refurbished for Henrietta. Behind it were two old whiskey barrels full of hickory nuts. Mother's canning jars with the glass tops were in crates to the left. Ella had replaced those with the newer mason jars.

In the back, they saw harnesses and paraphernalia that belonged in the stable with the horses, which had long since been replaced with automobiles. There was an old lamp Liz recognized from her childhood.

"There," said Thaddeus, pointing to the wall on the right.

Sure enough, from pegs on the ceiling hung four pairs of almost new skates. Liz pulled down the pair that had once belonged to her. "As I thought, they are a size too small. They won't do. My feet would be pinched."

"What about Mother's?" Thaddeus prodded.

"Do I dare? They are so special. It would be like wearing the slippers from *The Wizard of Oz.*"

"And almost as old." Thaddeus laughed. "Mother may have bought them about then."

"But…"

"C'mon Liz, it's not like Mother is going to be using them. I think she would be proud to know you are enjoying them."

"Well, okay. I'll try them." She sat down on an old stool and wiggled her toes into one skate. "What about your skates?"

"Perfect," Thaddeus said. "Just like the last day I wore them."

"Oh wait, we don't have skates for Richard."

"What about these?" Thaddeus looked at the size on Father's old skates. "They're a size eleven."

"They may be a tiny bit big, but I can give Richard some extra socks from his luggage." They gathered their treasures and returned to the house.

"Does Richard even know how to skate?" Thaddeus questioned with a twinkle in his eye.

Liz tilted her head to the side. "Well, there is a great shortage of ice in Hawaii, but Richard is originally from Minnesota. I would think he must have worn skates sometime in his life. But Thaddeus, after 20 years, I'm not sure I remember how."

"Aw, Liz, it's like riding a bike. You never forget. You will be tearing up the ice in no time."

"What have you two been up to?" Richard asked as they walked into the kitchen. "Ella has been looking for you."

Ella walked into the kitchen to check on dinner and stopped in her tracks.

"Who wants to go skating after dinner?" Thaddeus held up the skates and smiled broadly.

"Thaddeus! Where did you find those?" Ella asked, laughing.

"We found these in the garage attic," Liz confessed. "I'll have to wear Mother's and I think these will fit Richard." Liz held up Father's skates. "I assume you all have skates. Can't live in Wisconsin without skates."

"Of course," Ella said hesitantly and then smiled. "I think Mother and Father would love for you to wear them. John bought new ones for everyone last Christmas and I think they all still fit. We haven't been out this year yet. It has been a mild winter and skating hasn't come up. Let's discuss it at dinner, which by the way is almost ready."

*   *   *

Ella's Christmas dinner was delicious, and everyone was anticipating the ice adventure to follow. At dinner, Liz learned Richard had been a hockey star on his high school team.

After dinner, everyone rounded up their skates and they were off to the rink.

John and Ella floated gracefully around the rink. Both sets of twins were challenging each other, with David and Helen in the mix. Shirley was trying to teach Henrietta how to skate, but she was a bit wobbly. Ella watched her constantly from the corner of her eye,

Henrietta took a bad spill and Ella was quickly there to comfort her. She wasn't hurt but she insisted that Dr. John check the arm she fell on.

"Let me see." Dr. John moved the arm in several rotations. "Well, I think you will be fine, but Mama has the perfect cure for this kind of problem." He winked at Ella.

"Yes, I believe I have the perfect cure." She reached down and kissed Henrietta's arm. "All better now." They both giggled and Henrietta was back to her lessons with Shirley.

Richard ended up being the star on the ice that day. He swooped Liz up on one of his speed trips around the rink and carried her to the bench.

"Liz, your family is fantastic," Richard said. "I can't wait until our kids can share in this family."

Liz was startled. "Our children?"

"I know it's not going to happen soon, but I hope one day it will."

She smiled. "Me, too." Liz touched his cheek and accepted his gentle kiss brushing her lips.

"Aw c'mon," Thaddeus swooped in. "Time for mushies later, get on your feet. We are going to crack the whip."

Chapter Forty-three

In two days, they would be gone and Liz didn't want the magic to end. That evening as Jimmy, Buddy, and David recounted the tales of the day in the bedroom they were sharing, they admired Richard's military career and the medals he had accumulated. They talked of the different places the military had to offer. Thaddeus and Richard had both talked of exotic locations, adventure, and glory. They relived Thaddeus' tales of flying like an eagle in the sky and the boys devised a plan. The next day, they would visit the recruiter's office and enlist. It would be a surprise.

*   *   *

The boys were up early and out the door before Ella had a chance to ask where they were going. The recruiters spoke with each of the boys. Jimmy and David flew through their interviews and were welcomed as new recruits. David was a tad shy of his eighteenth birthday so he might be delayed a month or two.

The recruiter who met with Johnny noted the slight limp as he entered the room. The recruiter looked down at the form. "John Ellington?"

"Yes, sir," Buddy said and stood up straight and tall.

"What is up with the foot?" the recruiter asked.

Buddy knew immediately where the conversation was going. He wanted to be part of the boys' recruitment day and hadn't said anything to David or Jimmy, but he suspected it was a long shot he'd be accepted.

Buddy slumped a bit. "Was born with a club foot. My dad's a doctor and he operated. I can even run now," he said hopefully.

The recruiter took a deep breath. "Well son, I know you would do your best and be proud to serve your country, but we need physically fit men who would be able to keep up in the worst conditions. We need men who will run, climb, fight, and survive. If we put men who can't live up to our standards, we would not just put you in danger but also endanger your fellow soldiers.

"I'm going to give you paperwork for the physical, but I am pretty sure you will be rejected. Don't get your hopes up."

"Thank you, sir," Buddy said and joined Jimmy and David.

The boys left the recruiter's office, slapping each other on the back and hooting. Buddy was quiet.

"What's up?" Jimmy asked.

"I'm not gonna make it," Buddy replied.

"Oh man, why not?" David wanted to know.

"It's his foot," Jimmy knew immediately. "I'm sorry, Buddy." He reached out to put a hand on his brother's shoulder.

"It's okay," Buddy said and tried to smile. "I'm used to it. Besides, someone's got to stay here and hold down the fort." He punched Jimmy in the shoulder. "You guys go get 'em. I'm proud of you both."

"Your foot is much better," David encouraged. "Maybe you will pass."

"Fat chance," Buddy replied.

They knew Buddy was sincere and they resumed their boisterous jaunt home. Their paperwork completed, they'd scheduled physicals for the following week. It was time to break the news at home.

They were home in time for lunch. Ella had planned a special dinner complete with turkey and ham, sweet potato casserole, canned corn from last year's crop, and apple crisp served with ice cream they had churned in the morning. It would be their last meal together before Richard, Liz, and Thaddeus had to leave for their posts.

As they began to push their chairs away from the table, Jimmy said, "Everyone, wait just a minute. We have an announcement."

"Oh?" Ella said, curious. "What about?"

Everyone else smiled.

John awaited an elegant speech of gratitude and praise for their holiday guests.

Jimmy stood and cleared his throat. "Buddy, David, and I visited the recruiter's office this morning and we signed up to become members of the United States Army."

Jaws dropped.

The boys didn't know if they were pleased or terrified. It was true war was on everyone's minds. Ella had expressed her fear for Thaddeus whenever she heard of another step in the war in Europe.

"What?" Ella was shocked. "All three of you? You are just babies. David is just seventeen."

"Mom, we thought you would be proud." Jimmy held his hands up in dismay.

Ella choked back tears. "Proud yes, but I am scared out of my mind for Thaddeus, and I pray every day he will be safe. I don't know if I can handle worry for three more of you as well...and Richard, too. I even worry about Liz, though I feel more confident she will be safe. And even then, I can't be sure. Nurses are needed overseas, too."

"But Mama," David protested. "Roosevelt said we are not *going* to be in the war. He is aiding with supplies and ammunition, but we're not in the battle. Don't worry. We are going to be okay." He reached over and rubbed Ella's back.

"We will be fine," Jimmy added. "Don't worry."

Ella turned to Thaddeus. "Will *they* be fine? Will you be fine?"

Thaddeus hung his head, not saying anything.

"Thaddeus?"

"I was going to tell you later, Ella. I have been assigned to the British Royal Air Force. I will report to General Montgomery in England the first of the new year to begin training for special ops. You won't be hearing from me for a while. It's getting bad overseas."

Ella sunk into her chair and let the silent tears flow down her cheeks.

"Congratulations, Thaddeus," John said. "We hope you'll keep us informed as you can. Good luck to you."

"Thanks. We are well-trained; we can handle whatever comes our way," Thaddeus said somberly. "Definitely, I will write often."

Ella sat silently, tears flowing down her cheeks.

*   *   *

Friday the third of January, 1941, Ella stood at the door as her three sons left the house to report for their military physicals. Jimmy and David passed with flying colors. Buddy, however, was rejected because of his club foot. A 4F was stamped on his registration.

"Someone did one hell of a good job on your foot surgery, son," the doctor stated. "I didn't even realize you had a problem when you came here for the physical, but I am sorry, you are unfit for duty."

Buddy hung his head.

"The training is very vigorous, son. And out there in the field, your comrades need to be able to depend on you. You have been through a lot, and I have no doubt you would give it your all, but you do have limitations. We need boys at home, too, you know. You can always be a civil servant."

"It's okay," Buddy said and looked up at the doctor. "It's just that my brothers and my uncle are serving, and I hoped maybe I would pass, too. I'm used to rejection. I'll be okay."

Buddy picked up his jacket and slowly walked to the door. He looked back at the man. "Thanks, Doc."

"Good luck, son."

Buddy waited for his brothers in the waiting area. They soon came out hooting and waving their papers.

"Reporting for duty, Private James Ellington." Jimmy saluted to no one in particular.

"Private David Corrigan of the United States Army." He stood at attention and saluted the flag in the waiting room.

Buddy was silent. They both looked at him. "4F" was all he said as he shrugged.

"Man," Jimmy said, "so sorry man."

"It's okay," said Johnny. "You guys kick ass for me." He punched them both on their shoulders. They punched back and headed home. They laughed and joked about all the wonderful things ahead.

When Jimmy and David told Ella their good news, Ella took a deep breath and said, "I am proud of you boys. Just stay safe." Then, she turned to Buddy and smiled. "At least I know one of my boys will be safe."

"We report to Ft. Leonard Wood in three weeks," David said. "The day before my birthday. They said I'd be eighteen my first day of boot camp."

"Plenty of time to spoil us." Jimmy grinned and winked at David.

"Well, let's get started," Ella said. "I just baked chocolate chip cookies."

They all scrambled to the kitchen.

*   *   *

The three weeks dragged for the boys, but Ella never felt time speed by so fast. The family was together at the station platform to see the boys off. Ella gave each boy a hug, not wanting to let them go.

The twin girls kissed each boy on the cheek and held their hands not wanting to let go, especially David.

"You write every day," Ella commanded.

"Don't worry, Mama Ella," David tried to assure her. "We'll be home in no time."

They grasped hands and passed around hugs. John pulled each of them to his chest in a man hug.

Jimmy kissed his mother on the cheek and gave her a little nudge. "It'll be fine," he reassured her. He reached down for his duffle bag and for his ticket. He pulled out candy treats for Shirley and Henrietta.

Helen shuffled nervously, not knowing if she was more proud or more scared.

The train whistle blew. "C'mon David, we don't want to miss this train," Jimmy said. "Take care of yourself, Buddy."

"You, too," Buddy said, and slapped his brothers on the back. He swallowed the lump in his throat.

The boys jumped aboard and found a window seat. They watched the family wave to them as the train took them away to new adventures. Tears ran down Ella's cheek. She wiped them away with the back of her hand.

Slowly, the family walked to the automobile and Ella said a silent prayer. *Dear God, keep them safe and bring them home to me.*

Chapter Forty-four

In August of 1941, while in Maui, Liz and Richard attended a luau at a local celebration. Richard sipped his tropical drink and held Liz close. They were at a table on a cliffside looking out over the ocean, waves lapping at the shore, natives surfing the waves.

Richard gazed into Liz's eyes and gave her a long kiss. He was so handsome in his dress uniform.

She wore a green and blue summer shift, which accented her body in all the right places. The sun was setting. He took her hands in his, gazed into her eyes and choked up a bit.

Liz was beginning to worry. Normally, they laughed and talked and were carefree but now he was so serious. Was he ill? Was he being transferred? What was it?

Then, he dropped to his knee and said, "Liz Dewberry, will you do me the honor of being my wife?"

"Oh…oh." Suddenly it hit her. This was a proposal.

"Oh, oh." Liz didn't know what to say. If she said no, he might be gone forever. If she said yes, her career was over since married women were not allowed to serve in the military.

"Yes, yes, yes!" Liz was in tears, happy tears. "But Richard…"

"But what?"

"Can we wait until my tour is finished to be married? That's over a year away." Liz was troubled.

"Sure, but…"

"But what?"

"Let's have an official wedding with friends and family then, but what do you say about a secret Polynesian style wedding now."

"Oh Richard…" She didn't get to finish. He locked her in his embrace in a passionate kiss.

When she came up for air, she whispered, "Yes, yes. Let's do it."

*   *   *

In October, under a harvest moon, they tied the knot. It was an evening wedding with a traditional Hawaiian celebration. Liz and Richard invited only their best friends who they knew would not betray their secret. The remaining guests were natives they had come to know and love.

The ceremony began as Liz was transported via an outrigger canoe piloted by two paddlers from a hut to the beachside where Richard awaited her with the guests.

Liz wore a long-flowered dress and had orchids entwined in her dark hair.

Richard was wearing a white tunic over white loose trousers. He was barefoot on the sand shore awaiting her arrival by canoe. Liz smiled as she saw him on the shore, tan and so so handsome. Richard moved to the grove where the ceremony would take place.

Liz and the paddlers walked down the beach barefoot, led by a priest who chanted the traditional wedding greeting as he guided her down the aisle of flower pedals toward Richard.

He continued the chant as the couple exchanged leis within a floral garden while torchbearers stood at the perimeter. The wedding leis were elaborate containing plumeria, orchids, tuberose, pikake, crown flowers, rosebuds, vines, ferns, nuts, and seeds. All portraying the joy and fertility of the occasion. The *pu* or conch shell sounded, announcing to the world the special occasion. It was sounded to the east to Haleakala, the world's largest dormant volcano and house of the rising sun. Then, it was sounded to the north to the mountains and jungles where spirits gather.

West to the eternal and powerful ocean, and finally south toward the wedding couple.

They repeated the traditional vow. "*E Lei aku 'oeku'ualoha I ko'oula nou I kahi mehemeha*" which means, "Wear my love as a lei and as your companion in lonely places." Liz thought it was a beautiful vow. A tear of joy slipped from her eye.

They ate poi, pork roasted over a pit, and sipped pineapple drinks. They had no idea what was in them. They were drunk with love. They watched as hula dancers entertained them. Finally, with farewell greetings from their closest friends, Richard and Liz departed together on the outrigger canoe that had brought Liz to the ceremony. Liz curled into Richard's strong arms as they disappeared into the sunset.

"I love you, Liz Cornell," Richard said, and kissed her cheek.

"I love you, Richard." She smiled a secret smile knowing that she had finally found love again.

*   *   *

When Liz and Richard were on duty, home was the ship for him and the barracks for her…at least until Liz's tour was over. They'd found a bungalow, a native hut of sorts, that they called home when they had free time together.

Liz had dressed it up with the essentials. They slept in a hammock, cooked over a campfire, and dined on coconuts and pineapples.

The nearby natives invited them to luaus and served poi and other native dishes. When their leave was over, they returned to the duties of their profession but waited for the next time they would be together in their tiny tropical paradise.

Liz had never been happier.

Chapter Forty-five

In late June of 1941, Ella was hanging out laundry on the line outside when she heard an automobile stop in front of her home. John was at work; Buddy was home from med school where he was pursuing a career in medicine but was helping John at the clinic. The twin girls were away tutoring while anticipating their teaching positions come fall. Helen, now sixteen, had a part-time job at the library, which delighted her since she not only had exposure to all those books but also got to meet lots of people, including a few young gentlemen callers. Shirley was watching Henrietta inside the house. Shirley was happy to have a little sister to cuddle and play with and Henrietta was delighted to have Shirley there to play games and have tea parties.

Wonder who that is? Shirley will show them in if they are guests. Probably just a door-to-door vacuum cleaner salesman. Ella continued with her task, humming her way through.

Soon Shirley was at the screen door. "Mama, come here. There are soldiers to see you."

Ella snapped the clothespin on the towel she was hanging on the clothesline and hurried inside.

When she entered the house, she saw two military officers in full dress uniforms standing inside her front entry. Her heart pounded and her throat tightened.

One officer came forward and said, "Mrs. Ellington?"

"Y-y-yes?" She already felt the tears welling in her eyes. "Who?" she asked as her knees began to shake.

"Mrs. Ellington, your brother Thaddeus is missing."

"Missing, what do you mean missing?" Ella asked.

"Please sit down, Mrs. Ellington." He took her arm and led her to the bentwood rocker in the parlor. The other soldier followed them.

"Captain Dewberry was flying a mission over Paris when his plane was shot down. We have some reason to believe he survived the crash, though we can't be sure. The French military units are no longer relevant, but we have some resistance personnel who do rescue missions when possible. They were not able to locate Captain Dewberry, so we can only assume he has been captured by the enemy forces and taken to Stalag."

Ella tried to process this in her mind. *Thaddeus is alive.* "Wha…what will happen to him?" Ella tried to control her shaking hands.

"We don't know," the second soldier said. "I'm afraid prisoners of war are not treated well, particularly officers. We know your brother is strong. He volunteered for the mission, and he knew the dangers. I know that doesn't make this any easier for you. We can only pray he will come home safe and soon. If you hear from him, please let us know."

Ella nodded and stared hard at the soldiers. "They said the Great War was the war to end all wars, but it didn't end. We are still fighting for the same things. Hitler will not stop until he rules the world. When will this all end?" Tears once again welled in Ella's eyes and rolled down her cheek.

Henrietta crept to her side and cuddled in next to Ella. "It'll be okay, Mama. Daddy will make it better."

"Sweetie, Daddy can't fix this."

"Oh yes, he can. He can fix anything," Henrietta insisted. "He fixes broken people, and he makes everything better."

Ella reached down and kissed the top of her daughter's head. "There are some things even Daddy can't fix." Ella wished John could fix everything. She nudged Henrietta. "Why don't you go find Shirley. Maybe you can have cookies together."

Henrietta jumped up and scurried away to find her big sister. "You'll see Mama, Daddy will fix it. You'll see."

"Is there anyone we can call for you, Mrs. Ellington?" the first soldier asked. "Dr. Ellington, a friend, your pastor?"

Ella sighed. "No, thank you. My husband will be home soon." She showed the officers to the door and watched them leave. Then she closed the door and dropped to her knees and wept. "Oh, Thaddeus..."

In minutes, Ella composed herself. She picked up the phone and asked the operator to dial Dr. Ellington's office.

The receptionist answered, "Mallory & Ellington doctor's office."

"Gloria, is Dr. Ellington available? This is Mrs. Ellington."

"Doctor is with a patient right now, Mrs. Ellington. Can I have him call you back?"

"No," Ella hesitated. "Just leave a message. Tell him to come home as soon as he can."

"Is it urgent? Shall I cancel his appointments?" Gloria asked.

"No, no. It's important, but not urgent." Ella was cautious, not wanting to risk a party line listener spreading gossip. The doctor's office was a private line but there was a two-party connection. Some lines had many more sharing, but she still wanted to be careful.

"I'll let him know, Mrs. Ellington. Doctor has just two more patients scheduled. He should be finished in about an hour. Dr. Paulson, the new doctor, can handle any walk-ins after that."

"Thank you, Gloria," Ella said and put the telephone on the cradle.

*   *   *

At four p.m. John walked in the door. Henrietta had been watching for him. "Daddy, Mama has a broken heart and you need to fix it."

"Mama has a broken heart. How did it get broke?" John asked.

"Two soldiers broke it."

"Oh no. Let's go find her." John knew immediately this news was not going to be good. He had two sons in the army, a sister-in-law and her husband, as well as a brother-in-law serving, and he knew two soldiers knocking on the door would not be bringing glad tidings. "Where is Mama?"

Henrietta took his hand and led him to the kitchen.

Ella was sitting at the table with her head in her hands. She looked up and he saw the pain in her eyes. He knelt next to her and clasped her hands in his. "Tell me."

"It's Thaddeus…" Ella closed her eyes and retold the story the officers had told her.

John stood and gathered Ella into his strong arms. He absorbed the sobs that shook her body and caressed her hair as he listened to her sob.

"I told Mama you would fix it. Are you fixing it, Daddy?"

He sat Ella back down and turned his attention to Henrietta. "Crying can help wash away some of the hurt, and hugs and kisses help a lot, too, but there are some things I can't fix."

"But Daddy you can, I know you can," Henrietta insisted.

"This is going to take a lot of time and a lot of love, so I need your help. Mama needs all the love we have. We can't make the hurt go away but together we can make it better."

"I knew you could fix it, Daddy." Henrietta grinned up at him.

John smiled at his number one fan and ruffled her hair. *Oh, the bliss of innocence!*

Chapter Forty-six

The next day Liz received a telegram from John informing her that her brother was missing in action and considered a prisoner of war.

Liz had only been married a short time and the news hit her hard. She had grown up with Thaddeus. He was her partner in crime. She recalled the last Christmas when they were all so happy ice skating together. Thaddeus challenged her. Thaddeus was the one who convinced her to become a military nurse.

She thought of Ella and her fears that all who served would not be safe. She recalled her last plea to Thaddeus at the dinner table at Christmas. Ella must be beside herself. She must be worried sick for her boys, too.

Liz thought of her own husband and worried he could be sent to the front. She couldn't let that happen. She would make him promise to stay with her here forever in this tropical paradise. Thaddeus was a renegade. He was first to volunteer for dangerous missions. Richard wouldn't be so foolhardy. He wouldn't volunteer, and as long as the United States stayed out of the war, it wasn't expected he would be deployed to foreign waters.

She would remain safe on this base. Her time left in the military was close to a year. She would not reenlist. She wanted to start a family. They had discussed family. Richard would remain in the military at least until he retired in ten more years. They'd discussed the pitfalls military families faced. They had even discussed the possibility of dying in the line of duty. People die before their time every day due to illness and accidents. Police officers and fire fighters have dangerous jobs, too. A carpenter could fall off a scaffold, a storekeeper could be shot in a robbery, a pilot could crash.

A pilot could crash. Missing in action, prisoner of war... "Oh God, Thaddeus. Please don't suffer. Please don't suffer..."

Of course he is going to suffer. He is an officer, a prisoner of war in a hostile country. Oh, Thaddeus...

Tears streamed down her face.

*   *   *

As soon as she was able, Liz went to find Richard. She stood outside the majestic *U.S.S. Arizona.* This massive battleship, 608 feet long with a 97 foot beam stood in the harbor with the American flag waving proudly from its mast. This was the home away from home for her handsome lieutenant. She looked about but saw her husband nowhere on deck and did not have clearance to board.

She took a deep breath, closed her eyes, and thanked God this great giant would keep her husband safe. She would talk to him when he got off duty.

He met her at the hospital each night after duty. As soon as she saw him, she flew to his arms as he hopped off the jeep that brought him there. "Richard." She wrapped her arms around his neck and showered him with kisses.

He pulled her away from him, wiped her face of any tears and then drew her back in to comfort her as he caressed her hair. "What is it? Why all the tears?" He pulled her away and looked into her swollen eyes.

"Th...Thaddeus," she choked out.

"What about Thaddeus?" Richard asked, fearing the worst.

"He...he...he's missing," she managed to get out.

"Missing?"

"Y...yes." Liz wiped her nose. "His plane was shot down. They think he was captured in France and taken prisoner."

"He is strong, sweetheart. He will survive." He drew in a deep breath. "Come, let's walk."

They found a bench. He sat next to Liz and put his arm around her. She snuggled into his arms and felt comforted and safe. "Can I tell you something?" he asked.

"Of course," Liz said.

"If Thaddeus is a prisoner of war, it's not going to turn out well for him. He will never be the same if he does return. He could suffer injuries due to torture. You need to be strong."

Her body stiffened before the tears began again.

After some time, he asked Liz if she wanted something to eat.

"Not hungry," she replied. "Do you want to get something to eat?"

"No, no. How about a drink at the officer's club?"

She nodded.

They walked the few blocks to the club and found a table off to the side. Richard went to the bar and returned with food and two cocktail glasses. He handed one to Liz. He knew she had said she wasn't hungry, but she had to eat.

She took a sip. "Gin Rickey." She recognized the lime bite. She gulped down the remainder and handed the glass to Richard. "Another?"

"Whoa, whoa, whoa," Richard said and shook his head. He looked at her from the corner of his eyes. "You can't run from this, Liz."

He took her glass and returned with plain seltzer and a twist of lime. "We need to talk about this."

Liz inhaled deeply. She had been thinking about it. "You are right. You're *always* right. I need a furlough. I need to go home to Ella. She needs me. I need her."

"There's nothing we can do for Thaddeus except pray for his safe return."

*   *   *

The next morning, Liz found a payphone on the island. She stood anxiously in line. Finally, it was her turn. "Please be there, please be there."

The phone rang several times before Helen answered. Liz smiled at the sound of her niece's voice. "Hi girlie, how are you doing?" Before Helen had a chance to answer, Liz went on. "Helen, I don't have a lot of time. Is your mother there?"

"Sure. Mama!" Helen called out. "Aunt Liz, did you hear about Thaddeus?"

"Yes, I did. That's why I am calling."

"Mama hurry, it's Aunt Liz," Helen called out again.

"Tend to Henrietta," Liz heard Ella direct Helen as she took the phone. "Liz, is that you?"

"Yeah, how are you holding up?"

Someone was banging on the phone booth behind her, anxious to get the next call time.

"Ella, I don't have much time. I am going to try to get a furlough to come home for a leave. I just thought I'd let you know."

"Oh Liz, that is so sweet of you, but I am okay. John is so wise and such a comfort. There isn't anything we can do here. Why don't you wait until we have more news? If you come now, you may not be able to come if it becomes necessary."

Liz's heart dropped. She knew Ella meant if his body came home in a casket. She was silent.

"Liz, are you okay? Do you *need* to come home?"

"Yeah, I'm okay. Richard has been supportive. He is my rock. You are right, of course. I will write. I gotta go now. Give my love to everyone."

"Of course."

"And Ella, let me know if you hear anything more."

There was another rap on the phone booth. "Hurry up, we don't have all day."

"I have to go, Ella. Good-bye. I love you and I miss you."

"We love you, too."

Liz left the booth. Someone else entered and the banging began all over again. She stood there for a few minutes breathing in the sweet tropical air, staring at the sky. "Where are you, Thaddeus? Where are you?"

The long wait began.

Chapter Forty-seven

Months passed, and still there was no word about Thaddeus. Early in the morning on December 7, 1941, Liz was leaving her barracks to go to the hospital dressed in her white uniform and cap. It felt different today as she heard the buzz of airplanes in the distance.

Liz looked up. The planes were flying low. She heard the deafening sound of bombs exploding. Chaos erupted.

What was happening? Liz was suddenly aware they were under attack. She heard the ships being bombed in the harbor. A blaze of fireworks lit the sky, but it was not night, and it was not friendly entertainment.

Liz ran back to the barracks and shouted to the nurses inside. "Get to the hospital…stat!"

She ran out the door and dodged debris falling from the sky. It was more duck, cover, run, and pray. Smoke filled the air. Her nostrils burned from the smell. She dodged for cover.

"We are not at war, what is this?" She could not immediately comprehend it.

Someone in the crowd of people running near her yelled, "Run, the Japanese are attacking!"

People were running everywhere. More bombs exploded and the sound of machine gun fire seemed to come from all around her.

When she and the other nurses reached the hospital, casualties were already arriving. Their normal peaceful hospital with only a few beds occupied was suddenly a triage situation. There weren't enough beds, there weren't enough supplies, there were not enough doctors and nurses to handle it all.

Liz stood outside marking the foreheads of those she judged to be savable as they attempted to patch and prep each patient. Some waiting outside the hospital died in the arms of comrades. Thousands of wounded begged for attention. They did what they could. It wasn't enough.

The streets were filled with smoke. Wounded were dragged out of the clouds of smoke like zombies to the hospital doors. The air was filled with screams of the wounded and cries of the survivors. When it was over, more than three thousand people had died.

Casualties were placed in the hospital basement and in tents and barracks, which were set up as morgues. Identification was attached to each body. Every able-bodied person was summoned to help.

Liz had worked for thirty-six hours straight. She was exhausted. Where was Richard? He had reported for duty earlier the night before on the *U.S.S. Arizona*. He hadn't been admitted to the hospital here. There were two other hospitals, the Solace, a hospital ship in the harbor and an unfinished ship. She could only hope he was one of the brave men who were rescuing their crews. She didn't have time to think about it, and yet he was all she thought about.

The captain tapped Liz on the shoulder and in a weary voice said, "Go home, Liz, get some sleep. Be back at 1400. It was seven a.m. and all was quiet, except for muffled groans and cries from the pained, the wounded, and choked back tears from the staff.

Liz left the hospital and walked into a war zone. It was total devastation. This was the sickening sight of battle. The smell of smoke and fire, the destruction, the once beautiful island was now the scene of a horror movie. She had seen destruction on movie newsreels when she and Richard went to see new motion pictures, but somehow this was different, this was real. She fell to her knees and wept.

A passing soldier went to her. "Are you all right, ma'am?"

"Is anyone all right in this terror?" she asked, looking up at him.

He helped her to her feet and grimaced. She thanked him and staggered off.

Where could she even begin to look for Richard. It was quite a distance, but she ran to the harbor, looking right and left, hoping to see Richard and his ship.

Her heart sunk. The place the *Arizona* was supposed to be was empty. Debris filled the water. Bodies were being removed and carried to the barracks of no hope. It was clear the *Arizona* had not survived.

She held on to the hope Richard was still alive. She followed the men who carted the deceased away. Richard was not there. Where was he?

Liz moved on to the next barracks, her heart pounding, tears welling in her eyes. She moved among the rows of bodies in bags with name tags attached. She stopped long enough to read each name of the deceased.

She saw the name *Richard* and she gulped. No, it was Richard Peterson. She went through most of the thousand corpses, reading each name carefully before moving on. Each row gave her added hope that her husband was not there. But where was he?

Perhaps he was helping in another place she had not been or perhaps he was still among the missing. Tears once again stung her eyes. She reached up to wipe them away.

She was on her way down the final row when the name Richard sprung out at her. Liz once again fell to her knees as she gripped the body bag. *Richard J. Cornell, Lt 1st class.* She unzipped the bag to be sure.

No, it couldn't be! Liz wept uncontrollably.

She held her hand over her mouth to stifle a scream. "Richard, Richard. No, not Richard…"

*   *   *

Eventually, Liz made her way to her barracks. She removed her blood-soaked uniform, dropping it to the floor. She buried her face in her pillow and drenched it with tears. Out of sheer exhaustion, she fell asleep.

A little before 1400 hours, she put on a clean uniform and went back to the hospital. There was no time to mourn; that would have to wait.

New cots for the wounded were brought to the hospital. It was filled until there was no room to move. Still, there was not enough room. A barracks was set up as a hospital extension. More doctors, nurses, and supplies were requisitioned from the mainland.

Some of those people who sustained minor injuries were given medical leave and sent home to be treated by their local doctors. Those who were able were recruited to help as aides to the wounded. They were able to attend to the physically wounded, but those mentally scarred were another matter. Some people woke from sleep screaming, others flung out in their sleep and grabbed onto anyone close to them so they would not be alone. The chaplain worked double shifts and families needed to be notified.

Liz wanted to go home to Ella. Ella, who had been her comfort in life. Ella, who was there when her mother wasn't. Ella, who held her close when Charlie died. Ella, who cheered her up when she was down, comforted her when she was sick and encouraged her always.

She missed Richard. *Oh, Richard... Why?*

*   *   *

Still, there was no time to mourn. Telegraph lines were jammed. Liz needed to inform her family that she was okay and contact Richard's family about his death. Richard's family was anticipating a marriage one day. They were looking forward to welcoming Liz into their family. But now this.

Both families wanted to come to Hawaii. Richard's family wanted to be with their son's body and bring him home. Liz's family wanted to comfort her.

She tried to place another telephone call to both families, but phone lines were down. An air mail letter would have to do.

So, she wrote.

Please don't come. It is a war zone here. We are not sure if it is safe. There could be another strike. We are preparing for anything, but the island is badly damaged. The devastation is everywhere. The State Department won't let you come. They will transport Richard's body home. I am far too busy to spend time with anyone. We are dealing with many injuries and deaths.

She hoped the letters would arrive quickly.

A week later, Liz accompanied her husband's body to the transport plane and said her good-byes. He'd be flown back to Minnesota, and there, Lt. Richard J. Cornell would be laid to rest.

Liz placed a small cross outside their tiny hut and hung a lei of orchids on it. The natives looked on with shock, understanding. She said a prayer, shed a tear, changed her clothes, and went back to work.

There were so many who needed to be attended to. Some would survive. Others they tried to comfort, knowing they would not make it home alive. The days were long and exhausting, and the nights were filled with nightmares and sobs. Liz would lie on her bed and long for Richard's arms to hold her. She would hug her pillow and pretend it was him. In the morning, her pillow was soaked with her tears.

After a few months, there were no more tears to shed. Just the numbness of death and shattered dreams.

Every morning, Liz reported for duty and wore a smile, trying to cheer up the boys in the hospital beds. They would ask about their friends. Some got the sad news they didn't make it, others were fine and would visit. The visits were welcomed. It freed up more time for staff to tend to those wounded who had no one to comfort them.

Hawaii the island paradise Liz once viewed as heaven on earth, the beautiful place where she and Richard had met and shared their love was now a hell hole. She wished she could go back to the day when they were married, the special moments they'd shared.

Liz wanted to go home more than anything, but she couldn't, she wouldn't. There were lives to be saved and fellow soldiers to be cared for. Duty before all.

Chapter Forty-eight

On December 8th, the day after Pearl Harbor was bombed, President Roosevelt delivered his "Day of Infamy" speech and Congress officially declared war on Germany. The Country and the world would never be the same.

The Ellingtons were all glued to the radio for every bit of this tragic news. Ella was terrified for her siblings and her sons and for her countrymen. She prayed for their safety.

*   *   *

Milwaukee in the early 1940s was the twelfth largest city in the U.S. It was a manufacturing powerhouse, so in 1942, the switch from civilian to military manufacturing was relatively easy. Everything from components for the atomic bomb to military ship building took place in Wisconsin.

Ella listened to the reports with interest. How could *she* help?

Harley Davidson continued to manufacture motorcycles and sidecars in preparation to support the war effort. Motorcycles played an important part in the war effort and the Harley Davidson WLA was produced to U.S. Army specifications. The surfaces were painted olive drab or black. Chrome and nickel parts were blued or parkerized. To reduce nighttime visibility, the WLAs were fitted with an extra set of blackout head and taillights. Fenders were removed to reduce mud clogging. Accessories included a heavy-duty luggage rack for radios, ammunition box, and leather Thompson Submachine gun scabbard. Most did not have windshields or leg protectors. Oil bath air cleaners such as those used in dusty farm equipment were added as were changes to the crankcase to reduce water intake. The motorcycle was an efficient vehicle for scouting and courier duties, as well as radio transports and even radio suppression equipment.

Ella was fascinated with everything manufacturers were providing. More and more women she knew were taking up jobs in the factories.

Manitowoc Shipbuilding Company built 28 submarines for the navy during the war. More than 7,000 men and women worked round the clock 365 days of the year producing some of the best submarines.

Oshkosh Truck, once known as Four Wheel Drive Auto Company had begun military production in 1939 when they supplied Model W-700 trucks to the Air Corps bases. Their initial use was as snowplows to clear runways. Transport vehicles were built with three axels to allow for off road terrain. They carried arms, ammunition, and supplies to the troops. Oshkosh Truck expanded into other vehicles and tractors, which transported aircraft. Their contributions were highly recognized for excellence in the war effort.

Buddy wondered if what he was contributing as a doctor was enough. Maybe he should go to Hawaii or maybe he should help out at one of the manufacturing facilities. John convinced him that he was needed at the clinic where more and more veterans were in need of continuing help. Buddy decided to volunteer on his days off at the Veteran's Hospital in Milwaukee.

Allis Chalmers in Milwaukee, a major producer of agriculture and industrial equipment, placed their production on hold while they made Liberty ship steam engines, steam turbines, generators and electric motors, artillery tractors, and various other products for the military. They manufactured components for the Manhattan Project, which produced the first nuclear weapons.

Harnischfeger Industries prewar had experienced a business lag, but with the advent of World War II, Harnischfeger's was up to full production. The company cranes lifted tanks and heavy artillery in defense plants. Their hoists positioned planes on aircraft carriers. Other companies were busy across the nation, contributing to the war effort.

Milwaukee saw a surge in enlistments of both men and women. Grass roots values in the Midwest displayed a huge amount of sense of duty and responsibility to do their part in the war effort. Attacked by Japan on U.S. soil, the call to arms was answered in a big way. Even the Mayor of Milwaukee, Carl Zeidler, left his elected office to enlist in active duty. He joined the U.S. Navy and was assigned duty on the *SS LaSalle* serving in the gun battery. His merchant marine ship and all hands perished off the coast of South Africa in December of 1942.

Wisconsin, being a huge agricultural state, played a big part in keeping the military supplied with food. The focus was changed somewhat from wheat and barley to fresh produce, including potatoes, other vegetables, and meat. Meat packing had been a major industry in the state and now with the railroad and advanced refrigeration, it was booming.

With so many men going off to war and the need for military supplies, the women filled the vacated positions. Women all over the country flocked to manufacturing jobs. The need was great, and they stepped up to fill the positions of men who joined the armed forces to serve their country.

Ella could no longer stand by and do nothing. She went to work at the Heil and Company factory making blackout lamps to be used on air force gasoline trailers. Primarily a truck and trailer making company, its innovation in making electrically welded compartmental tankers and the first stainless steel tank truck for milk transport prewar brought the company much acclaim.

During wartime, the focus turned to aircraft refueling tankers as well as truck and tank bodies, and Rosie the Riveter became the symbol of the women workers. Although it was hard work, Ella personified that image when she became a welder in the factory. She believed everyone had to do their part, just like Liz and all the military personnel were doing theirs.

Dr. John was hard at work in the clinic. He kept very busy treating wounded soldiers home from the war as well as those struck with diseases, such as tuberculosis and malaria. It wasn't financially necessary for Ella to work since he and Buddy were so busy at the clinic, but she felt the need to do her part in the war effort.

Shirley took care of Henrietta when Ella was at work. Even school children did their part in the war effort. They held fundraisers to purchase war bonds. For every 25 cents, they could purchase a stamp for their war bonds booklet. $25 would purchase a war bond. The money would be used to purchase military equipment. Children across the nation emptied their piggy banks and contributed a staggering $715,000,000 to the cause.

Mrs. Johnson had a heart attack shortly after war was declared. She passed peacefully in her sleep at the age of sixty-five. She had a full life and a lovely funeral. The Ellingtons had embraced her as an extension of their family, and they were all saddened by her passing.

Ella hung her head and sobbed. *So much death. So much death.*

Chapter Forty-nine

In August of 1942, Liz went home. The taxi pulled up to the house on Astor Street. Liz paid the driver, took a deep breath, hoisted her duffle bag, and headed for the house.

Ella met Liz at the front door. She was a shell of the boisterous woman they had seen the last Christmas she was home with Richard in 1940.

"Oh Liz, I've missed you so much." She threw her arms around her sister, feeling her bones through her uniform. "Girl, don't they feed you in the military?"

Liz half-smiled and said, "More than I care to eat."

Ella held Liz at arm's length and saw the dullness in her eyes. Her sister had aged significantly and looked bone weary tired. Ella pulled her close again. "Come in, come in. Helen, take her bag upstairs."

Ella led Liz to the parlor. "Liz dear, what has happened to you?" She took her sister's hands in hers. They were ice cold.

Liz coughed. "I am *so* tired. Ella, you can't imagine what it has been like. So much blood, so many broken people. So much death." She coughed again.

"We were so sorry to hear about Richard. Are you okay?"

"No," Liz confessed. "I am numb. I never got a chance to grieve his loss. The hospitals have been full since the attack in December, there is no time to even sleep. I go to my bunk late at night and get maybe six hours of sleep if I am lucky and then I head back to the hospital. They are getting more new recruits now and shipping the wounded home as soon as possible, but we just can't do everything we should for those boys. And Ella, they are just boys." A tear rolled down her cheek.

Helen came into the room.

"Helen, could you make a pot of tea please?" Ella asked. "And bring a chicken sandwich for Liz. I think there is some leftover chicken in the ice box."

Helen took a deep breath and shrugged her shoulders.

"Please, Helen. I know you want to sit here with Aunt Liz, and as soon as you get back from the kitchen, you can join us."

Helen left the room before Liz continued her story. "I cry myself to sleep every night. That's the only time I have to grieve. Not just for Richard but for everyone. I don't even know if I can cry anymore. I just want to sleep forever." Liz yawned.

"You need rest, and lots of it," Ella said.

Helen came back and placed a small plate with a sandwich in front of Liz. Ella poured the tea.

Helen scampered back to the kitchen and returned with a slice of fresh blueberry pie.

"Oh my," said Liz. "The sandwich is much appreciated but I don't think I have room for pie."

Helen looked disappointed. "I made the pie myself. Just this afternoon."

Liz smiled. "Well, in that case, I will have to make room."

They continued the conversation with Helen informing Liz this would be her last year in high school. "I am so happy you will be home for my graduation. You will be home, won't you?"

"I wouldn't miss it," Liz assured her. "I am officially a civilian now. When I take off this uniform, it will go in the closet forever. I think I will have to go shopping for some new duds. Would you like to go with me?"

"Can we, Aunt Liz? We can shop together. I am going to need some things for school, too."

"It's a plan. I know it is very early but if you ladies don't mind, I am going to hit the hay. I am about to fall asleep here."

"You know where your old room is, no one is using it now," Ella stated. "Is there anything you need? Towels and shampoo are where they always were. I think you can find a toothbrush in the bathroom cabinet as well."

"Ella, you never change. We can always count on you to be prepared."

"I'll just take the pie back to the kitchen," Helen said and shrugged.

"No, you won't." Liz took the dish and set it next to her. "I'll take it to my room in case I get hungry later." She nibbled at her sandwich, then she coughed. Setting the plate with half a chicken sandwich on the table, she took the pie plate.

"Are you okay?" Ella asked again, concerned. She had visions of Rose and what she had endured.

"I'm fine. Just a bit of travel fatigue. Maybe I picked up a cold along the way. Summer colds are the worst." Liz was home and she should be happy, but instead she felt numb. Right now, sleep was all that was on her mind.

She went to her old room, glanced around at the familiar surroundings. It was good to be home.

She put a glass of water from the bathroom on her nightstand. She pulled off her uniform, dropping it to the floor. Then, she collapsed on the bed and fell asleep in her undergarments. In minutes, she sat bolt upright, breathing rapidly as panic struck her.

Liz stifled a scream. "Oh, dear Lord, make the nightmares go away."

*   *   *

When John got home, Ella met him with a hug at the door.

"Is everything all right?" he asked. John didn't find the greeting unusual, but normally he would find Ella curled up on the couch with a book or he would find her in the kitchen and greet her with a kiss.

"I...I think so. No, I think not. John, Liz came home today. She was very tired and so thin. She wasn't her perky self."

"Sprite has been through a lot this past year. She got married and lost her husband. She was in an active military zone. She has been living in warlike chaos and destruction and has seen death and dying all around her for months. That is not normal. We can't expect her to *be* normal. This is going to take time. She needs to heal, to grieve."

"I understand, but…but John, can you check her out? She is so thin. I think she might be ill."

"Of course. Let her get some rest. I'll talk to her in the morning. Meanwhile, why don't you plan a nice meal for tomorrow evening that you think she would enjoy. Perhaps after sufficient sleep she will be much better."

Ella smiled. "My husband, you are so wise. You may be right. She is exhausted."

John patted Ella on the arm. "Why don't you sit a moment and relax. You have been keyed up yourself. I know you worry about the boys and Thaddeus. Look at the bright side, Buddy and the girls are doing well. You've done a fine job raising this brood. They have all been through a lot and you have endured through all their pain. Liz will work through this, too."

"But Liz hides her pain. She didn't even tell me about her marriage until Richard died. She had to face that loss all alone. I understand why they kept the marriage a secret, but it breaks my heart to think of how she must have suffered alone."

"But now she has her big sister here and she is safe. Just give her time."

"Thank you."

"For what?"

"For being you. You are my rock. You always know what is best for all of us." She snuggled into John's arm and knew in spite of the chaos in the world, everything would be all right.

Chapter Fifty

Dr. John was quite shocked when Liz came down for breakfast the following morning. Her clothes hung on her, and her complexion was extremely pale. She appeared to be feverish. "Sprite, you need to come to the clinic. I'd like to run a few tests on you."

"Thanks, but I'll be fine. I just need some sleep. I am so very tired, but I haven't gotten much sleep for a long time."

"Exactly why you need to be tested. I can see you are run down. We'll take the tests just to be sure. You're a nurse, you understand the importance of early detection. You also know it is best to be cautious. It could be fatigue, but isn't it better to find out?"

She gave him a thin smile. "You're right, Doctor. I'll stop by later this morning."

When Liz arrived at the clinic, Dr. John ushered her into an exam room where he drew a vile of blood. He gave her a cursory exam and sent her home with a caution.

"Liz, until we get the results, maybe you should stay in your room. You need rest and are malnourished." He patted Liz's hand and sent her on her way. "Go right home. I should have some results later today."

"I will. I'll go right home and to bed...with pleasure," she said.

*   *   *

Dr. John was home early and found Ella finishing making dinner in the kitchen. He got right to the point. "Ella, Liz is undernourished and suffering from what is sometimes called battle fatigue. She told me she is troubled by nightmares…horrific nightmares."

"Battle fatigue? But Liz wasn't in battle."

"Well, not technically, but she was in a battle zone and saw more destruction, human destruction than many do in the line of fire. I think she will recuperate but she may need some psychological help, plus she needs a lot of tender loving care. Ella, Liz needs you more than ever now. I brought something to calm her nerves."

"Whatever she needs I'll be there. I'm really worried, John. She is not the same Liz."

Just then, they heard a scream come from Liz's bedroom. Ella ran up the stairs with John close at her heels.

Liz was flailing about in the bed.

Ella sat on the edge of the bed and wrapped Liz in her arms, rocking her like a small child, rubbing her hair and calming her with soothing murmurings. "There, there, Liz. It's okay, you are safe."

Liz had tears streaming down her face as she broke into deeper sobs. "Do you want to talk about it?" Ella encouraged.

Liz shook her head violently. "No, no. I just want it to stop."

Dr. John got his medical case and went back to Liz's room with a glass of water and a pill in his hand. "Here Liz, take this. It should help a little. Come down for dinner and we will talk…when you are ready."

They left the room.

A moment later, Ella peeked through the door and saw Liz was fast asleep.

"I don't understand, I don't understand," Ella said and bit her lip in consternation. "Are you sure she doesn't have some serious disease? She is so thin, and she doesn't eat. She sleeps all the time. She is not the person we last saw at Christmas."

"You are right, Ella, she is not. Battle fatigue used to be called shell shock. It has traumatized her. I fear she could become catatonic. She has no appetite, and she relives all of the horrific scenes she endured at the hospital over and over again. Young boys missing limbs, some with internal organs spilling out, some with severe head injuries, many with broken bones and broken bodies. People screaming in agony. I experience some of those things one by one, and it can be hard on a person. She experienced them continually for months, and then in the midst of it all, she lost Richard. Sprite is strong beyond all imagination. She will get better, but it will take time. A lot of time and patience and love."

*   *   *

Liz didn't get out of bed for weeks. She was elusive but not catatonic. Ella brought her soup and wouldn't leave until Liz would eat at least some of it. She brought fresh milk and tried to encourage her with pastries, pies, and cookies. Liz had no appetite but forced down a bit of food every time to make Ella happy.

Ella opened the drapes and the windows to let in sunshine and fresh breezes. She read to her and talked to her about mundane topics like what to have for dinner that night, even if Liz didn't listen.

Ella told her funny stories and encouraged the children to visit Aunt Liz, if only for a few minutes. They all left her room making sure they told Liz they loved her.

Dr. John checked on her daily and gave her sedatives at night, hoping they would bring a night without terror. He talked with colleagues regarding care and treatment of patients with shell shock and battle fatigue. During World War I, the assumption was the patient was a coward and were often reprimanded or jailed and then sent back into battle. Those with severe symptoms were looked down upon and sent home. Some suffered with deafness, blindness, and sometimes even convulsions. In later years, they determined the condition was not triggered by explosions or shells. It was determined to be battle fatigue, which was treated with rest and admission to psychiatric hospitals in severe cases. If hypnosis and medications did not result favorably, they often resorted to electric shock therapy.

Dr. John was not about to expose his sister-in-law to that kind of treatment. He didn't feel she was dangerous in any way. If anything, she was feeling sympathy and caring but plagued by nightmares. He decided to treat Liz at home.

Ella gave up almost everything to care for Liz. Of course, there were the children, but they were not babies anymore and were self-sufficient. Henrietta was six now and the older girls understood the situation most of the time. Ella tried to make them feel important and even involved them in Liz's care, promising them if they took very good care of her, she would be the Liz they all knew and loved.

Ella also leaned on Reverend Nelson for strength. He stopped by every week to see Liz. She seemed to enjoy his visits, or at least did not reject them. He encouraged her to try to let Jesus carry her burden. He said it would take time, listen to your doctor.

Liz listened to Reverend Nelson's message but was unsure. It sounded so simple. Was it a roadmap to recovery or just a bunch of hocus pocus? Liz chose to believe. To not believe left no hope. A life without hope was not an option.

Ella came to know Liz on her bad days. Cheering Liz up was not an option. Wrapping her in love and the comfort and safety of her arms was the only answer. Ella would waken to Liz's screams, and she would hurry to her bedside, spending the night in the chair beside Liz's bed. Every time Liz stirred, Ella was there to comfort her.

If Liz wanted to talk, which was rare, Ella was a most attentive listener. Sometimes when it was bad, Ella would crawl in bed beside Liz and hold her the whole night through.

Ella would make sure Liz ate every day, even if it was a cup of broth or a few nibbles of meat or fruit or vegetables. She tried to get as much sunshine and fresh air into Liz as she could. Even on a brisk fall day, a stroll down the walkway kicking the beautiful fall foliage was helpful. A stroll was worth it to feel the wind on her face and breath the cool air deep into her lungs.

Before winter set in, Liz was sleeping less and eating more.

Ella selected readings for Liz. The books were filled with hope and joy, never anything dark or depressing. She read books like Pearl S. Buck's *The Good Earth* and a few lesser-known books that had happier endings.

Even so, it seemed every book she selected for Liz had tragic incidents, murders, wars, pestilence, and death. *Our Town* was based on lives of deceased townspeople. They were all soon discarded. Ella eventually gravitated to books like Laura Ingalls Wilder's *Little House on the Prairie* and Bagnold's *National Velvet*. They were easy reading and were based on achievements, hope and purpose, as well as survival.

Slowly, Liz began to heal. She continued to eat more and slept less restlessly. By the summer of 1943, she was beginning to be the old Liz they knew and loved. Was she cured? Would she ever be cured? Probably not, because what she had experienced was part of her being. It could never be erased, but it could be put aside and managed.

*   *   *

Later in the year, Liz surprised John with a question. "Do you think I can help out at the clinic?"

"Are you sure?" he asked. "It gets really busy."

"Yes, I want to help. I have never wanted to stop being a nurse or even a doctor. I just... I just want to heal people. It's all I've ever wanted to do. It was all too much, too terrible, too impossible, too tragic. And too senseless in Hawaii."

"That it was. But Liz, you are not afraid of flashbacks? You have made such good progress, I don't want to see you regress. Is it too soon?"

"You know what they say, 'If you fall off a horse, you need to get back on.'"

He chuckled. "Yes Sprite, but you didn't fall off, you were trampled."

"I suppose you are right, but do you think I could try it for a while? Maybe a shorter shift to get my feet wet. I promise I won't fall apart. All through the worst part of the tragedy at Pearl Harbor, I didn't fail. I was able to put on the uniform and do whatever was necessary to aid all the wounded and dying. You have tragic accidents and injuries but nothing like the mayhem of those days. And not under the chaos and overwhelming pressures of the situation. I think I can handle it. I would like to try."

John wasn't as sure, but he knew Liz needed to move on. At least here, he could monitor her progress. "I could use the help. We had a measle outbreak last month. We have ten expectant mothers and Tommy Anderson is always breaking or spraining something. That boy needs to calm down."

"Let me try, please John? If it doesn't work out, just let me know and I will step aside. You don't even have to pay me."

He smiled at her. "Come to the clinic tomorrow. I will show you around and you can see to anyone who drops in. I have a few house calls to make in the morning and our other doctor is taking a few days off."

*   *   *

That evening, Liz set the table for dinner. Ella had been busy in the kitchen most of the afternoon preparing a new recipe she'd found in the latest *Good Housekeeping* magazine.

At dinner, Ella made a grand display of presenting the beef Wellington she had prepared. There were oohs and ahhs as everyone admired the meal, anxious to dig in. The smell tantalized their taste buds. Ella had outdone herself. She had been trying new recipes the past few months, but this was exquisite. They couldn't wait for grace to be said.

After much ado about the meal, John announced, "Sprite will be joining the clinic of Mallory & Ellington tomorrow as our nurse in charge."

There was silence as Ella looked from Liz to John and back again. Turning to Liz, she asked, "Are you sure? Are you ready?"

"I am." Liz nodded.

"John?" Ella took a deep breath and stared at John with wide eyes.

"I believe in Liz. She has made a lot of progress and we won't work her too hard to start. She can handle some of those pesky measle cases and take care of walk-ins while I am on my calls. She can lend a hand when two are not enough. She has convinced me she is ready."

Ella took a deep breath and blew it out through her mouth. "If you're both sure."

"Hooray! Auntie Liz is going to help Daddy," Henrietta squealed. Everyone laughed.

*   *   *

The next day, Liz reported to work at eight a.m. and Dr. John was there, waiting for her. He had already been in for an hour.

He showed her about the clinic. "Bandages are kept here." He opened a couple of drawers of gauze, medical tape, and various ointments. "Unless there is a major calamity, these should last at least three months."

He opened a closet, which held various braces, slings, and other paraphernalia for sprains and broken bones. He then showed her the sterilized thermometers, needles, scissors, scalpels, etc. Another area held what to the lay person might look like a tool shop or a torture chamber... hammers, tongs, clamps and knives.

Liz was familiar with most and felt very comfortable in the setting. As a military nurse, she had performed many tasks which only a licensed doctor would perform in a civilian setting.

Soon Gloria, the secretary/receptionist arrived. "What a glorious fall day. The leaves are showing off their autumn splendor in the morning sun and there is a nip in the air. It is so energizing."

She took off her coat and hung it on the coat tree behind her desk. "Anyone like some coffee?" she asked. She began to prepare a pot without waiting for an answer.

"Gloria, this is Liz, our new nurse. What's on the docket this morning?" John asked.

"Nice to meet you, Liz. I'm sure you'll like it here." Gloria shuffled a few papers on her desk and turned the page in her appointment book. "Your Associate, Dr. Paulson, will be in Madison for a seminar all this week. They are looking into treatments for polio. It is a horrible disease, and it effects many children. I hope they come up with a cure soon." She turned a few pages. "Dr. Ellington, you have a busy morning today. Mrs.

Thomas called, eight-year-old Elaine has come down with a fever and she would like you to stop by."

"She didn't call me last night, so I assume the aspirin did the trick, but I will stop by just to be sure," Dr. John said. "I am visiting old Adolph Martin. The Thomas home is on the way. Anything else?"

"Yes, Martha Albrecht is nearing her due date and she said their car broke down, so she won't be able to come in. It might be wise to check on her, because all of her other children delivered early."

"She has a midwife, doesn't she?" Liz inquired.

"Yes, but she prefers to deliver in the hospital. Her last birth was breach and the baby had a very difficult time. He is two now and seems to be fine physically but is a bit slow in his progress. He was eighteen months old before he walked and is just now starting to talk." Gloria continued down the page.

"Is that it?" Dr. John slipped on his coat over his suit. He took his satchel with everything he thought he might need and tucked a clean lab coat in the bag. "You never know when things get messy." He smiled.

"Just peruse the office, so you are familiar with where things are. We generally don't have a lot of crises while I'm away. Mostly a few scuffs, some sniffles, and perhaps Mrs. Jones. There is not a thing wrong with her, but she imagines all sorts of terminal problems. Just listen to her, give her a cursory exam, and assure her she will live. If she is overly anxious, there are some sugar pills in the medicine chest."

Liz laughed. "Placebo noted."

Dr. John left for his morning runs and Liz turned to Gloria. "I'd love some of that coffee."

*   *   *

Dr. John could not have been gone more than a half hour when there was a frantic rustling at the door. Mr. Anderson entered with an unconscious Tommy in his arms. "Got to see Dr. Ellington now."

Gloria jumped from her chair, opening the door to the exam room. "Put him here," she said and motioned to the exam table. "Nurse Liz, come quick."

Liz rushed around the corner. "What happened?" she inquired, immediately assessing the patient, making sure the boy was breathing.

"Tommy fell outa the apple tree," Mr. Anderson informed her. "Where is Dr. Ellington?"

"He's out on calls, Mr. Anderson," Gloria stated. "Liz, do you need help? We can get him to the hospital."

"I think I can handle this," Liz stated confidently.

Gloria left the exam room.

"Who are you?" Mr. Anderson wanted to know.

"Nurse Liz Dewberry Cornell, Dr. Ellington's sister-in-law. I have been practicing for over ten years and have treated injuries far worse than this."

He looked at her crisp white nurse's uniform and cap. "You a doc?"

"I am not, but I patched up hundreds of soldiers at Pearl Harbor. I assure you I can handle this." Liz continued to check Tommy's vitals.

"Mr. Anderson, have a seat there." She pointed to a nearby chair. "I am going to examine his leg and arm while he is still unconscious. It could be very painful. Then, I am going to wake him," Liz explained.

She worked quickly and soon determined there were no broken bones. There was a dislocated shoulder and a sprained wrist. She was able to pop the bone in his shoulder back in place. She had noticed earlier a deep gash on his forehead, which she compressed. "It's going to require a few stitches on his forehead."

"He's going to be okay?" Mr. Anderson nervously asked.

"A few bandages and some pain for a while, but he should be fine. No tree climbing until he is healed, though."

Tommy was starting to stir.

"Looks like he is going to wake himself," Liz said and smiled. "Hey Tommy, can you hear me?" Liz flashed a small light in Tommy's eyes.

Tommy looked into Liz's eyes and tried to get up.

"Whoa there," Liz cautioned. "No sitting up for you just yet."

Tommy winced at the pain but insisted he was fine. "I'm pretty tough. It was just a little bump."

"You have to make sure the branches are safe before you crawl out on them," Liz advised.

"I reached out for the juiciest red apple you ever saw," Tommy said. "It was a beaut, but I couldn't reach it. I needed to get out a tiny bit more but then I heard the branch break, and it broke behind me, so I had nowhere to go but down."

"Well, we need to wrap your wrist so you can't bend it. You are going to leave here with a sling so you don't move your shoulder until it is healed and then we need to take care of the gash on your head. First, I need to disinfect it. It is going to sting a little."

Liz dabbed the wound with an antiseptic that made Tommy shut his eyes tight and wrinkle his nose. "Sorry Tommy, but I have to make sure it is clean so it doesn't get infected."

"Don't hurt," Tommy blurted. He winced. "Much."

Liz proceeded to wrap Tommy's wrist while he watched carefully. "You are going to have a nasty bruise on your leg, but it should be fine in a few days." She put the sling around him.

"All done?" Tommy inquired.

"No, I'm afraid not. Now we must put a few stitches in that gash. I think three or four will do."

"What?" Tommy was horrified as he saw Liz prepare for the sutures. "Can't we just put a bandage on it?"

"I'm afraid you are going to need more than a bandage on that one. I'll fix it so you won't feel the sutures, but you will feel the shot I have to give you to numb the area."

Tommy gulped. "Do ya' have to? I can stand a lot and I don't like shots."

"Tommy trust me, the shot is going to be a lot less painful than putting in stitches without it."

Liz went to the medicine cabinet to see what kind of anesthetic Dr. John had available. She hoped she would find the newest anesthetic

Lidocaine, but it had only recently been available. The cocaine-based anesthetic would have to do.

"Ready, Tommy?" Liz asked as she prepared the hypodermic needle. Tommy squinted and gritted his teeth to prepare for the shot.

"We need two shots, Tommy. One on each side of the wound."

"Can't we just go with one? Don't know if my folks can afford two," Tommy said.

"Tell you what. Today, we have a special two for the price of one. Ready?" Before he had a chance to respond, the second shot was administered. "Now we have to wait a bit for the shots to work. Relax now, you won't feel a thing when I do the sutures."

Liz turned to Mr. Anderson. "I'll be back." She left the room to get that still illusive cup of coffee. As she passed the reception area, she noted an older lady sitting there nervously. She quietly addressed Gloria. "Who is the lady in the reception area?"

"That's Mrs. Jones. She is sure she is on her deathbed. She insists on waiting so she can get her medicine. Shall I give it to her and send her on her way."

"No, bring her into Dr. Paulson's exam room since he is out of town. I will see her while Tommy's shots take effect." She grabbed a quick sip of coffee.

Taking a breath before she entered, Liz stepped into Dr. Paulson's exam room. "Hello, Mrs. Jones, I am Nurse Liz Cornell. I am so happy to meet you. Dr. Ellington told me about your unusual case."

"I'm going to die, aren't I? I knew it. Why else would Doc talk to someone else about my problem," Mrs. Jones said.

"Well, Dr. Ellington was a bit concerned since your problem keeps returning. Can you tell me about it?"

"Can't breathe, can't catch my breath. Sometimes I get pains, but it isn't always in the same spot. Then, my heart races and I can't talk. Doc gives me medicine and it always helps, so if you could just give me the medicine…"

"Well, let me examine you." Liz took out her stethoscope and listened to Mrs. Jones' heart. It was beating strong and in rhythm, though perhaps a bit fast…not unusual in her panicked state. Liz took her blood pressure. Slightly elevated but within normal range. "Stick out your tongue and say ahh."

Mrs. Jones looked on wide-eyed.

"Mmm… Hmm…" Liz gazed off in deep thought.

"Is it bad? Am I dying?"

"Oh no, Mrs. Jones. I have seen cases like this before."

"You have?" Mrs. Jones asked.

"Why yes, I have and although the treatment is a little unconventional, I think it might help."

"What is it?" Mrs. Jones seemed oddly pleased at the new diagnosis.

"Well, I believe you have something very rare. It is something called Lonevitas. It strangely effects older widows. What I would like you to do is open up all of your drapes on a sunny day and go for long walks in the fresh air. It will help you to breath better."

Mrs. Jones looked a bit skeptical, but it did seem to make some sense. Fresh air could fill her lungs and help with breathing.

"Sometimes, it helps the time go by if you walk with a friend. Do you have a friend to walk with?"

"No, I'm afraid not. Esther passed and Agnes spends all of her time at the church. They have a quiltin' bee there and some other stuff. She doesn't have time. When she's not doing that, she's readin'."

"You know, Mrs. Jones, I just bet Agnes could use a little help at the church and maybe if she had someone to walk with, she would enjoy that, too. Especially now, when the fall colors are so beautiful, and in the spring, when the flowers bloom and lilacs smell so wonderful."

"I don't know…"

"Well, you will never know until you ask. Tell me you will stop by and talk to her. Sounds to me like you used to be good friends. That is what friends do."

Mrs. Jones stared at the wall. "Well, I don't want to bother her."

"Tell you what. You go home and open up all your drapes. Tomorrow, you stop by the church and see if you can lend Agnes a hand. If she gets done sooner, maybe she will walk with you. Just give it a try. If it doesn't work out, I have some other ideas that might help."

She smiled. "All right, I will give it a try, but can I get my medicine?"

"Of course, but be sure to only take it when you need it. We don't want you to overdose."

"I like you, Nurse Cornell, but I like Dr. Ellington, too."

"Thank you, Mrs. Jones. You take care and if you do what I tell you, I think you will be doing fine after a while."

Liz tended to Tommy's sutures and told his father to keep an eye on him because he had also suffered a concussion in the fall. He warned Mr. Anderson to keep him awake through the day and check on him a couple times during the night.

She took a deep breath and went back to her cold cup of coffee. It didn't matter because the entire Peterson family had crowded into the waiting room. All in varying degrees of pox. Chicken pox.

Liz dispensed calamine lotion and oatmeal bath and gave them instructions to not have contact with anyone else for at least ten days. No school for the kids.

"Hooray," went out the shout from all nine of them. She got them all out of the office quickly and sent them back to their quarantined home.

"Okay Gloria, get the disinfectant, we need to sanitize the place. They should not be contagious at this point, but we don't want to take any chances."

Dr. John returned about a half hour later to the smell of antiseptic spray, bleach, and everyone hard at work sanitizing the clinic. "Slow day, huh? Glad to see your enthusiasm in cleaning. It's important to keep our patients safe."

Liz threw the towel she'd been holding at the doctor. "Slow day... slow day? Let me fill you in on all you missed."

When she finished, not leaving out any details, Dr. John smiled. "Well, it looks like you passed the test. You are ready to join the firm of Mallory & Ellington."

Chapter Fifty-one

L iz continued to work at Mallory & Ellington for three more years. To her credit, Mrs. Jones did not return for her placebo. She rekindled her friendship with Agnes, and they were often seen at movie theatres and band concerts. They were invaluable help at the church and worked tirelessly. Mrs. Jones had found a purpose in life and Liz had reestablished her love for medicine.

On June 22, 1944, the Serviceman's Readjustment Act of 1944 was signed into law. Commonly referred to as the GI Bill of Rights, the law provided many veteran benefits. Prior to this, veterans had been a political football for decades. Finally, those who served would be recognized and assisted for their service. The bill established veteran-run hospitals, provided low interest mortgages, and granted educational stipends covering tuition and expenses for veterans attending trade schools and college.

Liz grasped the opportunity and enrolled at Harvard Medical School in Boston, Massachusetts leaving Wisconsin behind again. In 1936, the first woman admitted to Harvard Medical School was Fe del Mundo, a Filipino pediatrician. Del Mundo would have been rejected but her application was mistakenly thought to be that of a male applicant. This, however, did not open the door to women. That would take another decade. The first class of women was accepted into the school in September of 1945.

Liz's first application in July of 1944 was rejected. She missed the first enrollment but in September of 1946, Liz Cornell reported to class. She was in a minority, and it seemed as a female, she had to work harder to be recognized for her efforts. That didn't matter. Liz was used to competing in a male-dominated world.

She knew Dr. John missed her help at the clinic. Now that Buddy had his doctorate, he came to work at the clinic full time. Since Dr. Mallory was no longer giving John consults, the clinic was renamed Ellington & Ellington. Dr. Paulson had moved on to a small clinic upstate and Dr. John had hired a new nurse to replace Liz.

Gloria was still working at the clinic but often complained at the confusion of not only having two Dr. Ellingtons but two Dr. *John* Ellingtons. Liz looked forward to consulting with them both someday.

Chapter Fifty-two

In January of 1944, Jimmy and David had completed three years in service. They had signed on for four. One more to go.

Jimmy was assigned to a cleanup mission in North Africa. British and American forces had defeated the Italians and Germans, leading to the fall of Mussolini. It had been a bitter battle and as with most battles, it was left with a great deal of debris. Jimmy was one of the first to step into a designated area, which had turned out to be a heavily charged mine field. One misstep and it could cost your life.

Kaboom!

Jimmy didn't know what hit him. He dropped to the ground as the dirt and debris fell all around him. The troops gathered him up, being careful not to detonate any other hidden obstacles. They put his arms over the shoulders of two comrades, who carried him to safety. The medics patched him up and he was airlifted to the nearest medical facility. Jimmy's ankle was shattered. He was treated in Washington and then sent home.

Word was sent to the Ellingtons their son would arrive at O'hare Field in Chicago the following Tuesday. Jimmy would be released from service on a medical discharge. Dr. John received the call and was told by the commanding officer that Corporal James Ellington had served his country admirably and he would receive the Purple Heart for his bravery.

He also spoke to the hospital surgeon at Walter Reed Hospital where Jimmy had first been treated. The surgeon apprised Dr. John of Jimmy's medical needs going forward. He would receive further surgeries to mend his leg but would most likely walk with a limp.

Dr. John told Ella of the situation and assured her Jimmy would be fine.

Ella sighed, not knowing if she should embrace the grief she felt or if she should praise the Lord he was coming home and would be fine. Unsure, she did both.

She and John stood on the tarmac as Jimmy descended the plane. He was dressed in his dress uniform with a duffle bag slung over his shoulder. He was on crutches.

Ella gulped, then caught her breath. She put on a smile and ran to meet him. She flung her arms around him, almost knocking him off balance.

"Hey, hey," he said as he grabbed her for support. "I'm just learnin' how to use these sticks, but wow, it is good to see you."

A wheelchair was brought on the tarmac to assist him inside and through the aisles and gateways of O'hare. Dr. John brought up the car and they were soon on their way home.

Dr. John treated Jimmy's injury. It took two surgeries, but Jimmy was soon up and ready to start life anew as a civilian.

Buddy teased him. "Since you have acquired a slight limp, we finally are twins."

*   *   *

David was sent overseas, and the last Ella heard was that he was on a mission to France. She got shivers when she heard the news.

It was almost five years and still there was no word about Thaddeus. Hope was growing dim he would ever return home.

The movie theatre showed news clips on the war and every time Ella saw one, she said a prayer for Thaddeus, David, and all the boys in harm's way. Would there ever be peace on this earth?

Chapter Fifty-three

On D-Day June 6, 1944, the U.S., British, and Canadian troops stormed the beaches of Normandy. Among more than 24,000 troops who landed at 6:30 in the morning was Corporal David Cody Corrigan. The men were met with heavy fire. The shore was mined and covered with metal and wood debris and barbed wire. Casualties were high. More than 4,000 souls lost their lives that day. The country celebrated the victory but mourned the lives lost.

Several days later in Milwaukee, two officers knocked at the Ellington's door.

As she answered it, Ella began to shake. Her heart pounded hard in her chest.

She instinctively knew her son—Rose's son—was the reason for their visit. Her heart bled for David, David the little boy she met at the train station when they arrived from Oklahoma more than ten years ago. The little boy who was so confident and unafraid, despite the horrors he had witnessed as a small child. David, who had joined the circus on a lark. David, who brightened everyone's life with his smile. He'd reminded her so much of Thaddeus and his carefree spirit. David, who would've been twenty-two in three weeks. David, who was not grown in her body but was born in her heart.

She listened to the words of the two officers, knew what they were saying but heard nothing but the pounding in her ears. She fell to the floor and fainted.

Ella was home alone that afternoon and the officers stayed with her as they summoned Dr. John home. She woke long enough to see John's face briefly. The rest of the day was a blur.

No, not the day or the week. It took months for her to recover. She briefly recalled the service for David with his sisters crying. Poor Ella Sara and Emma Sue. They'd lost so much already.

Both girls had rushed home when they heard the news about David. After college, they had taken teaching jobs in West Allis. Through the years, they frequently spent time at home and would never miss a Christmas. But it never felt quite right with the boys away. This visit was particularly somber. They consoled each other, knowing now it was just the two of them. Sure, the Ellingtons had been wonderful substitute parents, but that's what they were—substitutes. They appreciated all they had been given and taught. They knew they were loved, and they were always there for advice or just a voice that comforted them. But in the end, the girls relied on each other. They knew this wonderful family would always be theirs, but their hearts could never release the family they once had.

The funeral was with full military honors. Bagpipers played "Taps" and Ella was presented with the American flag, which she graciously accepted but shared with Emma Sue and Ella Sara. That evening, although their hearts were heavy with grief, they shared stories of David's escapades through the years. It helped to salve the wounds left by his departure. They celebrated David's life. It didn't take away the pain but through it they endured.

The late summer air brought some relief and hope back to Ella, but she was still in a deep sadness. When would the war end? When would it *all* end?

*   *   *

August 14, 1945 was V-J Day and victory over Japan marked the end of World War II. Chaos was in the streets. Neighbors hugged neighbors and there was joy with the news the husbands, sons, and fathers would soon be returning home. Ella's job at Heil and Company factory would soon be manned by a returning soldier and that was just fine with her.

Ella was happy the bloody war was over. Maybe this one would be the war to end all wars. Had it been worth it? The bodies of more than 400,000 men were brought home in caskets. Millions had lost their lives throughout the world. For what? Greed? Power? It made no sense. David was dead. Richard was dead. Thaddeus was still missing. Yes, Ella was elated it was over but the joy she felt was overshadowed by all the grief she still felt.

How much can a body endure? How much can a family endure? How much can a country endure?

*   *   *

Fall was here. The girls had returned to their teaching jobs. Helen had moved out on her own. Jimmy had completed undergraduate studies prior to enlisting. He now began to pursue a degree in law at Yale.

Buddy was working with Dr. John at the clinic but still lived at home. A romance was budding. The new nurse that had replaced Liz was the sunshine in his life.

Liz was still at home as well but would be attending Harvard in a few weeks. Shirley was a gregarious teen. Her roots were nearly washed clean from her sordid past. Only on rare occasions was she spooked by a distant memory. On those occasions, she shuddered, took a deep breath and went on.

Henrietta was nine and filled the house with laughter. Life was back to normal, whatever that was.

Ella had been sitting on the porch, staring up at the fluffy clouds but now wiped her hands on her apron and went inside. Dinner needed to be made, laundry needed to be done. Factories were still grinding out products. John was still healing broken and ill bodies. But who could mend a broken heart?

And yet, Ella looked at the world around her. The leaves had fallen from the trees and the ground would soon be covered with a blanket of fresh snow. People would be bustling about with Christmas preparations and then, a new day would dawn.

Her mind went to all the countries devastated by the war. Cities and farms and businesses destroyed from the fighting and bombing. A large hole was in her heart for all of the lives lost but tomorrow would be a new day. A new beginning. Each day she would pick up and start anew. She would never forget, but Ella would endure.

DISEASE

DISASTER

Chapter Fifty-four

L ife did go on and was looking pretty good in 1948.
Ella Sue and Emma Sara were twenty-eight and on the verge of
becoming spinsters. Like Ella, both had gone to school to become teachers. They shared an apartment in West Allis, a suburb of Milwaukee.
They both taught at Lane Elementary. While attending a teacher's conference in Chicago in the fall, neither had an inkling how this conference
would change their lives.

Ella Sue was mesmerized by Chandler Cummings, a professor of law at
Marquette University. He was a keynote speaker at the conference and Ella Sue
was quite smitten. After his presentation, she made a bold move to meet him.

"Professor Cummings, your presentation was fascinating."

"Ah, Miss," he glanced at her nametag, "Ella Sue Corrigan. And what
part did you find fascinating?" Professor Cummings seemed genuinely
interested in what she had to say.

"Well, um, all of it." Ella Sue shrugged and smiled demurely.

"Well then, did you agree with the point of neutrality in government
participation in education or do you go with the opposing viewpoint?"

*What did he say about all of that? I don't recall the discussion. I guess I
was preoccupied with his dashing looks. Especially his cute mustache.*

"Really, I have not made up my mind," said Ella Sue. "I think I need
to do more investigation into the issue."

The professor glanced at his watch. "I'm finished here today but
I would like to continue this conversation. Could I buy you a cup of
coffee?"

Ella Sue hated coffee. "Yes, I would like that. Um, where would you like to meet?"

"I'll just call down to the valet and have my automobile brought around so we could leave together. That is, unless you need to be somewhere else right now."

"Just give me a moment to let my sister know I will be going. She would be a dreadful mess if she couldn't find me later."

"Certainly, meet me right here in…let's say 20 minutes?"

"Perfect." Ella Sue turned and dashed off to find her sister. Emma Sara was already seated at the next seminar they were to attend.

"Emma, you are on your own. I am having coffee with the gorgeous Professor Cummings. You will be fine, won't you?"

Emma Sara made a face. "But you don't like coffee."

"Does it matter?" Ella Sue raised her eyebrows. "This is the perfect Professor Cummings."

"Go, go. I'll be fine." Her sister shooed her.

*   *   *

Ella Sue dashed off to her professor and Emma Sara smiled at the fellow who had slipped into the seat next to her.

"Twins?" he asked.

"Yes, how did you guess?" Emma Sara quipped. She noticed he did not have a ring on his finger and was a handsome specimen himself.

"Oh, just a lucky guess. Tom Sanders." He offered her his hand.

"Emma Sara Corrigan." His hand felt warm, and he held on a bit longer than necessary.

"Have you heard this lecturer before?" she asked, curious.

"No, but I've heard he is quite good."

The lecturer took the podium. His speech, Emma Sara was sure, was quite enlightening, but her mind was on Tom Sanders and the spicy smell of his cologne.

During break, Tom and Emma Sara tried to discuss the topic but it was clear neither of them had been paying attention.

"Do you like coffee?" Tom asked.

"I think I do," she answered honestly.

Tom gave her a questioning glance. "You think you do?"

"Can I get tea?"

"Sure, let's go." Tom took Emma Sara's hand and they slipped out of the building like two school kids playing hooky.

*   *   *

Six months later, both girls were engaged and planning a double wedding for May of 1949.

The wedding took place at the Presbyterian Church with Reverend Nelson officiating. Helen was their maid of honor, along with Chandler's sister, Bernice. Shirley was a bridesmaid, along with three bridesmaids who were friends from school. Buddy and Jimmy served as grooms-men. The grooms each had brothers who filled the role of best men and additional groomsmen. It was quite an impressive entourage with 10 attendants plus flower girl and ringbearer. Henrietta was the flower girl, though a bit old at thirteen for the role. Tom's nephew, Tony was ring bearer. He, too, was older, which was not traditional. Ella Sue and Emma Sara didn't care. They wanted to include everyone.

Ella was elated that the girls had finally found their true loves and delighted with their choices. A double wedding. Wow! Ella immediately stepped into the role of mother of the brides. Of course, she and John would pay for the wedding, and it would be a grand affair.

The brides were each stunning in their white southern belle style dresses and tiaras with short veils. The bridesmaids wore mint green taffeta with tulle shawls. The maids of honor wore a darker mint-colored dress with black heels. Ella had found a brocade suit with a pill box hat and John wore a grey tuxedo and gave the brides away. He walked the aisle with one on each arm and a proud smile on his face. The grooms wore white tuxedos with a grey ascot. The groomsmen were handsome in their grey tuxedos.

The reception was held at the Pfister Hotel in downtown Milwaukee. John and Ella spared no expense. It was an affair to be remembered by the 300 guests.

The sit-down dinner consisted of roasted chicken, wild rice, braised vegetables, and piping hot rolls. They marveled how the rolls could be so hot at such an elaborate affair. But it was the Pfister after all.

Ella wondered at how the nest was getting smaller. Shirley and Henrietta were still at home, but for how long? Emma Sue and Ella Sara had moved out some time ago but were close to home and visited often. Now they would be living in Minnesota. Things would be different as they started families of their own. Their family of ten definitely was shrinking.

Buddy was working at the clinic but still lived at home. Jimmy was away at Yale on a GI loan from his time in the service. Yes, indeed the nest was shrinking.

Chapter Fifty-five

It was the summer of 1949. Henrietta was an energetic and intelligent thirteen-year-old. She loved to read, but most of all she loved the outdoors. She would spend winters on the ice-skating rink and summers swimming with her friends at the lake front. The beach was walking distance from their home, so this became almost an everyday event. Henrietta was a strong swimmer and couldn't wait until she was old enough to be a lifeguard.

It was an idyllic time in the nation. The depression and World War II seemed a distant memory. The economy was blossoming. It seemed a safe time when kids didn't need to be attended to all the time. If you were at a friend's house, that mom was in charge. If friends were at your house, your mom was in charge. You'd better not break the rules because you would be disciplined, and your parents would hear exactly what transpired and then you would be disciplined further.

Children addressed their elders by their surname and there were no excuses. If you had an accident and got a scraped knee or cut finger, the mom in charge had iodine or mercurochrome handy and would patch you up and send you home.

One day, Henrietta was playing in her neighbor's yard with their children, climbing the old apple tree and looking for a crispy summer treat. They sat on the porch savoring the sweet taste of the Braeburn apples. Henrietta's leg was bouncing. She tried to stop it, but it wouldn't stop.

"You gotta pee?" her friend Karen laughed.

Henrietta shook her head. "No, my leg just wants to jump."

"Okay then, I'll get the jump rope." Karen scampered away and returned in a minute with two jump ropes. "I challenge you to jump longer."

Henrietta swung the rope but on the first jump she fell to the ground.

"Get up. I'm already at twenty," her friend counted. "Twenty-one, twenty-two, twenty-three...come on, get up."

Henrietta tried but she *couldn't* get up.

Karen tried to help her. Henrietta was scared.

Just then Karen's mom came to sit on the steps with a glass of lemonade. She lit a cigarette and watched the girls struggling and laughing. A minute later, she stomped out the cigarette and went to the girls' assistance.

"What's the matter?" she asked.

Henrietta was crying and she rarely cried.

Mrs. Arthur lifted Henrietta and helped her to her house. Ella heard the commotion and met them at the door.

"I think Henrietta fell and hurt her leg. She can't seem to walk. I noticed she has a fever, too. You better have Dr. Ellington look at her," Mrs. Arthur said.

"Oh my," Ella said and thanked Mrs. Arthur. She helped Henrietta up to a chair in the parlor. She felt her forehead. Mrs. Arthur was right. "Child, you *are* burning up. How did you fall?"

"I fell when I tried to jump rope, but it wasn't the jump rope. My leg was jumping and felt funny before we started to play."

"Does it hurt?" Ella asked.

"Not all the time but it does hurt."

"When your father gets home, he will check it. In the meantime, I think you should go to bed and get some rest. You may have the flu."

Henrietta got up and headed up the stairs. Halfway up, her leg once again failed her, and she crumpled on the stairway.

Ella went to her aid and tucked her into bed. "You get some rest, and you will feel better later." She put her hand on Henrietta's forehead and kissed her gently. Then, she pulled the shades down but left the window open for the soft summer breeze to fill the room.

Ella didn't call Dr. John, but as soon as he arrived home she told him to check on Henrietta.

"I think she has the flu, John. She is tired and weak, and she has a fever." She explained Henrietta's fall but added, "I think she might have sprained something playing jump rope, or maybe it was just a cramp."

"I'll check on her, Ella," John said and went upstairs.

*   *   *

"Hey Henri, how is my girl?"

Henrietta looked up groggily at her father and smiled. "My head hurts."

"Your head? I thought it was your leg?" he asked.

Dr. John felt her forehead and took out a thermometer from his bag to check her temperature. It was 102 degrees. "Well, that's not good. How do you feel?"

"I am so tired, Daddy. I just want to sleep…and my headache is really bad."

"What about your leg?" He lifted the covers and turned her on her back. Her leg began convulsing.

John checked her leg, took a deep breath, and exhaled slowly. "I think we need to do a few tests. I don't have everything I need here but we can check you out in the morning. Hopefully, you will feel better then. Get some sleep. Do you want something to eat?"

"No, I just want to sleep." Henrietta yawned.

"Mama will bring you something. I will check in on you later."

John walked slowly down the stairs. *I hope I am wrong.* Although the war was long over, there was another battle the country faced, and John feared it was in their home. This new enemy was polio.

*   *   *

The next day, Henrietta didn't want to wake up. She ached all over. She tilted her head down to her chest in a stretch and a pain shot down her back. Her breathing was labored.

John checked on Henrietta, but she seemed worse.

He took Ella aside and sat her in a chair for the news. "Ella, we need to get Henrietta to the hospital right now." He was very serious.

"Oh, no, John. Will she get better?"

"If we don't leave soon, she won't," John said.

Ella got Henrietta dressed and they took her to Milwaukee Children's Hospital where she had a spinal tap.

As Ella sat patiently in a waiting room, John came from the lab with a serious look on his face.

Ella's eyes widened and she gulped, "What is it, John?"

"I am afraid Henrietta has polio. We need to get her help immediately. I am making arrangements to have her admitted. They have an excellent respiratory facility here and an area devoted to victims of polio."

"Oh John, will she be okay?"

"This is a horrible disease and unfortunately, there is no cure. Ella, pray she will have a mild case and be better very soon. It is important to tackle the problem early."

Ella began to sob. "What about the others? Her friends? Our family? It is very contagious. I don't know anyone who has it. Where did it come from?"

"We will get answers, but right now we need to get Henrietta the help she needs."

Ella gulped back tears, yet a couple slipped down her cheek.

"Ella, Ella. We need to be strong for Henrietta now. Dry your eyes and come with me while we tell her."

*   *   *

They went into the room where Henrietta lay. She wore a hospital gown and was half asleep. She struggled to pull her eyes open. "Can I go home now?"

Ella sat on the cot and pulled her daughter to her. "Sweetheart, Papa has something to tell you."

"Hey there, Henri." He smiled softly and took her hand. "It looks like we have a big problem here and I am afraid you won't be going home just yet. I am making arrangements for you to stay at this hospital for a little while longer and get some treatment. Henrietta, you have polio."

Henrietta's eyes got bigger. "I've heard about polio in school. Some of the swimming pools are closed to prevent it from spreading. But Papa, I don't know anyone with polio. Am I going to die?"

"No, you're not going to die, but we need to treat you now. Polio can get bad quickly and we need to stop it as soon as we can."

"Can we go home to get my things?" Henrietta pinched her lips together to stop the tears.

"No, you can't take anything with you. You will be in quarantine," Dr. John said.

"What is quar-an-tine?"

Ella wiped away a tear that escaped from her daughter's eye. "They need to make sure the disease doesn't spread, so everything you take with you needs to be burned. You won't be allowed visitors but…"

"I can't see *anyone*? Not you or Papa or my friends? What about starting school or seeing my classmates?" Henrietta couldn't hold back the streaming tears any longer.

Ella gathered Henrietta into her arms and rocked her while she stroked her long brown hair. "We will see you as often as we can and as soon as we can. Let's get you better first."

Henrietta curled into a fetal position on the cot and sobbed. Soon, the exhaustion overtook her and she was fast asleep.

"Oh, John, the poor girl," Ella said, grasping his hand.

"I know, Ella, I know. This isn't going to be easy."

*   *   *

Not long after, Henrietta was admitted. They had one last long hug before she was placed in a room with a glass window to the hall. Ella and Dr. John were not allowed in.

A woman gave Henrietta a fresh gown, removed the first gown she had been given and took the clothing that she had arrived in at the hospital and sealed it all in a laundry sack. The sack would be taken to the incinerator. Dr. John and Ella were advised to do the same with the clothing they had on that day and were given strict instructions to sanitize their home. The woman also told them to advise all who had been in contact with Henrietta to do the same.

The draperies on the window to the hall opened and they both smiled their support. They blew their daughter kisses and waved before they turned to make the long trek down the hallway and back home where they had to inform the other children, neighbors, and friends as to what had transpired.

Thankfully, most were very supportive and kind to Ella and Dr. John. One neighborhood family, however, exited quickly and locked their door, warning their children to stay away from the Ellingtons. Apparently, they were sure Dr. John had brought it home to his family and would bring the virus home again. In truth, Dr. John had not treated any polio patients.

Needing something to do to keep from getting emotional, Ella took care of the sanitizing of the home while Dr. John removed all bedding and gowns in Henrietta's room. Then, he set about sterilizing and sanitizing the entire area.

"You can't be too careful, Ella," he said as he passed by her on his way to the backyard. Ella scrubbed down the kitchen cabinets, stopping only to blow her nose and wipe away her tears. Then, with even more purpose, she scrubbed harder.

*   *   *

Ella placed calls to Jimmy, Ella Sue and Emma Sara, as well as Helen and Liz apprising them of the situation. They were all aghast and asked what they could do. "Send cards and pray," was the only advise she could offer. This was the one time she was happy that her nest was emptied. At least, she didn't have to worry about them for the moment.

Buddy was advised to sanitize the clinic and to stay at a hotel until they knew their home was safe. Dr. John also asked Buddy to stand in for him for a while.

When they'd come home with the news, Shirley was scared. "Will I get it? Will we all get it?" Tears welled in her eyes. She choked back a sob. "Will Henrietta die?"

Dr. John pulled Shirley to his side. "I will be honest with you, Shirley, we don't know if she will live. All I can tell you is this is a wonderful hospital, and the doctors and nurses will give her the best of care. We can only pray."

Ella left the room to contain her own emotions. John could handle this much better than she could.

"Papa, why don't you make her better? We trust you."

"Sweetheart, trust me. The doctors at the Children's Hospital can take far better care of her than I can. Polio is their specialty. They will do everything possible to get Henrietta well."

"But Papa, will we get it, too?"

"We have sanitized everything in this house. I doubt a single germ could survive. Your mother did a fantastic job. We don't know a lot about this disease, but it seems to not affect entire households. Usually just one family member is afflicted but we can't be too careful."

"So, will she be better soon?"

"That would be a miracle, but we can hope. This may be a very long recovery."

"What can I do? Can I go see her?"

"I'm afraid not. Mother and I can go but we have to be careful, and we can only see her through a window or with caps and gowns on to protect us."

Shirley wiped her eye. "But…"

John kissed the top of her head. They sat in silence for a long while.

Chapter Fifty-six

Henrietta was tired the rest of the day and slept through the night. In the morning she felt better, but the nurse told her that her temperature was now 103 degrees.

The nurse brought her a breakfast tray, but her appetite was not enough to eat more than a few bites. She also noticed she couldn't reach the juice at the back of her tray with her left hand. She tried again, but upset the tray and spilled food all over the floor. The clatter alerted the nurses even before Henrietta had time to ring the call bell. She burst into tears.

"Oh, my sweetie," the nurse said. "It's okay. I'll get another tray. Don't you worry about it." She smiled, assuring Henrietta.

"No, I don't want another tray. I'm not hungry."

"Okay, you just relax. I'll bring you a new juice."

Henrietta sniffled. The nurse left to get the juice.

By noon, Henrietta could not move her left arm at all and was having trouble breathing.

The doctor on call came by to see her and said to the nurse, "She needs a respirator." They placed her in an oxygen tent where they monitored her. She continued to deteriorate the next two days.

A nurse urged her to drink but she had difficulty. The doctor checked in frequently. Henrietta wondered if she would survive.

At one point, the doctor sat by her side and explained to her there was more than one kind of polio. "Henrietta, I know your father is a doctor so I'm going to explain some things to you, so you understand what is happening to your body. There is spinal polio, which causes paralysis in the arms and legs. That is the most common type."

Henrietta gave him a solemn look. "That is what I have, isn't it? That's why I can't move my arms and legs."

"Yes, I think so, but there is another type of polio. It's a respiratory polio. Respiratory makes it difficult to breath."

Henrietta didn't have to ask. "I have that, too."

"Don't you worry. We will take good care of you, but you have to try to eat and drink to keep your strength up."

"Will I die here?"

"No, Henrietta, you won't die. We will do everything possible to help you get better." He patted her on the leg and left the room.

As she watched him leave, Henrietta realized she couldn't raise her hand to wipe away the tears that fell from her eyes. She cried even harder.

*   *   *

In the polio unit, an iron lung was brought into the room for Henrietta. It was a monstrous machine, with hoses dangling from it. The nurses assured her she would feel much better once it was set up and breathing for her.

They were right. What a relief to breath. Henrietta was surprised the bed inside the tube was so comfortable.

As the day went on, her legs ached. She told the nurse about it and soon discovered Henrietta had lost the use of both of her legs. She could feel their hands reaching in from the portholes on the side of the iron lung to rub her legs, but she was unable to move them when they asked her to or when the doctor used his rubber mallet to check her reflexes.

Her parents came to visit and spoke to the doctor. Everyone in the room was dressed in hospital garb and masks.

"Hello, Henri, how are you feeling?" Dr. John asked.

"A little better, but my legs won't work," Henrietta whispered.

"I know, Henri, the doctor told me. Be strong."

They couldn't touch her, but they assured her they were there for her and would stay as long as they could. They left at the designated time and blew her a kiss.

"We will be here every day for you," Ella assured her. "I will see you tomorrow. I will pray for you to be better soon."

Henrietta could not leave the iron lung without gasping for air, so any bathroom duties had to be accomplished by bed pan, which was handled through the portals. The only time she was off the machine was for a few seconds when the bed inside the lung needed to be changed.

Most of the work was done through the portals but the final tightening of the sheets to maintain her comfort required opening the machine. They would warn her when they were doing that part and Henrietta would remember what it was like to hold her breath while swimming. She would close her eyes and pretend to be in a deep dive. The iron lung worked her lungs compressing then releasing, so it was doing the work of the lung muscles for her.

Henrietta's head extended outside the lung, so she was able to talk, to be fed and to read. The lung was equipped with a mirror set at an angle so she could look toward the ceiling but read from a book propped open on the device. Turning pages, however, required assistance.

A new doctor came in and explained to her there were different kinds of polio.

Henrietta had been in the hospital for several weeks. Over the shock of having the disease now, she said, "I know, spinal and respiratory. I have both."

"There are *three* kinds of polio. The third is called bulbar polio. Bulbar is the most serious. It impairs a patient's ability to talk and swallow. You have some problems swallowing and we believe you have that polio as well."

Henrietta closed her eyes and pretended she was asleep. She didn't want to see anymore, she didn't want to hear anymore, she just wanted to die. But the *swoosh, swoosh* of the iron lung worked to keep her alive.

After a considerable amount of time lamenting the fate she was dealt and praying death would be painless, she came to the conclusion she could survive. She would survive. She would do everything in her power to walk again.

Her parents were allowed in the room, of course with the necessary caps, gowns, masks and gloves. Her mother stood with unshed tears in her eyes trying to be strong for Henrietta while she was torn apart inside. This was her baby.

Henrietta assured them she would not die. "I'm strong, Mama. I can do this." She had been reading stories of polio survivors that a nurse had given her, and she was determined to be one of them.

"That's my Henrietta," said Dr. John, squeezing Mama's hand.

Mama smiled at Henrietta. "Yes, sweetheart, fight with all your might."

*   *   *

Dr. John spoke quietly with Dr. Webster in the unit. "What can we do? Is there any facility in the country that can help her?"

Dr. Webster shook his head. "I'm sure you know this, but unfortunately, there is no cure for polio. There is nothing more we can do unless the body decides to heal itself. It often does, but it takes time."

"How much time?" Dr. John pressed. "I hear FDR has a place called Warm Springs…I believe it is in Georgia. He treats polio victims there."

"Yes, they have had some success, but I am afraid Henrietta is not a candidate for the facility. It would require she be able to breath and to swallow. It is a great facility aiding paralytic limbs, but Henrietta has more needs. She can only be relieved with the respirator."

"I've heard about Sister Kenny's steam therapy," Dr. John said. "Will you be implementing a treatment like that."

"Let's step out into the hallway, shall we?" Dr. Webster motioned to the door and Dr. John followed him. "Our plan is to implement therapy as soon as Henrietta can be removed from the lung and breath on her own, at least part-time. We cannot rush this. Polio has its own time frame. Some patients recover quickly, some will be in an iron lung for months, even years. Some as you know don't make it. We have great hopes for Henrietta. It has only been two weeks and although we have not seen signs of improvement yet, her attitude is a great factor in getting her well."

"What are Sister Kenny's credentials?"

The doctor pursed his lips together. "More important than her credentials is knowing her treatments are proven to work and quite frankly, we have no other options."

"I see," Dr. John said, glancing into the window to Henrietta's room. Ella was still speaking with their daughter. "Tell me about her treatment process."

"As I'm sure you know Elizabeth Kenny is an Australian bush nurse. Her treatment consists of two parts. First, she administers hot packs. They might be steam-filled wool towels or boiling water into which the wool is dipped, wrung out, and applied to affected areas. In either event, the towels are steaming. Of course, not enough to burn the patient but nevertheless, very hot. When they cool to lukewarm, they are replaced with more hot towels. This continues for about an hour. This treatment is used until the patient regains mobility in the affected limb.

"The second part is exercise therapy. Polio patients experience spasms which tighten the muscles. They then need to be stretched to regain their mobility and strength. This can be a painful process. Some consider it torture but eventually the muscles comply, and the patient will in time regain the use of these limbs. We will keep working with Henrietta. She is strong and I believe she will make a recovery."

John took a deep breath, realizing all that can be done for his daughter is being done. "Thank you for your time, Dr. Webster."

The man nodded, and John went in to get Ella so they could return home. Buddy was handling the patient load currently, but he wanted to check in to make sure there were no severe cases he needed help with. Besides, he needed a distraction. He was a doctor yet he felt helpless to cure his own daughter.

*   *   *

After a few months of being in the iron lung, Henrietta was able to swallow and her speech, although never fully impaired, became stronger and more natural. They attempted to remove her from the lung for short periods of time, but Henrietta was soon gasping for air. She needed to let the lung work for her.

Several more weeks went by. Little by little, she was able to breath on her own. It was time for Sister Kenny's magic.

The treatments were excruciating at first and Henrietta begged the therapist to stop.

That didn't happen. Henrietta was told it was the only way she would be cured, so she endured the pain and sighed a sigh of relief each time it was over.

Soon, she began to regain mobility. It started when she lifted her hand without thinking to scratch an itch on her nose. It had been maddening to not be able to do even that. She still couldn't, but she did raise her hand, didn't she?

She tried again. She moved her fingers. Then, she called out to the nurse.

The nurse came running. They feared something had gone terribly wrong.

"Look, look," Henrietta said. "I can move."

The doctor was summoned immediately. Other nurses came to the bedside as well. All were smiling at Henrietta.

The doctor asked her to move her hand again.

She did. Then her fingers.

He asked her to move fingers on the other hand, but there was no such result. Neither was there any movement in her legs. In any event, they were all elated. This was the first indication Henrietta was on her way to recovery. But it would be a long haul ahead.

Her parents came to see her that afternoon and she showed them her progress.

They were overjoyed.

"Henrietta, Henrietta. We are so happy and so proud of you. It is hard but look. This is the first step," John said.

*   *   *

Over the next two months, Henrietta regained movement in both hands and arms and was soon able to read and write on her own. The days were so much more pleasant now that she could return to some of the activities she loved.

At first, she was a little clumsy but gradually the dexterity improved. The other good news was now she didn't need to rely on the iron lung, and she was in a new room with roommates. She shared a room with three other girls who were in various stages of recovery.

Henrietta made many friends at the hospital. Mary was fifteen and a long-term patient. She had been there for four years. She could also use her hands, but it looked like she would not regain the use of her legs. She was told they were trying to secure a place for her at Warm Springs. There was a long waiting list. Mary's family was wealthy but rarely came to see her. Holidays and her birthday were assured but any other visits were a surprise.

Barbara's parents came to see her when they could, but they had moved to North Dakota where they had a wheat farm. Chores kept them busy, but her mother always managed a month stay at least once a year. Barbara looked forward to her visit. Most of the time, her dad stayed home and took care of the other kids and business. Barb had spent her last two birthdays at the hospital and the nurses tried to make her feel special on her special day. The hardest was Christmas. She was seventeen and her siblings were twelve and ten. The family felt it was important to not disrupt the "little ones" on the holiday. It was just too much to do to bring them all to Milwaukee.

Maggie's parents came to see her often since they lived in town, but their visits were getting more infrequent. She was only ten, so the girls all participated in Maggie's world, making sure she got all of the things she needed. They arranged a celebration for her every time she accomplished one more feat. Maggie was starting to walk with "sticks" and the girls were her cheerleaders. All four girls became fast friends and knew they would be friends forever.

Now that she was in this new ward, Henrietta's family still came every day. Sometimes it was just her mother and sometimes one of her siblings, but she was always sure someone would come.

Her parents were supportive of all her roommates as well. When they brought treats, everyone got treats. When an occasion such as a holiday or birthday arrived, they brought gifts for everyone. They got to know the girls well.

Ella was interested in all of Henrietta's new friends. She had become aware through time that they did not all have frequent visitors.

"Mary, I heard you like dolphins," Ella said.

"I love dolphins. I hope one day I will be able to swim with them."

On the next visit, Ella brought Mary books about sea life and even got her a dolphin brooch.

"Barbara, I understand your family moved to a farm in North Dakota. How do you like farm life?" Ella brought her farm magazines and a picture of a border collie to hang on the wall near her bed.

They played wishing games. Of course, all the girls wished to be well and home with their families.

"What if you were all better, what is your wish for your future?" Ella asked.

Maggie spoke first. "I want to be a ballerina. I always wanted to be a ballerina. I love to dance."

Ella bought a jewelry box with a dancing ballerina on top for Maggie.

Henrietta wanted to read so many stories, and she never lacked for books. She liked the Nancy Drew mysteries and read every book she could get her hands on. Then, she passed them on to her roommates. Ella kept her well supplied with books that they all enjoyed.

*   *   *

One day when the doctor came by Henrietta was very frustrated. She had made many attempts at walking, but her legs were like rubber and didn't hold her up. She complained to Dr. Webster. She had seen others progress faster than she could, and no one wanted to walk more than she did.

"Why can't I walk?" she asked.

The doctor gently explained. "All cases are not the same, Henrietta. Some are more severe than others. When you have polio, the virus destroys the nerve center, the muscles controlled by the nerve center are paralyzed forever. Sometimes the damage is not total, and the paralysis is temporary. The muscles are weakened but it is possible to regain strength in those muscles again. It takes time and a lot of hard work."

"Is my damage total?"

He shook his head. "I don't think so. I can't tell you how much strength will return to your limbs, but I believe you will walk again some-day. The question is, do you believe you will walk?"

She grinned. "I do. You'll see. I will."

"Good, back to work." He winked at her. "Here comes your therapist now."

Henrietta didn't mind the hot packs as much now. She didn't know if they were not as hot or if she was just getting used to it. The therapy had gotten easier, too. Although with every bit of progress, they increased the intensity. But if she could walk, it was worth it.

*   *   *

One day about a month later, Henrietta was helped up from her bed and noticed she could move her toes. She wanted to jump up for joy. "Look, I can wiggle my toes!" she said to her friends.

The nurse and the girls all celebrated the moment with her. It was only a moment but a wonderful moment. At least now she could sit in a wheelchair and wiggle her toes.

Gradually, she got movement back in her right leg and soon after the left leg responded. She was still far from walking, but she was thrilled the damage was not permanent.

Henrietta got measured for "sticks." She would soon try to walk.

She managed to get up from her wheelchair but couldn't move more than a step or two forward. At least, she was now able to go to the bath-room with assistance.

The doctor had discussed the possibility of leg braces but felt the muscles would strengthen faster without the dependency of braces. They could always consider other options later if needed.

When her parents heard the news, they stopped by that afternoon to speak with Dr. Webster.

"The sticks or polio crutches are used in place of standard crutches because of the underarm pressure," Dr. Webster explained. "The sticks have bands that secure around the upper arm and have a handle to hold. They have a pole like leg. Often, they are used in combination with leg braces."

"I am familiar," Dr. John stated. "This is good progress. Will she need to continue with the hot compresses?"

"For a while yet until she regains the strength in her legs to be mobile. Then, she will be able to go home."

"Thank God for Sister Kenny," Dr. John said. "What order is she from? I would like to make a donation."

Dr. Webster smiled. "Oh, Sister Kenny isn't a nun. Sister is a military term in Australia. It is like a lieutenant in our armed forces. She was a nurse and was commissioned sister during World War I."

"I just assumed she was a Catholic Sister."

"Many do, but if you want to help, donate to the March of Dimes. FDR's struggle with polio led to the creation of the National Foundation for Infantile Paralysis. As I'm sure you know, that was the original name for poliomyelitis, which we've shortened to polio. The foundation is now the March of Dimes. They champion the fight against polio, aiding in vaccine research. If we can eradicate this horrific disease, you can thank that organization. They need all the help they can get."

"Thanks. I will look into it," Dr. John said with a smile.

"Of course, as you know, many of your expenses for Henrietta's long stay have been taken care of by the March of Dimes' funds. You are fortunate to have some financial advantages, but polio has no economic parameters. Many of our patients have no means to pay the medical costs incurred by this disease."

"Thank God for the March of Dimes," Ella said.

*   *   *

It was one year and four days from the time Henrietta was admitted to the hospital until she was released. Finally, she was not quarantined and her friends could visit. With her father at her side making sure she didn't fall, she climbed the three steps into the house on Astor Street.

John and Ella had set up a bed for her in the parlor. It was too early for her to climb the staircase to her old bedroom, but it was great to have her home again.

Home was quiet. Almost too quiet. There were no more swooshing sounds from the iron lungs, no more clattering of bed pans and other equipment as the nurses scurried about doing their daily chores. No more clamoring roommates or therapists coming with their torture sessions. Henrietta still had a long recovery, but now Ella, John, and her siblings could be there to support her and help where they could. She was home but far from recovered.

Chapter Fifty-seven

E lla was looking forward to school starting in a month. Henrietta had been able to keep up with her classes with the assistance of a tutor. She had missed a year but working into the summer had caught her up. She still had to have therapy and she tired easily. Ella tended to her needs, getting her to her therapy and doctor appointments, fixing her meals, making sure she was comfortable and on track to health.

The tutor John hired had continued with Henrietta for the first year she was home. Some of her old friends from school visited her and she kept in touch with her three hospital friends.

Ella Sue and Emma Sara had moved to Minnesota with their husbands after their marriage and started families of their own. Women were still not allowed to teach after marriage and both girls accepted that readily. Ella hated that they were so far away. They kept in touch via mail and an occasional telephone call, mostly to check on Henrietta's progress. Ella missed them terribly and longed for the times she could hold her grandchildren.

Jimmy was away at law school and Buddy was busy working with Dr. John at the clinic.

Shirley was another issue entirely. Before Henrietta's illness, she and Shirley had spent a lot of time together. Now Shirley had little time for Henrietta and when she did, it was bitter.

Ella realized that Shirley had been the baby long before Henrietta came along, but that was years ago. Shirley hadn't minded sharing time with a baby, but did she mind all the time and attention Henrietta had required when polio hit?

Ella wondered if this was a rebellious teen thing or something more serious. It was getting frustrating for her. Whenever Shirley was asked to do things for her sister either by getting something for her or by staying with her while Ella did the shopping, Shirley grudgingly complied, sometimes with a deep sigh or an eye roll. Or even by saying, "Fine, it is all about Henrietta." Then she would feel bad about her actions and spend time alone in her room or try to compensate by doing something nice for her sister. It was all very confusing for Ella.

It was September of 1950 and John and Ella decided Henrietta needed some entertainment. They purchased their first Zenith television set. It had a sixteen-inch black and white screen. *Howdy Doody* was the first show on after the set was delivered. It was placed in the parlor where Henrietta would have the prime viewing spot, but the chairs were arranged so the whole family could enjoy the entertainment.

The family watched *Milton Berle Comedy Hour* and *The Imogene Coca Show*. There wasn't a lot to see and sometimes the reception was bad. Sometimes, it was like watching through a snowstorm, but it was a novelty and occupied time.

Even so, Henrietta preferred her books. The books she had acquired at the hospital had to remain there but Ella's trips to the library would always produce a book or two each week that she enjoyed.

*   *   *

One day, as Shirley was in her room pouting, Ella came in and asked her if she could help fold the laundry.

Shirley burst into tears.

Ella rushed to her side. "Sweetie, what is the matter?"

"Nothing."

"Obviously something is. Tell me about it." Ella sat on the bed next to Shirley and cradled her in her arms. She wiped Shirley's tears.

Shirley sobbed. Shirley was one of the all-time hard sobbers. Not able to talk and sobbing long after the tears stopped. Ella was aware and waited a while for her daughter to get down to a sniffle.

Finally, Shirley was able to get out some of her thoughts. "Henri… Henri…etta is sick." Sniffle. Sniffle. Sniffle.

"Yes, sweetie we know. She is very sick, and we are all trying to make her better. Don't you worry, she will get better."

"I know she will, but I want her to be better now. Because…"

"Because what?" Ella prodded.

"Then you and Daddy won't forget my school play."

Ella gulped. "Shirley, we won't forget. It is this Friday, right?" She tried to process all that was going on. She ran through the calendar in her mind, John's schedule, her own appointments, and of course Henrietta's many appointments for therapy.

"It was last Friday," Shirley whispered. She hung her head and shut her eyes. "Nobody came."

"Oh honey, last Friday? I am so sorry."

"It's all right."

"No, it is not. Why didn't you remind me?" Ella asked.

"Henrietta had a bad day."

Ella recounted the events of last Friday. Yes, Henrietta had therapy. She had a small cold and developed some respiratory problems. John came home. Then there was the fuss with Helen, and oh my… They did forget Shirley's play!

"Oh Shirley, I am so so sorry. I don't know how but I will make it up to you."

"It's okay. Henrietta is your child and she needed you."

Ella looked aghast. "Oh no, Shirley. No, no, no, no, no! You are my child, too, and you are all important to me."

"But she was born to you. She is more important."

"Shirley, Shirley." Ella took her by the shoulders and looked into her eyes. "Don't you ever think that. Yes, Henrietta was born from my body, but you were born in my heart. We *chose* you to be ours. Don't ever think you are less important."

Shirley looked down, still sniffing.

"I am so sorry, Shirley. I love you with all my heart."

Shirley looked away for a minute. Then turned toward Ella and threw her arms around her neck. "I love you, Mama."

Shirley was never forgotten again. She enjoyed sitting in the parlor and watching television with Helen and Henrietta, too.

Henrietta was determined to graduate with her class. Ella and John were so proud of her. And so was Shirley, comforted by the thought that she was the chosen one.

Chapter Fifty-eight

In June 1950, North Korea invaded South Korea and the news set Ella on edge. Not another bloody war. They still had had no word on Thaddeus. He had been missing in action for ten years. Hopes of ever recovering him were small and hopes of him returning alive were even smaller.

Now, they were not just dealing with the Korean war, but a cold war was brewing. President Truman received the NCS-68 report outlining the U.S. policy with regard to the Soviet Union. The result was an aggressive military expansion and ramping up of the nuclear weaponry. A policy was enacted for containment of communist nations.

*   *   *

In 1950, now twenty-five, Helen had her own apartment in Milwaukee. She was a teacher at Edison Elementary School. When she wasn't at school, she was busy marking papers or planning the curriculum projects. She was a very dedicated teacher, but she had one other passion that took up any spare time she had. His name was Joey Carlson.

Joey was a handsome lad from across town. For everyone who knew Helen, Joey was an enigma. He was nothing like her. Helen was the dedicated, sensible teacher devoted to her students. She attended church services every Sunday.

Joey wore a leather jacket, drove a Harley Davidson motorcycle, and worked at the Harley factory. He didn't seem to have a care in the world.

He didn't have a lot of money, either, and what he did have, he spent freely. He loved kids from a distance. He was quite the charmer, and his friends would say he could charm a snake if it didn't bite him. Joey was twenty-three, two years Helen's junior but age didn't seem to bother either of them.

Joey would swing by Helen's apartment and coax her onto his bike, and they would ride off like the wind with her long hair whipping in the breeze. It was a whirlwind courtship.

It was the fall of 1950, and a brisk but beautiful day. "Hey doll, let's go for a ride." Joey seemed more serious than usual.

It was a Saturday and Helen had been grading papers. She hadn't planned on going anywhere and looked down at her attire. She had on a pair of baggy slacks and an old sweater.

She said, "Hold on a minute." She went in her bedroom to get a jacket. It was warm but she knew it was much colder riding on the motorcycle.

She hopped on and he swung around. They were on their way to God only knows where. It was like that with Joey; he never made plans. Where they were going was wherever the bike took them. That was okay with Helen. They rode for hours with her arms snug around his waist.

It was dusk when Joey finally pulled into a secluded grassy area off road. "We need to talk."

This didn't sound good. Helen slid off the bike. "What's wrong?"

Joey reached into his pocket and pulled out a sheet of folded paper. "Got my notice today."

Helen took the paper and snapped it open. She read:

Joseph J. Carlson, report for duty on or before September 15. You are number 253 on the draft and your number has been called. Upon reporting to your local unit at the National Guard Armory, 6592 76th Street, Milwaukee, Wisconsin, you will be given a physical and your assignment. You will have 48 hours there before going to Fort Leonard Wood in Missouri to begin your boot camp training. Failure to report can result in incarceration.

Helen dropped to the ground. Joey sat down beside her. "Joey, tomorrow is September fifteenth. You need to report tomorrow."

He picked up a stone and threw it as far as he could from his sitting position. "Damn, I don't want to go to the army and I sure as hell don't want to go to Korea. They don't even call it a war. It's a conflict. Shit, it's a war. People are getting killed over there. For what?"

"I know it doesn't seem fair. None of us wants another war. But you *have* to go. It is your duty. I'll be here when you get home. I'll write you every day."

Joey reached around her waist and kissed her passionately. He put his hand behind her head as he dropped her to the ground, covering her body with his. He kissed her neck and her eyes, and his hands began to hungrily grope her body.

"Joey, we can't..." Helen protested.

Joey wasn't listening as he reached for the zipper on her trousers.

She grabbed his hand. "I have no protection. Do you?" she gasped, wanting to continue as much as he did.

"I don't care," he whispered. He covered her mouth with his to stifle any more protests.

They lay on the grass drinking in the intoxicating wine of kisses and savoring the heat of the moment, the tingling of their touches, the passion of their bodies speaking without words. Every sense known to mankind surged through their bodies and they were one.

She opened her body and her soul to him, and he entered with hunger and urgency. And then it happened all over again, but this time she was taking in all of the senses. The fresh grass around them, the spicy aftershave he wore, her lavender perfume mingled with the sweat from their bodies. The taste of the salt gathered on his chest and on her breasts. The sounds of birds in the trees and the soft breeze rustling the first fall leaves. They gazed into each other's eyes and the world was theirs alone.

She ran her fingers through his thick brown hair. He gently kissed her ears and eyes, her throat and lips. Neither wanted to have this time end. If only they could stay in this moment forever.

Forever was cut short. Reality required Helen to get back to her papers and her classroom. Joey had to report to the recruitment center in the morning.

His day was full and at the end, he was handed his marching papers. He'd be on a plane to Fort Leonard Wood the next morning. After school, Joey met Helen at her apartment. They began their evening just as they had left off the day before. They spent most of the night together.

Joey made a quick trip home to pick up some last-minute things for his duffle bag. Helen went with him to the airport, and they said their good-byes. She was sure Joey was her one true love and she knew in her heart he felt the same.

Or did he? He'd never said.

It didn't look like he would be home for Christmas, but Joey would be for Thanksgiving. The family would all be together. It could be a wonderful time for an engagement party.

Joey climbed the steps to the plane and blew a kiss to Helen.

Helen left the tarmac with a smile on her face but a heavy heart. It was only ten weeks, but it might have been a lifetime.

*   *   *

In the barracks, Joey reported for duty and then stowed his gear. He put a pin-up of Marilyn Monroe on his locker door. He kissed Helen's picture and hung it below. And then, he kissed two more pictures and hung them beside Helen's.

A soldier passing by did a wolf whistle. "Are you in the barracks or did you die and go to heaven?"

Joey laughed. "Two naughty bitches to fill the lonely nights and one to take home to Mama."

"So, which one's the cherry?"

"Okay, okay, three naughty bitches. Ate the cherry this weekend."

They both guffawed as his new buddy slapped Joey on the back.

*   *   *

Helen was true to her word and wrote to Joey every night before she went to sleep. Their letters were steamy.

Joey wrote every day for a week but then started making excuses.

They really work you out here. Up at four a.m. and hard exercise all day. Long hikes and obstacle courses. Dropping dead by night.

I miss you.

Joey

The letters were shorter and fewer as time went on.

Helen tried to keep the intimacy going but without the reciprocation, she felt cheap. She told Joey how much she loved him and missed him, but later her letters turned to more serious matters.

First, she tried to be cute and flirtatious.

Hey Joey,

When you come home, why don't we be naughty and elope?

Helen

Joey's response was:

Uh, uh Babe. You can be naughty but no eloping. What would your mother say?

Dear Joey,

That's the idea of eloping, Joey, we don't tell her.

Joey did not respond.
Helen wrote again.

Wouldn't you love to see a cute little Joey running around?

Joey's response:

I'd rather chase you around, girl. Don't think the world is ready for two Joeys.

Helen was trying to break the news to Joey gently and slowly. At first, she wasn't sure, but it was now eight weeks, and it was official. Helen was pregnant. Should she tell him, or should she wait until he got home?

She decided to tell him. He would be home in two weeks, and they could get married. Yes, she had to tell him now. She wrote him.

Dear Joey,

You know how much I love you. I want to spend the rest of my life with you. I have news I hope will make you as excited as I am. The world is ready for two Joeys. Come summer, there will be another Joey or maybe a Jolene. Joey, I am pregnant with your baby. I hope it is a boy and I hope he looks just like you. I know you will make a wonderful father.

I think we should get married when you come home at Thanksgiving. It will be too late if we wait. We don't want our son to grow up without a father. We have to do the right thing for him (or her). Just let me know and I will make an appointment with the pastor or if you want, we can go before the Justice of the Peace. You will have to get a blood test and we will have to get a license so that will have to be the day before Thanksgiving.

It will be simple, just the two of us and then a Thanksgiving celebration with our families. I will invite your mom and sister. It will be so nice. We will have lots to be thankful for. And you won't ever forget our anniversary. How can you forget Thanksgiving?

Joey, I love you so much. I can't wait for you to get home.

All my love,

Helen

Helen ran to the mailbox every day, hoping for a letter from Joey. Then, a few days before Thanksgiving a letter arrived. Helen tore it open immediately. There was none of Joey's playful flirting in his response.

Dear Helen,

I won't be coming home for Thanksgiving. Some of my new buddies are planning to go to Vegas for a last wing-ding before we are sent to war.

I know a guy in Milwaukee who can take care of things. We will have to work quick because if this baby is mine it must be getting close to three months. Are you sure it is mine? You're a good-looking dame and there are a lot of lonely men in Milwaukee.

I'll send you the guy's name. I think he wants $300.00, but don't you worry about that. I'll take care of the money part. Let me know when he needs the money and I'll wire it to you.

Take care of yourself.

Joey

Inside the letter was a note with the name and phone number of "the guy." Helen was aghast. This was not the reply she'd expected. She ran to her bedroom, threw herself onto the bed, and cried until she could cry no longer.

What can I do? I can't give up this baby. I will have to quit my job. Where will I live? This will be humiliating. What will my friends say? What will Mother say? What kind of life will my baby have?

Joey wrote another anxious letter to Helen asking if the job was done. Asking if she needed the money. Finally, Helen sent one short letter back to him.

Joey,

GO TO HELL!

Helen

Chapter Fifty-nine

Thanksgiving came. Ella had prepared a spectacular traditional meal. All the children and spouses were in attendance and they were making plans to get together again for Christmas. Ella was concerned about her daughter. Helen had picked at her meal and seemed to have something on her mind.

Ella served a dessert choice of pumpkin or apple pie, and everyone commented on how delicious the pies looked, but did they have any room left to eat dessert?

Ella suggested they clean up first and have pie in an hour. So, the women cleared the table while the men gathered in the parlor to watch television.

John got out a bottle of bourbon and poured shots all around. The fellas lit up cigars and pipes and discussed the politics of the day. The election had been held earlier in the month and there was much excitement about Ike taking on the presidency. Although the election was completed, the presidential debate continued in the Ellington parlor.

Those who had been in favor of Adlai Stevenson as president were afraid Eisenhower's military background would undermine the social programs established during the Roosevelt presidency. Truman had backed those and was a strong supporter of allies, and through the Truman Doctrine, supported all nations in the war against communism.

The Eisenhower supporters liked the idea of a five-star general in charge. Eisenhower, for the most part, supported the Truman agenda with regard to defending foreign nations against the communist Soviet Union. He also expanded some of the Roosevelt social programs such as Social Security. They differed in that Truman's support for the defeat of communism was primarily financial, the Eisenhower Doctrine was to provide both military and economic support. The Ellington family was divided. Hadn't there been enough war?

The argument was moot since the election was over. The conversation turned to the Korean conflict. Helen's stomach tightened.

Since World War I, the U.S. had occupied South Korea while the U.S.S.R. had occupied the North. Communist China fueled the flames, and the South came under attack in 1950. Military intervention brought on the Korean war, although formal declaration of war was never enacted. The cold war was the underlying reason for the Korean conflict. A fear of communism was rampant in the country fueled by Republican Senator Joseph McCarthy from Wisconsin, who waged a campaign against communism by accusations made against citizens with little or no substantive proof. His targets were politicians, entertainers, and educators. Many were charged and jailed only to later have their convictions overturned. This became a real issue in 1950. It became another issue on the presidential campaign trail. McCarthyism had to be stopped.

When the dishes were put away, carts of pie were brought to the parlor. Apple pie with ice cream and pumpkin loaded with fresh whipped cream. Everyone was still full, but it was Thanksgiving after all, and everyone took a slice. Everyone except Helen.

Scattered about the room, some of the fellas found a place on the floor. Ella suggested they take turns stating what they were thankful for.

Dr. John started. "I am thankful we have been able to get control of polio. It is still a threat, but I believe a vaccine is on the horizon."

Henrietta, who was for the most part back to normal except for a limp and some shortness of breath, said she was thankful to be better and back in school.

Twenty-year-old Shirley had recently become engaged. She snuggled into her fiancé on the love seat, waved her hand and said she was thankful for her husband-to-be. He squeezed her tight and returned the proclamation.

Jimmy and Buddy, with no one on their arms tonight, were thankful for their successful careers and promising futures.

Ella Sue and Emma Sara, visiting from Minneapolis where they were raising children of their own, each expressed joy over their families and homes. Their husbands did the same. They each hugged their children. A boy for Emma Sara and a girl for Ella Sue.

Liz hesitated and then said, "I am thankful for everyone in this room."

Ella agreed, but then added she was thankful the war was over. John reminded her that although Korea was not officially a war, for all practical purposes it was, and it was escalating.

"And I pray it will be over soon as well," Ella said.

"What about you, Helen? You seem awfully quiet," Buddy inquired.

"Well…" She hesitated, not sure what kind of reaction she would get. "I'm pregnant," she blurted out and burst into tears.

Ella was stunned for a moment. She had thought something was off with Helen.

No one said anything.

Shirley was closest and she reached out to hug her sister. She wiped her tears and looked into her eyes. "That is wonderful, Helen."

"No, it's not. Joey wants nothing to do with me or the baby. I am going to lose my job. I have no idea how I will support him." Helen sobbed. She reached for a tissue and blew her nose.

"Joey?" Ella Sue and Emma Sara said at the same time.

Jimmy and Buddy were speechless.

"The biker guy?" Ella asked, finding her voice. "He's the father?"

"Mhmm," Helen nodded her head and looked down at the floor.

Jimmy went straight to the legal ramifications. "He can't just ignore the fact he has a child. At least we can charge him medical fees."

"He wants me to get rid of the child," Helen said.

"You aren't considering it, are you?" Jimmy asked. "It is illegal, you know."

"No, no. I won't have an abortion. But I haven't figured out how to support the baby…or myself."

"Have you considered adoption?" Buddy weighed in.

Liz crossed the room and sat on Helen's other side. "We can do this together. We can figure it out. Do you want the baby?"

Helen looked at her, surprised. "Yes of course. It's my baby."

Liz nodded. "Then, you shall have your baby."

"We have plenty of extra room here. You can move back home," Ella suggested.

"I can babysit," Henrietta added.

"Just look in the kitchen. We have plenty of food," John said.

"See," said Shirley. "That's what family is about."

Helen smiled, her eyes brimming with tears. "And I am so so so grateful."

They took turns hugging Helen and offering their support. It was a good Thanksgiving after all.

*   *   *

It was June 1, 1951, and Helen had been sitting quietly, knitting, when she began to feel pains in her abdomen. Gas, she thought. It had been a problem in recent weeks. She gave it little thought. She put down her knitting and took a stroll around the room, stopping to peek out the window.

There it was again. A pulsing pain. This one was sharper.

"Ohhh," Helen breathed and looked down at the puddle between her legs.

It was early afternoon. *What should I do?*

"Mother, Mother!"

*   *   *

Ella came running.

Helen had a helpless look on her face and Ella knew immediately what had to be done. First, she had to turn off the oven. Everyone would have to fend for themselves for dinner tonight.

Helen's hospital bag had been packed for a few days. "I'll get your bag," Ella said. "You go get cleaned up in the bathroom. I'll find a clean dress for you."

Next, Ella called the doctor's office. Within minutes John, Buddy, and Liz were all aware of the situation. Ella grabbed the mop to clean up the floor. In fresh clothes, Helen got another pain.

"Time those," Ella instructed. "We have plenty of time."

In a half hour, it went from ten minutes to five minutes apart. Helen had three pains in fifteen minutes.

"I'll get the automobile." Ella brought it to the door and Helen got in. By the time they reached the hospital, the pain was almost constant.

On the first of June 1951 at 6:22 p.m., Melissa Jane Ellington came screaming into the world. She was a healthy seven-pound, eight-ounce girl with lots of her father's chestnut brown hair. Her mother had been put to sleep and was still very groggy.

The nurses cleaned the baby, wrapped her, and presented her to the family who had all gathered in the waiting area. It was clear everyone was proud and happy.

"What a beautiful little girl," Ella said. "Where is Helen? Can we see her?" Ella wanted to see the joy on the new mother's face.

"She is still a little groggy. We will get her ready and you can meet her in the recovery room. The aide will show you the way." The nurse retreated into the delivery room as the aide led them down the hall to another room where the family chattered and anxiously awaited Helen.

*   *   *

After about thirty minutes, Helen still had not been seen. John felt this was a bit unusual, so he went to find out what was keeping her. Maybe they were put in the wrong room.

A nurse met him in the hall. "Dr. Ellington, we have run into some complications with your daughter."

"What complications?" Dr. John asked. The baby delivery was a standard procedure.

"Just come to the delivery room. The doctor will talk to you."

John followed at a rapid pace down toward the elevator and to the delivery room.

"Wait here," the woman said.

John was left in the waiting area outside the OR. He wanted to go in and scrub, but he knew it was not a good idea for someone emotionally attached to interfere.

Soon, the doctor came out from the delivery room. He stripped the mask from his face.

John noticed blood on his scrubs but was not immediately alarmed. Sometimes, birthing could get messy.

"Please sit," the doctor instructed.

John sat. "What is it?"

"I'm sorry, we were not able to save her."

"What? We just saw the baby. She is perfectly fine."

"No, no. The baby is fine. It's your daughter," the doctor clarified.

"What happened? What do you mean, you were not able to save her?"

The doctor sighed. "Unfortunately, Helen started hemorrhaging shortly after the birth. It appears uterine atony is the cause. She started hemorrhaging while she was still under anesthetic. It seems the normal muscular contraction did not take place. Coagulation did not occur, and we were not able to stop the hemorrhaging. It doesn't happen often, but it is a common cause. I am so sorry."

Dr. John pinched his eyes shut to hold back the tears. He picked up a magazine from the table and slammed it onto the table. "Damn, damn, damn."

He glanced at the doctor. "May I see her?"

"Certainly."

Dr. John walked silently into the delivery room. On the table, he saw his first-born child. The love of his life. Still, pale. Her body covered with a sheet but her face visible.

He sobbed and sobbed and sobbed.

He heard Helen's doctor walk silently from the room, giving John time alone with his daughter. How would he explain this to Ella?

Chapter Sixty

Ella mourned Helen's death deeply. It had been a lovely service at the church but a hard one. Helen was so young. She had so much to live for. Why was her life cut so short?

"Helen, Helen. My first born. My blessed baby. My life. Be assured your daughter will be safe in our hands. She is a beautiful baby," Ella whispered as she stood next to her daughter's casket, tears streaming down her face.

Ella insisted baby Melissa would be raised by them. It was strange having a baby in the house at first. All the children had grown up. Shirley and Henrietta were still at home. Shirley worked at the library and when she wasn't there, she was with her fiancé. They were busy planning a fall wedding.

Henrietta adored Melissa and wanted to spend all her time pampering her. She was far too old for dolls, but this was like having a live doll. Melissa loved all the attention Henrietta provided.

Henrietta had progressed well and was attending high school. She was a normal sixteen-year-old, but she still had some respiratory restrictions. Because of these limitations, choosing a career was difficult. She was not given encouragement by her therapist as far as holding down any job requiring normal hours. She had considered nursing or teaching but rejected both of those. She finally decided to go to a community college for two years after high school during which time she could decide.

John had encouraged Henrietta to be assertive, but Ella wanted to protect her daughter and hovered over her like a mother hen. Now with a baby in the house, life was very different.

Without Helen being there, Melissa had to be fed formula. There was the constant washing of diapers and changing of clothes. Melissa was a good baby, but she suffered from acid reflux issues. Night cries at two a.m. were a real chore.

"I sure didn't plan on being a mother and grandmother all at the same time," Ella said one night. God made mother's young for a reason." At fifty-two, Ella struggled to keep up. She really appreciated Henrietta's help. Despite all of the adjustments, Melissa was growing up to be a healthy, normal and energetic child.

Chapter Sixty-one

Liz had graduated from Harvard Medical School and was offered a prestigious position at Marshfield Clinic located in the middle of Wisconsin.

The hospital was founded in 1916 by six prominent physicians in the area. Patient care, research, and education were their primary focus, and this common focus had stood the test of time. They hosted scientific meetings for many doctors who came to learn cutting edge techniques. This shaped the Clinic's character for decades and they were renowned for their forward thinking and expertise. In 1924, they joined in partnership with the University of Wisconsin's first medical preceptor program. It was truly an honor to be a member of their staff. In 1951, upon her graduation with high honors, Liz was one of the first female physicians to be added to their program

John offered his sincere congratulations. Ella beamed with pride at her sister who had overcome overwhelming adversities. All her nieces and nephews echoed their congratulations.

Dr. John had hoped Liz would become a part of their clinic but now he had to think about adding another physician on staff. Buddy was a great doctor and Dr. John felt blessed to have him on staff, but he realized he would need to add at least one more doctor. After all, at fifty-five, he knew he had maybe a decade of service to contribute, and the clinic was growing.

*   *   *

Buddy was thoroughly captivated by one Rachel Forrester, the nurse who had replaced Liz five years earlier. Rachel was quite efficient at her job but a bit on the shy side. She was the daughter of Emil and Carol Forrester. Carol had always been the traditional submissive housewife and taught her daughter to "know her place." Rachel did not buy into the idea yet tended to be shy among those in authority. Particularly men. She was wonderful with patients and reliable to a fault, willing to forgo any personal indulgences to care for others.

At first, Buddy recognized her as a cute girl-next-door type. She was very capable and personable but whenever he stood too close, she would move away. When he boldly asked her if she had plans for the weekend, she invariably had some noble cause she must attend to.

For some time, he thought perhaps she was spoken for or that she found him unsuitable. However, as time went on, she let down her guard and they even shared moments of light humor.

One unusually quiet afternoon in 1951, he took advantage of the situation.

He sighed. "I need a cup of coffee. Nurse Rachel...care to join me for a cup in the kitchen?"

"Well, I need to..."

"It can wait," Buddy countered. "Come relax for a few minutes."

"Well, I guess..."

"You aren't going to make me drink my coffee alone, are you?" he asked.

Rachel almost laughed. "Well, I guess I can take a little time."

"I assure you; you won't be fired. You're a hard worker. You deserve a break."

They talked about their families. Buddy told her about all the siblings and how they had become one loving family.

Rachel told him of her family's struggles during the Great Depression. Her father had been a milkman. Dairy farmers in the countryside had been hit hard by the Great Depression. Milk prices fell so low that the milk distributors were paying farmers less for their milk than it cost them to produce it. He relied on farmers for his income, but they couldn't pay so he found himself out of work. There were no jobs to be found. They soon lost their home and everything they had. Had it not been for her father's brother taking them in, they would have ended up in the poorhouse. Her father eventually found work, but they never fully recovered. Still, they had hopes for the future.

Their ten-minute break turned into a half hour and a bit beyond until they were summoned by Gloria to tend to a walk-in patient.

After work that evening, Buddy asked Rachel to go to a movie.

She smiled and accepted graciously. From that time, there was no hesitation or awkwardness in their relationship. Buddy was in love and so was she.

Their relationship grew over the next year. In winter of 1952, they became engaged. Rachel was not able to attend the Ellington Christmas because her mother had recently passed away.

In late summer of 1953, Buddy took Rachel to a picnic in the park. "We've been engaged for several months; what do you say we get married?" he asked.

"When? How? My mother passed away and my family has no means to put on a wedding. I saved a little but not a wedding grand enough for your family."

"Okay, next Saturday. Let's elope."

"What? Buddy, we can't."

"Why can't we? You love me, I love you. I can buy a ring; we can get a license. What else do we need?"

"But Buddy, what about Mama Ella. Won't she be crushed?"

"Mama Ella has her hands full with a toddler. She has enough on her mind. Yes, she may be a bit disappointed but I'm sure she will be happy. She likes you...a lot."

"I like her, too, and I don't want to hurt her. She revels in the things her children do."

"Rachel, it makes sense. When we get back, we can celebrate with her quietly. You'll see."

"Oh, Buddy." She threw her arms around him and showered him with kisses.

He chuckled. "Save a few for later. We have plans to make."

That evening, they decided to get blood tests and a license right away. They would take a week off from work. They would be married by a Justice of the Peace and honeymoon in Niagara Falls. It was Labor Day weekend so they would only be gone for four days.

"But Buddy, if we both take off from work, won't your parents figure out what we are up to?"

"Hmmm, that is a dilemma." They mulled around several excuses, none of which worked. Finally, Buddy had a solution.

"I can take time whenever I'd like so I'll move some appointments around and ask Dr. John to handle things I can't change. I'll tell him I'm visiting a friend. There is a new doctor starting this week. He can handle any walk-ins."

"Well, that's fine, but what about me?" she asked.

Buddy scratched his chin. "Wait 'til Friday and tell Dr. John you need to be with your father who is gravely ill."

"But Buddy, I can't lie to Dr. John. I have *never* lied to him."

Buddy shrugged. "Well, then I guess you'll have to tell him you are eloping."

Friday rolled around. All systems were a go. Rachel went into Dr. John's office and shut the door. "Can I talk to you for a minute?"

"Of course, Rachel, sit down. You look a little nervous."

"Well Dr. John, I am." She twisted her handkerchief and cleared her throat. "I need to take off this coming week. Something has come up."

"Tell me, my dear, how can I help?" Dr. John asked, giving her a sincere look.

"Will you promise not to tell anyone?"

"Doctors are pretty good with confidentiality. Of course. What is it?"

Rachel smiled. "Buddy and I are eloping."

"Wait'll I tell…"

"Dr. John, you promised," she chided him.

"Yes, my dear, your secret is safe, but you know Ella will be very disappointed…in the wedding arrangements, not the marriage. She will be thrilled to have you as her daughter-in-law."

"I know, but it feels like the right thing to do with a new baby in your house and the passing of my mother. It makes sense financially, too."

"Make it what you want. I am sure Buddy can afford a wedding and of course Ella and I would help."

"You are so thoughtful, but Buddy and I considered all the options. This is what we both want. We don't need all the frills and attention. We just want to be married."

"Well then, you have my blessing, and I am sure I will have Ella's wrath when she finds out I knew." He chuckled. "You kids go and be happy."

"Thank you, Dr. John," Rachel said, smiling.

She rose to leave, and Dr. John stood with her. He gave her a hug and a kiss on the cheek. "Welcome to our family."

Chapter Sixty-two

Melissa was a happy and inquisitive toddler. She reminded Ella so much of Helen. Even though there were no young boys in the household to emulate, Melissa was becoming quite the tomboy just like her mother. She played with other neighborhood children, but preferred playing with the boys.

At four, Melissa announced she was going to be a cowboy when she grew up. Ella laughed. "No sweetie, you will have to be a cowgirl."

"Nope, gonna be a cowboy like Roy Rogers." She loved *The Roy Rogers Show* on television.

"How about if you be Dale Evans?" Ella encouraged.

"Nope, Roy Rogers."

Soon Roy Rogers was no longer on air, so Melissa found a new hero in the Cisco Kid and the Lone Ranger. Ella was a little worried this cowboy era wouldn't come to an end for Melissa. She never played with dolls, but she was thrilled to strap on her holster and play cowboys with the neighborhood boys.

But the cowboy era did end. Still, Melissa continued to enjoy time with the boys. Softball, climbing trees, or swimming. She became adept at all sports. She liked volleyball but couldn't understand why the rules were different for boys and girls.

Melissa was especially fond of Aunt Liz who encouraged her sense of adventure. Liz came as often as she could. She told stories of her own childhood when she'd played games with her brother Thaddeus and wasn't afraid of worms and bugs. Neither was Melissa.

Liz told Ella, "I think we have another budding doctor in the house." Melissa loved catching frogs or butterflies and showing them off to Aunt Liz. She hated to see Liz return to Marshfield. Whenever Liz had some time off, she loved to spend it with Melissa.

*   *   *

As Melissa grew, she became aware of the injustices in the world. She often wondered what life would be like if her mother had lived. The mother she only knew through pictures and the occasional stories the family shared. She sometimes wondered about her father but decided that he meant nothing to her since he had long before made the decision that she meant nothing to him.

Melissa sometimes saw children being picked on by bullies and she always came to the defense of the underdog. Even resorting to physically knocking sense into the heads of some bullies. Sometimes, the person she defended would ask, "Aren't you afraid?"

"Naw, they are all cowards," Melissa replied. "Otherwise, they would pick on someone their own size."

She heard broadcasts about Dr. Martin Luther King and decided he was a brave man. She couldn't understand why any human being would hate another simply because of the color of their skin. Dogs and cats come in many colors and sizes, but we don't pick on them because they are black or white or spotted or whatever.

She learned in history about wars. Lots of wars and lots of people died in wars. She decided all wars were bad. *Whoever heard of a good war? Well, maybe we have to beat up the bullies.*

Aunt Liz thought Melissa should be a doctor, but Melissa thought there were enough Doctor Ellingtons. Maybe she could be president and fix all the problems. But she was told that wasn't likely since she was a girl.

"Why not," she'd ask. "I don't see men presidents fixing much. They just get us into more wars and they don't know how to stop."

She was grateful for her family. Aunt Liz was fun. Mama Ella was so full of love. Papa John was the smartest person in the world and all of the rest of the family were very special to her. Yes, she liked her life. It was good. Life was an adventure.

Chapter Sixty-three

M elissa turned nine in 1960. Until this time, her world had revolved around television personalities and the music icons of the day. It was the era of pop culture and Motown records was the hottest ticket in town. Motown was the birthplace of The Supremes, Gladys Knight, Lionel Richie, and numerous others.

Elvis, "The King," was waning since his induction into the army, but he was a legend never to be forgotten. Ed Sullivan brought these great performers and many more into homes every Saturday night. Melissa was entranced. The teens were enthralled, and parents were mortified when Elvis was brought on to the stage. His musical gyrations were appalling to the over 30s but adored by teens. Although Melissa was not yet a teen, she too was drawn into the culture of the day. She was a precocious child, inquisitive and opinionated.

Being an only child growing up in a household of adults, she became aware of issues beyond pop culture. It was an election year, and the house was divided. Whenever people gathered, the conversation would turn to politics. Would it be the charming and handsome Senator John F. Kennedy from Massachusetts or the seasoned politician and former vice president from California, Richard Nixon?

To the gentlemen of the house, it was clear that Nixon should win the presidency. After all, he served under their beloved Ike. He was an avid foe of communists and would be best suited to handle the likes of Nikita Khrushchev of the Soviet Union, our primary adversary. A cold war was evolving and the nation needed a strong leader. Besides, if Kennedy, an avowed Catholic were to win, the country would be under the control of the Pope himself.

"Nonsense," cried the women of the house. Kennedy was the right choice. He was a man of diplomacy and would not involve the nation in yet another war. He was a man who knew the perils of war, having been wounded in active duty as a Naval Lieutenant in 1942. He was Commander of PT-109, which went down under attack in the Pacific theater during World War II. His actions in saving his surviving crew after the sinking of PT-109 made him a war hero.

Although he was very wealthy, he felt compassion for the poor, the elderly, the disabled and above all the Negro, who had been discriminated against by Jim Crowe laws. Yes, indeed. Kennedy was the better choice for president.

Melissa absorbed it all. She sided with the women of the house. Besides, Kennedy was so handsome. He could be a movie star and he had a very cool New England accent. Both the men and women in the Ellington house assured her those traits were not considerations for choosing a president. Melissa didn't argue, but what difference would it make. She couldn't vote anyway.

In November, the point became moot when John F. Kennedy was voted the 35th President of the United States.

*   *   *

The road was not easy for the new president. Tensions had been festering between the Soviet Union and the United States. Fidel Castro invaded Cuba in 1959 and was now in control of Cuba just 90 miles from our shores. This did not please the president, who quickly banned the import of Cuban sugar to the U.S. This was approximately eighty percent of their export revenue. The U.S.S.R. quickly allied with Cuba and purchased their sugar.

The CIA had a plan to sneak into Cuba and retake the country. JFK was hesitant but listened to his advisors and initiated the plan that had been formulated by the previous Eisenhower administration.

The attack took place in April, 1961. It turned out to be a total disaster. We were outnumbered and the secret plan had been intercepted on faulty radio equipment. Many lives were lost, and it became an embarrassment to the U.S. and its president. The brief skirmish lasted less than 24 hours but "the Bay of Pigs" incident was a failure that history would note.

John was quick to respond. "See, I knew it. Kennedy is too weak, too unprepared to lead this country. We're just lucky it didn't end up as World War III and on our soil."

"Don't forget, it was initially formulated by your military leader Ike," Ella argued.

"Don't you forget, it was Ike who signed the Civil Rights Act into law last year."

The conflicts did not end there for the countries nor for the Ellington family debates.

Melissa was doing homework in her room. John and Ella sat together on the sofa in the parlor.

"I'm scared," Ella confessed. "There is so much talk of nuclear arms and any negotiations for disarmament stalled. Even France tested its first A Bomb in the Sahara Desert. In the *Sahara Desert*. My God, what are they doing there?"

"It seems like the world can't live in peace. The Soviet Union scares me. Their Nikita Khrushchev is a maniac. At a meeting of the United Nations, he pounded his fists on the desk and picked up his shoe and banged it on the podium, railing against capitalism. Earlier, he even spoke the words 'We will bury you.' That is the action of someone who is out of control. At the very least, it looks like we have to be on guard." John shook his head.

"Do you think we should build a bomb shelter? The president is advising it."

"I don't think we need to go that far just yet."

"Oh, John." Ella curled into the comfort of John's strong arms.

*   *   *

The chaos continued in 1961. The U.S. launched its first test of the Minuteman I intercontinental ballistic missile. Khrushchev built the Berlin

Wall, separating communist controlled east Germany from the democratic west, as well as dividing the whole European continent. The Russians sent the first man into space. The Vietnam War officially began with American helicopters and 400 U.S. personnel landing in Saigon.

"John, the whole world is going to explode. What is happening to humanity? I don't believe any people around this globe want war and yet the leaders of all countries are on the verge of annihilating everyone. There seems to be a race for the biggest and baddest weapons and threats for the safety of everyone. Do they not know that a nuclear war would destroy the world? The U.S. alone has a stockpile of weapons that could destroy the whole world three times. Don't they know that nuclear fuel has a half-life of four billion years? Are they all insane?" Ella was near tears. Being the journalist she once strived to be, she did her research.

"Ella, Ella." John comforted her, drawing her into his protective embrace. "It seems like the world is tearing apart at its seams, but these are not stupid people. They talk the talk, but no one wants nuclear war. They all know what happened at Okinawa and Nagasaki. It is more a war of words than actions."

"But what if any one of them is truly insane? And it's not just words. We were drawn into war in Vietnam. That's on foreign soil, but what about Cuba? It is a hot box just 90 miles from our shores. John, I think it's time to listen to our president and build a bomb shelter."

"I hardly think it's necessary but if it gives you comfort, we can look into it."

"Yes John, I think it's time."

There were shelters throughout the city designated for public access. A plaque outside the entrance of the building would identify it as a safe haven, though the number of occupants would be limited by its size. People were encouraged to build their own fallout shelter. Although often referred to as a bomb shelter, it was designed to protect the family from fallout for a period of two weeks.

There were many citizens who scoffed at the idea. Many claiming they would prefer to die instantly than to have a prolonged exposure. Others proclaimed it to be a rich man's fantasy. At the cost of $1,200 to $1,500 per shelter, it was out of reach for the less influential.

Construction began in an area of the backyard on Astor Street. It was approximately a ten-foot by ten-foot structure with eight-foot ceilings. Many watching the construction declared it to be a concrete tomb with its eight-inch reinforced concrete walls.

Inside, it was furnished with barrack style bunks, an oven, minimal dishes and cookware, a space heater, lamps, a toilet, and a cabinet to hold canned goods, other non-perishable food items, medical supplies, toilet paper, tools, flashlights, and batteries. It was equipped with electricity and phone service, although they were uncertain if those would be operable. In addition, blankets, bed linens, and clothing for two weeks were stored beneath the cots. Of course, five-gallon water jugs were a necessity.

Upon completion, they observed their home away from home. Ella gulped. She was glad it was built, but if anything, it increased her gloom over the current state of affairs.

John squeezed her hand. "Honey, welcome to your new home. Let's hope it is like any insurance—necessary but never needed."

Ella responded with a thin smile and headed for the house. Once again, John was right.

*   *   *

Wasn't there any good news?

Spirits rose in the race to space. The U.S.S.R. launched its first manned spaceship, the *Vostok*, carrying Yuri Alekseyevich Gagarin on April 12, 1961. Less than a month later, the United States launched *Freedom 7*, carrying Alan Shepard on May 5. Up until this point, the U.S.S.R. was one step ahead of the U.S., but on May 25 Kennedy announced in a speech that the United States would lead the charge in landing a man on the moon. Spirits soared. The country found something positive to rally around.

Melissa was excited and it was the talk around school. But there was something even more exciting happening in Melissa's world. It seemed there was a new band formed in Liverpool that was taking the world by storm. They called themselves the Beatles.

Chapter Sixty-four

Ella's hopes were dashed on October 22, 1962, when President John F. Kennedy came on television to announce that Cuba had Soviet missiles in Cuba directed toward the United States. A U-2 flight over Cuba on October 14 had taken photos of Soviet weapons being installed. This was followed by a confrontation between the two leaders. There were threats of nuclear war.

Was this an imminent threat or another of Khrushchev's mind games. In any event, with Cuba just 90 miles from the nation's shores we could not take chances.

Ella watched in horror, clutching John's arm.

John had a sober look on his face. "This can't be good."

"What will we do? We can't have another war. We just can't."

"If Khrushchev deploys those missiles, we'll need to retaliate. This is going to be a true test of our president's resolve," John said.

"Thank heavens, we built the shelter but there is not enough room for everyone. What will we do?"

"We will go on as we have been and hope it doesn't come to that."

"Pray, John, pray." Ella clutched him tighter.

President Kennedy announced that he was placing a naval blockade around Cuba, cutting off all entry of supplies to the country and denying Soviet entrance as well. Khrushchev, who up to this point believed Kennedy to be a weak and unintelligent leader, met his match.

Khrushchev wanted his threat to crumble this young president into submission, but he stood his ground. After some discussion, Khrushchev ordered the removal of missiles and shut down the missile bases in Cuba. He had a newfound respect for this president. They were far from friends or allies, but they were able to communicate. All United Nations agreed that nuclear armaments and threats were to be met with severe consequences.

President Kennedy had gained the confidence of the people of the United States and globally. And John's.

The world sighed a sigh of relief. And so did Ella.

Chapter Sixty-five

⌒⌒∽〉∽⌒⌒

In November of 1962, Ella woke up one morning and discovered a lump in her breast while she was getting dressed. She worried for a moment and then passed it off as a cyst in her ducts. The doctor had told her earlier she had some fibrous cysts there. But this one was different. What could it be? Later that day, she talked with Liz and told her of the discovery. She was so happy Liz was home for a time. Under Liz's direction, Ella scheduled an appointment with her doctor.

When Melissa got home from school, she heard muffled talking coming from the parlor. It was Mama Ella and Aunt Liz.

"Ella, you have to be strong for Henrietta and Melissa. You need to continue the fight," Liz said.

Mama Ella was sobbing. "What is the use? It is over."

What is that about? What is wrong? This is clearly not something they want to tell me right now.

Pretending she'd just arrived, Melissa went back to open and shut the door, leaving the storm door bang when she called out, "I'm home."

She heard some shuffling and Aunt Liz came around the corner. In a cheerful tone, she inquired about Melissa's day. "Come to the kitchen, Melissa. I made cookies this morning. Chocolate chip, your favorite." She shuffled Melissa past the parlor door and into the kitchen.

Meanwhile, Ella headed into the bathroom to wash her face before joining Melissa and Liz in the kitchen. When she arrived, her eyes were puffy. It was obvious she had been crying.

"Mama?" Melissa said hesitantly.

"What, dear?" Ella asked as she turned to pour a cup of tea.

"Mama? What is wrong?"

"Oh, nothing, nothing."

"Mama, something is wrong…tell me," Melissa insisted.

Ella waved a hand in the air. "Nothing, nothing. I'm just tired. I think I will go lie down for a while."

Melissa watched as Mama Ella made a hasty departure.

Melissa turned to Liz. "Aunt Liz, what is wrong?"

Liz took a deep breath. "We will talk about it later, I promise."

*   *   *

A few days later, Ella was sitting in the office of Dr. Meyer, her gynecologist. Dr. Meyer leaned forward with one hand on his knee and the other fisted over his mouth. "Ella, I am afraid we have some bad news." He hesitated a moment.

Ella watched him silently with wide eyes.

"I am afraid you have breast cancer," he said.

Ella gasped. "No, no. Are you sure?"

"Well, the lump could be benign, but I don't want to get your hopes up."

Ella gave a sigh of relief. In her state of denial, she would only believe the lumps were enlarged cysts.

"We will schedule you for surgery. If the biopsy shows the lump to be benign, you can go home in a day or two. If it is malignant, we will do the surgery immediately to remove your breast."

"*Remove* my breast? I will be a freak. Can you just remove the lump?"

"I am afraid cancer doesn't work that way," Dr. Meyer said. "Cancer spreads, and we will want to try to take it all. You would be fitted for a prothesis so you will appear normal to anyone who sees you."

Ella gulped. "I will *not* be normal. My husband will see me. I *will* see me." She had not had the surgery and already she felt violated, half a woman.

"Your husband is a doctor; he will know it is just body tissue. You will always be the woman you are today. Go home and talk to him."

*   *   *

John in his wisdom, made things understandable. "I love you for the woman you are. What is important is what is inside you, Ella. It doesn't matter if you are fat or thin; it doesn't matter that your hair is streaked with grey. It doesn't matter that you have developed a few wrinkles. In fact, I find them very appealing. It wouldn't matter to me if you have one arm or two or one leg or two. I will always love you, my dear.

"Look at Henrietta. Do you love her any less because she had polio? Look at Melissa. Do you love her any less because she has no mother? Look at all of our children. Because of their adversities, we chose them. Are they loved any less? Or do we love them more?"

"You are right, of course," Ella said, and hugged him. *John made perfect sense. He always did. But what would he know? He's not a woman.*

*   *   *

Two weeks later, Ella had a major mastectomy and was fitted with a prosthesis. She hated it and felt less a woman for it. But with time and a loving husband, she began to feel normal.

She did well for a year, feeling more confident with each passing month.

On Melissa's eleventh birthday, Ella went in for her regular checkup. This time, the report was not so positive. A lump had appeared in the other breast. A second diagnosis with the same thing was not encouraging.

That night, John held Ella's hand as she told the children the startling news.

"It's okay, Mama," Henrietta said. "I'll take care of you like you have taken care of me. You'll lick it just like I did polio. I know you can do it."

"Mama, you will be fine. No one is stronger than you. Look at all you have endured," Shirley encouraged.

"This birthday really sucks," Melissa chimed in. "I want a present from you. A very important present. Get well. I love you so much, Mama Ella." She rushed over and threw her arms around Ella and kissed her cheek. Then, she reached up and wiped a tear from Ella's eye.

"I love you, too, Melissa," Ella said.

*   *   *

Once again, Ella endured another mastectomy. She struggled with a treatment that made her very ill. She soon learned the cancer had come back stronger and spread to more lymph nodes and other parts of her body. There was nothing more they could do.

Ella had now accepted her fate and as she always had endured, she once again pulled herself together and tended to business. She arranged for Liz to care for her twelve-year-old granddaughter if John couldn't.

She took care of everything that needed to be taken care of, including the details of her own funeral, John's eventual funeral, and wrote letters to each of her children. There was nothing more to be done.

*   *   *

On November 22, 1963, the family gathered around Ella's bed. She lay in a hospital bed in a semi-conscious state. All eight of her children were gathered together. Well, seven of her children and Melissa, who had become yet another child not born of her body but born in her heart. The radio played soothing music as they took turns holding her hand and expressing their love to her.

John held her hand last, giving her a kiss on her forehead like he had done once long ago on their first date. "I love you, Ella Dewberry Ellington. I always will."

"Oh, John, I love you." Ella looked around her, first at her loving husband, and then at her family, and in that moment, she was at peace.

At 1:38 p.m. EST a special report broke in on the radio. It was Walter Cronkite's voice announcing President Kennedy had been assassinated.

At 2:38 p.m. CST Ella Ellington, still holding onto her husband's hand, closed her eyes and passed away. She'd been a loving mother, a devoted wife, a true friend, a survivor who had endured the pain of all whom she loved. She'd fought against the evils in the world but had succumbed to the one battle she could not win. Her family wept deeply for their loss.

Epilogue

 ⁂

lmost sixty years later.

A   Melissa and her daughter, Victoria were sitting by the fireplace in their Astor Street home. Melissa was poking the embers and thinking about all the strong women who had preceded her in this house.

Her great grandmother, Sara, who had fought valiantly and sacrificed everything.

Her grandmother/mother, Ella, who had lived through the trials of the Greatest Generation. Ella, who had endured the pain of her loved ones who went to battle and lost their lives.

Her Aunt Liz, who had loved and suffered the tragedy of lost love, not once but twice. Dr. Elizabeth Dewberry Cornell, a trailblazer in her field. Dr. Cornell had died tragically in an automobile accident in 1978 at the age of seventy-one.

Her real mother, Helen, who gave her life while bringing life to her.

And her Aunt Henrietta, who had suffered through polio and dealt with the effects of post-polio. Henrietta, who would not succumb to her disabilities but graduated college and became a research librarian. However, after spending 20 years in a wheelchair, Henrietta lost her battle in 1996 at the age of sixty.

Her twin Aunts Ella Sue and Emma Sara, who had lost their brother David in World War II and before that, who had lost their father to suicide, and their mother and brother to the Dust Bowl. Amazingly, these women had overcome all the pain they endured and grew to be beautiful, smart women raising children and grandchildren of their own. They'd passed away a year apart in 2000 and 2001.

And her Aunt Shirley, who was taken from the hell of her childhood and raised up with Mama Ella's strength and gave her a new lease on life. Shirley, that desperate child who became a renowned psychologist. She'd passed away in 2005 but her legacy lived on.

She thought of the men, also. Papa John, who had been there for every step she took. He had outlived Mama Ella and he missed her companionship all his days.

Uncle Thaddeus, whom she'd never met but heard stories about all her life. His body was never recovered, and Mama Ella's heart broke every day, but she endured.

Uncles Jimmy and Johnny whose optimism and smiles had warmed her heart. Both gone now, too.

Uncle David, whose mischievous nature had driven Mama Ella crazy, or so Melissa had heard. But oh, what Mama Ella would have done to have more time with him.

"Mom," her daughter Victoria said, drawing Melissa out of her thoughts. "Women have accomplished much in the past, but remember, your generation made their mark as well."

"Yes, we did," Melissa said and smiled at her. "Yes, we did. But we are not done. Your generation must finish the job Great Grandma Sara started 100 years ago."

The march goes on.

Acknowledgements

A book cannot be completed without the assistance of numerous people who give input as well as support and encouragement along the way. My sincere appreciation to all who contributed.

I would be amiss not to mention my dear grandmother Emma Grunske to whom I dedicated this book. Grandma taught me my religious values, my strength and resiliency, and by example, she showed the strength and fortitude of women. She lived in the Greatest Generation and suffered through the trials of the Great Depression. Her husband, my grandfather, was seriously injured in a farm accident and my grandmother took up the reins of primary breadwinner in the family, going to work first in the hospital kitchen and later as a factory worker. She raised her three children and me. She still found time to prepare Sunday dinners and holiday meals well into her seventies. She always made time to smell the roses, taking pride in her flower gardens, especially her geraniums.

My son, Jim Parfitt was an invaluable aid to me in coming to my rescue when I needed technology assistance. He developed my website, fixed my computer problems, and offered advise along the way. I am also grateful for his being the best son a mother could ask for. A man I am proud to call my son.

Research is extremely important in writing historical fiction. I spent five times the time researching as I did writing. Historical facts are easy but sometimes details are even more important. What kind of wine did they drink in 1912? How to drive a Model T Ford (you get a manual).

When were flashlights invented, when was tissue manufactured? Some information sources are not reliable, so two or three resources became necessary, sometimes four or more. I thank all the people in libraries, museums, and historic societies who were so willing to help me.

I can't tell you the number of Ken Burns documentaries I watched as well as other movies such as *Midway* and *Pearl Harbor*, which brought the era to life and provided a visual of the life in this era.

I thank Brittiany Koren, my editor for keeping my timeline accurate and providing insight into making this the best novel possible.

I thank Jackie Lohr Burkat for her first-hand knowledge of polio and her assistance in getting me in contact with other victims of this terrible affliction. And further, for providing me with contact information for March of Dimes and Research hospitals.

I thank my Pastor Josh Fite for theological support. Most of all, I thank God for inspiration and the gifts He gave me to make all this possible.

About the Author

Flo Parfitt is a lifelong student, attending schools, seminars, workshops and other educational programs throughout her life. She attended Northeast Wisconsin Technical College and Downer College in Milwaukee. Most recently, she completed a program at Rubart Writing Academy and currently is enrolled in Lifelong Learning Institute at University of Wisconsin-Green Bay. She worked as a business manager at Everson, Whitney, Everson & Brehm, S.C. law offices, Seering & Company Advertising Agency, and Warner Bros Television.

She's published in several trade journals including the Wisconsin Bar Journal, Callaghan's Law Office Management, Integrated Office Technologies "The Word", "Footsteps", a writer's showcase published by the University of Wisconsin-Green Bay and other publications.

She has worked with Court Appointed Special Advocates (CASA) for abused and neglected children and various charitable causes. She is a member of the League of Women Voters, The Green Bay Area Writers Guild, and Authors & Allies writers' groups.

Flo is in the process of writing a trilogy based on more than 100 years of American history. She writes historical fiction with an emphasis on strong women. The first in this series, *Sara's Sacrifice*, was released in October of 2019 and sold in nine countries. The novel is about a suffragette who sacrificed everything. Book two, *Ella Endures* follows Sara's daughter, Ella from Prohibition and the Great Depression through WWII. *Melissa's March*, book three will feature two more generations from the feminist movement of the 70s through the Me Too movement today.

For more information on Flo and updates on her publications, visit her Facebook page @FloParfittAuthor.

CPSIA information can be obtained
at www.ICGtesting.com
Printed in the USA
JSHW030327020222
22495JS00001B/10

9 781951 375638